Vegas Pursuit

(Fleeing Sin City)

by

Patrick Shanahan

An Authors OnLine Book

British Library Cataloguing Publication Data.
A catalogue record for this book is available from the British
Library

ISBN 978-0-7552-1556-0

Authors OnLine Ltd
19 The Cinques
Gamlingay, Sandy
Bedfordshire SG19 3NU
England

This book is also available in e-book format, details of which
are available at www.authorsonline.co.uk

Acknowledgements

My gratitude goes out to the following people whose contribution has enabled me to get this book into print.

Thank you then to Sharon Shrubb not only for her helpful comment and ability to pick out my errors but also for her enthusiastic promotion of my work; to Steve Skarratt who, once again, gave up his time to provide advice on grammatical errors and inaccuracies in the text; to the lads who made my Vegas research all the more enjoyable – Charles, Gaspar, Quincy and Emmanuel (the hardship of research in the bright lights of Vegas under jet-lagged conditions should not be underestimated!); to Richard Taylor of BT Graphics for providing the cover design.

I should also like to acknowledge all of the establishments in Las Vegas that appear in this book, in particular the Paris, the Bellagio, the Venetian and Caesar's Palace hotels. Although none of the places mentioned are connected in any way to the production of this work, or indeed to any of the entirely fictitious events that appear in the story, each of them made my stay in Las Vegas a very pleasant one.

Finally, thank you to Penny again for her patience and support and the encouragement she continues to provide for my writing ambitions.

Patrick Shanahan
May 2013

1

Perhaps it was fate that had decided at this particular stage in my life, just five days away from my fortieth birthday, that the law, in all its different guises, should become so finely integrated into my every day existence. The links seemed too many to be mere coincidence and as I caught sight of the flashing blue light in my rear view mirror, I resigned myself to the thought that a higher power was definitely at work. My mind raced through the list. A newly established relationship with a police woman; a succession of entanglements that had resulted in a recent court appearance that, with the help of a lawyer, I had managed to extricate myself from with minimal damage; and now a summons which I was on my way to answer.

I killed the engine and sat gripping the steering wheel as I awaited the approaching police officer. Then, recalling the night before, I popped an extra strong mint in my mouth hoping that I didn't still smell of beer. My finger pressed the button on the window console to my right and I watched as the glass slid downwards. A glance at my watch showed that it was twelve minutes to ten o'clock. My appointment was for ten. If I had entertained the slightest chance that I would make it, that thought evaporated as the police officer stopped by my door.

'Good morning, Sir,' he said, as he fixed his cap firmly to his head. 'Do you know why I have stopped you?'

I had a good idea.

'Good morning officer. I was probably going a tad too fast

perhaps,' I said, trying to keep the tension from my voice as my anxiety level increased.

'Well Sir, you're right. You were going too fast but as we don't measure speed in tads, to be more precise, you were clocked at thirty-eight miles per hour. Are you aware of the speed limit in this location?'

He placed both hands on the passenger door where the window had been and leant towards me.

'It's thirty...thirty miles an hour officer,' I said, trying hard to affect a contrite tone when I really wanted to say, '*Bugger off please. I wasn't breaking the land speed record. I was doing thirty-eight. That's only eight miles an hour more than the limit. Everybody does it. Shouldn't you be out catching crooks? So please go away because you are going to cost me three points on my licence if I miss my appointment.*'

He leant forward again, his head turned to the left as if he was looking for something on the back seat.

'Yes, it is Sir. Correct. Thirty. So, tell me why you were doing thirty-eight.'

My fingers began to drum a beat on the steering wheel as I contemplated a question that had no real answer. 'I know it's no excuse but I was in a rush. Loads of traffic this morning and I'm late for...err...somewhere I need to be...at ten...ten o'clock.' I glanced at my watch as I said it. 'In...err...ten minutes.'

He turned to face me again.

'Is it a matter of life and death then Sir, this appointment that has caused you to break the law? You understand that is what you have done. Broken the law.'

I felt the flush rise to my face. I had to explain myself and deal with the embarrassment.

'I'm sorry officer. No, it isn't life and death but I am late... late for...look, this is going to sound stupid but I am late for a...a speed awareness course.' I reached over to the passenger seat, picked up my appointment letter and handed it to the surprised looking police officer.

He took it from me and began to read. I glanced at my watch

again – nine minutes to ten. The directive from the course had clearly stated that if you were late you would be barred from taking part. I gritted my teeth and glanced up at the police officer, willing him to read faster. I noticed that his surprised look had been replaced by a look of bemusement.

He finished reading the letter and looked at me.

'Let me get this straight. I have stopped you because you're speeding and you're on your way to a speed awareness course? Correct?'

I nodded.

'You'd think you'd know better, Sir, in such circumstances.'

The thought flashed through my mind. Why would I know better? I haven't been on the bloody course yet. I let it go.

'I know officer. It's just that I am running late, what with this rush hour traffic, and they say that I won't be allowed to take part if I turn up late. And that will cost me a sixty-pound fine on top of the ninety-five I have already paid for the course and I will get three points on my driving licence too. I know I shouldn't have been doing thirty-eight. I am really sorry and I –'

'Slow down Sir.' The police officer's tone cut across a sentence that I realised had started to ramble and was in danger of becoming a full-blown grovel. 'Look, I could give you a ticket right now but on this occasion I'm not going to do so. Instead, I'm going to give you an opportunity. And you know why?'

An opportunity? How about an opportunity to be on time for my course, I thought. But that was out of my control and the shrug of my shoulders and wide-eyed look of surprise told him that I had no idea why he was being so considerate.

'I'll tell you why. Only because you are about to go on this course. I'm not in the habit of letting lawbreakers off the hook but since you are about to be educated on the dangers of speeding I am going to give you this opportunity to learn from your experience. I hope you will take it. But be warned, Sir, if you ever cross my path again and I find that you are exceeding the speed limit by so much as one mile an hour, I will throw the book at you.'

He walked off to his car. My shock at this unexpected outcome turned to relief. My relief quickly turned to anxiety as I caught sight of the time. Five minutes to ten. I was a good four miles from the hotel that was hosting the course and I knew I could not possibly make it on time. Why had I not taken that early night I had promised myself? Why had I agreed to meet up with Cecil? I had succumbed yet again to his insistence.

The night before I had walked in to MacFadden's at 6.30pm, straight after work, summoned there by Cecil in a mid-morning phone call. MacFadden's Bar or Fad's as it was known, was my local in Kingston. In the last few months, it had seen a transformation from run down, tired dive to a vibrant and exciting cocktail cum wine bar. With the extra revenue that its newly acquired reputation had afforded it, the owner, Carlos MacFadden, had splashed out on improvements. A coat of red paint had transformed the exterior wooden window frame and gleaming, gold painted lettering, emblazoned above the window, announced that this was MacFadden's. The front entrance was also painted red with a thin white border outlining the doorframe and the bar name inscribed in white through the glass pane at its centre. Above all this, a red awning covered a small external seating area in which four aluminium tables with wicker-backed chairs stood empty, awaiting night time revellers.

Inside Carlos had managed to add the sort of small cosmetic touches that gave the bar an ambience that was a cross between a local pub and cosmopolitan wine bar. The floor had been polished and re-varnished to highlight the natural grain of the wood, yet emphasise the scratches and wear of many years of activity. An inspired blend of lighting threw shadows where intimacy was required and illumination where the spotlight was sought. Around the tables that lined one side of the room small, white vases of flowers brightened the harshness of dark wood surfaces. I could only think that the floral display was the result of a female influence, perhaps Abigail, a young lady with whom Carlos had been having a dalliance for some weeks. He had also been true to his natural preference for the local pub scene and had retained a vast selection of draught beers and ales as well as the more trendy cocktails.

As I walked towards the bar, I felt some satisfaction that in a small way I had helped with the transformation. A brief reference to marketing at a time when business was slow was all it had needed to galvanise Carlos into action. My reward was that I had a decent local in which to while away some downtime. A couple sat sipping wine at a table near the front entrance window. The remaining tables were unoccupied.

Cecil was already at the bar perched on a stool talking to Carlos, who saw me first.

'Hola Mateo. How are you doing? Long time no see amigo.'

It appeared that the South American side of Carlos's personality had taken precedence over the Scottish side on this particular afternoon but, as always with him, it could flip at any time. I shook his outstretched hand just as Cecil turned to face me.

'Geezer, how you doing?' He stood up, grabbed me in a firm handshake and playfully punched me in the right shoulder.

'I'm good Ces but what's with the urgency? What's going on? You ok?'

'Mate, take a seat. Carlos get this geezer a beer.'

'No, Carlos. No beer. I'll just have a coffee, cappuccino or something.' I turned back to Cecil. 'I have that speed course in the morning I told you about. Got to be on my game,' I said, trying to head off a potential session at the outset. For once Cecil didn't try to talk me out of it.

Carlos turned to the back of the bar placed a cup on the metal tray of the Espresso machine and pressed a button. The machine hissed and spurted into life. I turned to Cecil curious to hear whatever it was that warranted the meeting.

'So, what's this all about Ces? What did you want to talk to me about?'

Cecil sipped his beer straight from the bottle, his dark brown eyes taking on a twinkle as he placed it back on the bar.

'It's your birthday soon mate. Right?'

'Yeah, it is. On Saturday. Why?'

'I thought so. Your fortieth, ain't it?'

'It is, yes, but what's that got to do with anything?'

'Well you bin a bit quiet about it. Not said fuck all in fact. I thought you might be up for a few beers seeing as how it's the big four O. You planned anything?'

I was about to answer when Carlos placed the cappuccino on the bar next to me. Cecil pushed a ten pound note towards him to cover the beer and the coffee.

'Well, no, nothing planned. I hadn't really thought too much about it.'

The truth was I had given it some thought but was considering the sensible couple thing with Louise as opposed to the wildness of a night out with Cecil. That was the real reason I had put off discussing my birthday with him. There was always going to be conflict when approaching a significant birthday. Do something to include the family, party big style with your mates or have a quiet one with your other half. Given the years of partying that Cecil had managed to talk me into, I had settled on the last option.

'Probably just have a meal with Louise or something, pretty low key,' I said and waited for the reaction.

'Low fucking key? What's with you now? Got a bird in tow and you're doing a mumble swerve on your mates.'

The reaction was more or less the one I had expected. I began to justify my decision.

'It's not like that Ces. Just that…you know, I've done all that partying and I kind of promised myself I'd be settled down by the time I hit forty. I've told you all that before. But, we can have a beer if you're up for that.' I picked up my coffee, took a sip and wiped away the froth that smeared my top lip.

Cecil stared hard at me for a moment as if checking that I was giving him my full attention before he spoke.

'A beer? Geezer, it's your fortieth. You don't just go for a beer on your fucking fortieth, do ya? You go out and party large. Big style.'

I knew what Cecil's persuasive nature was like and I could see

6

he was about to get on a roll. He slugged the last of his beer, shoved the bottle towards Carlos and ordered a second one.

'Get us another Budvaar Carlos while I try and talk some sense into this geezer.' He ran both hands through his thick head of 'Irish' hair, as he called it, as if the action would stimulate some serious, logical thought processes that would indeed make me see sense. He then turned towards me and looked me directly in the eyes.

'Mate, it's your fortieth. It's not like you're pushing seventy. You ain't retired yet. So…here's the deal. We're going partying mate, proper partying. You listening? We...are...going to...'

He stopped mid-sentence, leaving me hanging. Going to what? Going to KFC for a chicken bucket? Going to party all night? Going to hook up with some hardcore strippers? Going to drop dead after indulging in some drug fuelled sex party? I waited for Cecil to deliver.

'Going to…Vegas geezer.'

The meaning of the word *Vegas* didn't register at first. I stared blankly at Cecil as my brain performed a high-speed search through the full lexicon of words that had been stored over a lifetime in its left inferior frontal gyrus. It settled on the wrong definition.

'Vegas? I'm not going clubbing tonight, Ces. I told you, I have that speed awareness course in the morning and I can't turn up there looking like a vagrant who's spent the night –'

'It ain't a nightclub you nobhead,' Cecil interrupted. 'I'm talking about Vegas. Las fucking Vegas. Sin City. Oh yeah mate… Las Vegas, Nerrrfuckinvaaaardaaaar.' He took a large swig from the fresh bottle, his eyes never leaving my face as he awaited my reaction.

'What are you talking about Ces,' I said, still trying to register the information.

He rolled his eyes and waved his beer bottle in front of me as if it would focus me on what he was trying to say.

'Mate…how can I put this in simple terms that a geezer pushing forty might tumble? It's your birthday Saturday, right?'

'Yes.'

'Well, on Friday, this Friday, we're going to Las Vegas to celebrate and party big style.'

I stared blankly at Cecil, unable to gauge whether or not he was serious.

He noticed.

'What you not getting? Five nights in Vegas. A man of your age has to celebrate these things proper. Go some place where there ain't geezers in football shirts. You know whatamean? That's how we roll now.'

Vegas. Las Vegas. It finally dawned on me that Cecil might be serious. That this was the urgent news he had brought me down to MacFadden's for. A flurry of thoughts suddenly buzzed in my head as I stared back at the bright-eyed enthusiasm all over his face.

'You're serious? 'But…what about…?'

'Course I'm serious. You're hitting forty mate. You gotta live like a Pharaoh. Go large. Anyway, do I look like somebody who's gonna mug you off with some bollocks about Vegas?'

'No, sorry Ces…I didn't mean…I meant…what about work and Louise. I don't know if I can get the time off. And who is we anyway?'

Cecil's face cracked into a grin and he reached for his beer.

'So you gotta apply for time off with the bird now have ya?'

'No, I meant work but…well, I mean I ought to at least talk to–'

'Chill mate. It's sorted. Louise is cool. I talked to her and I sorted work for you as well. You got time off on both counts.'

'Work? What do you mean sorted work? Did you–'

'Geezer, shut up and listen. Here's the deal. I rang your boss, invited him for a lunchtime beer, told him the mumble and it's sorted. Told him to keep it quiet. Bit of a birthday surprise and all that. He's cool with it. Nice geezer. Spoke to Louise too and she knows the score. She's a good girl. She thought it was a blinding idea. She ain't gonna stop you having a bit of a party for your big four O. Anyway, you only bin together two minutes and you don't want some bird whose gonna start laying the law down soon as you get together. Mate, there are geezers doing twenty year stretches now in some fucked up marriage cos they let some bird dictate to them after five fucking minutes. So you go with this Vegas thing and you're putting a marker down for the whole relationship deal. Yeah?' The brown eyes were intense, checking to see if I'd grasped the relationship concept. Clearly, he wasn't convinced I had and it needed more emphasis.

'I mean, she's a bird right. Birds have that relationship crap going on. It blinds them. Mate, they start off on heels and before you know it, they're doing all that legging and flat shoes shit. So, you put down the marker and it keeps them on their toes. Keeps your rogue gene alive too. They love it.'

'Blimey Ces. It's not that bad. Louise is her own woman. I don't think I need to be anything other than who I am with her… you know. Odd she never mentioned anything to me though about the trip.'

'She wouldn't mate. I told her it was a surprise too so that's why you ain't heard nuthin from nobody.'

I was too shocked to speak. It appeared he was deadly serious. Cecil seemed to have the whole thing covered. I didn't want to think too much about what he might have said to my boss or how many beers he might have fuelled him with and I knew I could talk to Louise later to find out what she really felt.

Cecil continued.

'So, mate, once I got the formalities sorted it was just a little matter of putting a crew together and –'

'A crew?'

'Yeah, a crew to take down Vegas.' He made it sound like an invasion. 'So, we all got together and decided we'd all chip in and treat ya to the trip. All you're gonna need is some big bucks to party with.'

Once again the shock washed over me but this time mixed with a sudden glow of warmth towards Cecil and his generous and thoughtful nature, something that was often missed by people because of his cloak of bravado.

'Blimey Ces, you *have* got it sorted. Who else is going then?'

'Mate, that was the hardest bit. There's a lot of lightweights out there. They all reckon they're up for it but when it comes to pulling the trigger they come up with lame fucking excuses. So just the four of us. You, me, Carlos and a geezer from your office…whasisname…Jasper Kane.'

I was still registering the crew information when I caught sight of Carlos pulling a beer from a pump to my left.

'Hey, Carlos. So you were in on this Vegas thing?'

Carlos scratched his bald head, gave a slight shrug of his shoulders and cracked a grin as if he was relieved to be unburdening the secret he had been told to keep.

'Correctamundo laddie. We're gannae party. Need a break myself anyway. My two wee lassies, Hanka and Janka can take care of things here.'

I turned back to Cecil. 'So how did Jasper Kane get in on the act? I don't even know him that well. He seems a nice enough bloke but I only know him through work. He's got a bit of a reputation for the ladies though.'

'That's no bad thing mate. No harm in having a good wingman on the crew when it comes to Vegas ladies. When I went to see your guvnor at the office, I got talking to Jasper and told him what I was sorting. We went out for a few beers a couple of nights later and he's on board. Nice geezer.'

'Bloody hell Ces. Look, it's a hell of a surprise and I am still a bit gobsmacked but I do appreciate what you've done. Seriously.'

'Geezer, it's what mates are for. You can't be sitting around on a big birthday in some Italian restaurant pushing fucking spaghetti round a plate. Now you're with a bird there's a danger you'll turn into one of them sad sacks that finish work on a Friday night and go home and do pontoon. You ain't going down that easy. Got to keep the dream alive.'

I had to laugh. Cecil was sure to keep the flames of his dream fanned without any help from anyone else and anyone in its glow would be swept along with it. I stood up to leave.

'Whereya going mate? Might as well have a small one now yer here.'

'I told you Ces I can't stay, got the speed course. Got to be sharp and anyway, I'm collecting Louise from work later.'

'Mate, what's with you…a fucking speed course. A show ya face job. You turn up, sign your name and then doze off while some nob bangs on about driving too fast.'

'Yeah…but Louise…'

'Relax, geezer. It's sorted. I told her you were coming out with me to sort the Vegas thing. She understood. She's getting a sherbet.'

'Sherbet?' Carlos said, his forehead scrunched in a quizzical frown.

'Yeah, Carlos. A sherbet mate. A cab. Taxi. Sherbet dab. Geezer, what is it with you? You bin here twenty years and you still don't speak the lingo.' Cecil turned back to me. 'So you on the programme? A few liveners tonight and we sort the Vegas details. Tumble?'

'Looks like it mate,' I said, resigned to the fact that Cecil had removed all barriers to starting a night on the tiles. As if to emphasise the fact he ordered two beers and shoved one in front of me.

'You know Ces, with all that organising I'm surprised you didn't persuade my boss to join the crew and come along for the ride.'

Cecil winked at Carlos and said, 'Nah, mate. The bloke's pushing forty. We don't want no old geezers on this mission.'

2

I pulled into the hotel car park at eleven minutes past ten, grabbed my appointment letter and ran towards the entrance. A sign pointed the way to reception.

Being late and not knowing where to go creates a mind-set bordering on panic and it was in this frame of mind that I approached the main reception. A long marbled top counter ran the length of one wall. The only receptionist on duty was on the telephone. She wore a navy blue uniform with a silver framed name badge that said her name was Lucy. I stood at the desk, half leaning over the front in the hope that my eager looking pose would induce the receptionist to drop everything and attend to my needs. It didn't. She continued with the call. I stood on tiptoe, leant further forward and assumed a wide-eyed, intense facial expression that I hoped would convey the fact I was in a massive hurry. The message did not get through. The receptionist remained engrossed in a call that was nothing more than a simple reservation booking. My fingers rapped out a fretful beat on the counter top. Finally she raised her eyes, acknowledging my presence but as I was about to speak she stretched out a hand, the palm turned towards me, one finger extended upwards, in an indication I took to mean that she would be with me in a minute.

I didn't have another minute. I had used up too many already. The receptionist's brief moment of recognition gave me the opportunity to interrupt.

'Excuse me,' I said, in a hesitant whisper, the polite side of my brain not really wishing to intrude but the agitated side screaming at me to find out where I was supposed to go, 'I'm here for the... err...speed...'

My sentence trailed off as I realised that my intrusion had had no effect. She was still engrossed in her call. I glanced around to see if there was anyone else I could ask for information and in an attempt to psych myself up for another go at getting her attention. The hotel lobby seemed to be devoid of any other people. Several sofas and armchairs filled the floor space behind me. Two tall yucca plants stood either side of a large window that looked out onto the car park, their fronds straining towards the daylight. To one side of the plant to my left a gold framed notice board was positioned on a raised stand, silver lettering pinned to a black velvety surface. In front of the sofas, two low coffee tables had several cups and saucers scattered randomly across their surfaces, clearly indicating that human activity had taken place at some stage.

I turned back to the reception desk.

'Look...err...Lucy, I am really sorry to interrupt but I am here for the course...the speed course...I'm late and I really need to –'

Lucy looked up and placed her hand over the telephone mouthpiece.

'I will be with you in a moment, Sir.'

'I just need to know...to find out...where the course is...some information...'

As I said the word, I stopped in mid flow. Information. The board. The notice board behind me. An information board maybe. I ran across the floor towards the window and stopped in front of the gold framed panel. Speed awareness...where was it? Speed... speed. I caught sight of the key words - speed and conference. Room B, Ground Floor.

I practically broke down the door of Room B, such was my rush to get in. My hurried entrance caused the audience to swivel around as one in the direction of the hastily opened door. At the far end of the room a surprised looking executive type in a dark blue suit stood in front of a white drop down projector screen, mouth open as if his script had been ripped from his hand.

'Sorry. Sorry I'm late,' I blurted out. 'It's a long story. I'm not too late am I?'

The executive type regained his composure in an instant.

'Never too late my friend, despite the fact that it's nearly twenty past ten. Now who are you?'

'Yes, I know. I'm sorry. My name is Matthew Malarkey. I'm booked on the course. I'm really sorry about being late.' I realised I was overdoing the apologies.

'Well, welcome Matthew, take a seat. You can catch up as we go along. I am Robin Hargreaves and I am running the course today. We're having a coffee break at eleven fifteen and we can do the formalities then.' He turned towards the white screen. 'Right, let's crack on.'

Relieved at having finally made the course I took a seat at the end of a row in the middle of the room. The adrenaline that had been pumping through my system began to dissipate as I settled in my seat. Robin Hargreaves picked up where presumably he had left off before my entrance but my attention began to focus on my surroundings rather than on what he was saying.

'...are in an age of instant demand...'

I estimated that the room was filled with around thirty to forty other people, all smartly dressed, an even mix of male and female. The thought flashed through my head, as I viewed my fellow miscreants, that we law breakers all looked fairly normal.

'...it's about expectations...you know that feeling when you are standing at an ATM and your cash can't come out fast enough...'

The age range appeared to be between early twenties up to late forties. Speeding wasn't just the domain of boy racers it seemed.

'...when you surf the web you need instant access. It's all about speed in this day and age...'

A wave of tiredness washed over me as I surveyed the room. The sudden drop from hyper unease to quiet inactivity had hit my concentration levels. I knew I had to focus in order to get through the course successfully but I was just catching snippets of Robin Hargreaves's delivery.

I sat upright and stared ahead in an attempt to apply my full attention.

'...a Traffic Management system that allows you to monitor traffic activity so you never go over your limit...'

My interest picked up. That sounded useful.

'...successfully achieving speeds up to two hundred and forty times faster than the national average...'

Who was going that fast, I wondered. What did he say? Two hundred and forty times faster than the average? That couldn't be right. What was the average anyway? My mind started to tick. I was on the course because I had been doing forty-six in a forty mile an hour speed limit area. If someone was going two hundred and forty times faster than thirty that would mean they were doing…I pulled my iPhone from my pocket and tapped on the calculator icon…7,200 miles an hour. Seven thousand, two hundred? That couldn't be right. I must have misheard.

I leant towards the person on my right, a woman in her twenties.

'Sorry,' I whispered, 'did he say two hundred and forty?'

'Excuse me?'

'Sorry…I didn't quite catch what he said. Did he say two hundred and forty times faster than the…err…limit…the average…limit, thing?'

'Oh…erm…yes, I think so.' She turned away and looked to the front again.

I concluded that she must have misheard too and tried to focus my attention on what was being said.

'People are demanding faster speeds and we are encouraging that demand...'

I knew that there had been Government discussion on increasing the speed limit but I was not aware anyone was encouraging it.

'Our platform is based on super-fast network capacity and our unique fibre optic system is capable of delivering some of the fastest broadband in the world.'

Broadband.

I turned again to the woman on my right.

'Sorry to interrupt again but did he say *broadband*?'

'What? Broadband? Yes, he did say broadband.'

I detected a slight note of irritation in her voice. She turned away.

'But I thought this was about speed awareness. What's broadband got to do with it?' I asked, risking her disapproval.

She turned sharply to face me, the irritation at my continuous interruptions now plain on her face.

'Yes, it is about speed awareness and broadband has everything to do with it. Look, I realise you were late and you have missed the introduction but if you listen you'll catch up. Now I really would like to hear what is being said. My company has paid a lot of money for me to be on this seminar.'

'Your company paid for you to be here? Err...do you have a company car then?' I asked, a little confused since I had paid my own way.

'I beg your pardon? A company car? What are you on about?'

'I mean...you know...were you speeding in a company car?'

'Speeding? I wasn't speeding in anything. Look, I told you, I want to hear what –'

'Yes, sorry...I know...but you wouldn't be here if you hadn't broken the law too, would you?'

'Listen, Mister...Mister whatever you said your name was. I don't know what you want or who you are looking for but this is definitely a case of mistaken identity. I haven't broken any laws at all. I am here because I want to be here. Because I work in an IT department and I want to learn about next generation broadband delivery. Now if you don't mind I would like to listen to what is being said.'

Next generation broadband delivery. The words penetrated my skull but I brushed them aside by forming another question.

'Err...are you sure you're on the right...the right...' *Next generation broadband delivery*. The words swirled around my head refusing to be dismissed so simply. '...the right course?'

My newly made acquaintance did not reply. She simply stared

directly at me as if I had asked her to remove her clothes and dance naked for the entire gathering.

'*DashNet Internet Solutions has anticipated the growing demand for bandwidth and committed the capital investment that will make these superfast speeds possible…..*' Robin Hargreaves's enthusiastic delivery rang in my ears as I contemplated my own words - *right course*.

A shockwave began its heated ascent from the pit of my stomach and rushed rapidly to my face, its sudden impact causing me to jump to my feet in an uncontrolled reaction.

'The right course…is it the right course?' I shouted out, causing the entire audience to turn in my direction.

A brief look of dismay darkened Robin Hargreaves's features.

'The right course, Mister…err…Matthew. The right course for what?'

'Yes, the right course…am I on…I mean, is this the course… the right course…for…speed awareness?' I asked, my sentence struggling for coherence as I waited for an answer.

'Well, sure it is Matthew.' Robin Hargreaves scanned the room. 'You guys are all in the ISP business, right? As carriers you want to deliver better and faster broadband wireless to your consumers. We at DashNet Internet Solutions are here to show you how to do just that.'

At that point I knew that my next question was pointless but I couldn't help myself.

'No, I mean…the course…isn't it for people who have been going too fast?'

A low murmur echoed around the room, interspersed with a few stifled chuckles. A smile played on Robin Hargreaves's lips. He glanced towards a window to his right as if looking for composure before he replied.

'Quite the opposite Matthew. Today is for people who want to go faster. People who want more speed. For those who want to get hold of the latest innovations and –'

'Shit…bollocks.' The expletives silenced the room. I spun around and sprinted towards the door.

Back in the hotel lobby I rushed over to the noticeboard. I skimmed the list looking for Conference Room B. I found it. *DashNet Internet Solutions-The Need for Speed Conference.* Definitely room B. My gaze scanned the rest of the list. A hairdressing product launch in room C; a doctor's medical conference, room D; I could hardly read the letters such was my rush as my stress level heightened.

'Come on, come on…where are you?'

Surely not the wrong hotel too?

'Are you ok, Sir?'

I heard the voice from behind and turned to see Lucy, the receptionist that I had tried to engage earlier, standing to my right side. Out from behind the main desk she looked taller, her hair tied back in a tight ponytail.

'Err, yes…no…I was just talking to the...the…err…no, look I am trying to find the National Speed Awareness Course. The driving thing…for people who have been speeding. I'm supposed to be attending it today and I'm late.'

'That's in one of our meeting rooms, Sir. This is the Conference list,' Lucy said, a kindly smile lighting her face. 'The National Speed Awareness course is in Meeting Room four.' She pointed to the left. 'Take the corridor over there, past our first four guest rooms, turn right at the next corridor and Meeting Room four is on the right hand side.'

'Thank you very much Lucy,' I said and raced across the lobby in the direction she had indicated.

A quick swerve to my left and I was in the first corridor, its lighting somewhat dimmer than that of the main lobby. I caught sight of the first guest room on my left and ahead I could just see the junction where the passageways met. My next view was an unwanted close up of the corridor carpet accompanied by the clatter of crockery and metal. Why do people have to leave their used breakfast trays on the floor outside their rooms? My foot caught the unseen tray sending me, a half filled coffee pot, a plate, a cup and two partially nibbled bits of toast, headlong in a heap. I had no time to contemplate the surprising situation I found myself in. I jumped to my feet, tried to brush off the coffee spillage that adorned my left trouser leg and headed for the passage to my right. Two rooms along I found a door labelled Meeting Room 4.

I knocked and entered without waiting for a response. Inside five rows of chairs were set up, theatre style, facing the front of the room where a squat sergeant major type stood in a short sleeved white shirt, arms folded across his chest. Behind him, a screen displayed two cars on what appeared to be a motorway. To one side a flip chart had a large circle drawn in black marker with the figure thirty in its centre. All of the seats were occupied by a varied mix of people who had all turned to see the cause of the interruption.

The *sergeant major* spoke first.

'Can I help you?' he said in a curt, direct tone.

'I'm here for the speed awareness course,' I said.

'And you are?'

'Matthew Malarkey. I should be booked on the course.'

He walked towards a table on one side of the room and picked up a clipboard that he seemed to scrutinise for longer than was necessary. Finally, he scratched his semi-shaven head and said, 'Well Mister Malarkey, the good news is you are in the right place and you are indeed booked in. However, the bad news is that you are now almost forty-five minutes late and I am afraid I cannot accept you on the course.'

'But, I got held up. I'm really sorry. It was not my fault.'

'I am sorry Mister Malarkey, those are the rules. If you check your confirmation letter it clearly states that if you are late, you will not be admitted to the course.' His expression under the semi-shaven skull took on an even more sergeant majorish look as he emphasised the point.

'I know,' I said, 'but it was out of my control...there were hold ups and I got stopped by the police for...for...' I decided not to finish the sentence as I took in the expectant look of the audience.

'Well, I am sorry but we can make no exceptions. It is your responsibility, having agreed to take up the offer of the course, to ensure that you arrive in plenty of time.'

I could tell there would be no negotiating. The sergeant major's expression left no doubt. I turned to walk away. His voice cut through the silence again.

'Mister Malarkey…one moment.'

I wheeled around to face the front, a moment's optimism that he must have had a change of heart lifting my spirits. He raised a hand and pointed in my direction.

'You appear to have a bit of toast stuck to your jacket.'

My hand clasped at my jacket lapel, my fingers encountering a sticky marmalade goo attached to which was indeed a slice of half-chewed toast. I pulled it off, slid it into a pocket and walked out.

3

I strolled briskly through the reception area intent on heading straight to my car when I caught sight of a clock on a wall ahead of me. Almost five minutes to eleven. The realisation that I had nothing planned for the rest of my morning dawned on me. I had booked the day off so I was certainly not going to go to the office. I didn't fancy going back home and killing time. Missing the speed awareness course was going to cost me a fine and three points on my licence. I was already out of pocket for the course and I decided I might as well make the most of the day that I had unexpectedly gained. I switched direction and headed across reception towards the wall with the clock.

The marble tiled floor of the reception area gave way to a polished wood surface and I found myself in a spacious room with a long curved bar to my right. Behind the bar a thin young man, his pale complexion heightened by a black waistcoat and bow tie, was placing cups on to a tray. In the middle of the room, several round wooden tables, each with three deep, bucket-style leather seats tucked neatly against them, were scattered in a semi random pattern.

'Can I get you anything, Sir?'

I looked in the direction of the bar to see the young barman in full service mode. The smell of fresh coffee swayed my response.

'Thank you. Yes, a filter coffee please. With sugar.'

'Take a seat Sir and I will bring it right over.'

I pulled out one of the bucket seats and slumped into it, facing towards the reception area. The sudden sense of quiet triggered a flood of thought. How had I got myself into another predicament? Why were these calamities always happening to me? My past legal mishaps had not long been resolved. I seemed to be dogged by irksome situations that, to me, were beyond my control. Or maybe it was something I was doing? I was less than a week away from my fortieth birthday and it was time my life settled into some stability.

My moment's introspection was brought to an end by the sound of a tray clinking on the table as my coffee cup was placed in front of me with two cellophane wrapped biscuits balanced on a saucer.

'Thank you,' I said, as the barman turned and walked away.

I reached for my top pocket and checked my mobile for messages. A text from Cecil mockingly hoping I passed the course but nothing to distract me from the moment. A moment where I had to decide what making the most of the day would involve. I picked up my mobile again and dialled Louise. It went to answerphone.

'Hi Louise. It's Matthew. Just wondered what you were doing for lunch? Got some unexpected free time. I'll explain later.'

I tapped the 'end call' button, picked up a teaspoon, stirred the sugar into my coffee, and thought about where I might take Louise for lunch. My thoughts were interrupted by the jangling ring of my phone.

'Matthew? It's Louise. You ok? I missed your call. I was in the shower.'

'Oh, hi Louise. Yeah, I'm fine. What are you up to? Fancy lunch?'

'I'm working. I told you this morning. One o'clock shift through till ten tonight. Anyway, I thought you were on that course?'

'Yes, I am. Well sort of. I–'

'Sort of? How do you mean sort of?'

'Well I'm in the hotel where the course is but not actually on the course. I was late. They wouldn't let me on it. And now I'm just having a coffee and trying to decide what to do next.'

'Don't tell me. You and Cecil. Another late night?'

22

I took a sip of coffee and began an explanation.

'Kind of but not *that* late. I was in bed by two but the traffic this morning was really bad and I ended up running late. Then when the road was clear I was rushing and got stopped by your lot?'

'My lot?'

'Yes, your lot. The police.'

Louise Penny had been a police officer for several years. In fact if she had not been a police officer we may never have met. Our paths had crossed when she had almost arrested me six months earlier on a crazy night when I had brought part of Regents Park to a standstill running around in a gorilla suit. It was a period of my life when I was looking for something, looking for love and I had found Louise. My ill-judged escapades on an internet-dating site, another series of mishaps that had befallen me, had almost guaranteed that we would never get together but somehow, against the odds, we did.

'So what happened?' Louise asked. *'You know you're going to be fined now and get points on your licence and that will affect your insurance, don't you?'*

I was about to answer when I caught sight of what appeared to be two groups of people heading towards the bar area from different directions.

'I'll tell you all about it when I see you. Looks like it's about to get crowded in here. I'll probably just finish my coffee and be on my way. Catch you later.'

'Listen. Why don't you pick me up after work and come over to mine. We can have a quiet night in with a bottle of wine.'

'Ok. Sounds good. I'll see you at ten. Bye.'

The bar was suddenly full of people many of whom I recognised as having been in the conference and meeting rooms I had visited earlier. Soon the bucket seats were fully occupied by chattering groups. I caught sight of the sergeant major filling a coffee cup at the bar. Behind him stood Robin Hargreaves helping himself to biscuits from a large doily covered plate. They must have let both groups out at once for a break. So much for organisation. I didn't fancy revisiting my embarrassment with DashNet Internet's super salesman and nor did I wish to speak to the Speed Awareness sergeant major who had summarily dismissed me from his educational course. I was about to get up and leave when a voice caught my attention.

'Excuse me, is this anyone's seat?'

She was tall, thirtyish, brunette, her hair settling in a loose wave on her shoulders. I was slightly taken by surprise by her interruption and even more by her good looks. She must have taken my lack of response as an indication that no one else was due at my table.

'Do you mind if I sit here? Nearly all these tables are occupied and I don't really know anyone.' She pulled out the seat opposite mine, placed her coffee cup and saucer on the table and in the same fluid movement slid onto the seat. Her tight black skirt rode up above her knees as she adjusted her position.

'Hi. I'm Erin. Erin Farrell. I hope you don't mind me joining you.'

I detected the hint of an Irish brogue.

'No...err...not at all. Of course. I'm Matthew. Matthew Malarkey.'

'Oh yes. You are the young man that came into the course late. I thought so.'

I felt the blush flood my cheeks, not sure as to whether it was the flattery of being referred to as a *'young man'* that had caused it, or the embarrassing memory of my brief appearance in the Speed Awareness course. I raised my coffee cup to my lips in a sub-conscious attempt to hide my lack of composure only to find that I had finished the contents. I tipped the cup further back to make it appear that I was finishing the drink, aware of the fact that Erin's eyes were was still upon me. My focus remained on her as the cold dregs at the bottom of the cup dribbled down my chin. I lurched forward instinctively, wiping my face with the back of my hand and hoped she hadn't noticed.

She appeared not to have noticed or at least pretended she hadn't.

'Well don't worry you are not missing much. It's all terribly tedious. All that lecturing. Banging on about speed limits on country roads and motorways. I mean who wants to spend their morning looking at pictures of speed signs and listening to that short, bald chap going on about stopping distances in his holier than thou, I'm an *ex driving instructor who never breaks any laws whatsoever*, pompous manner.'

'Flatulent self importance if you ask me,' I said, pleased that someone shared my disapproval.

A broad smile flashed across Erin's face, creasing tiny laughter lines either side of her green eyes.

'An old fart, yes. To be honest I feel like a naughty schoolgirl being kept in after class. I wouldn't even be here if it weren't the better of the two options. I didn't fancy the points on my licence so I am taking the medicine. Anyway, looks like you will have to take the points then Matthew.'

I tried to dismiss the picture that had popped into my head of Erin Farrell as a naughty schoolgirl.

'It looks like it, yes.' I placed my cup back on the table and stood up. 'Excuse me a moment. I'm just going to get another coffee and I'll be back. Can I get you anything?'

Erin shook her head and said she was fine.

Two large coffee thermos pumps were positioned in the middle of the bar for delegates to dispense their own coffee. I placed a fresh cup under the spout and pressed the black button on the top of the unit.

'Hey Matthew. So why didn't you stay for the seminar?'

I turned to see Robin Hargreaves standing behind me, coffee cup in one hand, wafer biscuit poised in the other.

'Oh, there was a mix up. It was the wrong course.'

'The wrong course? DashNet Internet Solutions is at the forefront of high speed broadband delivery in this country and –'

'No. I mean the wrong place. I made a mistake. I got the speed thing mixed up and went into your meeting by mistake.'

'Yes, it appears he was meant to be in mine.'

The voice materialised over my right shoulder. The sergeant major. Instantly I saw an opportunity to perhaps retrieve the situation, try to get back on the course, and perhaps save my licence. I turned to face him.

'Yes, I was meant to be on yours. I'm mortified at missing it. I was looking forward to it too. I've just been talking to that lady over there and she's been saying what a great course it is so far.' I pointed in Erin's direction and caught sight of the sergeant major's eyes light up. Either he had the hots for Erin or he was flattered that someone might have found his course interesting. I tried to seize the moment.

'Look, sarge…I mean…err…' I glanced at the name badge that was clipped to the top pocket of his shirt. Phil Travers. 'Phil… err…Mister Travers…I wondered if there was any chance I might just slip in at the back and get the benefit of the course. I'm sure I could catch up with what I've missed. The lady over there has sort of updated me. Maybe I could do some homework or something?'

'You were late. You know the rules,' he said, his features taking on a stern look.

'I just made a mistake and went into the wrong course so technically I wasn't late. I –'

'He was late for my course too,' interrupted Robin Hargreaves.

Thanks a bunch Mister bloody interfering Hargreaves. I put my cup on the bar and turned towards him.

'I wasn't even meant to be on your course so I couldn't have been late. You can't be late for something you're not meant to be on, can you?' I turned back to the sergeant major. 'If there is any chance of getting back on, Mister Travers, I would appreciate it. I'm here to learn about…err…speeding…you know, to make sure I don't get caught…err…I mean, do it again.'

'Look you were late. The fact is, you were late for this gentleman's course too and that tells me you were running late. So you would not have made it to my course on time anyway. It says quite clearly in the paperwork that if you're late you will not be allowed to participate.'

I appeared to be getting nowhere.

'Ok, I was late because I was rushing and made a mistake, that's all. A simple mistake. Anyone can make a mistake.'

26

'That's the problem Mister Malarkey. Everyone is rushing these days. That's why I run these courses,' he said, a smug look crossing his features. 'And why precisely were you rushing?'

I picked up my coffee, grabbed two biscuits and turned to walk away.

'I was rushing because I was stopped by the bloody police for…for…oh forget it.'

I sat back down at the table with Erin. She smiled as I shuffled into the seat.

'You looked to be in deep conversation over there Matthew. Everything alright?'

'I was trying to persuade the sergeant to take me back onto the course. All I did was make a simple mistake and go into the wrong room. Now he's not having it because I was late.'

Erin crossed her shapely legs and placed her cup onto its saucer.

'The sergeant? That's funny. He is a bit like that isn't he? He's an ex-driving instructor apparently. Bit of power gone to his head I think. So why are you here anyway? What did you do wrong?'

'I was doing forty-six in a forty zone and got flashed. What about you?'

'Oh I'm much more of a villain than you. I was doing sixty-nine on what I thought was a dual carriageway, on my way to the airport, a whole nine miles an hour over the limit. Bad girl. Still it's much more fun breaking the law than being a goody-two shoes all the time, don't you think?'

I ignored the question recalling past mishaps with the police. 'I thought it was seventy on a dual carriageway?'

'Apparently not. According to Mister Driving Expert in there, I was on a single carriageway with two lanes and the limit is sixty. Bloody confusing if you ask me.'

'That was unfortunate then. So you thought you were within the speed limit but were in fact nine miles an hour over it?'

'Yes. Very unfortunate. Nine…my unlucky number.' She smiled and picked up her coffee again.

'And mine seems to be six by that reckoning then,' I said. 'We wouldn't be here but for my unlucky six and your unlucky nine.'

I caught the mischievous twinkle in her eyes as she stared over the coffee cup.

'Err, well, anyway, I hope you caught your flight,' I said. 'Missing your flight wouldn't have been a good way to start your holiday.'

'Oh no, I wasn't going on holiday. I work there. I'm a flight attendant. You know, cabin crew. Always rushing to the airport.'

'Sounds exciting. I love airports. As a matter of fact I'm flying off myself on Friday.'

'Trust me. When it's your job day after day the excitement soon wears thin. Where are you off to?'

'Vegas,' I said, feeling a sudden rush as I used just the latter part of the name, as if I was an old hand, a seasoned visitor to the city.

'Ooooh, Las Vegas! Nice. On Friday. Have you been before?'

'No first time. A birthday trip. My birthday. I'm looking forward to it.'

'Oh you'll love it. You'll be mesmerised. Mmmm, a new boy in Sin City, eh.' The green eyes flashed mischief again as she said it. 'How exciting. I have a weekend off. Much rather be in Vegas though.' She picked up her coffee again, red tipped fingers gently tapping the side of the cup as she held it in front of her. 'Where are you staying?'

'The Paris, I think. I only found out last night. Bit of a surprise to be honest?'

'The Paris? I know it. I've not stayed there but I know the Strip quite well. I've had a drink or two in there. It'll be great. How long for?'

'Just the five nights...I think.'

'That's about enough in Vegas sometimes. Who are you going with? A girlfriend, I expect.'

'Oh, no. Not at all. It's a lad's trip. Well you know, guys only.' I was slightly taken aback at my eagerness to emphasis it was a trip with the boys. Perhaps it is a male response to brush over the subject of girlfriends when in the company of attractive women, almost as if the mention of another female diminishes the male's appeal. I felt a rush of guilt. 'It was all organised by my friend and anyway my girlfriend is visiting a friend this weekend so maybe we will go another time.'

'Ooooh, when the cat's away, eh?'

I felt myself blush but I didn't know why. Erin saw it.

'I'm embarrassing you Matthew. Forgive me. I'm just teasing.' She stretched out a hand and gently patted my arm, as if soothing away my sudden discomfort. 'Anyway what do you do for a living?'

'I'm in the leisure business. A marketing manager for a chain of health clubs. Conditioning Centres is how we brand them. I was on my way to visit a corporate client when I triggered the speed camera.'

To my left a rustle of movement and the clearing of cups signalled that the coffee break was coming to an end. Erin caught my glance at the course delegates leaving their seats. She picked up her handbag from the floor, finished her coffee and stood up.

'Looks like we are back in class, Matthew. Lucky you having the day off. Nice to meet you.' She smiled warmly and held out her hand.

'Nice to meet you too Erin,' I said as I shook her hand. 'Good luck with the rest of the day. Hope it isn't too dull.'

'Thank you. Have a fantastic time in Vegas. I know you'll love it.' The smile lit up her eyes again. 'Do you have a business card? Some of my colleagues are always talking about joining health clubs.'

I reached into my jacket pocket for a card and stretched out my hand. I noticed a moment's astonishment flicker across Erin's face.

'Well, Matthew, very kind of you to offer but…erm…that's actually a bit of toast.'

4

The night before the trip I stayed with Louise. I pulled a soft white pillow down close to my shoulders and stretched out.

'Isn't it a fabulous idea?' Louise said, as I reached across and stroked her hair. 'Las Vegas for your fortieth. Cecil is such a great guy and he thinks the world of you. I said you'd love it.'

'You did? You encouraged him? What about you and me?'

'We can do something to celebrate when you get back. Look Matthew, you know how I feel about you but that doesn't mean to say we have to live in one another's pockets all the time. Sometimes it's good to have your own space, to do things with your friends. Stop worrying. I know you like a bit of a party from time to time and there is no reason why you can't see your friends just because you have a girlfriend now. I do have girlfriend status now, haven't I?'

I caught the playful wink and smiled at her. I had been looking hard enough to find someone and now that we had found one another, I didn't intend to mess it up.

'You go out there and enjoy yourself Matthew. Don't be worrying about me. I will have a lovely few days with Sheryl before she goes back to Toronto. Can't believe her six months is nearly over. I will miss her when she goes.'

Six months had flown by so quickly. Sheryl had been with Louise the first night I had met her properly, in MacFadden's. (I didn't count meeting her whilst I was in a gorilla suit, going to a date's fancy dress party, as a proper meeting.) I remembered the

30

evening in MacFadden's clearly; how I had made a total fool of myself, spilling my drinks and inventing an alter ego, to avoid looking foolish. Just to avoid being recognised as the idiot in the gorilla suit. Sheryl was Canadian, a forensic scientist working with the Metropolitan police on a short time assignment. She had hit it off with Louise and they had become good friends. She had also hit it off with Cecil and they had been seeing one another on a fairly casual basis over the previous few months.

'Well, you two will always keep in touch, won't you?' I said. 'And it's great to have a friend abroad as you will get invited out to see her too.'

'You're right. I know. But I am definitely going to miss her. She's been such great company. Anyway, I have a surprise for you.' She jumped off the bed, grabbed her bathrobe and disappeared down stairs. A few moments later she returned carrying a large, gift wrapped package. She pushed the box across the duvet towards me. 'A pressie for you darling.'

'For me?'

'Of course it's for you, silly. Who else has got a birthday in this room?'

'But it's not until Saturday.'

'I know that but you won't be here on Saturday, will you?'

'That's true. So, it's a birthday present then,' I said, stating the obvious but still taken aback by the size of the box.

'No. It's a homemade bomb and it is designed to go off in thirty seconds unless you start unwrapping it right now. Come on then. I'm excited. Open it. Let's see what it is.'

Louise half sat and half knelt on the bed, her face wide-eyed with anticipation. I started to unpick the wrapping, slightly puzzled about the way women got excited about the opening of presents that they had bought when they already knew exactly what was in the box. The final piece of wrapping came away to reveal two square boxes. The first one that caught my eye had the words *Canon EOS1100D* emblazoned across the shiny exterior. The bold central picture of a camera registered immediately.

'Wow, Louise. That's fantastic.'

I tore at the lid of the box to reveal the shiny, serious looking piece of photographic equipment that was enveloped in a plastic bag inside it. I lifted it out and felt the light but sturdy sensation it created in my hand.

A broad grin spread across Louise's face.

'I thought you might like it. You're always taking pictures on your mobile so time to get more professional.'

I picked up the second box and stared at the print. *Tamron AF70-300mm lens.* I pulled open the lid and lifted out a long black zoom lens.

'Blimey, you have gone for the full package. A zoom lens too.' It was heavier than the camera itself and had a series of numbers encircling the circumference, none of which meant anything to me at that point.

She saw my slightly puzzled look.

'There are loads of instructions with it. You can read them on the flight. I put the battery on charge yesterday so you should be able to try a few practice shots. Now let's get some sleep. You have an early start tomorrow.'

'It's brilliant Louise. A fantastic present. Thank you so much.' I leant across and pulled her to me intent on giving her a big hug. A playful giggle accompanied her outstretched hand as she held me off.

'Hey, come on. We need to get some sleep if we are going to be up at 5.30.'

'Ok, ok, but I want a few shots of you first. A quick try out.'

Flicking a switch on the casing, I powered up the camera and pointed it at Louise. She tossed her blonde hair back and affected an exaggerated model-like pose. I squeezed the shutter button and heard the whirr of the camera motor as it captured my first picture. A glance at the display on the back revealed the shot. Almost perfect.

'That's cool. It must be on automatic,' I said. I raised the camera again and fired off another three shots. Each time Louise adopted yet another exaggerated pose, playing to the lens.

'Ok, now close your eyes, tilt your head back and put the back of your hand across your brow. Good…that's it. Hold it there.'

As Louise adopted a drama queen pose I shot out my left hand and pulled her dressing gown open. At the same time I hit the camera button. Her reaction was a mere nano-second slower than the camera shutter.

'You bugger. What are you doing?' She grabbed a pillow and clumped me straight round the head.

I caught the twinkle in her eye as I took evasive action.

'I'm a respectable police officer. I don't want shots like that all over the internet. Now put it away Mister Malarkey and go to sleep before I cuff you up and frog march you down the station.'

The alarm shattered the deep slumber I had been in at precisely 5.30am. Louise was already up making toast. An hour later my luggage was in the car and we were ready to go.

'Have you got everything Matthew?' Louise asked.

'Yep, all in order and ready to go.'

'So, where's your camera then?'

'Oh...sorry, yes. I left it on the table. Hang on.'

I came back out to the hallway carrying the camera, the zoom lens and the boxes. Louise shot a swift glance in my direction, disappeared into the bedroom and appeared a minute later carrying a large, black rucksack with the Nike Swoosh emblazoned across it.

'Here. Take this. You won't need all those boxes. Leave them here. All you need is the equipment, the charger and the instruction book. Put it all in the bag and keep it together.'

'Oh, ok, good idea. I can stick my video camera in there too,' I said as I dropped the cardboard boxes on the hallway floor.

'There's a pocket in the front too. You can put your passport and books and whatever else you want to take with you on the plane in there. Now let's get moving.'

We pulled up at the passenger drop off point outside Terminal 5, Gatwick Airport at 7.40am. The flight was at 11.25am but Cecil had insisted we meet at 7.45. I had no idea why he thought we needed to be there nearly four hours ahead. In his assumed role of trip organiser, he had been very specific about the timings when we had met up in MacFadden's. He had been reluctant to elaborate when I'd questioned him, insisting that it 'makes sense to get there early.'

The cool morning air drifted across my face as I opened the car door and stepped onto the pavement. Louise flipped the boot and I grabbed my suitcase. As I extended the handle she reached out for a hug.

'I'll miss you Matthew. You have a fantastic time, ok.'

'I'll miss you too.' I held her tight, breathing in her scent, a lingering embrace that embodied how close we had become in the last few weeks. My mind was racing, a mix of regret at leaving Louise behind and excitement at the prospect of the trip ahead.

'Ok, now have you got everything? Passport, tickets, wallet...?'

'Ces, has the tickets. He told us he'd give them to us at the airport.' I checked the inside pocket of my jacket for my passport. It wasn't there. 'My passport. I haven't...'

Louise saw my sudden concern as I fumbled through every pocket.

'Matthew! Twit. Your hand luggage. It's still on the back seat.' She reached through the back door and pulled out the Nike rucksack. The passport was in the side pocket. 'Bit early to slip into holiday mode. You can chill when you get there. Just make sure you don't lose that passport or you're going nowhere. Put it in your jacket pocket. You're going to need it soon anyway. Now go on. I'll see you next week. Call me.'

She kissed me firmly on the lips and pushed me in the direction of the terminal entrance.

5

It was Carlos I saw first.

'Hola Mateo. How's aw wi ye? Cómo estás?'

A broad grin cracked across his face as he spoke. What he lacked in height he more than made up for with personality. He had a tendency to slip into a dialect that veered between broad Scottish and flowing Spanish when he was drunk, or excited, or both. I hoped that at that time of the day it was simply excitement.

'I'm good Carlos. Where's the boys?'

A nod of his head in the direction of a W H Smith newsagent revealed their whereabouts. Jasper Kane walked towards me, a couple of newspapers tucked under his arm. Cecil followed behind.

'You made it Matt. Good to see you,' Jasper said, his hand outstretched in greeting.

'More important, glad you decided to make the trip Jasper. Good to have you on board.'

Cecil looked me up and down, a half smile playing across his face.

'We thought you'd bottled it geezer. We bin here half an hour already,' he said.

'I'm hardly going to duck out of a trip to Vegas Ces, am I? Anyway, what's all the mad rush about? We've got plenty of time?'

'Mate, the holiday has just begun. Got to maximise it. You'll see. Now let's get checked in. Got a little surprise for ya.'

Within forty minutes our bags had been checked, we had passed through security and passport control, and were airside. Cecil led the way heading for a stairwell at the far side of the terminal. At the top of the stairs he led us through a door, marked *VIP Hospitality*, into a wide spacious lounge. Along one side, floor to ceiling windows showered daylight into the room and allowed a panoramic view of the airport runway system. To our right a row of executive style chairs lined the window area. In front of these, a number of soft cushioned sofas stood in a rectangle around low oblong tables. To the left there was a cafe style seating area and several more rows of sofas hugging similar tables. In the centre a long bar ran half the length of the wall.

'Nice in here, lads,' Jasper said, 'Good choice Ces.'

'It's gotta be done mate. Might as well start the trip on the right note,' Cecil replied as he lowered himself into one of the sofa seats next to Jasper and picked up a menu.

'So what's going on Ces,' I asked, feeling that I was the only one not in the loop. I placed my rucksack by the side of the sofa and sat down opposite Cecil. Carlos sidled in on my left.

'Mate, it's your birthday trip, right. So a little hospitality is in order. We booked it for ya. Everything's on the house. Little surprise. That's what mates do? So what we having then lads?' He didn't wait for an answer but replied to his own question. 'Gotta be Champagne to start a birthday trip, I reckon.'

Carlos and Jasper nodded agreement. I was the only dissenter.

'Bit early to start on the booze, Ces. It's only twenty-five to nine.'

'Geezer, what's the matter with ya? You gotta acclimatise, ain't ya. We're going to Vegas right? So right now in Las Vegas it is... let's see.' He raised his left arm in the air in an exaggerated fashion and pointed to his watch. 'It's not long past midnight. Twelve-thirtyish to be precise. You wouldn't object to a little livener at that time of night wouldya?'

I ignored the fact that Cecil's twelve-thirtyish wasn't exactly precise.

'No, but I don't know about you but my body clock's still in UK time. I fancied a bit of breakfast to be honest,' I said.

'Breakfast. You'll get breakfast mate. They got it all in here. Chill geezer. It's your birthday do.' He waved at the waitress and placed the order.

Within two minutes an ice bucket was brought to the table, the Champagne uncorked and four glasses at the ready. Cecil didn't wait for the waitress. He grabbed the bottle, wiped away the glistening water droplets and stretched across the table to fill my glass.

'Cheers mate. No lightweights on this road trip,' he said, winking at Carlos and Jasper. When the remaining three glasses were filled Cecil raised his in the air. 'To Vegas, lads.'

The first sip caused a grimace, not because there was anything wrong with it but simply because it was still so early in the day. I wasn't quite used to the sparkling, bittersweet tang of Champagne when I should have been drinking tea.

Cecil noticed.

'That's what I mean mate about getting acclimatised. You gotta prepare your body. It's like an athlete who's gonna compete at altitude. He's gotta put the work in first so that when he gets there he's right on the programme. Yeah?'

I wasn't sure that Cecil's analogy was quite appropriate given the difference between disciplined training and outright indulgence but I remembered what Louise had said. 'Enjoy it.' I raised the glass in my own toast.

'To Vegas boys...and thanks. Thanks for this. Thanks for the trip.'

'Vegas.' My three travelling companions raised their glasses again and in unison gulped down most of the contents.

The Champagne didn't take long to hit the spot and I knew I should eat something. I ordered breakfast. Poached egg with Hollandaise sauce, tomato, mushrooms and bacon. Cecil ordered more Champagne and bacon rolls for the boys.

'Not a bad looking little waitress,' Jasper said, his grin matching whatever thought was racing through his mind.

'Do me a favour,' piped up Carlos, 'They all start to look good once the bubbly slips down.'

'No, mate, I caught a little twinkle there. She was giving me the once over. I know the look, don't worry about that.'

'Well, you'll get your chance to put yer skills on show, Jas, she's on her way back,' Cecil said.

Carlos and I both turned round and caught a fleeting glimpse of the waitress carrying a loaded tray of food. Our next view of the food was altogether more enduring as it sailed through the air straight over both Cecil and Jasper, who had taken instant evasive action when they saw the trajectory of the waitress's tray. As the tray reacted to gravity, an assortment of breakfast items were deposited fairly and squarely onto the lap of an elderly, pinstripe suited businessman who was sitting on a sofa behind. Luckily most of the contents landed in a copy of the Financial Times that rested on his lap, but the eggs Benedict hit him square in the chest, covering his white shirt and navy blue tie in bright yellow Hollandaise Sauce. For a brief moment, as the reality of what had happened took time to sink in, it occurred to me that the yellow livened up the tie a touch and made him appear less formal. Clearly taken by surprise the man sat frozen in disbelief as one half of the muffin slid down the gooey liquid and dropped onto his newspaper. For a while he didn't react and just stared at the muffin as if he was thinking, '*I didn't order this.*' With our attention focussed on the besieged businessman we hadn't noticed the waitress. From my right I caught sight of something moving on the floor. Climbing to her knees, the waitress looked devastated.

'I am so sorry,' she said in the direction of the businessman who had finally looked up from the breakfast in his lap. 'I didn't see it. I'm sorry. I tripped. It was the bag. I couldn't help it.'

The bag. The word reverberated through my head. The bag. What bag? Surely not? I jumped to my feet and glanced at the floor next to my seat. My bag was not there.

'What bag?' I blurted out.

'This fucking bag geezer.'

I turned to see Cecil leaning back to retrieve my Nike rucksack, which had slid further along the floor and slightly behind his seat. He held it out towards me.

'It's yours ain't it? What you doing leaving it in the fucking gangway? My breakfast is all over that geezer sat behind me now.'

The waitress was back on her feet frantically trying to help the businessman remove the mess from his shirt. He seemed to be taking it all in good part, which was a relief.

'I didn't think Ces. I just put it down. It was just the surprise of this place. I didn't think. We'll get some more food.'

'What's in it anyway? Weighs a ton.'

'Just my cameras and stuff. It's hand luggage.'

'Well, here stick it under yer seat. I don't want that little waitress chucking our Champagne over everybody as well.'

I took the bag from Cecil and stuffed it under my seat as he'd suggested. Cecil turned towards the man behind him.

'It wasn't the waitress's fault my friend. It was ours. My mate's bag in the way. It's his birthday. Bit of high spirits. Accidents happen. Let me get you a drink or something.'

Cecil applied the charm. Our new acquaintance, on route to Rome, was gracious enough to accept his offer. Cecil ordered more Champagne. Another round of breakfast was delivered.

Approximately two hours later we made the last call for our flight.

6

There is a sense of anticipation when you first enter an aircraft, heightened by the fact that you are finally on board, the point of no return. The start of an adventure. I dropped into my seat relieved to have been in the first phase of seat numbers to be called to board. The Champagne breakfast had started to kick in and I had begun to feel pleasantly drowsy. Cecil sat in the window seat with Carlos in the middle one. Jasper's seat was across the aisle in the centre row to my right. He leant across to me as I fastened my seat belt.

'Gonna be a good one Matt, Can't wait to get there.'

I smiled back at him, clicked the buckle into place and stretched my legs out under the seat in front. As soon as we were airborne I intended to recline my seat fully and catch up on a few hours sleep. Ahead of me, along both sides of the aircraft, passengers bustled around trying to get what seemed like oversized hand luggage into the overhead bins, blocking the progress of others as they stuffed their personal paraphernalia into the available space. Others stood in a semi-crouch in their seating space, wrestling with coats and jackets as they tried to remove them without smacking their neighbours in the face with a flailing arm. I watched as several ducked back out into the aisle again to place the clothing overhead causing yet more hold ups. A flight attendant walked slowly through the cabin checking that hand luggage was stowed safely. When she was satisfied that all was well she slammed each huge bin door firmly into place.

And then it dawned on me.

My own hand luggage. My rucksack. Where was it? I hadn't placed it in an overhead locker. In fact I didn't remember carrying it onto the plane. I tried to get to my feet but only succeeded in performing what appeared to be a convulsive jerk forward as my seat belt arrested my movement and I was yanked back into the seat.

'Shit. My hand luggage. Bollocks.'

'What's up Mateo?'

I heard Carlos speak but was too busy tugging at the belt buckle. As the belt fell away I stood up and I hit the flight attendant call button in the panel above my head.

'What's going on Mateo?' Carlos asked again.

My sudden burst of activity had alarmed passengers around me. A low chatter had broken out. People had begun to point at me.

'My bag, Carlos. I think I left my bag. My bloody bag...my hand luggage...in the airport lounge. I got to get it back. I don't remember taking it on the plane.' I stepped into the aisle but was confronted by one of the flight attendants, a young man in his early twenties.

'You pressed the passenger service unit, Sir. Can I help you?' he asked.

'I have to get off the plane,' I said. 'It's my bag. My bag. I placed it under the seat. It's going to go. I have to get off.'

The young steward went pale, his facial expression changing from helpful customer service mode to the stern look of anxiety.

'Stay calm please Sir. Your bag is under a seat? Where?'

'Yes. It is. In the aircraft...the aircraft lounge place. Under the seat. I need to get off before it goes.'

'Can you tell me what is in it Sir?'

The commotion and the pointing along with the sense that I might have lost my birthday present from Louise had unsettled me. In addition, several glasses of Champagne had begun to take a toll on my thought processes and my response was not as coherent as it should have been.

'Well...err photo...erm...equipment...it's got a telescopic...

41

thing for shooting...what do you call it...' I tried to recall what I had read on the box. 'A telescopic attachment...for shooting long range. You know...what are they called?'

'A sight. A telescopic sight Sir?'

My mind refused to focus. 'Kind of...yes...a –'

'Wait there Sir.' The young steward turned abruptly before I had a chance to finish my explanation and beckoned a more senior looking colleague forward. The two huddled together in a secretive whisper. An elderly woman in the seat in front had clearly caught snippets of the conversation and felt the need to inform her travelling companions. Within seconds, a murmur was travelling through the seated rows about a *'bag under his seat that's ready to go off.'*

As the hubbub began to grow into a general wave of loud chatter, the older flight attendant announced that he was calling security.

I tried to protest.

'No, you don't understand. I left the bag under a seat in the airport lounge. The hospitality bar, whatever it's called. I need to get off the plane to –'

'I'm afraid we can't let you off the aircraft Sir. You need to wait here,' the younger flight attendant said.

Cecil got to his feet.

'What's going on geezer? The whole fucking plane is in uproar over your stupid bag. Leave it. It's caused enough aggro already.'

I turned back towards Cecil.

'I can't leave it. It's got my camera in it. The one Louise bought me for my birthday. And my telescopic sight...photo lens, I mean. I can't lose it all. My passport is in there too.'

'Your passport? Hang on a minute you nob. You can't have left your passport in it or you wouldn't be on the fucking plane would you?'

Cecil had a point. I reached into my jacket pocket and sure enough, the passport was there. Carlos tugged at my jacket.

'Hey, Mateo. Relax. Look you're on the plane now. You have your passport. You can get to Vegas. No sense in trying to get off over the bag. The security people will find it and you can ask them to send it on to the hotel or something. Maybe they'll do that, I don't know. Might cost you a bit, but what the hell. Don't forget we only have five nights there so you can't lose any time. The point is to get to Vegas. Comprendo?'

'Makes sense, Matt,' Jasper said, 'No point in spoiling your trip over a bag, eh?'

'Mate, Carlos is right. Just tell them to send it to the Paris, Las Vegas. It's where we're staying. OK?' Cecil added to reinforce the sensible approach. 'Then we can get this baby off the ground and check out the drinks trolley.'

I sat back down in my seat. They were right. It did make sense. I was devastated that I had lost my bag but had a sudden wave of optimism that it could be resolved. My optimism was short lived. The senior flight attendant returned. Behind him, two armed police officers walked down through the aisle towards me. As they approached, the flight attendant stood to one side, pointed in my direction and let them pass. The older of the two police officers stopped in front of me, legs apart, a scowl crossing his features. The facial expression was either his standard demeanour for intimidating suspects or a genuine irritation at having a break interrupted.

'Good morning Sir. Can you step out into the aisle please.'

I did as I was told.

'You appear to have a problem with a bag I hear.' His sidekick stood slightly behind him looking over his shoulder. 'Where is this bag?'

'I left it…in the hospitality lounge in the terminal,' I said, half hoping that they would just fetch it and let us get on with the flight.

'Whereabouts Sir? We need to know its exact location.'

'It's under the seat…where I was sitting…I'm sorry to have caused so much bother officer,' I said.

'Bit late to be sorry now Sir. I understand you've been saying it's about to go off.'

I was beginning to get the distinct impression that he was not too sympathetic towards my predicament.

'Well yes…I mean, no…I mean…go off? No, it's just left there. Somebody will get it.'

'Apparently you are in possession of a telescopic sight for long range shooting as well.'

I took a deep breath and tried not to look at the weapons both men were carrying.

'It's a…yes…a…you know, a telescopic lens…in a camera bag. Why? I just want to get off so I can sort it.'

I made a move forward. There was a general murmur around the cabin. The police officer stretched out an arm and placed his hand on my shoulder.

'You stay where you are Sir. You're going nowhere until I say.'

Cecil jumped to his feet. 'Officer, what's the mumble here? Can we not sort this?'

'It's nothing to do with you Sir. I'm talking to this gentleman.'

I held both hands up in front of me in a placatory action.

'Ok, ok. Easy. I just want to get it before it goes. That's all.'

'It's on a timer is it? Have you set it off? I need to know right now,' he said, his voice taking on a sharp, urgent tone.

A timer? Most cameras had one.

'It could be. Look, we're wasting time here. Somebody's going to get it,' I said.

As I finished speaking, he beckoned towards his sidekick. They both stepped towards me.

'Right Sir, I've had enough of this messing about. You need to come with us.' He placed a helpful hand under my right elbow to encourage me forward.

I shrugged it aside. 'It's ok,' I said, 'I'll leave the bag now. Perhaps you could send it to –'

'Get moving. You're coming with us.' His helpful physical encouragement was more pronounced this time as he tugged my arm and pulled me forward.

Again I protested. 'Look, there's no need, I –'

I was manhandled along the gangway by the two police officers, my right arm suddenly twisted behind me and shoved up against my back.

Cecil stepped out into the aisle and started to follow. 'Hey, let go of him geezer or I'll –'

'Get back to your seat, Sir, unless you want to get off this aircraft too.' The stern voice of the copper meant business.

'Leave it Ces. Not worth getting involved,' I called out over my shoulder. 'I'll sort this out and be back.'

Cecil realised there was no point in pursuing it.

'Ok, mate. Get it sorted and get back here. See you in Vegas.'

They led me to a holding room and asked for my passport. I waited five minutes until a heavyset man, in black framed glasses and a tight white shirt entered the room. The buttons of his shirt struggled to contain his belly. He sat down at a table opposite me, introduced himself as Detective Inspector Richardson from Aviation Security and began to flick through the pages of my passport. Then the questions began.

'So which organisation are you with then Mister Malarkey?'

I thought that an odd place to start, wondering what my work had to do with anything.

'Organisation? I…erm, do memberships. I'm in conditioning centres. Improving people's lives through –'

'What's the aim of that organisation Mister Malarkey?'

'The aim? Well, it's to focus people on their well-being through conditioning. To have an impact on the public mindset so that they –'

'You extremist groups are all the same. You think that your way is the right way, don't you?' He leant across the table so that his face was just a few feet from mine. 'Conditioning, yeah. I know your type. Playing with people's heads. Brainwashing. That your game is it?'

It was clear he wasn't in the best of shape himself but I thought it was a bit of an overreaction to label the sale of gym memberships as 'brainwashing.'

'I wouldn't say that. We are only trying to make a difference in people's lives. To the way they view themselves. Anyway, what's this got to do with my...' I hesitated as the words finally made an impact on my brain. 'Whoa...wait a minute. Did you say extremist groups? You did...didn't you? You think I'm a...a terrorist?' The shock of what I realised he had said sent a wave of panic straight through me, the anxiety tightening my chest so that my breath came in deep, rapid fits. I needed a glass of water. There was none there. I asked my interrogator if I could have a drink. He walked to the door and called down the corridor. A few moments later a jug of water and two glasses were delivered to the room. The brief interruption gave me time to compose myself.

'Listen Mister Richardson...Detective Inspector. There's a lot of confusion here.' I explained how I had left the bag behind and how I had tried to tell the two police officers that I had just forgotten it. I told him that all it contained was a camera, a video camera and a John Grisham book. I had done nothing more than mislay it. I had been in the hospitality bar and left it by mistake under the seat. I left the bit out about the waitress tripping over it. I didn't feel that it was necessary to make myself look any more foolish than I had already. I was simply on a birthday trip to Vegas. I asked if they had checked the bag out yet.

'The area is under police control at the moment checking for explosives and weapons. We have evacuated the whole terminal and have a bomb disposal team, dogs and weapons experts there at the scene now Mister Malarkey,' DI Richardson said.

'You've done what? Evacuated the terminal. But there's no need. There are no explosives, no weapons.'

'You told the flight attendant you had a telescopic sight for shooting long range. I am taking your threat very seriously.'

'No I didn't. I didn't say that. I said I had a telescopic...tele... telephoto lens. For a camera. I just couldn't think of the name in the confusion. I have just got the thing. It's new. There is no threat. I can just go and get the bag if you like and you can let everyone back into the terminal. All those people will be delayed and their holiday plans upset and –'

'Don't tell me how to do my job Mister Malarkey. We need to follow procedures. You should have thought of all that before you decided to play your little hoax on the aircraft, if that is what it is.'

'But I didn't do anything. I told you. I just forgot my bag. It was a mistake. It is harmless It only has my cameras in it. I've told you that.'

Detective Inspector Richardson's gaze never softened. It was clear he was not going to accept my story until he had been through his own checks. I sat back in my chair, exasperated at this turn of events that now found me back in the airport terminal instead of on the flight to Vegas.

'How long will this take then?' I asked. 'I need to be on that plane to Vegas.'

'It takes as long as it takes. The safety of passengers is our priority. If it is clear that the bag is harmless, as you say, you will be re-united with it and can be on your way. We will have to carry out some background security checks on you too. I'm afraid there is no chance of you being on that flight. That plane will be long gone by the time you leave here. You wouldn't want to get back on it anyway even if you could. Which, I might add, you can't. You wouldn't exactly be Mister Popular. You've already delayed it long enough. Your luggage is being off loaded as we speak.'

At 12.45, approximately one hour and forty minutes after leaving the flight I was released by security. Reunited with my bag and luggage I wandered into the terminal. I was still dazed by the events that had caused me to miss my birthday trip and devastated at the fact that I would not be with the lads after they had gone to so much trouble. I sat for a moment and pondered how I was to get home. '*See you in Vegas,*' Cecil had called after me. I stood up and began to walk towards the terminal exit following the sign for trains. Heavy hearted I passed through an assortments of travellers, business people and holiday makers, some tugging their luggage purposefully in the direction of check in points, others standing staring at departure monitors that reeled an endless stream of brightly numbered flight details across dark screens. Flights to all corners of the world, none of which included me. As I stared blankly at yet another screen, a sudden burst of positivity surged over me. Flights. That's what they do in airports. Hundreds of them. I was already in an airport. If I was going to see the lads in Vegas I knew what I had to do.

I rushed across to the nearest information desk full of renewed enthusiasm.

'Good morning. Could you tell me when the next flight is to Las Vegas? I need a single seat, just one way.'

The receptionist scanned a screen in front of her.

'Nothing available here today Sir,' she said. 'I can get you out on Sunday morning. Everything else is fully booked until then.'

My optimism had dipped faster than a fairground roller coaster.

'Isn't there anything? Anything today at all? I can't leave it until Sunday. I am booked to return on Wednesday night.'

The lady was helpful. She trawled through her computer screen again. Finally she looked up.

'As I say Sir, nothing at all from here but I can get you one today direct to Las Vegas from Heathrow. It leaves at 16.15, arriving at 18.45 US time at McCarran International.'

'Fantastic. I'll take it.' I checked my watch. Five past one. I could get a taxi to Heathrow and be there in time. That way I'd only be roughly four and a half hours behind the lads. We had been due in to Vegas at 14.10.

'It's coming in at £1,428 one way, Sir.'

'How much?' I gasped at the cost.

'I am afraid that you are paying full rate for such a late booking. There is only one seat left.'

Decisions. Sometimes a pivotal moment is reached. Pull the trigger and go for it or miss the moment and possibly regret that you were not decisive enough.

'I'll take it.' I was only going to be forty once.

I left Gatwick in a taxi at one thirty. Just over an hour later, at two thirty five, I was at Heathrow. Check in was straightforward. I kept a watchful eye on my hand luggage, my only distraction being the Duty Free shop where I bought a bottle of Bombay Gin. With the hectic morning I had been through I was tempted to open it there and then.

Half an hour before flight time, I walked through the boarding tunnel and stepped through the aircraft door. As I reached out my boarding pass for inspection my mind was focussed on nothing more than getting to the right seat with my hand luggage. I hadn't noticed the familiar face but I heard the greeting.

'Hello. How are you?'

Erin Farrell.

7

We were thirty minutes into the flight when she came to see me.

I had been browsing through a copy of the Washington Post given to me by a fellow traveller, an American businessman who had slipped into a gentle slumber in the seat next to me. The paper was a typical mix of sport, crime and social comment.

Redskins face the New Orleans Saints and their pass-happy offensive attack on Sunday; Nationals blast six homers for second consecutive night; Lawyer to testify in political sex abuse case; Police probe link to organised crime in $2m Baltimore wages heist; Homebuilders in Las Vegas have been able to increase both sales and prices this year.

It is never easy trying to digest another country's news. Unfamiliarity perhaps. I was glad of the interruption.

'So how did you manage to get yourself on my flight Matthew?' Erin asked, a dazzling smile lighting her perfectly made up face.

'It's a long story.' I didn't feel too inclined to explain my earlier predicament.

'Well we have ten hours to Vegas. Plenty of time to tell me.'

'Oh, it's not that exciting. I mislaid my hand luggage and missed my original flight. Pretty stupid really.'

Erin's smile changed to a puzzled expression.

'But I got it sorted,' I said, trying to keep it simple as I didn't want her to realise exactly how stupid I had been.

'Oh dear. But you got it back then?'

'Yes, I did. It has my cameras in it, one of them brand new…a birthday present. I would have been really upset if I'd lost it. Anyway, it's safely tucked away in the overhead locker now. Lucky to get it back I suppose and very lucky to get another flight today as well.'

'Yes and my flight too. How wonderful. So where are your friends you told me about?'

'They're all on the flight I missed. Bit ahead of me. Anyway, so how come you're working? I'm sure you said you were doing something this weekend?' I said, to change the subject.

'I was but one of the team went down with flu so I stood in for her, but I get a few days stopover so that'll be good.'

'A bit of a holiday for you too then,' I said.

'Absolutely. Perhaps we can meet up for a drink or something if you're not too busy with your pals when you all catch up. You're at the Paris, aren't you?'

'That's right. Sure. That would be good,' I said, flattered that she wanted to meet me.

She pulled a pen from the top pocket of her white shirt. 'Here. Take my mobile. Give me a call.' She scribbled her number across the top of the Washington Post, tore the section off the paper and handed it to me. The American businessman stirred in his seat.

'Now speaking of a drink would you like a glass of Champagne Matthew?' Erin asked.

'I'd love one. May help me get some sleep too. It's a long flight.'

'Actually, I did look to see if I could get you upgraded but we are completely full on this trip.' She noticed the American. She leant forward in his direction, her eyes focussed directly on him. 'I'll bring you a glass of Champagne too Sir, if you'd like?'

It was almost impossible for him to refuse her offer. She turned and walked back along the aisle. The American tapped me on the arm.

'Hey buddy. Howd'you do that? That's one good looking airhostess. Love the uniform and that ponytail. Howd'you manage to get her number? You Brits are real smooth talkers.'

'Oh...err...no. It wasn't like...I kind of know her. Just coincidence. We met recently on a speed course.'

'Speed dating? You think that works? I was thinking of doing that maself.'

'No. Not speed dating. Just a driving course thing. Long story actually.'

'Well I got time buddy. We got ten hours on this baby. By the way, I'm Bill. William Earp to be precise.' He held out a hand.

'Earp?' I said. 'As in Wyatt? Wyatt Earp?'

'Yup. One and the same name but no relation.'

'Well pleased to meet you Mister Earp. I'm Matthew. Matthew Malarkey.'

'It's Bill, Matthew. Call me Bill.'

Bill Earp was probably in his mid fifties. He had a jovial, approachable face, heavy eyebrows, dark hair that appeared to have been enhanced with a bit of colour and a firm handshake.

'Bill it is,' I said. 'So have you been to England on business or on holiday.'

'Vacation mostly but I had a business meeting this morning with some potential investors. That's why I'm still all dressed up in this suit and it sure isn't the most comfortable of things on these long haul flights, I gotta tell ya. I own a car rental company in Vegas. WEN Car Rental. Short for William Earp Nevada. We specialise in the big Cadillacs. Something a bit more in yer face. You know, the Eldorados, DeVilles, Broughams. Something to give the customer a bit of a real American feel. Too much competition out there in the rental game with the big boys like Hertz, Avis and Alamo. So I figured I'd specialise.'

'Sounds good, Bill. I'm not too familiar with Cadillacs I must say, but as long as business is good.'

'Yeah, it sure is Matthew. Good times. Say, why don't I give you my card. You're on vacation, right? If you feel like a drive out somewhere give my office a call and mention my name. I'm sure we can do you a good deal buddy.'

We landed in Las Vegas at 18.45, right on time. I checked my watch. It still had UK time, 2.45am. I spun the hands back and gained a whole evening. I grabbed my camera bag, slung it over my shoulder and joined the queue to leave the aircraft. As we waited to exit, Erin pulled me to one side.

'I hope you enjoyed the flight Matthew,' she said, a broad smile lighting up her face.

'Yeah, I did thanks. It's definitely a long one. I'm shattered. I was up at 5.30 this morning. Looking forward to getting some sleep.'

Erin cast a pretend shocked glance in my direction.

'Matthew. You're on holiday for goodness sake. In Las Vegas. You can't sleep the minute you get here. If you go to bed too early you'll never acclimatise.'

'You sound like Cecil. That's what he says.'

'Who?'

'Cecil. He's my friend. He's one of the guys on this trip.'

'Well he's right. Look, I'd recommend you check in have a couple of drinks, take a walk around, maybe check out Caesar's Palace and just take in the atmosphere. I'm booked in there myself so we might run into one another. Caesar's is great at night, all lit up, the fountains, the atmosphere. Maybe play a bit of poker or something. You never know, first night luck. A few hours or so and you'll be ready for an early night by Vegas standards. Then tomorrow you'll be fresh.'

'Sounds like a plan Erin. I might just do that.' I turned to re-join the exit queue.

'Matthew wait. Here, before you go, I have something for you.'

I watched as she reached into her bag and pulled out a vibrant dark flower. She handed it to me.

'What is it,' I asked, slightly bemused. I'm a bloke after all and flowers didn't register too highly on the interest scale.

'It's called Primula Gold Lace, a member of the primrose family apparently. Just a little keepsake...for luck. We all need it in Vegas.'

I took the flower and examined the soft, scallop shaped petals. Dark red, almost black, each of them edged with a thin golden border. A striking sunburst of yellow splashed from the centre and faded into the dark hue of each petal.

'They were a gift,' Erin said. 'From an old lady who I looked after on a flight to New York. She was a nervous passenger. She grows them in her garden. So she made a bouquet for me and then sent it to the airline. I made some of them into buttonholes. Here, let me put it in your jacket.' In a deft flurry of fingers she pinned it to my lapel and stood back to admire her handiwork.

'There you go. Let's hope you hit a winning streak. Now have a fab time. Don't forget to call.'

McCarran taxi drivers queued in a long line to load excited passengers and ferry them towards the bright lights of Las Vegas.

'You wanna go the quick route?' my driver asked.

It sounded sensible to me. I didn't know any better. It was only later that I realised it was 'the quick route' because it took us at speed down the freeway, but it was the longer option and more expensive. To my right familiar names passed in sequence, names I'd read about but had never seen. The Mandalay Bay with its Y shaped tower; the Luxor, a bright column of light spearing the night sky from the apex of its huge pyramid; the towers of New York New York replicating the Empire State and Chrysler Buildings. Each of these landmarks illuminated and enhanced the extravagant light show that was the Las Vegas strip.

As the taxi veered towards an exit marked 'Flamingo Road' I pulled my mobile from my jacket pocket and tapped out a text. *'Ces. Made it into town. Where can I hook up with you guys?'* The driver took the car around in a rectangular route onto Las Vegas Boulevard. A few moments later, he took a left turn into a wide short section of road in the middle of which was a replica of the Arc de Triomphe.

'There you go buddy. Paris Las Vegas.'

I paid the fare and stepped out of the car. My first proper view of The Strip, a long colourful, brightly lit corridor filled with chatter, noise and expectant faces. High above, the vivid illuminations had created a sheer black expanse of sky as the aura of light pollution drifted upwards. To my left stood the Eiffel Tower. To my right a giant, colourful hot air balloon with the word '*Paris*' emblazoned

54

in white lettering across the front. Behind me, a low rumble intensified into a deep roar. I turned to see huge columns of water spray high into the air, outlined against the pink-lit backdrop of the Bellagio hotel, like giant dancing white spectres in the midst of a synchronised ballet. I had arrived in Las Vegas.

The reception area of the Paris was something to behold, more akin to a stately home than a hotel lobby. Its tall white columns, inlaid with an ornate golden latticework, supported a high ceiling from which several elaborate crystal chandeliers cast their light over the glossily patterned floor. A long white and gold reception desk ran the length of the room. I queued with numerous other guests waiting my turn to be checked in. When my turn came the receptionist checked my reservation, swiped my credit card for 'extras' and handed me two keycards.

'Room 1164 Sir. Enjoy your stay.'

'There's just me,' I said, 'you've given me two keycards.'

'It's a double room Sir, so you have a spare one.'

I stuck one in my wallet and kept the other in my hand. My mobile buzzed in my pocket.

'Where are ya, geeze? Glad you made it.'

'Hi Ces. Just arrived at the Paris. In reception. Where are you guys?'

'Mate, we're just having a few liveners over at the Hyde Bar in the Bellagio. You comin over?'

'I just got checked in. I was going to get a shower and get changed.'

'Geeze, it's your first night. You're already nearly five hours behind the rest of us cos of your cock up with that fucking bag. Just dump your gear and get yourself down here. What room you got?'

'1164. You?'

'1170. See you in the Hyde bar then.'

'Hang on Ces, I've been rushing about all bloody day. I fancy a bit of a chill first.'

'Mate, you don't chill in Vegas. What's wrong wivya? Tell you what. Get your gear sorted and we'll come and meet you over

there. There's a little bar inside the main casino called the Central Lobby Bar or lounge or something. Come outta reception, walk towards the lifts and it's on your left. You can't miss it. It's a round bar. We'll meet you there in half an hour. Ok.'

Typical Cecil. Everything was urgent where a night out was concerned. And I could tell he'd already sunk a few *liveners*.

8

Le Central Lobby Bar, a slightly elevated circular bar that overlooked the casino floor with its slot machines and roulette tables, was easy to find. It stood under a light blue-sky ceiling that covered the whole casino. The sky formation was enhanced with painted wispy, clouds, the whole effect designed to create a timeless quasi daylight that would insulate the reveller against the demands of a ticking clock. The bar itself was surrounded by several tall, sculpted marble columns supporting an ornate dome shaped roof, its glass centrepiece revealing the blue of the artificial sky above it. Below the dome, a circular decorative unit housed four flat screen televisions each showing an American football game, positioned so that the programme could be viewed from all round the bar area. I ordered a beer and took a seat at one of the tables adjacent to the main thoroughfare where I could watch passing visitors and guests make their way along tree lined, cobblestone paths that replicated the Parisian boulevards of long ago. Couples walked hand in hand, stopping occasionally to browse the merchandise in quaint French boutiques. Groups of tourists strolled past under the wrought iron street lamps that lined the walkways, some pulling suitcases behind them as they headed for the lifts, others dressed up and ready for a night on the town. On the far side of the bar area an orchestra of slot machines jangled and hummed as their brightly coloured screens dropped rows of random lights into a co-ordinated picture arrangement that decided the fate of hopeful punters. Further back, groups of gamblers crowded around green baize tables, engrossed by the spin of a wheel or the turn of a card. I sipped my beer and waited for familiar faces. I didn't have to wait long.

'Geezer. Good to see ya.' Cecil strolled towards me, his arms held out in front of him in a welcome embrace. Carlos and Jasper followed in his wake. A back slapping bear hug welcomed me to Vegas. 'What the fuck is that in your jacket?'

I glanced quickly at where Cecil had pointed hoping that I hadn't been got at by a low flying pigeon.

'It's a primrose...a primula flower or something. I was given it by one of the flight attendants. She said it was for luck.'

'You pulled the air hostess on the way over, geezer? Respect mate. Getting the party started,' Cecil said, a broad smile cracking his face.

'No Ces. Not like that. I kind of knew her...she's around town for a few days...it's a long story. I'll fill you in later.'

Jasper Kane stepped towards me and grabbed my hand.

'Good to see you Matt. Bit touch and go there on that flight. What was all that about anyway?'

'You wouldn't believe it. They thought I was a bloody terrorist. They thought I'd left my bag in the lounge with a bunch of explosives and a weapon in it. Can you believe that?'

Cecil burst into loud laughter. 'A terrorist! Mate, you? Did you see the way that copper manhandled you off the plane? You didn't put up much of a fight for a fucking terrorist.'

'I'm hardly going to fight the police on an aircraft Ces, am I?' I said, slightly indignant at the suggestion that I wasn't a fighter. 'I've told you before I did some martial arts stuff when I was in my twenties. Bit of Kung Fu actually. So I could have got myself out of it I reckon...if it'd been the right thing to do.'

Cecil was still laughing. 'Well your twenties were a while ago now mate.'

'Take no notice of him, Mateo. He's...what is it? Pulling your rope,' Carlos intervened.

'Chain, nobhead,' Ces said. 'Pulling your chain is the expression, Carlos. Anyway, let's get some beers in. We're standing round like a bunch of tarts yacking on a street corner.' He pulled a chair out from the table and sat down, a clear indication that someone else was getting the drinks.

'Lagers all round then lads?' Jasper asked.

Cecil held his hand up as if to make some profound announcement.

'Jaz, I'm a connoisseur of beer, mate. A little Leffe will do me. Can't be doing that lager shit. Some of them lagers out there you wouldn't pour on a dog in the summer.'

Jasper returned to the table. A waitress followed with a tray of drinks.

'Cheers, lads. So where we going tonight,' Cecil asked, as he placed his beer on the table.

Three expectant faces looked at me as if it was suddenly my decision. It was my birthday trip but I was whacked.

'I'm just going to have a couple I reckon and get an early night. I'm knackered. I want to be fresh for tomorrow. I mean it is my birthday.'

'You might be right Mateo. It's been a long day. How about a nice meal somewhere and then get some sleep,' Carlos said.

I saw Cecil's eyes widen. I could have predicted what was to come.

'Sleep. Nice meal. What the fuck is wrong with you geezers? You don't come to Vegas for a nice fucking meal. You all fucking deranged? You ain't here for a nice fucking meal in a friggin restaurant. You come to Vegas to nail birds, do drugs and party twenty-four seven. You turning into lightweights on me now?'

'Well I'm on that programme boys,' Jasper said.

'Hang on Ces,' I said, 'I didn't mean every night. I meant, you know, tonight...what with all the travelling and that.' I suddenly felt guilty since Cecil had gone to the trouble of organising the trip for me. 'I'm no lightweight.' I picked my beer glass up from the table and took a long draught, perhaps in some sub-conscious need to disprove Cecil's lightweight accusation. 'Anyway, Ces, you don't do drugs.'

'Yeah I know. It's just an expression. My drug is adrenaline,' he said with a surreptitious wink to no one in particular. 'The point is lads, when in Vegas you party like a wild dog, right?'

Partying like a *wild dog* held little appeal for me given the day I had been through. There had to be a solution that would suit everyone's needs.

'Tell you what boys, why don't we take a trip up to Caesar's Palace. The hostess on the flight said it was alright up there. She said she might be up there too. You never know, she might have some mates. And if any of us wants to come back here early then at least we've had a bit of a party on the first night. You up for that Carlos? '

Carlos scratched his bald head and sat back in his chair.

'Sure Mateo. Sounds good. Then maybe we can all meet up in the morning for the Bellagio breakfast. They say it is worth a visit.'

'That all you worried about, mate? Your next meal,' Ces asked. He didn't wait for an answer. 'Yeah, I'm cool with Caesars. We didn't get up that way this afternoon.'

My solution seemed to meet with approval. 'Great. Now let me get a couple of pictures.' I pulled the Nike rucksack from under my seat and grabbed the Canon camera.

'The infamous terrorist bag,' Jasper said, laughing. 'You're not taking that out with you tonight are you Matt after that palaver today?'

'Just tonight Jas. May as well get a few shots of the boys on tour.'

I took several shots of the guys in various poses. The waitress took a couple of group shots for us. We sunk a few more beers and I recounted my escapades with Gatwick security.

Las Vegas Boulevard, The Strip, was in full flow. A crisp breeze cooled the night air. Rows of palm trees divided both sides of the highway, its two lanes almost gridlocked with slow moving queues of traffic. Neon lights on every building caught the eye in a blaze of flashing colour. Groups of men stood around flipping small photo cards and handing them out to whoever would take one. Each of the cards had a photo of a topless or scantily clad woman with a phone number and a slogan indicating their availability. We wandered through the early evening crowd, the Bellagio to the left, past Bally's until we reached a pedestrian bridge that crossed the Strip. On the far side stood Caesar's Palace, its striking white facade illuminated by bright spotlights that gave it an almost supernatural glow. Its centre was dominated by the towering mid-section of the building, atop which the name 'Caesars Palace' was displayed in huge red letters. We stopped in the middle of the bridge and I took a picture of the lads. Behind them the Strip glittered against the deep, black of the Nevada sky, the sidewalk bathed in a pink hue by the merging of a multitude of coloured lights.

On the other side of the bridge we made our way down a wide flight of white steps onto the main concourse. A vast silver-lit pond sprayed jets of water high into the air directly in front of a magnificent semi-circular *porte-cochere* canopied entrance. The underside of the canopy was layered in a step effect that enabled it to rise as it jutted forward, each layer edged with a decorative plaster cornice. Numerous rectangular recesses were set into the layers concealing rows of striplights that cast a subtle glow onto a mock cobbled courtyard. Either side of the main entrance, tucked into a series of ornate alcoves, a display of replica Roman statues looked out upon bellboys opening limousine doors for arriving and departing guests. I fired off a few more shots on the Canon trying to capture as much as I could without aggravating the guys who were impatient to begin the night out.

We strolled through an opulent Roman themed entrance, past a life-sized statue of Julius Caesar that stood in the centre of a long, white tiled floor, into an impressive circular lobby. Its sculpted domed ceilings, marble columns and semi-spherical lighting units, hanging like a glowing galaxy of golden planets, created a complex splendour that was both brash and theatrical all at once. Further along we crossed an ornately patterned marble floor rotunda, past a beautiful statue of three semi-naked 'nymphets' standing back to back in the middle of a circular fountain, water trickling in a steady stream beneath their feet.

'Lads, hang on. Just a quick shot in front of the statue,' I said, halting their progress as they strolled in the direction of the casino. 'It won't take a sec.' Again I clicked off three or four pictures. Cecil's patience appeared to be wearing thin.

'Geezer, we got the whole trip to do the fucking tourist thing. Let's get going. We got some serious partying to do.'

The marble flooring gave way to an intricately patterned carpet that led us directly to the Palace Casino. The casino was huge, the usual mix of slot machines, gaming tables and money change desks along one side. Jasper and Carlos went straight for the slots. A few dollars slid in, a press of a button and the cash was gone for good in a whir of lights and humming acceptance. Cecil and I watched for a while and then wandered off in the direction of one of the roulette tables.

'You ever played mate?' Cecil asked.

'No, never tried it,' I said. 'What about you?'

'A couple times in London. A bloke I used to work with would do the casinos now and then. I'd go along but never much luck though. No fucking idea of how you're supposed to angle it. All seems pot luck to me mate but I'll give it a go if you fancy it?'

'I'll watch for a bit Ces, get the hang of it. You go ahead.'

The truth was I didn't feel too confident. I had never really gambled. The occasional bet on the Epsom Derby or the Grand National horse races was about the extent of my experience. The fact that the table was surrounded by a crowd, all of whom seemed to have a substantial number of gaming chips stacked in front of them, didn't help either. They all looked like they knew what they were doing. Cecil walked round to the centre of the table and blended into the action. He never did suffer confidence issues. I decided to take a walk around.

I crossed towards the middle of the room. An enormous round lighting gantry, its rows of tiny bulbs fanning out like giant batwings from a golden chandelier at the centre, highlighted groups of semi-circular gaming tables each of which had a croupier stationed behind it. I went over to one of the tables that had just three people at it, an elderly couple and woman in a long black evening dress, her reddish brown hair scraped up into a severe, tight bun. I stood back to watch what was going on. The croupier was petite, very pretty, her eyes hinting at an Oriental background. A badge on her white shirt said, '*Maria.*' She noticed me immediately, a customer service thing I assumed.

'Hello Sir. You want to play?'

'Oh, no. It's ok. I'm just watching. Not sure even what it is you're playing,' I said, genuinely confused by the table lay out that had a series of geometrical shapes printed on it, each containing a word that meant nothing to me.

'It's three card poker Sir. You can win one million dollars. It's very easy. Why don't you try? I can show you.'

'Very easy to win one million dollars,' I said, laughing, but hoping there might be some truth in the statement.

'Oh no, not easy Sir, but possible. Are you from Australia?'

'Australia? No, I'm from England. London. On holiday... vacation.'

'Oh ok, welcome to Las Vegas.' She smiled warmly and picked a deck of cards out from under the table. 'I like your flower. What is it?' she asked, pointing to my jacket.

'It's a...erm...a gold...primula...primrose. I can't remember its proper name. Something like gold lace or something. I was given it. For luck. '

'It's very pretty. Let's hope you have lots of luck. Now let me show you how to play. First you place a bet, minimum ten dollars. Ok.' She pointed to the shapes on the table that contained the words '*ANTE*' and '*PAIR PLUS.*'

'You must decide how to bet. The ante bet, you bet that your hand is better than mine, Ok? The pair plus bet, you are betting that you will get a pair or higher. Then you get three cards ok, and I get three cards. You check your cards and decide if you want to play. If you do you must place another bet here.' She pointed to a circle that said '*PLAY*' on it. 'It must be at least the same as your original wager. I have to have at least a Queen to play. Ok? So if your hand beats mine you win on your ante bet and if you have a pair or better you win too.'

I had a basic idea of the poker format but that seemed too easy. 'What, a million dollars?' I said.

'No. Not a million. You only win a million if you have the Ace, King, Queen, Jack, ten and nine of Diamonds. Ok, why don't we try a dummy hand so you get the hang of it.' She looked at the couple standing next to me and the woman in the evening dress. 'Do you mind if we just try a couple of dummy runs to help this gentleman?'

'Sure. You go ahead,' the man said. He then turned to me. 'My name's Pete and this is my wife Martha. We're on vacation. Flew in from Philadelphia yesterday.'

'Pleased to meet you. I'm Matthew. Look, I didn't mean to interrupt your game. I was just watching.'

'Hey, it's no problem, Matthew. We're almost done now. Martha won fifty bucks and I won thirty so that'll get us a nightcap. You go ahead son, see if you can't get that jackpot.'

I turned to the woman on my left. 'Sorry about this,' I said. 'I hope you don't mind a beginner.'

She smiled at me and I noticed the carefully applied vampish make up.

'Everybody's got to learn sometime. You go right ahead,' she said, her accent clearly American, but its precise location unidentifiable to my untrained ear.

I placed my camera bag on the floor in front of me and slid onto one of the stools positioned around the table. Maria dealt me three cards and then three for herself. I had a pair of fives. She had a Queen and two threes.

'There you go. You would have won for real there,' she said, smiling encouragingly.

We played two more dummy hands and I won both times. I pulled out my wallet, cashed a hundred dollars for chips and decided to play for real. If I lost the hundred I'd quit. Put it down to experience. My first hand turned up a pair of sevens. Maria had a Queen, a seven and a four. Another winner. My twenty dollar bet returned eighty dollars. I played another hand and won with a pair of nines, twenty dollars this time. My third hand was a losing one, twenty dollars back to the table, but I was beginning to like the simplicity of the game. I was eighty dollars up. I decided to play some more. As Maria slid the three cards towards me, I noticed a tall, dark haired man approaching the table. He stood on the far side of Pete and Martha, placed a pile of chips on the table and without saying a word nodded to Maria to deal him in. My hand won me sixty dollars. Pete and Martha folded their hands. The stranger won eight hundred dollars. The American woman in the black dress lost twenty.

Pete offered his hand.

'I'm done son. Good to meet you. Looks like your lucky flower is working. Martha and me are heading off to bed. Getting kinda late now for us old folk.'

'It was good to meet you both too,' I said. 'Have a great holiday.'

They wished me luck and went on their way. The tall stranger glanced in my direction.

'Are you English? I recognise the accent,' he said.

'I am, yes. From London. On holiday.'

'London. I know it well. I studied at Oxford when I was a student.'

Even though his own accent was the perfect model of cultured English, I detected a slight intonation, possibly Spanish or perhaps even Italian. He placed a hundred dollars in bets on the table and turned back to face me.

'My name is Arturo. Arturo Magana-Gallegos.' He held out a hand.

'Good to meet you Mister Magana…err…Mister Gallegos,' I said, as I shook his outstretched hand.

He smiled broadly revealing gleaming white teeth, their brightness enhanced by his tanned face and the dark shadow of a day's stubble. 'Please. Call me Arturo. And you are?'

'Oh, sorry. Matthew. Matthew Malarkey.'

Arturo flicked his fingers through his black hair so that it flopped to one side. I noticed tiny flecks of grey around the temples. The grey caused me to assume he was in his forties.

'Well good to meet you too Matthew. London. Yes, I know

London well. I had some good times in the city. One day I will go back. I like Europe.'

'Where are you from Arturo?'

'Me? I am from Argentina. Buenos Aires. I have a polo ranch in Luján not far from the city. I used to play professionally when I was younger, twenty years or so ago. Expensive hobby now. I come to Las Vegas from time to time. I like to gamble…for fun, you know. Now let's play some poker. We are keeping these pretty ladies waiting.' He gave Maria a playful wink and placed fifty dollars on the *ante* and *pair plus* positions. The woman in the black dress smiled and made a twenty dollar bet.

I did likewise but just ten dollars on each position. We played for half an hour or so. Arturo gave me the benefit of his poker knowledge, which seemed to work for me but not for him. By then I was three hundred and fifty dollars up. Arturo had lost a thousand. The American woman seemed to be slightly ahead. She kept herself very much to herself but I assumed she was just focussed on her game. It crossed my mind if Arturo had been more focussed on his game he may have had more success. Instead, he seemed to concentrate on my play.

Despite my winning streak I was beginning to feel tired, jet lag and time both kicking in. I had resolved to play one or two more hands before calling it a night when I caught sight of Cecil at an adjacent table. I walked across to see how he was getting on.

'How's it going Ces?' I asked.

'Ok mate. Just getting the lay of the land. How you getting on? Winning?'

'Thanks Ces. Yeah, I'm three-fifty or so up. It's not a bad game this…well, when you're winning. What about you?'

'Lost a couple hundred. Jas has too but I think Carlos is just ahead. Who's the geezer you're chatting to?'

I turned back in the direction of the table I had just left. Arturo was loading some chips onto one of the squares.

'Oh, just some bloke from South America. He was giving me a few poker tips. Bit of a pro I think, although I reckon if he concentrated on his own game a bit more he'd clean up. Not complaining though. His tips seem to be working for me so far.'

'Right handy then geeze. I'd hang on in there until your luck changes. If you're on a streak you wanna rinse it.'

I smiled at Cecil. There had to be a more scientific approach to gambling than just *rinsing* your luck. I wasn't sure what it was and I knew I wouldn't be in Vegas long enough to learn whatever skill was required to beat the casino. It was a bit of fun and if I came out with a bit more than I started with, that would be success enough for me. I hadn't come to Vegas to try and break the bank.

Cecil interrupted my thoughts.

'Anyway, we're going down the road to the Bond Bar in a minute. You coming?'

'I don't know Ces. I'm just going to play a few more hands, finish this drink and then go back to the hotel. I'm knackered to be honest. I want to feel at least half human for my birthday tomorrow. After all that was the point of coming here. I need a good night's sleep.'

'Geezer, don't give me that gotta sleep thing. You got Irish genes like me right? The Irish didn't do that sleeping crack. They did things, like built fucking New York...yeah? Mate, in the time we're talkin here they'd have built another two fucking miles of motorway. Am I right or wrong?'

'I know, I know Ces but –'

'There ain't no buts geeze. You're in Vegas. You're winning, there's plenty of action out there. What's your problem?' He stared at me, a sort of astounded *are you for real* look, as if I was the only person who had ever come to Vegas and actually decided to go to bed at night. I caught the expression and knew he needed a plausible explanation.

'There's no problem Ces. Just...you know, a bit jaded. Been a long day. To be honest I've had a shit day in fact, no offence or anything. I mean I'm glad I came and I appreciate the trip. But all that hassle at the airport has...well...it sort of threw me. It's aggro, isn't it. I'll be up for it tomorrow and then we can party as much as you want. Break all the rules, eh?'

I had no idea what rules I intended to break at all but I knew it would appease Cecil's aggrieved sensibilities. In his world he had gone to the effort of organising the whole trip on his best mate's account and now his best mate was deserting him and going to sleep, of all things.

As we spoke the American woman in the long black evening dress brushed past me, wandered across to Cecil's table and took a seat. I glanced in her direction but she looked away.

'Who's that then?' Cecil asked, nodding towards the woman.

'No idea. Just another gambler trying her luck I suppose.'

'She ain't too bad from behind. You see that look mate? It looked like she knew you or she's got the hots for you.'

'Hardly Ces. I've just got to Vegas. She was playing on my table for a while. Must be hoping a change will bring some good luck. Who knows? Anyway, look, I'll definitely be up for it tomorrow. I just need to crash tonight. I'll have my party legs tomorrow, no problem. It'll be a great trip, one we won't forget.'

Cecil's expression lightened.

'Yeah, mate it will, count on it. OK, it's your shout but if you change your mind about going all lightweight tonight the Bond Bar is in the Cosmopolitan, just past the Bellagio. You can't miss it. It's rammed with blinding birds. Might see you there then.'

Since Cecil had only arrived in Vegas that day I wondered how he had such informed local knowledge. But I also knew that Cecil could find a party in a Buddhist monastery and had a knack for picking up the tips on the local scene and passing it off as his own opinion.

'We'll see Ces,' I said.

'Ok geeze. If I don't see ya, we're meeting up in the Bellagio for breakfast tomorrow. Carlos's little mumble. Ten sharp.'

I watched Cecil head off and then turned back to my table. A waitress approached and I asked for a gin and tonic. At the card table another couple stood and watched proceedings. Arturo was the only one playing. I placed a thirty dollar bet and focussed on Maria dealing the cards.

'A friend of yours I take it,' Arturo said as he examined his cards.

'Yes, he is. One of the guys I'm here with. Cecil. Loves a party but to be honest I'm worn out so I will save my partying for tomorrow. I think I need to get some sleep,' I said, as I sipped the gin and tonic.

'Makes sense my friend. Sometimes it's difficult though when you travel a long way. Your body clock takes time to adjust. You should do what I do. Take one sleeping pill, a shot of bourbon and you sleep like a child.'

'That just what I could do with, to be honest,' I said, fighting back a yawn. 'Don't have any sleeping pills though so maybe I'll give the bourbon a try.'

Arturo stuck a hand into his inside jacket pocket and pulled out a packet.

'Here, take one of mine.' He handed me the packet. 'Take a look, just so you know what they are. I often play in the casinos until five, six in the morning so I always have them to get my sleep the next day.'

I took the packet and examined it. It had genuine branding and declared that the contents aided *insomnia relief*. I turned the pack over. Active ingredient *Diphenhydramin*. I had no idea what that was but then again I had no idea what was in a simple aspirin either. Arturo took the packet from me, pulled out the plastic insert and popped a pink pill from its bubble.

'Here. Put it in your wallet Matthew. If you want to take it you have it there.'

I won another hundred and fifty dollars and decided to cash in my chips and quit while I was ahead, at almost one in the morning. Before I left I unpinned the buttonhole from my jacket.

'Maria. Here, you have this. It seems to have brought me a bit of luck and since you helped me learn the game I think you should have it.'

Maria took the primrose from me and pinned it to her blouse.

'Oh thank you. It's very unusual. What did you say it was?'

'Gold lace or something. A primrose I think. I don't suppose it matters as long as you like it. It suits you.' I reached for the camera bag. 'Here, let me take your picture before I go.'

Arturo stepped towards me, one arm outstretched.

'You can't take pictures in the casino.'

'That's right,' Maria said. 'It's against the rules. You know, in case you are cheating or planning something. It's very strict in here.'

'Oh, I see. Shame. Ok. I don't want to get arrested or thrown out,' I said, a little taken aback.

'No, not a good idea,' Maria answered, her smile lightening the moment

I picked up the bag and slung it over my shoulder.

'Oh well another time maybe, when nobody's looking. Thanks for the game. I'm shattered.' I said goodnight to Maria, shook hands with Arturo and headed for the exit.

As I walked through the lobby I heard someone call my name. 'Matthew. Hello.'

I turned to see Erin Farrell walking towards me.

'Nice to see you. Are you settled in?' she asked.

'Hi Erin. Yes, all sorted. What are you doing here?'

'I told you. I am staying here...remember? I was just meeting up with a friend I sometimes see when I get into Vegas. But no rush. Why don't we get a drink together?'

She looked great. Her hair tied back, black fitted trousers, a silver top that sparkled under the lobby lights and a short black jacket. But I was exhausted. I knew I'd be no fun.

'I'd love to Erin but I'm out on my feet. I'd be worse than useless...erm, I mean, you know...no fun. I'm going back to the hotel to get some sleep.'

Her eyes widened in mock hurt. 'Oh I see, rejection –'

'Oh no Erin. It's not like that. You look great and –'

She reached out a hand and patted me on the arm.

'I'm teasing you Matthew. I know what it's like with all that travelling and jet lag. Luckily I'm used to it. You get some rest and perhaps we can have a drink tomorrow or something. You have my number.'

I strolled down the Strip back towards the Paris. The fresh air and a five hundred dollar profit had put a temporary spring in my step. Beginner's luck it may have been but five hundred dollars was a good win. I did a quick estimate in my head – three hundred or so pounds I reckoned. As I reached the hotel, I caught sight of the Cosmopolitan and the Bond Bar across the street a little further along. I felt guilty at leaving the boys early especially as they had treated me to the trip. I decided to nip across and have one drink before bedtime. I would buy them a couple of beers from my winnings, grab that bourbon and head off to bed. Before I crossed over I opened my wallet, took out the sleeping pill that Arturo had given me and swallowed it, just to be certain I had an undisturbed night.

Cecil, Jasper and Carlos stood at the front end of a brightly lit rectangular bar crowded with thirty something revellers on all four sides. High above the main window that looked out on the Strip, three square pods hung from the ceiling. In each one, a skimpily dressed dancer interpreted the pumping bar beat with her own mix of twist and spin moves.

Jasper saw me first.

'Hey, Matthew. Paaaaaaaaarteeeeee aneeemaaaaal.' Clearly Jasper had indulged in a few. 'How'd you get on? Ces said you were on a winning streak when he left.'

'Not bad came out ahead.'

'What, d'you hit the jackpot then?'

'Of course I did mate. Well, enough to get you boys a few beers tomorrow on my birthday anyway,' I said with a wink. I decided to avoid getting into too much detail mainly because I intended to stick around for one drink only and then get to bed. I realised if they knew I had come out five hundred up the party might really start.

'Great. Look forward to that then. Anyway, what you having, mate?'

'I'll have a bourbon please Jasper.'

Cecil stared straight at me, his brown eyes inquisitive.

'Bourbon? You going native all of a sudden geezer?'

71

'Just fancied it Ces…and I'm not staying before you say anything.'

'What, you have a win in the casino and you ain't staying?'

'Well, yeah, I did, but not exactly the million dollars though,' I said, trying to dismiss the topic. 'Look, I'll make it up to you all tomorrow, yeah, birthday drinks all round. Splash the cash. Right now I'm just staying for the one.'

'So how much did you win, mate? You was doing ok when I left.'

A bourbon was placed on the bar in front of me. I took a large gulp and placed the glass back down. Clearly, Cecil was not going to leave my winnings alone. Turning to the group I said, 'Bloody difficult to hit the jackpot guys. I managed to come out with five hundred large but I'll do the drinks thing tomorrow. As I say, I'm only staying for the one tonight. Right.'

The *one* turned into three on the excuse that it was my birthday. My protests that my birthday was tomorrow met with an argument that it was already tomorrow back in London and that as it was the early hours of the morning in Vegas tomorrow was now today. I found it hard to argue with the logic.

At around two thirty in the morning I left the Bond Bar and crossed the street unsteadily to the Paris. My head had started to spin, my vision blurring as the bourbon and sleeping pill combined to dull my senses and create disorientation and confusion. I stopped by the Central Lobby Bar and ordered a coffee in an attempt to clear my swirling senses.

'Hi, you have any luck then?'

I turned in the direction of the voice but the speaker's face swam in front of me like an image from the hall of mirrors. I tried to focus but the image was too blurred. I heard the voice again.

'We met in Caesar's. Are you Ok?'

'Two dollars, Sir.'

I heard the bar tender this time, his voice distorted as befuddlement gripped my senses. I reached for my wallet, but it slipped from my grasp as I attempted to open it. In the hazy distance that was now the best my vision could muster, I saw its black almost shapeless image on the floor by my stool. I reached out to get it and pitched forward onto the floor. I struggled to my hands and knees, gripping the base of the barstool. My hearing seemed to be the last of my senses to succumb to the mix of sleeping pill and alcohol.

'Thanks, lady. Don't worry about the tip. Just get this gentleman outta here.'

It was the last words I heard.

9

It was the vibration of my mobile on the hard wooden surface that woke me. Jet lag, stress, the sleeping pill and several drinks had combined to create some sort of chemical reaction in my body that caused me to remain prostrate on the bed, unable to raise the will to move a muscle.

The night before flashed through my mind, like the light from a torch being shone into dark corners until shadowy outlines are revealed. The shapeless edges failed to materialise into a visible picture. I had no recollection at all of getting back to my room. I must have crashed out at around three o'clock in the morning. Nearly midday as far as my body clock was concerned. No wonder my head was in a state of flux. The heavy curtains blocked out any daylight, the darkness of the room adding to my confusion.

With great effort, I rolled across the empty expanse of king sized bed and reached for my mobile. Through bleary eyes, I saw that it was twenty minutes past ten. The screen told me I had three missed calls and one text message. I clicked the phone icon. The calls were from Cecil, two at around three forty-five and another at five o'clock in the morning. Cecil clearly pissed and drinking and dialling. I pressed the text icon. *'Happy Birthday. Have a fab day. Love you. Louise.'* My birthday. I had woken up 40 years old but felt twice that age.

I pulled myself into a seating position. I vaguely recalled that we had arranged to meet at the Bellagio for breakfast. What time we had arranged was outside my memory capability at that point. I lifted the bedside telephone and dialled Cecil's room. No answer. I walked to the window and pulled back the curtains. The bright blue of a Vegas day smashed across my eyes like the glare of a searchlight, the sun glittering on the hotel rooftops across the Strip. I tried Cecil again. No answer. I called reception.

'Can you put me through to Room 1170 please.'

A short silence and the voice came back, 'Sorry Sir the guest in 1170 is not responding. Would you like me to leave a message?'

I didn't want to leave a message. I could call on Cecil's room on the way down.

I threw on some shorts, a tee shirt and some boat shoes and grabbed my wallet. There was four hundred and fifty dollars left of the money I had won in Caesar's Palace. I took out four hundred and put it in the safe. Next, I went to the bathroom and glugged down a pint of water to alleviate the raging thirst that had suddenly hit me. Then I picked up my keycard from the dressing table and headed for the lift. A shower could wait. Cecil's room was on the floor below. As I walked the long corridor with its blue patterned carpet and cream wall, my head gave way to a lightness I had not experienced before, an almost disembodied state as if my mind was several steps ahead of me waiting for my physical presence to catch up. At 1170 I rapped the wooden door.

'Ces. You awake mate. It's me…Matt.'

No response. I thumped the door again. 'Ces. You in there? We're supposed to be meeting for breakfast. You awake?'

Still no response. I looked at my watch again. Almost ten forty. Perhaps Cecil had already left for breakfast. I vaguely recalled him saying something about ten sharp. I didn't have room numbers for Carlos or Jasper so I decided to get across to the Bellagio.

Outside the sky was clear, the air fresh and the sun already warm and glowing. A gentle breeze flicked at the fronds of the row of palm trees that separated the two sides of the carriageway. The street buzzed with activity, car horns urging the traffic forward, crowds wandering along the sidewalks in that slow gait that is the pace of tourists in no hurry. I crossed the road and walked up the long pedestrian ramp that bordered one side of the enormous lake that fronted the Bellagio. At the top I made my way across the wide expanse of the lobby area, turned right across the casino floor and then realised I had no idea where I was heading. I stopped and asked a porter who directed me to the Buffet restaurant area. I stood in a line in a long arched corridor and waited to pay for breakfast. There was no sign of the others so I assumed they were already in there. Within five minutes a waitress led me into the main dining area, a vast open plan room that featured an assortment of food stations spread across the whole floor. As I pulled out a chair at my designated table I caught sight of Carlos sitting alone on the far side of the room.

'Hey Carlos,' I called out as I approached his table. 'Where are the others?'

'Mateo. Buenos dias. You made it,' Carlos replied through mouthfuls of scrambled egg. 'You look like cagada. I thought you went to bed early?'

'Cagada? What's that anyway? English today please Carlos. I'm having enough trouble making sense of things as it is without you confusing me more.'

'Yes cagada. Crap. You don't look so good,' he said, pointing his fork in the general direction of my face. 'What happened?'

'Nothing happened Carlos. Well nothing that is unless you count getting up at five in the morning, a missed flight, getting arrested, having to find another flight, a ten hour journey, arriving late, several drinks, three large bourbons and a sleeping pill designed to take horses out of the equation.'

Carlos laughed. 'You sound pissed off Mateo? Forget it. You're here now. It'll be a great trip. Don't you worry.'

'I'm sure it will mate. I'm not pissed off. Just feel like I've been hit head on by a truck. Knackered still to tell you the truth. Anyway, where's Cecil and Jasper? Ces said ten o'clock here.'

'Do me a favour Mateo. There was no way Cecil would be here for ten. I left him and Jasper in the Bond Bar at just after three o'clock this morning. They were still drinking and talking about going on to a lap dancing club. I went back to the hotel and went to bed. Haven't seen either of them since.'

'I tried ringing Cecil this morning and I tried his room but he's not answering. I reckon he is either still out or crashed out in his room big time. Don't blame him though. My head's throbbing and it's my bloody birthday too.'

Carlos swallowed the remainder of his scrambled egg and wiped his mouth with a napkin. 'Mateo. I'm sorry pal. I forgot. Happy birthday to you. Look, you go get some breakfast and some juice. It'll make you feel better.'

'You're right. Good idea mate. Back in a minute.'

To my fuzzy, muddled head, the choice on offer was far too much. In addition to the usual cereals, eggs and bacon that I was used to at breakfast there was a choice of Italian, Japanese, Chinese, and American cuisine. Plates of seafood, crabs and shrimps piled high; roast beef, a variety of meats and cheeses. Several of the food stations were packed with salads and vegetables of every kind. An army of white hatted chefs stood behind sizzling pans and boiling pots, cooking to order. It meant making a decision and I wasn't up to it. I grabbed a plate, filled it with fresh fruit, poured a glass of tomato juice and went back to the table.

'Have you seen the food Carlos? I can't believe it. They've got…everything. I just saw some Japanese asparagus. It looks delicious. I might try some with a bit of roast beef.'

'Aye laddie. They have whatever you want.'

I gulped down the fruit and tomato juice in the hope that the vitamins and minerals they contained would soon hit my system and make me feel more human.

'I'm just going to get something else Carlos. You having any more?'

'No, I'm full mate. Maybe just a coffee.'

I returned to the table with a plate of roast beef, the Japanese asparagus and a heap of broccoli.

'That'll liven you up Mateo,' Carlos said.

'I hope so mate. I must get a picture of this lot. I've never seen so much…'

My sentence trailed off as the cold shiver ran down my back

from the base of my neck. The thought zipped through my head, *'Shit! My camera. I don't remember bringing my camera back last night.'* A wave of panic followed the cold shiver.

'What's the matter, Mateo? You've gone white as a ghost. You feel sick?'

'No. No Carlos. I can't remember what I've done with my camera. You know, in my bag. It must be in the room. I hope so.'

'I think you had it with you last night when you came into the Bond Bar. I am sure you had a bag, yeah, a black bag…on your shoulder,' Carlos said. 'Is that the one you lost in the airport?'

'Yes. But that's good. I had it with me. It must be in my room. Just that I don't remember going to bed last night or even getting to my room.'

I finished my breakfast feeling slightly more reassured. I told Carlos I was going back to the Paris to check for my bag. He walked back with me as far as the Central Lobby Bar.

'I'll have a coffee and I'll wait for you here Mateo in case the others come down. You want anything?'

'Get me a Bloody Mary Carlos, please. My head's spinning.'

I pulled my keycard from my pocket and let myself into my room in a hurry, anxious to see if my bag was there. I checked everywhere. Under the bed, in the wardrobe, in the bathroom but there was no sign of the bag. I raced back to the lift and went straight to reception. Nothing handed in. I headed straight over the road to the Cosmopolitan. Nothing there either. They took my name and hotel room number in case anything turned up. I went back to the lobby bar and found Carlos sipping a coffee.

'Any luck?' he said.

'Nothing. I don't understand it. I had it in the Bond Bar but it's not there now. It's not been handed in here and it's not in my room. So, what's happened? It must have been stolen. Maybe I left it on the floor or something and someone has taken it. I came in here before I went to bed. I sort of remember trying to get a drink…a coffee or something…yeah, right here. Bollocks. That camera's worth a lot of money too and it's my birthday present from Louise.'

'Hey, mate. Calm down. I'm sure it'll show up. Somebody will hand it in. If they check the pictures they can trace you.'

Carlos's words hadn't made me feel any more reassured. I pulled up a seat and watched as the barman placed a white napkin on the bar followed by the Bloody Mary, complete with two floating green olives, a large stick of celery and a straw. Carlos pushed the glass in my direction and left two dollar bills on the bar.

'Get this down you. It'll liven you up,' he said.

I glugged down two large sips from the bright red concoction. The spicy zing hit the back of my throat causing my eyes to squeeze tight shut as I absorbed the impact.

'Blimey, that's got some kick, Carlos,' I said as I put the glass back down on the napkin.

'Aye. Hair of the doggie, mate.'

I was halfway through the drink when my mobile rang.

'*Where are ya, geezer?*'

'Cecil. Where are you more like? You didn't make it to breakfast.'

'*Nah, fuck that. Didn't get to bed till eight o'clock this morning. Anyway, what's the mumble with you? Kept that quiet didn't ya.*'

'Kept what quiet Ces? What do you mean?'

'*Mate, don't give me all that. I got your bag in my room.*'

'My bag? You got it? Fantastic. Thanks Ces. Thought I'd lost the bloody thing again.' The sense of relief that washed over me lifted my spirits. For a moment I felt a burst of energy that wiped away the jet lag, the late night and the effects of over indulgence. Suddenly I could enjoy my birthday. 'Anyway, what am I supposed to have kept quiet?' I picked up the Bloody Mary and waited for an answer.

'*Geezer, you're talking to me right. Don't try pulling the old mumble swerve on me. Your win…in Caesar's.*'

'My win? I told you about that last night mate. Five hundred. Remember? I said I'd treat you all to a birthday drink. I owe you a large one at the very least for finding my bag. Is my stuff in it? I'm not having much luck with –'

'*A large one. You win half a fucking mil and you wanna splash out on a large one? You having a giraffe geeze?*'

'Half a what Ces? What did you say?' I asked, giving Carlos a wink and a shrug in response to his enquiring expression. I heard Cecil's next sentence with a mix of shock and incredulity.

'*Half a million mate. Half a million US dollars. D'you want me to spell it out?*'

I grabbed the Bloody Mary and took a large hit, my senses not quite grasping what was going on.

'You still pissed Ces? What the bloody hell are you on about?'

'*What I'm on about mate is I've got your bag in my room and there's half a million dollars in it that you won in Caesar's. You with me? You told us you won last night. Tumble?*'

My brief moment of positive energy crashed through the floor. I had no idea what Cecil was talking about but a sense of foreboding quickly filled the space where my positivity had been.

'Ces. Hold on. You in your room? 1170 isn't it? I'm coming up?'

I downed the remainder of the Bloody Mary, chewed up the two olives that had sunk to the bottom of the glass and got to my feet. Carlos stared at me expectantly.

'Be back shortly Carlos. Cecil has my bag but I think he's hallucinating or something. Catch you in a minute.'

I reached room 1170 and banged on the door. Cecil opened it wearing just boxer shorts, his hair dishevelled, his eyes barely open enough to see out of.

'You just got up Ces?' I asked, as if it wasn't blindingly obvious.

'Yeah mate. Only had four hours. Come in.'

I walked through the room straight to the window where I pulled back the heavy drapes. A stream of daylight changed the room from dark to light in an instant.

'What the fuck mate. What you doin?' Cecil asked, screwing up his eyes and scratching his crotch through his boxers at the same time.

The room was a state. Cecil's trousers were flung over the

back of an armchair, his shirt crumpled on the floor. An empty Champagne bottle stood on the bedside table alongside two glasses that were still half full.

'Looks like you had a bit of a party in here Ces,' I said.

'Yeah. Looks that way,' Cecil answered, looking about him, almost as if he was a visitor to his own room. He sat down on the edge of the king-sized bed that dominated the centre of the floor, lowered his head and ran both hands through his thick head of hair. I waited for him to say something. Even though I was anxious to get my bag back, having seen the state of Cecil I considered there was no rush. Clearly he was winding me up about the bag.

'Listen mate. Bit of a fess up. I borrowed a bit of money from you last night and I've spunked most of it on gambling and booze.'

'Borrowed money? When was that? I don't remember giving you any money.'

'From your winnings. I took –'

'What winnings Ces? What are you on about? What's this half a million stuff anyway? And where's my bag?'

'It's in the wardrobe.'

I opened both doors of the large wooden wardrobe that stood against the wall at the end of Cecil's bed. There was no sign of the bag. I checked the top shelf. Nothing there either.

'There's nothing here Ces. No bag. You must have put it somewhere else?'

'It's there mate. I stuck it in there last night.' He rolled back across the bed, picked up one of the Champagne glasses and sniffed the contents as if he was considered drinking it. His screwed up expression told me he'd thought better of it. 'My fucking head's bad geezer. Gotta get some water.' He stood up and wandered unsteadily to the bathroom.

I checked the wardrobe again. I looked on top of it just in case he'd lobbed the bag up there. Nothing. Next I pulled out all the drawers, even though they were too small for a rucksack full of camera equipment to fit into. Each of the drawers was empty except for the last one I looked in. I saw the bundle tucked at the back, reached in and pulled it out. Wrapped in a money band was a wad of one hundred dollar bills. I stared at it for a moment, unsure of what I was looking at. I walked to the bathroom door where Cecil was staring at himself in the mirror as if trying to recall who he was or how he got there. I held out the wad of notes.

'Is this yours?'

Cecil's brown eyes flashed into full wakefulness. He grabbed the cash from me.

'Where's the rest geezer?'

'The rest? What rest?'

'Mate, there was a whole load more like that in your bag. Fifty fucking bundles at ten thousand dollars a shot in fact. I counted a couple of bundles to see how much was in each.'

Despite the shock of what I had heard stunning me into silence, my brain automatically went into calculation mode. Fifty bundles. Fifty...fifty times ten. Five hundred.

'Five hundred thousand...that's five hundred thousand dollars Cecil,' I blurted out, the words a direct product of my calculation rather than any deliberate rational attempt to make sense of what he had said.

'Fucking right it is geezer. That's what I told ya. The five hundred large you won in Caesar's, right?'

I stood for a moment and stared at Cecil. He tilted his head towards me, his hands either side of the sink propping himself up in a half stoop. I waited for some explanation but none came.

'I didn't win five hundred thousand dollars Cecil. Where'd you get that idea? I won five hundred, that's all. Five hundred US dollars. Five double zero. I told you that last night. Do you think I wouldn't have mentioned it if I'd won that amount of cash? I win half a million on my first night in Vegas and I don't even mention it?'

I caught the wave of shock cross his face before he replied.

'You said five hundred large, right? So I thought you meant five hundred bucks but when I saw what was in the bag, I'm thinking fuck's sake, he meant half a fucking mil. I misunderstood.'

'Misunderstood? I reckon it's me that's misunderstanding here. Five hundred dollars win on your first night *is* large in my book.'

I pointed to the wad of notes. 'So, tell me, how come you've only got ten grand then in the drawer if you reckon you had half a million dollars? Where'd you get it anyway? You winding me up? Some sort of birthday stunt? It's not that funny if it is. There's no bag in your wardrobe mate. So where's my camera bag?'

'Fuck the camera Matt. What d'you mean no bag? It was in the wardrobe,' Cecil answered. His use of my first name always told me he was worried about something. He walked out of the bathroom across to the wardrobe and began searching just as I had a moment earlier. After a minute he realised that I was right. There was no bag.

'I told you Ces...'

'Shut it for a minute. I gotta think, he said and plonked himself on to the large blue sofa that was positioned in front of the window. He stuck both feet up on the coffee table in front of him and began to scratch his balls again in earnest. His silence had begun to unnerve me. What if he wasn't winding me up? The first day of the trip hadn't gone to plan as far as I was concerned and what if the second day was about to go down the pan too?

I needed to stay calm and not allow the panic that was beginning to surface take hold. I walked across to the bedside table, picked up the Champagne glass and necked the contents. I almost brought it up again as the bubbles fizzed back down my nose and the smell of perfume wafted over me. As I placed it back down I noticed a red trace of lipstick around the rim of the glass.

Finally Cecil spoke.

'Mate, sit down and let's look at this thing, ok. After you left the Bond Bar, I found your bag on the floor stuffed up against the base of the bar. I remember thinking what a nobhead you are with that fucking bag. Anyway, I called but you weren't picking up. I was sposed to be going to some lap dancing club with Jasper but, being a decent geezer, I thought I'd take the bag back to you first. Jas said he'd meet me at the club later after I dropped it off. I get to your room and there's no answer so I decided to stash the bag in my own room. I thought I'd check it to make sure all your gear was in there, although I have to say it felt full enough. So I open it up and it's full of fucking cash. No cameras, just bundles of dollars. Each bundle had a hundred one hundred dollar bills. I counted out two lots of $10k bundles. I'm telling you mate, there was fifty bundles exactly. So I try you again on the dog and still no answer. So I'm thinking you must've won it playing three card poker at Caesar's. I mean you definitely said you'd won five hundred large. So when I saw it…well, I just told ya. Easy mistake to make.'

'Mistake, Ces? Not that bloody easy. There's a bit of a difference between five hundred and half a million,' I said, as it began to dawn on me that Cecil sounded too serious and looked too hung over to be weaving an elaborate birthday hoax. The remaining wad of notes had to be proof enough that he was for real. 'So where's the money now then?' I asked.

'Hang on a minute geezer. I'm trying to tell you aren't I? So I put the bag in the bottom of the wardrobe thinking we'll sort it out in the morning and I go back downstairs to go meet Jas. I get down as far as the Lobby Bar and there's a few people there hanging out, couple of nice looking birdies too so I reckon I'll have a little drink and see what happens. Worst case I'll catch up with Jas bit later. Anyway, I'm sitting there with a Jack and coke and this bird comes up and starts giving it to me big time. I mean, I'm minding my own business geezer and she's full on. Not a bad looker either. We have a few drinks, a bottle of Champagne and we go try the casino. Mate, I told you. I know fuck all about roulette right, but she wants to play the tables. Before I know it I've blown seven hundred and fifty dollars on a friggin ball bouncing round a wheel and two more bottles of Champagne. I only had twelve hundred for the whole fucking trip and it's still day one. I'd already done two hundred in Caesar's not to mention a few beers after we got here. She wants to play blackjack next and I've done my cash. I need to get hold of some more green ones.'

'Wait a sec Ces, I don't get it. I mean, you didn't have to gamble. That's not like you. Thought you'd be trying to do the deal with her?'

'Yeah, I know, but I'm in Vegas. Going large geeze. I'm living it big style. Mate, I'd had a few drinks. Party like a wild dog, right. You know the mumble.'

I wasn't convinced I knew Cecil's *mumble* at all. The way I saw it was that if I'd lost most of my spending money I'd be calling it a day. Cecil's earlier admission that he had *borrowed a bit of money* from me began to take on a frightening certainty in my mind.

'But couldn't you have got some more cash with your card or something?' I said.

'Look mate, I wasn't thinking straight was I? You'd had a big win as far as I knew, there's geezers winning a stack load of chips all round me and my luck had to change. I had a hot bird on the mumble and I'm thinking I gotta keep the dream alive. I figured that I can't keep fucking losing so I needed to get some more dosh in a hurry, right. Easiest thing was to borrow some wedge from the bag in my room. I mean, after all mate, you said you'd sort us out the next day right, so I thought I'd just get ahead of the programme.'

'I said I'd get a few drinks Ces, not finance your whole frigging party scene.'

'Yeah I know. But I was on a roll. I run up to the room, grab one of the bundles and –'

'What, ten thousand dollars? Why the bloody hell would you think you need ten thousand dollars Ces?'

'Mate, I told you. I wasn't thinking. I'd had a few right, and the bird was coming on strong big time. I knew the old hashmadishmalacka was on if I played it right. One hot bird geezer. You shoulda seen the body on it. I spose I was just giving it large. Cut a long story short I lost eight thousand dollars and blew another five hundred on booze.'

I couldn't quite take in what Cecil was saying. It was as if he was relating a story about someone else.

'Fucking hell Ces. What? Eight and a half grand. You blew eight and a half grand of my money?'

'It wasn't your money you nob, was it? I'm just telling you what happened.'

'You know what I mean. You only took it because you thought it was mine, didn't you.'

'Geezer don't get all self fucking righteous now. I'm telling you what happened, right. Anyway, I grab a bottle of bubbly and me and the bird go back to my room. Then she fucking pulls the swerve. Tells me she wants paying for the hashmadishmalacka. I told her I don't pay birds to shag'em. I'd already spent a load of dough on her showing her a good time in the casino and she wants me to pay her for a shag.'

'Well she was a hooker then Ces, wasn't she?' I said, 'You've been turned over by a hooker.'

'Mate she wasn't no hooker. I said that to her and she said she was a high class escort. You know, the type that spends time with… how'd she put it? Oh yeah, discerning gentlemen who want a good time in Vegas. She wanted paying for her time she reckoned.'

'So a hooker then, Ces. I mean if she was willing to have sex with you, that was part of the spending time deal and in my book, that's a hooker however you dress it up. So what happened?'

'Nothing mate. I told her I ain't paying. Last thing I remember I was lying on the bed. I must've crashed out cos I don't remember her leaving or anything.'

The realisation of what had probably happened then hit me. 'So, she must have taken the money with you out cold or it would still be here wouldn't it?'

'Yeah, fucking bitch robbed us geezer.'

'It wasn't our money Ces. She hasn't robbed us.'

Cecil stood up and walked towards the bathroom. I heard the tap running as he called out to me. 'Well if it wasn't your money, where'd you get it?'

'How should I know? I thought it was my camera bag didn't I? I didn't know I was walking round with half a million dollars in my bag. When I left you guys in the Bond bar I wasn't feeling that great. I'd taken a sleeping pill and was all over the place. Don't even remember getting back to my room let alone whether I had the right bag. You sure you picked up the right one in that bar? What did it look like?'

Cecil emerged from the bathroom with another glass of water. 'What d'you mean what did it look like? It looked like a fucking bag mate. A black rucksack, the one you bin carrying about since you left London.'

'Did it have the Nike logo on it?'

Cecil sat on the edge of the bed and squeezed both temples between the finger and thumb of his right hand, perhaps an attempt to stimulate the threads of his memory. He turned his head and stared at me for a moment as if I had asked a question on the theory of relativity.

'Yeah, mate. It did. Yeah. It was identical to the one you had in London.'

'Well then Ces, it looks like I have someone else's bag. Or did have. Some poor tourist is walking round Las Vegas right now looking for their money.'

Cecil began to laugh and shake his head at the same time.

'What's so bloody funny Ces?'

'Geezer. Get real. Trust me. No ordinary tourist walks round with half a fucking mil stuffed into a rucksack. Not even in Vegas. You got some villain's wedge.'

Villain. The word sent a streak of unease straight through my stomach. I wiped the palms of my hands on my shorts and stood up, mainly to stop the anxiety taking hold.

'But that's just it Ces,' I said, 'I haven't got the money. It's been nicked. What have we got left?'

Cecil rose up from the bed and went over to where his trousers were draped across the armchair and began to rifle through the pockets. He pulled his wallet from a back pocket and flipped it open revealing a wad of notes, which he took out and spread on the table.

'That's about right mate,' he said, staring at the dollar bills. 'Fifteen hundred bucks left. I told ya. Eight large on the tables and five hundred on booze.'

'So, we have the ten grand bundle plus the fifteen hundred left. We need to hang on to that then. I'll take it and put it in the safe in my room.'

'Might as well stick it mine mate now you're here. They're all the same.'

'You reckon...it's not our cash, you know.'

Cecil caught my hesitation. He had already blown eight and a half grand and I naturally had a moment's doubt. But he was my friend and I trusted him. I wanted him to know that too.

'Ok, Ces, you stick it in your safe. It's not a lot left out of half a million dollars anyway.'

'No mate it's not,' Cecil replied. 'Looks like that bird's made off with four hundred and eighty thousand dollars of somebody else's money.'

10

I met up with the others down by the pool at around two o'clock. The afternoon sun had attracted a crowd. Situated on the first floor of the Paris the octagonal pool was a sure fire suntrap. Each angle where the corners of the poolside met was linked by a large plinth on top of which stood a huge decorative pitcher. Behind these, the shape of the pool was outlined by a row of cream planters that broke up the expanse of grey and white concrete tiling with bursts of greenery and vibrant purple and orange flowers. The giant legs of the replica Eiffel Tower straddled one corner of the poolside whilst the tower itself threw a long shadow across the far side of the pool and halfway up the tall multi-windowed hotel facade.

Carlos and Jasper were already by the pool, Carlos spread out on a white sun lounger, a beer on the ground next to him. Jasper was sitting on the edge of the pool, his legs dangling in the water, watching ripples radiate across the aqua-blue sheen of the surface as smiling bathers took tentative steps down the steps next to him. I placed my towel and a canister of sunscreen down on a sunbed next to Carlos. Jasper greeted me first.

'Matt. Happy birthday mate. Sorry I missed breakfast this morning. I was shattered. Overdid the partying last night. You know what it's like. First night and all that.'

'No worries Jasper. What did you do then?'

'I was supposed to meet up with Cecil in some lap dancing club down the Strip but he didn't show. I got talking to one of the girls in there and, well you know. Ended up back at hers. Got out of there at midday.' He flashed the killer grin, the one that presumably had got him a ticket to some besotted girl's apartment for half the day. 'Talk of the devil. Ces. Mate. Where you been?'

Cecil strolled across the poolside, a blue and white striped towel thrown over his shoulder, a bottle of water in one hand. He threw the towel down on a vacant sun lounger and sat on the wall of one of the planters.

'Don't ask Jas. Crazy night.' He took a long swig from the bottle, wiped his mouth and said, 'Boys we got a problem.'

'A problem? What problem?' Jasper asked, a look of concern emerging on his face.

Cecil pointed in my direction.

'Birthday boy here has fucked up again with that fucking bag of his.'

'Did you not get it back?' Carlos asked, sitting up and looking directly at me. 'I thought you said Cecil had it.'

'You had it last night Ces,' Jasper said. 'I thought you were taking it back to the hotel?'

'Nah, mate. I ain't got it.' Cecil said. 'Anybody fancy another beer? You're gonna need one when I tell you this shit.'

He ordered four beers from a young dark haired waitress in a white bikini top and began to relate the events of the night before. When he'd finished there was a silence. A silence that indicated a shift of mood. A shift I felt totally to blame for. The lads had been good enough to organise the trip and everyone had been looking forward to it. I needed to lighten the mood, to get the party spirit back in spite of the tension I personally felt. I sat on one side of my sun lounger, grabbed the can of factor fifteen moisturising sun tan spray mist, and pressed the button on the top of the can. A burst of white liquid splashed across my chest.

'Well, look lads whatever's happened it's still my birthday,' I said, as I rubbed in the sun cream. 'So let's get a few more beers in and enjoy the day. I mean I am only forty this one time and you boys have all got together to take me out here so let's not let anything spoil the trip, right. I mean it's only...well...only half a million dollars. Could be worse, eh? Could be a million.'

'Yeah, too right,' Jasper shouted. 'Come on boys. Let's party. Happy birthday Matt. I'll get em in.'

'What are you going to do Mateo? You gannae report it to the polis?' Carlos asked, slipping into his Scottish side, a sign that the beers were taking effect.

'Well, I've thought about –'

'Geezer. Are you losing it? You don't go to the Old Bill. Mate, you do that and you're opening a whole world of pain, ok.'

Cecil's sudden intervention took me by surprise just as I was trying to spray more of the sun cream onto the back of my neck. A scream immediately behind me heightened my surprise.

'What are you doing you jerk?'

I turned in the direction of the question. A red haired woman was staring straight at me, the left side of her face and hair covered in white liquid.

'I could sue you for that. You nearly blinded me,' she shouted, as she wiped away a dribble of the liquid that had run down onto her blue bikini top.

Realising what I had done, I flung the sun oil onto the lounger and grabbed my towel. I scrunched it into a ball and tried to wipe the white liquid off the woman's head, galvanised by the words blinded and sue and the fact that, as she was an American, she may very well take that last course of action. I couldn't risk it.

'Get off me,' she shouted, waving her arms above her head. 'You're a goddam British yob, aren't you? Out for trouble.'

I stepped back. 'I'm not a British yob. I'm sorry it was an accident. I must have had the nozzle pointing the wrong…' My sentence tailed off as a sense of familiarity kicked in. 'I know you don't I?'

Her stare was disdainful, her response scornful.

'I don't think so.' She pulled a towel from her bag and began to wipe her face. 'You're an Australian yob then. All the same.'

'Look, I said I'm sorry. I didn't realise you were that close behind me. It was an accident.'

Jasper intervened. 'Leave it Matt.' He turned to the woman,

knelt on one knee next to her and flashed the Jasper Kane smile. 'You alright love? It's only sun oil. It's not in your eyes is it?'

Her demeanour changed in an instant. 'It's ok. I'll be fine. Thank you, young man.'

'It's Jasper. And you are?'

'Kimberley. And this is my friend Lana.' Kimberley pointed to a woman who had been stretched out on a sunbed a few feet away from her but who, on hearing the commotion, had sat up and was leaning on one elbow looking to see what was going on. Kimberley was probably around thirty-five years of age and once her face had relaxed from its initial angry frown and she had wiped away most of the sunscreen, I was convinced that I had seen her before. I could also see that she was quite attractive. On the other hand, her friend Lana was not quite as physically appealing. Her features were plain, almost non-descript and ordinarily she would have gone unnoticed particularly given the high percentage of stunning wannabe models that seemed to frequent Las Vegas. However, she had clearly only applied sunscreen to her exposed limbs and had forgotten her face completely. As a result, her features were redder than her crimson all in one swimming costume that was stretched tightly around a podgy physique. The overall look was not helped by her short cropped black hair and excessive black eye liner.

Jasper gave a cursory nod in Lana's direction and turned his attention back to Kimberley, who was towelling the remainder of the sunscreen from her red hair.

'Nice to meet you, Kimberly. All cleaned up now? Anyway, could be worse,' he said, nodding in the direction of Lana's scarlet face, 'at least you're getting a bit of extra protection now from this wonderful Las Vegas sun.' He shot a glance at me and I caught the surreptitious wink. 'It is factor fifteen after all,' he said, a hint of a chuckle in his tone. 'Look, I'm just getting some drinks for my friends. Let me get you one.'

I was grateful for Jasper's intervention. I was worried enough about the bag incident and I didn't need to get myself into more difficulties. I turned back to Cecil, who had watched the whole incident and clearly found it highly amusing.

'Ruined that bird's hairstyle there mate,' he said. 'Who is she? She looks familiar?'

'No idea Ces. Anyway, you don't think I should report it then?'

'Nah mate, it's only a bit of sun cream. She'll survive.'

'Not the bloody sun cream Ces, I meant the –'

'I'm winding ya mate,' he chuckled. 'Chill.'

'Chill? How can I chill? We're in the shit big time. Half a million dollars. I reckon we have to report it to the cops. It's the only way.'

Cecil's face turned serious, his eyes screwed up against the sun as he turned fully in my direction.

'Listen to me mate. First of all, if you do report it, the cops are gonna keep you here while it's sorted out. They're gonna be asking all sorts of questions about how you got hold of half a million dollars. And what you gonna say? You found it? You don't even know how you got it. Suppose it's dodge, which I reckon it is, you're gonna be right in the frame for whatever mumble has gone on. The cops ain't gonna swallow a story that's got no explanation are they? I'd lay low mate if I was you. See what happens first and then we can make a move when we know what we are dealing with.'

'So where did you get it Matt?' Carlos asked.

'I don't know. You heard what Ces said earlier. He found it in the Bond Bar. Look, when we were in the hotel last night I had the bag with me. Yeah? I know I did because I took some photos in the hotel bar. Remember? When we left here I still had it because I took some more pictures on the way up to Caesar's.' I watched them all nod in agreement. 'Then when we went into Caesar's I took a few more shots. Remember? In front of that statue...fountain thing.' Three heads nodded their agreement once more. 'Then in Caesar's we all split up. But I had the bag with me when I left. I remember because I was going to take a photo of the croupier, Maria, but she stopped me. She said it isn't allowed on the casino floor. I am sure I remember walking down the Strip on my own with it. But it's not the sort of thing you think about is it? And you said this morning, Carlos, that you are sure I walked in the Bond Bar with it, didn't you?'

Carlos nodded again.

'So, ok, it looks like maybe I have mislaid it in the Bond Bar. I reckon someone's picked it up by mistake. If that's the case they'll probably go back to the bar at some point to see if their bag is there and then return mine with the cameras. Then we just take their bag back and let them have it. Simple. Problem solved.'

'But you went there today Mateo and they didn't have it,' Carlos said.

'No, they didn't but maybe it was too soon. Maybe whoever picked up mine hadn't realised the mistake yet.'

'Simple you reckon?' Cecil said. 'You're forgetting one thing you fucking nobhead. You ain't got no bag to give them, have you?'

I stretched out on the sun lounger. The warm sun felt relaxing on my skin. I wanted to lay there and just fall asleep.

I walked back down the corridor to my room determined to enjoy my birthday and not worry about what had been said at the poolside. On reaching my door I couldn't find the keycard. It wasn't in my wallet and nor was the spare one. I searched the pockets of my shorts but it wasn't there. I searched them again just in case. It definitely wasn't there. I'd let myself into my room on at least two occasions that morning. I hurried back down to the poolside to see if it had fallen out by the sun lounger. Nothing there either. As I made my way back to the hotel entrance I stopped and asked at the towel kiosk if a keycard had been handed in. It hadn't. It had to be in my room then with the spare. I must have left it inside. Back in the lobby I queued up at the information desk to tell them I was locked out of my room. I was told I would need to be met by security in order to get back in and that I would need to identify myself once I got there.

When I reached room 1164 a security guard in a light blue shirt, dark blue trousers and a peeked hat was waiting for me. I thought at first he was an airline pilot and had made a mistake with his room.

'Mister Malarkey?' he asked.

'Yes. It is. Sorry to drag you up here but I've locked myself out.'

'I'll need some ID Sir once we open the door,' he said as he swiped his card through the lock mechanism.

I wasn't prepared for what I saw as we walked in. Either room service had prepared the room whilst under the influence of hallucinogenic drugs or I'd been burgled. The mattress had been dragged off the bed and lay propped against the window ledge. The bed linen was rolled up and piled into a corner. A metal pedal bin had been pulled out and lay on its side. My wardrobe doors were wide open and every item of clothing flung into a crumpled heap on top of the base of the bed. My wash bag lay on top of the television for some reason, completely empty, the contents strewn over the carpet. Most worryingly of all, the mini safe door was wide open.

'Bit of a party in here last night Sir, I see. I need some ID now,' the security guard said.

I recovered my composure at the sound of his voice and went straight to the safe. It was completely empty. My passport, driving licence and the four hundred dollars I had left were missing.

'My passport's gone,' I said.

'So you got no ID then Sir,' the guard said.

'I do, but it looks like somebody has taken it. It's gone.'

'So you saying you been robbed, Sir?'

'I don't know. Yes. Maybe. All I know is I didn't leave my room like this.'

'Well we don't know if it is your room Mister Malarkey, Sir. Do we? Because you don't have any ID, Sir.'

The word *robbed* was still reverberating in my head. Robbed. Why would anyone rob me? How did they get into my safe? It had my PIN code. I had nothing of real value. Another shock wave struck me, in the form of Cecil's words, *you got some villain's wedge*. Why would anyone want to rob me? Unless... unless they thought I had half a million dollars in the room. It was then that I spotted my keycard on the bedside table. I must have left it there before I went to the pool.

'Mister Malarkey. I was saying, we don't know if it is your room Sir.'

I heard the security guard's voice and snapped out of my thought process. 'What? We don't know if it...of course it's my bloody room. I wouldn't be dragging you all the way up here to let me in if it wasn't, would I?'

'Well stranger things have happened Sir. You could be planning to break in and rob it.'

'Oh I see. Are you for real? You think there's a run on room 1164 then? People queuing up to rob it. Except I seem to have turned up a bit too late in that case because it looks to me like somebody else got here before me. Blown that one then. And you think that part of my robbery plan is to call hotel security to let me in? Really? Maybe I thought it was a good idea to have an hotel employee as an accomplice. Novel idea that, eh? You don't happen to have a bag with 'SWAG' written all over it do you? Because if the first lot of robbers have left anything then maybe you and I can clean up big time.'

The guard took a step back.

'There's no need to be that way Sir. I have to establish whether this is your room or not. I'm just doing my job.'

'I'm telling you, it is my friggin room. You check with reception. Mister Malarkey. Booked into room 1164.'

'That's the point though Sir you can't prove you are Mister Malarkey because you have no ID.'

'I know that. That's because I have been...look, I have my wallet. My cash card is in here.' I pulled my wallet from my pocket, opened it and took out a bank card. 'There you go. See... Matthew Malarkey. And what's more, I swiped a credit card at reception when I checked in...for extras, you know.'

'It has to be photo ID Sir. I'm sorry but you could have found the wallet. I'm afraid we're going to have to go back down to reception, report this and call the police now that –'

'No. Not the police,' I shouted. 'I'm sure we can sort this out and I have the keycard now anyway,' I said more calmly, as I noticed the guard's alarm at my reaction to the police.

'Yes, but it was me who let you into the room, Sir. We still need to identify you.' He pulled his radio from his belt and raised it to his face.

'What are you doing?'

'If you're unwilling to come back down to reception Sir, I'm going to need back up.'

'Back up?' I repeated the word but I realised I had no choice. I told him I would co-operate. He closed the room door and we walked back down the corridor towards the lifts. As we approached the lift area, I noticed something red sticking out of one of the waste bins that stood by the wall. I walked over and there was the familiar red cover of a British passport. The passport had somehow opened up as it was discarded and had lodged at the top of the bin. I turned it over and sure enough it was mine. I turned back to the security guard who was standing by the lift pressing the button.

'There you are. My ID,' I said, holding the pages open. 'No need for any more fuss now, is there?'

He checked my photo, looked me up and down to ensure the likeness and handed it back. 'What's it doing in the garbage Mister Malarkey?'

'Oh...err...well...I...well, I sometimes...when I am in hotels, leave it somewhere else...somewhere unusual...you know...in case I forget the code to the safe. So, it makes sense not to...err... lock it away in case I can't get at it. I must have forgotten what I did with it last night. Bit of a late night. You know...party thing. You can tell by the state of the...the messed up room.'

The guard stood and stared at me. He seemed to be deciding whether to believe me and save himself the bother of an official report or to report me as a deranged lunatic that had thrashed a room. 'So, the robbery you mentioned?'

'Robbery?' I felt the blood drain from my face. The corridor began to spin as I experienced a lightness in my head that disorientated me for a moment. I reached out for support as I stared at the guard, wondering how he had found out that half a million dollars had gone missing. Unfortunately, the support

I had reached for turned out to be the lift doors and they opened just as I leant back in that direction. The lack of something solid to compensate for my weight shift caused me to lose balance. I twisted in a half turn as I felt the loss of control but could not prevent myself stumbling into the open lift just as Kimberley, the woman that I had sprayed with sunscreen by the poolside, emerged. My momentum took me straight into her. Instinct caused me to reach out with both hands to prevent her from falling as I stumbled forward but I only succeeded in gripping the top of the sarong she had wrapped around her. The flimsy blue and green material came away in my hand leaving her in nothing other than the bikini she had been wearing at the poolside. Such was her shock at the unexpected collision that she lost her footing and collapsed on the floor of the lift, taking me with her. I heard a clatter as the contents of her beach bag spilled over the floor. For a moment, I lay on top of her staring into her eyes, too surprised to move. She stared back, a sudden recognition flickering into her gaze.

'You! You goddam jerk. What're you doing jumping on me?'

I was about to answer when the lift doors closed and the lift began to descend. Just as they closed tight shut I managed to blurt out the word *accident*.

'Another freakin accident? Too many for my liking. I'm going to report you. You're a goddam menace. Get off of me.'

Her angry toned shocked me into action. I pushed down with both hands to lever myself upright and at the same time I brought my right foot forward to get a grip on the floor. It came down on something long and cylindrical in shape causing my foot to roll back behind me. The loss of grip on the floor threw me forward again and back on top of the prostrate Kimberley. She began to scream and pummel my shoulders with her fists, just as a short ringing sound signalled that the lift had come to a stop. I rolled my weight to one side to try and get out of reach of her flailing fists. As I did so, my left hand came down on the long cylindrical object. Instinctively I gripped it and raised it up just as the lift doors opened in the main lobby. Three Japanese tourists, a nun and two suited businessmen, both carrying brief cases, stared in open mouthed dismay into the lift. Kimberley stopped screaming as we both stared directly back out from our prone positions at the six people who had been about to enter the lift. I noticed the nun pointing at me, her eyes agog, her face a crimson mask. My own face must have registered total astonishment as I realised what I was holding in my hand. A large, pink, silver tipped vibrator protruded proudly from my clenched fist. Kimberley, lying flat out on her back, legs splayed wide, suddenly realised what was happening.

'Oh my fucking life. Gimme that.' She shot out a hand and made a grab for the end of the vibrator.

I hadn't expected the sudden movement and didn't let go of it properly as she snatched at it. The rapid jerk in my hand caused it to twist and it started to buzz. Both of us let go at the same time. It dropped to the floor and rolled towards the dumbfounded crowd at the lift entrance. One of the businessmen reacted first. A swift kick of the rolling object sent it back into the lift. Next, he reached round the door and pressed one of the buttons, saying as he did, 'You two love birds ought to have some privacy in there fella. Way to go buddy.' The doors closed and the lift began to ascend.

I managed to get to my feet. I reached out a hand to pull Kimberley to her feet. She declined and stood up by herself, her face like thunder. To try and diffuse the situation I began to pick up the remaining contents of her bag including the wayward vibrator. I handed it to her. Her eyes had turned black with murderous intent as she snatched it from me.

'You'll pay for this. You will pay for this outrage. This embarrassment. I will report you. Sue you. Your butt won't know what's hit it by the time I'm finished with you,' she screamed, as she stuffed a hairbrush, sun cream, after sun, hairbands and a bottle of water back into her bag along with the still buzzing vibrator. She then grabbed the sarong that I tentatively held out to her, in an effort to save her further embarrassment, slung it over her arm and hit one of the buttons on the lift as it ascended. Within seconds we had stopped at the same floor where we had made our impromptu departure. Standing outside was the security guard.

Kimberly stormed straight out of the lift past the startled guard.

'You haven't heard the last of this. Your ass is toast, you jerk.'

I began to chase after her along the corridor. I couldn't have another person threatening to report me.

'Mister Malarkey. Your room.'

I heard the security guard call after me. I signalled to him to wait. I caught up with Kimberley outside her room as she began to fumble through her bag for her keycard.

'Get away from me. I warned you…you…fraudster.'

'Whoa. Fraudster? Hold it a minute lady. Look before this gets out of hand let's just calm down and –'

'I am fucking calm you stupid sonofabitch. You assaulted me. Twice in one day. Now get outta my face.'

I ignored her rage and held both my hands up in front of me, palms towards her, in an attempt at placating her.

'Ok, ok. But look, I realise it was an embarrassing situation and I am really very sorry it happened. You may not think so but it *was* another accident. I have no reason to assault you. I'm just on holiday. There is no sense in suing anybody. I mean look at this way. If that happens I'm going to have to give my version of what happened too and I will have to mention your...err... your toy, won't I? And that will only mean more embarrassment. No sense in that, is there?'

Her face changed. The dark rage that had clouded her eyes seemed to subside a little as she contemplated what I'd said.

'Don't get me wrong. It's fine by me and I have no problem with what you carry in your bag. Each to their own I say, but it's probably best that it's your secret and it doesn't come out in front of all and sundry. Perhaps I can get my friend, Jasper to buy you another drink. Just as an apology or something.'

She swiped the keycard in the lock and turned the handle of the door. As she pushed it open she looked back over her shoulder.

'Ok. We will say no more. But you keep away from me. Got it?'

As she shut the door I walked back along the corridor. The security guard was standing waiting patiently.

'Mister Malarkey. You wanna get back in your room or not?'

I nodded.

'And what about this robbery? The one you say happened in your room.'

A sense of relief ran through me as I realised what he had been referring to earlier.

'Oh, that. No, there was no robbery. I was...err...I don't know, just having a bit of fun. English humour. Look, I will tidy up the room. If there is any damage I am happy to pay for it. I am sure there isn't. Just a bit of mess. There is no need to go to any fuss. Who needs it anyway?'

There was a moment's hesitation in which he seemed to be making the decision about whether to report me or let me back in. I held my breath. Finally, he started to walk back towards my room.

11

Three hard raps on my door woke me.

'You in there mate?'

The sound of Cecil's voice shook me back into reality. I leapt off the bed and opened the door. Cecil was standing in the doorway dressed up for a night out, black jeans and a pale blue shirt that had red trim on the inside of the turned up cuffs and two thick red and white vertical stripes running down the left side.

'Geezer. What you up to? It's twenty past seven. We're supposed to be out partying. It's your birthday mate. What you doin?' He strolled past me into the main room. 'What the fuck happened here? Why're all your clothes all over the floor?'

After I had got back to my room I had begun to tidy up but once I had thrown the mattress onto the bed I felt so exhausted that I had stretched out hoping to catch a half hour nap. Clearly I had been asleep much longer. I told Cecil how I had found my room on my return and my concern about the fact that someone had broken in and taken my money and driving licence but that I had no idea why anyone would have done so or why they would have taken my passport and then ditched it.

'Mate, it's obvious, innit. Somebody is either trying to find out who you are or stop you leaving the country. They're the only reasons anyone would be looking for your passport. I don't reckon they were after your cash or nuthin. How did they get hold of it anyway? Didn't you put it in the safe? You didn't just leave it lying around did you?'

'No I didn't. It was in the safe with the cash and my licence. They must have opened it while I was out at the pool.'

'What? You mean sussed your PIN and just opened the door?' Cecil cocked his head to one side, a puzzled frown creasing his brow.

'I don't know Ces. Yes...maybe. Who knows.'

'What PIN you using mate?'

'1,2,3,4,' I said, 'keeping it simple.'

'Simple. Fucking simple. Why didn't you just write it down on a post-it note and stick it on the fucking safe door? Would have saved whoever it was, having to use his brain for two seconds. Good job you didn't put what's left of the other dough in your safe then, ain't it? Geezer, don't you know that half the fucking world is dumb enough to use that PIN sequence. That or four zeros. Any villain worth his salt is gonna try that combo on a hotel room safe before he does anything else. It's a *come and get me* combination. I hope that ain't your bank card PIN too.'

'No, it's not,' I said, stung by the criticism. 'I just used it as... well, a temporary thing. Easy to remember. Anyway why would anybody want to know who I am or stop me leaving the country?'

'Geezer, did it not occur to you that when we've just mislaid half a million friggin dollars that isn't ours, somebody's gonna want to find out who's got their dough and then buy plenty of time to make sure they get it back. If you can't leave the States they got more of a chance of getting hold of it. I told you, didn't I? It ain't no little old lady who just got lucky in the casino and has absent mindedly misplaced it. Nah mate. It belongs to some villain, like I said, or somebody who ain't walking on the right side of the line if you get the mumble.'

'Bloody hell, Ces. I'm in the shit now then, aren't I? Whoever they are, they know who I am and they are going to come looking for me. I can't stay in the hotel. I have to get out of here. And how did they get in the room anyway? There's no sign of a forced entry.'

'Duplicate keycard or something mate. Who knows.'

'Or they have my other one...the spare. I left one of them on the bedside table when I went down to the pool earlier. Had to get security to let me in. I can't find the other one. I've definitely got to get out of here.'

Cecil didn't respond. He simply started to pick up my clothes from the floor and place them in the wardrobe.

'What are you doing Ces? I told you I got to get out of here,' I said, taken aback by Cecil's nonchalance.

'Shut up Matt and listen.'

It was the word '*Matt*' rather than the abrupt '*shut up*' that shocked me into silence. Twice in one day he had used my first name, although this time he seemed to be taking more care to hide his concerns.

'Look, we don't know who the money belongs to so you either do a runner and try and sit it out until it's time to fly back home or you do nothing. If you do a runner that fucks up the whole trip and in any case somebody is still gonna want their dough back so they're still gonna be lookin, right up until that plane gets off the ground. And if you start hiding it makes it look like you got something to worry about. Makes it look like you're involved. If you do nothing, just carry on as normal then somebody is gonna find you and we start to get to the bottom of this. Whoever it is knows who you are now, right? So you gotta play dumb. Carry on as normal. That's the only way any villain's gonna believe you.'

'Yeah, but what if they don't Ces?' I said, as I paced the room.

Cecil finished putting my stuff back into the wardrobe. He turned towards me and grabbed my arm, halting my nervous pacing.

'Geezer, sit the fuck down and chill. Look, I dunno whether they'll go for your story or not but it's true ain't it? You just leave the bit out about spending any of it and –'

Panic gripped me at the thought of the potential consequences of being responsible for the loss of five hundred thousand dollars. I jumped to my feet.

'Oh, that's great Ces. Leave the bit out about you blowing the best part of ten grand so it looks like I've not only taken their cash but started spending it too. Drop me right in it, eh? We wouldn't be in this mess if you'd left the bag alone would we? And now you want to distance yourself from the whole thing. Great.'

Cecil took a step towards me, his barrel chest pumped out, his face contorted with pent up anger, a jabbing finger cutting the space between us.

'Is that right is it? We wouldn't be in this mess if I'd left the bag alone, yeah? What about if you'd looked after your fucking bag in the first place, you fucking twat? How about that then?'

The sound of my mobile ringing broke the tense moment. I picked it up from the table, glad of the unexpected diversion.

'*Happy birthday to you. Happy birthday to you. Happy birthday dear Matthew, happy birthday to you.*'

'Louise. Blimey…err…I mean, hi honey. How are you?'

'*I'm good Matthew. Just finished a late shift. How are you doing? You having a good time? How's Las Vegas.*'

'I'm...err...fine...yeah, it's good. Lot's going on. I was just getting ready to go out.'

'*You ok? You sound odd.*'

'I'm odd, yes…I mean, I'm good. Just tired. You know, still a bit jet…jet lagged. What time is it with you?'

'*It's just gone half past three in the morning. I finished at three and just got home. I started work at two o'clock this afternoon. I was going to call you earlier but I had such a busy day and what with the time difference, I wasn't sure what you'd be doing. Did you get my text?*'

'I did, thanks. Yes, Vegas is great. Not seen a lot of it yet but got a few more days. We're out tonight somewhere. Not sure where yet. I was just...err...just chatting to Cecil...sorting the...err...night out.' I looked across at Cecil who was sitting on the end of my bed staring at his shoes, deep in thought from what I could see.

'*Is he ok? Party mood I bet. Say hi from me. How's the camera? Have you taken loads of pictures?*'

'The camera. It's...yeah...its...I've taken a few. Not had much chance yet. I've –'

I looked at Cecil who had glanced in my direction at the word *camera*. His left hand was making a slicing motion just below his chin. I realised he was trying to tell me not to mention the bag incident.

'I've got...err...plenty of time. Anyway, honey, I'd best let you get some sleep. I've got to hit the town with the lads. Us youngsters have some partying to do.'

I heard Louise's giggle as she spoke. *'Well as much partying as a forty year old can handle. You take it easy at your age.'*

'I will. We'll celebrate properly when I get back. Get some sleep. Don't want you dozing off on duty.'

'I'm off to bed right now. I have a long day but I'm seeing Sheryl tomorrow and we're having a few days together before she goes back. She sends her love to Cecil. Tell him.'

We said our goodbyes and I cut the phone call. Cecil spoke first.

'That Louise? She ok?'

'Yeah, she's fine Ces. She said Hi to you. She's seeing Sheryl tomorrow. She told me to tell you that Sheryl sends her love.'

Cecil ignored the remark but I could tell by his face that it had registered. I knew he had got to like Sheryl over the past few months but as her return to Toronto drew closer, he had begun to see less of her. He would never say it directly but I knew it was because he had a fear of being hurt again. He ran both hands through his hair, stood up and walked across the room to where the pedal bin lay on its side where it had fallen when the room was ransacked. As he stood it upright something slid to the bottom. He flipped the lid and reached in. As his hand emerged from the tall metal canister I saw that he was holding a fistful of cash. He reached in again and pulled out what looked like my driving licence and a room keycard.

'These yours mate?' He stretched out his hand and handed me the driving licence, a wad of dollars and the keycard.

I flicked through the notes.

'It's the rest of the cash from my winnings. I'd left it in the safe with my driving licence. And that's my spare keycard. So they did have it. They must have just chucked everything when they got what they wanted – the passport.'

'Yeah, looks like it mate.'

'So, it was definitely not a robbery. They would have taken the cash if it was. They were just after the passport.'

'Or looking for the bag. They must've used your card to get in then just dumped it in the bin with the rest of the stuff in your safe once they found there was no bag and they had your passport.'

'But…how did they get my card?'

'Who knows, geeze. Anyway, listen, I was thinking. No sense in you and me falling out over this shit. I ain't trying to save my own skin. I'm just trying to talk some sense. I meant that you don't mention spending any of the cash because you don't want anyone thinking you were taking the piss and spending their wedge, right? So you let them think that fucking tart who stole the bag has spent it. I mean, after all she wouldn't have taken it if she wasn't gonna spend it and you can bet your bottom dollar that she's already had a little shop up. Then tomorrow you go back over to the Bond Bar again and ask if your bag has been handed in. That way it looks more legit. You look like you genuinely lost your own bag and you're still looking for it. The thinking is that anybody who's done a runner with somebody else's cash isn't gonna be walking round town in plain sight asking questions about a bag, ok? So it backs up your story that it's been nicked from you. All you can do at the minute.'

Having just spoken to Louise, a career police officer, the law was on my mind.

'I still think we should go to the police Ces. It makes sense to get some backup in case this gets tricky.'

'Mate. Not a good move. Told ya. They are gonna take some convincing and then you gotta explain why, once you found a bag of cash, you started spending it.'

'Yeah, but can't I just say nothing, like you said earlier, and just make out I know nothing about spending any of it so it looks like the escort girl has spent it?'

'You could do, yeah, but once you involve the feds mate and you ain't told them the full mumble, they're gonna suspect you of something the minute they find out. Maybe even implicate

107

you and make out you and the girl are in it together. The point is, we don't know whether that cash is legit casino winnings or something else. If it's something dodge like I told ya before, you could then be in the frame for whatever else is going on.'

'Like what? What are you saying?' I asked, a multitude of scrambled thoughts running through my head.

'What if it's drugs money, geezer?' Cecil saw my reaction. 'Don't look so fucking worried I'm not saying it is. But if for example it was, then the police are gonna be lookin at you too to see if you're involved.'

I began pacing again. 'Christ Ces. This sounds like one fucking mess. I need a drink.'

'We'll get one in a minute if you just get your arse in gear. Now –'

'What if the escort girl lets on that there was ten grand missing? And what about the ten grand she left behind? We forgot about that didn't we?' I stopped by the window and turned round to see Cecil's reaction.

'Listen mate. Don't let it all get out of hand. I ain't forgot about nuthin. That's all tucked away. Do what I said. Go looking for your camera bag tomorrow at the Bond Bar. If the money belongs to a villain and they come after you, their main interest is in getting it back. Once they track down the bird they ain't gonna believe no story about it wasn't all there. And the ten grand is insurance, right?'

'Insurance?'

'Yeah, insurance. I'll keep the wad in the safe in my room. If anyone doubts your story, you give them the ten grand as proof of your good intention. You tell them that the bird must have dropped it when she nicked the bag and was leavin in a hurry. You found it under the bed later and you didn't spend it. It's a long shot and it gets us some time but let's see what turns up first. And the beauty of it is, if you don't need to mention it we get to hang on to it. Plus we got an extra fifteen hundred from the ten I spent. Tumble?'

'You're joking Ces. I'm not –'

'Geezer. Trust me,' Cecil interrupted. 'Sometimes you gotta

walk on the wild side. That's how we roll now. It's all a gamble mate. Every woman you marry, every car you buy, every job you take. All a trade. A trade between what you think you can do and what you know you can get away with. Yeah?'

I said nothing in reply. Cecil was my best mate. Somehow we had always come out ahead. I had no idea who or what we were dealing with so I started out with a degree of innocence, an inability to suspect the worst. Cecil sounded sure, in command, unruffled and as usual, he saw a way to benefit. We were in Las Vegas, a city where every single night somebody somewhere played a gamble that stretched them beyond their means. Sometimes they came out lucky. Maybe it was my turn.

I walked towards Cecil, my hand outstretched.

'I'm sorry Ces. I didn't mean anything earlier. You know, about covering your own tracks or anything. I was just...you know... worried.'

Cecil ignored my proffered handshake. Instead he grabbed me in one of his back slapping bear hugs.

'No problem geezer. I know what you meant.' He let go of me and looked at his watch. 'You seen the fucking time mate? Five past eight already. We're supposed to be out there living like Pharaohs, not stuck in a hotel room worrying about what the fuck's gonna happen next. I told Carlos and Jasper I'd see them downstairs in the bar at eight, have a couple there and go over the Hyde Bar. Get yourself sorted. We got a fortieth birthday to celebrate.'

'I know Ces. But suddenly I feel old, you know.'

'Old? Mate. You're a Jedi, like me. There's Jedi age and human age. Jedi age goes more slowly geezer. There are some forty year olds who act like they're sixty. Mate you're still a cool dude. Get showered up and I'll see you downstairs in twenty. You up for that?'

I had to smile at Cecil's reassurance.

'Ok, mate. I'm on it.'

'Good man. Get out there and close the show.'

I walked towards the wardrobe looking for something to wear. I glanced back at Cecil standing there, a confident grin on his face, the anticipation of a night out gleaming in his eyes.

'Nice shirt, by the way Ces. You're looking good yourself.'

'Mate. It's my *get it shirt*. No bird in Las Vegas is gonna resist this shirt. The white ones are coming down.' He turned to leave, opened the door and hesitated. 'Mate, you're gonna have to weigh me in with some cash. Done all my dough, ain't I? I'll square you back home. What you got left of your winnings? Four hundred? Yeah, that'll cover me.'

12

The Bellagio was a frenzy of activity. A crowd of people stood around the enquiries desk in the front lobby each seeking a bit of information that would shape their evening. Slot machines hummed and chimed, spinning out their eagerly awaited verdict – fortune or misfortune – to hundreds of focussed eyes, tunnel-visioned on their fate as the images dropped into place.

We strolled across the main entrance floor in a line like Reservoir Dogs, four Brits abroad intent on a good time. With the buzz of distracting activity all around us I hadn't noticed her purposeful stride until she was practically on top of me. A blonde vision in a golden, figure hugging, sleeveless cocktail dress approached me, her tanned and toned legs displayed to maximum effect by the mid-thigh finish of the hemline. Her outstretched hand reached for my hand.

'Hi. How are you doing?' she said, her voice soft but confident, the accent revealing a Southern drawl. 'I'm Brooke.'

I thought she must be a *meeter and greeter* for the casino.

'Oh, hi. I'm Matthew. Nice to meet you,' I replied.

In the instant that our palms connected, I felt the impression of the folded card that she had slipped into my hand. In a reflex action my fingers closed around it.

She smiled broadly, the whiteness of her teeth enhanced by the carefully applied pink lipstick.

'Welcome to Las Vegas Matthew,' she said, her gaze holding mine, almost as if she was seeking recognition that I had understood some subtle, secret message that had passed between us.

For a moment I couldn't break the spell that had gripped me. Brooke managed to do it for me. Moving past me, she glanced back over her shoulder, the hint of a wink fluttering around one eye.

'I have friends too,' she said and walked on.

I stood and stared as she walked away. Her blonde hair swayed lightly as she moved, her toned calf muscles accentuated by the high heels that matched her golden dress. I turned back to the boys, each one of them still staring at the departing Brooke, a look of admiration clearly visible on their faces.

'Wow. Did you see that?' Jasper said unnecessarily, his eyes wide with appreciation.

'Welcome to Las Vegas indeed lads,' Cecil responded. 'Oh yeah mate. You'd go mad on that. Do coke off her belly all night long. The whole lot.' He turned to face the three of us. 'Now that's what we came to Vegas for boys. That's the standard. The gold standard my friends. Let every man take note.'

The word *note* focussed my attention. I opened my still clenched grip to reveal a plain card folded neatly in half. I unfolded it and stared at the pink lettering displayed across the glossy, white background.

Brooke. Blonde Barbie. Las Vegas. Call or text (712) 631 7643.

I had been done by the classic Cecil '*how are ya,*' the move he pulled on club doormen, usually with a ten pound note that would cross their palms in a friendly handshake, followed by a fast track entrance to London's nightlife.

'What you got there Mateo?' Carlos asked.

'She gave me her card mate. She must have took a shine to me. Maybe it's the cool black jacket,' I said, my ego flattered that she had signalled me out amongst the four of us as we had strolled across the casino.

'Give us a gander at that geezer,' Cecil said, snatching the card from my grip. He stared at it for a moment, looked up and handed it back, a grin all over his face. 'Mate, she's an escort. She ain't got the hots for you. She's more interested in your cash. She can't be more than twenty-three.'

Jasper came to the rescue of my rapidly deflating ego.

'Yeah, but all the same Ces she did walk up to Matt. He's not a bad looking fella for forty. She could've gone up to any mug in here, couldn't she? I mean if she's working the floor for blokes she thinks might have money it's always gonna be better for her if she likes what she's looking at too.'

I winked at Jasper to acknowledge his support. I dismissed his reference to my age and the word *mug* as just his way of putting things.

'Yeah, see Ces. Jasper's right on the money,' I said and slipped Brooke's card into the top pocket of my jacket, for no reason other than as a memento of my moment of ego. As we walked on I stuck an arm around Cecil's shoulders. 'One up for me on the *get it* shirt then Ces,' I said, pushing him playfully in the back as I removed my arm.

'Nights barely started geezer. Barely started.'

There was a short queue at the entrance to the Hyde Bar. The bar itself stood to one side of the casino floor. A red roped barrier, separating the queue from the main walkway, directed the line towards a glass doorway set back into a short corridor that was the access point to the bar. Inside the rope barrier and either side of the corridor, two tall, muscular doorman in tuxedos controlled entry. Several shapely girls in short dresses and Venetian masks shimmied along the queue, their concealed identities highlighting their allure.

'Must be some sort of theme night,' Jasper said. 'Those chicks are hot.'

As he spoke one of the girls, her blue eyes sparkling beneath the white, gold trimmed mask, twirled past us, her gaze direct but the expression on the lower part of her face fixed and serious, creating a doll-like, surreal aura.

Within five minutes we had been ushered through the glass door and into the full impact of the Hyde Bar's classy, discreet, upmarket image. The soft glow from strategically placed lights picked out specific positions across the room, dispersing light and casting shadows, creating a sensual ambience that enticed and enthralled the visitor. The most eye catching feature was the large expanse of window that ran across the entire length of the room and overlooked the huge pond and fountains of the Bellagio. Further on the view took in the Strip and the Paris Hotel opposite, its golden Eiffel Tower reaching high into the blackness of the sky. The central floor of the bar contained a mix of long sofas and soft armchairs, each positioned around low mahogany tables. Behind the bar the staff wore a variety of Venetian style masks reflecting the style of the girls outside.

We were shown to a table by a tall, stunningly attractive waitress whose tight dress just managed to reach the tops of her thighs.

'Hi, I'm Geraldine. What can I get you guys,' she asked as she handed a drinks menu to Carlos.

We ordered four Bombay Gin and tonics with fresh mint. Within five minutes Geraldine had returned with the four drinks perched on a silver tray. As she set each one down onto the table, it was clear that she had perfected the art of table service whilst wearing an impossibly short dress. A straight back and a distinct bend of both knees, ensuring they stayed firmly pressed together, enabled the bottom of the dress to stay fixed to her thighs. Had there been any movement it would not have gone unnoticed.

'That is what I call a shapely pair of legs,' Jasper said, as he lifted his glass from the table.

'What's that song? You know...Chuck Berry, he sings that line, *she looks like a model on the cover of a magazine...*' I said, but was met by puzzled stares.

'You can tell she works out,' Cecil chipped in.

'She may well do,' I said, 'but judging by the way she does that knee bend I reckon it's like doing a set of squat thrusts at every table night after night. I'm not surprised she's got legs like that.'

Carlos raised his glass. 'Hey, you cucarachas. We're supposed to be celebrating Mateo's birthday here. C'mon, let's get this wee drink doon and get the party spirit gannin.'

It didn't need much encouragement from anyone to get in the party mood. I for one had already had a fraught two days and I needed some light relief. Two more gins followed in quick succession. The mood was relaxed, banter flowing back and forth. A group of people began to move towards the window, which was open across the entire length of the room. In an instant, several jets of water spurted from the centre of the lake high into the air. Gasps of appreciation echoed across the bar. Cameras pointed in one direction as the full display of the Bellagio fountains went into their choreographed dance.

'You gottae get a picture of that,' Carlos said, poking me in the shoulder.

'I can't, can I. I lost my bag or did you forget Carlos?' The memory of my predicament hit me suddenly. I dismissed the thought as quickly as I could. I wanted to have a good night and I knew I could worry about it all the next day.

'Och, sorry mi amigo. I forgot. Must be these wee drinkies. Sorry.'

'No worries Carlos. I can get a picture with my mobile anyway.'

We watched the display for a few minutes more and sat back down.

Geraldine approached the table with four small shot glasses.

'Guys, that gentleman over at the bar sent these over for y'all. It's Jägermeister.'

Four heads turned at once. At the bar behind us, a man in a khaki coloured shirt and black chinos sat nursing a small shot glass similar to the ones Geraldine had just delivered. He looked familiar, sandy coloured hair, thinning slightly at the front and a cheerful round face, but I couldn't place where I might have seen him before. My suspicions suddenly kicked in. A stranger sending over drinks. What if he was something to do with the missing cash? He raised his glass in a *cheers* salute on catching our collective gaze.

Cecil was the first to acknowledge him, raising his glass in a similar salute and draining it in one neck-jerking hit. The rest of us followed Cecil's lead, the impact of the shot causing my eyes to squeeze tightly together in some reflex attempt to absorb the taste. The guy at the bar necked his shot, left his seat and walked across to our table.

'Guys, I hope you didn't mind my little interruption but I wanted to buy this fella here a drink.' He pointed directly at me.

I had a sudden fear that the boys were pulling a birthday stunt on me and that he might be a stripogram.

'Yeah, I thought it was you buddy,' he said, a broad grin playing across his pale features. 'Any guy who makes out with a chick in broad daylight in a hotel elevator is alright by me. Way to go buddy.'

Three heads turned in my direction. My face flushed scarlet as I realised he was the businessman who had kicked the vibrator back into the lift when I had inadvertently fallen on Kimberley, the woman from the pool.

Cecil turned and looked directly at me, the surprise clearly showing in his eyes.

'Geezer. What's the mumble? You kept that quiet. You ain't said nuthin.'

I tried to laugh it off, still acutely embarrassed by the incident, but Jasper was on it.

'Who was it then Matt? Spill the beans?'

'No one. Just that Kimberley from the pool. I ran into her in the lift and –'

'You tried it on with that Kimberley bird Matt? She's not a bad looker –'

'No, it wasn't quite like that Jasper. Look, I'll explain later.'

'Well, I wouldn't blame you if you did,' Jasper said. 'She had a bit of a twinkle in her eye when I was chatting to her. Might even give it a shot myself.' He turned towards Carlos. 'Hey, Carlos. What d'you say me and you do the old double act on her and her mate...what was her name?'

'Lana,' Carlos replied.

'Yeah, that was it. Lana. What do you reckon?'

Before Carlos could reply, Cecil offered his opinion.

'You seen her face? Redder than the fucking toxic avenger.

She's a troglodyte mate. It only takes a couple of mutations and you lose your Kennel Club certificate and trust me, she's lost it.'

'That's a bit harsh Ces,' I said. 'It's only a bit of sunburn.'

Cecil rolled his eyes and shook his head slowly to emphasise his dismissal of my comment. He beckoned our visitor to sit down and invited him to join us for another shot.

'Thanks buddy,' he said and slid onto the sofa next to Carlos. 'Guys, I'm Richard. Richard Heydon the third, to be precise. I'm on business from Chicago. Staying over this weekend. You guys from the UK, right? On vacation? Looking for a bit of action here in Vegas, I guess.'

We introduced ourselves and I explained that the trip was for my birthday.

Richard Heydon told us that he was a rep for a gun manufacturer in Chicago and was in Nevada servicing all the local outlets.

'Yeah I visit Vegas about three times a year, just to keep up with clients and show our new lines. It's all strictly licensed. I carry a couple of cases of stock, hand guns, ammo, a few semi-automatics, Ruger, Smith and Wesson but all under lock and key. I mostly make out I sell textiles just so, you know, my real business don't get known to the wrong ears, if you know what I mean. But, hell, you guys are from outta town, so I reckon you're cool.'

I suspected that it was the shots rather than any assessment of our *out of town coolness* that had loosened Richard's tongue.

'Say, maybe we can get together for a beer before you go back home,' he said. 'Maybe some of that good old English charm will rub off on me and we might get lucky with the chicks. What d'ya say Matt?'

I nodded agreement in a placatory fashion rather than any conviction that I wanted to accompany him on a trawl for women. I also wasn't sure that *chicks* was quite appropriate when you hit middle age. Somehow he had me down as a ladies' man and had totally missed the fact that, if that was what he wanted, Jasper was his guy. Perhaps it was the fact I was clearly nearer his age.

'I got a dinner date myself tomorrow,' Richard said to no one in particular. 'Ran into a nice looking lady earlier today, by the name of Kate. Some hot ladies in Vegas. You guys had any action apart from Matt's little escapade in the elevator?'

'Just got here mate, but the night is young. Another shot, boys?' Jasper said, as he looked around to catch Geraldine's eye.

Another round of shots was delivered, followed by several more drinks. Richard became more exuberant and talkative. I got the feeling that he was trying to be one of the boys and impress with his references to women and the guns he traded. The boys began to lose interest as the bar began to fill up and their attention was taken elsewhere. Cecil and Jasper got chatting to two girls. Carlos went to the bar and never came back. Eventually Richard left for his room saying he had a busy day come Monday morning and he also wanted to be fresh for his Sunday dinner date. Before he left he pulled a business card from his pocket and slid it towards me.

'Don't forget that beer Matt. Call me, ok.'

I picked it up from the table and popped it in my top pocket. As I did so, I felt the shape of another card in there. I pulled out Brooke's card and, for a moment, contemplated it. It was probably the booze that made me consider the possibility of calling, but I thought of Louise and came to my senses. I pushed both cards into my wallet. And then I spotted the folded up bit of newspaper. I took it out. Erin Farrell's number, on the strip torn from the Washington Post. I'd promised her I'd meet up for a drink. The boys were all otherwise engaged. It would do no harm. A friendly drink and a chat. Always handy to know someone who worked for an airline. I punched the number into my mobile.

'Erin? It's Matthew. From the flight...and the...the...err...speed course.'

I heard her giggle.

'*I know who you are Matthew. Nice to hear from you.*' Her soft Irish lilt was almost musical on the phone.

'Well you said to call. I wondered if you fancied that drink. For my birthday.'

'*Of course I do. As a matter of fact I'm over at the Paris right now. To be honest I was hoping I'd run into you. You hadn't called so I thought I'd see if you were about. I'm in the Chateau Nightclub, in the Terrace bar. Just come through the hotel entrance and go up the stairs. There's a sign. You can't miss it.'*

'Ok, I will be over shortly. Just got to find the boys and tell them where I'm going. Catch you in a minute.'

I found Cecil and Jasper in deep chat up mode with two attractive girls from Texas. They, not unsurprisingly as far as I was concerned, were fascinated by Cecil's mannerisms and accent. He seemed to be giving Jasper, who had the seriously appealing good looks, quite a bit of competition. I pulled Cecil to one side.

'Ces, I'm just going over to the Paris, to the nightclub up on the roof. Just spoken with the hostess I mentioned from the flight I was on, and arranged a drink. Why don't you come over?'

'Oh yeah? Doing a little mumble swerve on your own then geezer.'

'I'm not doing anything. Just said I might have a drink with her that's all, so I am. Come over with me.'

'Mate, I will do but right now I'm on a roll with these little stunners. One of them thought I sounded like Ray Winstone. Told her I was his cousin. She's only gone for it. They like all that movie star stuff and the accent. Laying it on large now.'

'Oh, ok. Well if you're busy I –'

'Not busy mate. I'll be there. Got to have a bottle of Champagne on your birthday, ain't we? Me and Jas'll bring these birdies over too and we can have a bit of a crack. Where's Carlos?'

I pointed across the room. 'He's at the bar chatting to the bar staff. I reckon he thinks he's still at work. Give him a shout when you're leaving Ces and I'll see you all over there.'

'Will do geeze. See you about half hour.'

13

The Chateau Terrace was part of the Paris Hotel's Chateau Nightclub complex. Located above the main casino there were three separate bars on two levels, the Nightclub, the Terrace and the Rooftop Garden, each with their own distinct style and ambience.

I walked up the stairs from the lobby to the first floor and headed for the Terrace bar. It seemed like a party was already in full swing, a lively crowd of Vegas revellers enjoying the pumping music and spectacular views across the Strip from the open-air terrace. As I walked to the centre of the bar area I could see Bally's and Caesar's glowing against the dark blue hue of the night sky to my right and, to my left, Planet Hollywood, the Cosmopolitan and, in the distance, the towering beam of light from the Luxor. The main bar area was long and spacious although most of the floor space was occupied as the DJ cranked up the party atmosphere. Four rectangular leather seating units held the centre of the floor, each of them fully occupied with a succession of gorgeous girls and good looking guys. The perimeter wall, that overlooked Las Vegas Boulevard, was lined by a series of cabana style seating areas, their arched canopies supported by short ivy entwined columns.

I ordered a Jack and Coke at the bar. As I handed over payment, I heard the familiar soft Irish tone behind me.

'Hello Matthew.'

I turned to see Erin's green eyes twinkling over her raised glass of Champagne. She looked stunning, in an olive green, three quarter sleeved, scooped neck, panelled dress. Her makeup was perfectly applied, just enough dark eye liner for emphasis, the sheen on her hair picked out by the waves of coloured light that bathed the terrace in cycles of brilliance and shade. Her shoes were high, sexy and matched the colour of her dress perfectly. As she stood in front of me, the contrasting light patterns gave her a mesmeric, bewitching appeal that caused me to stumble for words.

'Oh, Erin...hello....hi. Good to see you. You look...err...how are you?'

She smiled at me, but I couldn't tell if she had noticed her impact.

'Well, truthfully I'm a little tipsy. Bit too much of this bubbly stuff. But it is Saturday night after all and it is Las Vegas so I make no apologies,' she said as she clinked her glass against mine. 'Cheers. Are you having a wonderful time?' Her eyes sparkled mischievously. She was in high spirits and I detected a slight slurring in some of her words.

'Yeah, it's great,' I said. 'Great to be out having fun. Can I get you a drink? More Champagne maybe? I'm celebrating after all.'

'Celebrating? What...a win? Did you win on the casino?'

'No. No such luck. My birthday.'

'Oh, of course. You did say. Silly me. I thought my flower had brought you some luck.' She placed a slender hand on my arm. 'You all on your own then tonight? No friends?'

'No, no...they'll be over later. They're in the Bellagio. The Hyde bar.'

'Good. That means we can have a bit of time alone then for a little while.'

I caught the surreptitious wink and couldn't miss the beaming smile. Here I was in Las Vegas, music pumping, bright lights flashing, drinks flowing and an attractive woman flirting outrageously with me. And yet a few months earlier I had been trawling through a dating site looking for love. I had found that love when I met Louise but it was sod's law that, now I was spoken for, other opportunities were presenting themselves. I dismissed the thought and decided to enjoy the moment.

I downed the Jack and Coke and ordered a bottle of Champagne. May as well push the boat out I thought. I'm only forty once. The barman placed it in an ice bucket on one side of the bar and poured out two glasses.

'Cheers Erin,' I said as we touched glasses.

'Cheers to you Matthew and a happy birthday.' She raised the glass and took a sip, her eyes never leaving my face. 'So, what have you been up to then? Anything exciting?'

'Well not a lot to be honest. This is only my first proper night out really.'

'Oh, you really didn't go out then last night after I saw you in Caesars? I thought you were just trying to be good and that the bright lights and pretty ladies would soon change your mind.'

'Well, to tell the truth I did have a few drinks in the Cosmopolitan with the boys before bed. The Bond bar. D'you know it?'

'The Bond Bar. Nice. Yes, I have been there once or twice before. So no lap dancing clubs for you? Straight to bed?'

'More or less, yes. Had a quick look around the casino downstairs but I was too exhausted and a little bit...err...well, drunk and jetlagged by then.'

She smiled and moved a little closer. 'So no excitement for you then on your first night.'

'No, nothing exciting,' I said, wondering if she thought me dull.

She moved closer still, leaning forward so that her cheek was almost touching mine. The soft curl of her hair brushed my face. Her scent drifted over me, a sweet fragrance but with an edge, like citrus fruits, heady and intoxicating. Her breath gentle, warm in my ear as her voice took on a low whisper.

'Well, I am sure we can change that tonight, Matthew.'

For an instant I felt faint, as if my brain had been temporarily deprived of oxygen. The mix of drinks, the flashing colours of the bar, the movement of the crowd, the throbbing music, all merged into one fleeting hallucinogenic moment that caused me to step back and gulp the night air. The blue lighting that speckled the front and side of the Cosmopolitan building in the distance, blurred into a single sapphire pigment. I gripped the bar and let the fresh air clear my head.

'Are you ok?'

At the sound of Erin's voice I focussed and lifted my Champagne glass to style it out.

'Yeah, I'm fine. I –'

'You looked like you went into a trance. Something I said?'

'Oh no. Nothing. I was...just...thinking...about...you know... how great it is to be in Vegas. All the colours, the lights, the music...what's that perfume you are wearing?'

'It's Burberry. Why? Do you like it?'

'Oh yes. It's...great. Just wondered.'

'Well in my job I get plenty of time to check out duty free,' she said as she hoisted the Champagne bottle from the bucket and began to pour it. 'C'mon, let's have more Champagne. Us Irish girls don't stand on ceremony when there's a party to be had. We need to boogie.'

The Champagne flowed. Erin moved to the music with no hint of inhibitions and a natural rhythm that gave full vent to her enthusiasm for a party. Her extrovert manner made me relax, to let go and enjoy the moment.

We were interrupted by Cecil and Jasper and the two Texan girls.

'Alright geeze. You're going for it then,' was Cecil's greeting.

'Hi Ces. Yeah, great little bar isn't it.' I turned to Erin. 'Erin, meet my friends Cecil and Jasper. They organised the trip for me. Guys, this is Erin.'

'Pleased to meet you Erin,' Jasper said stepping forward and taking her hand.

Cecil looked Erin up and down. 'How you doin? Matt tells us you're an air hostess?'

'We like to call them flight attendants now,' Erin replied.

'Do we? That's just all that political correctness bullhang, init? They're all air hostesses where I come from, darlin.'

It was as if Cecil was laying down a marker. Establishing roles.

He had seen something in those green eyes, something that made him realise he was not dealing with a pushover and that Erin wasn't the usual type that he ran into in nightclubs.

I caught a brief flash of irritation cross Erin's gaze.

'Take no notice of Cecil,' I said. 'He likes a wind up.'

Cecil stretched out a hand. 'Yeah, I'm winding you luv. I got the Irish genes myself, like Matt here. You're amongst friends. Pleased to meet you.' He took Erin's hand as if to shake it, raised it to his face and kissed her fingers just below the knuckles. 'Get us any cheap flights, can ya?'

Erin's face cracked into a smile. She slapped Cecil around the upper arm.

'Sure aren't you the right cheeky bugger.'

'So where's Carlos then?' I asked, relieved that the moment had lightened.

'Mate, he's still over in the Hyde bar. He's doin that fucked up corkscrew dance of his with two Mexican birds he got chattin to and talkin a mix of that Scottish Spanish lingo he gets into. Geezer's off his nut when he's had a few. I told him we was comin over here,' Cecil said.

'Oh, he sounds like fun,' Erin said.

'Oh yeah he's fun alright if you like some geezer talking half pissed Spanish and half pissed Scottish to you all night. The geezer cracks me up. No idea what the fuck he was going on about when we left him.'

I caught sight of the two Texan girls giggling behind Cecil.

'Aren't you going to introduce us to the ladies then lads?' I said.

'Oh yeah mate. This is Morgan and this is Destiny. They're both from Dallas, Texas,' Cecil said, indicating the girls in turn.

Destiny was tall, good looking, leggy and blonde, no more than twenty-two with eyes that seemed to be permanently impressed with everything around her and a wide appealing grin. Morgan was a brunette, slightly shorter than Destiny but extremely attractive. Her hair was loose and flowing, her full lips enhanced with glistening, bright red lipstick. She was around the same age as Destiny but her sophisticated expression made her look slightly older. Both girls were wearing dresses that showed off shapely legs, a style that seemed to be the Vegas fashion. It was clear from where they were standing that Morgan had paired up with Cecil and Destiny with Jasper.

Morgan spoke first. 'Pleased to meet y'all. I hope you're having a great time.'

'Yeah, pleased to meet you,' Destiny chipped in.

'Nice to meet you both too,' I said. 'Have you been to Vegas before?'

'No, it's our first time,' Destiny replied. 'It's so exciting here and I can't believe we met Ray Winstone's cousin on our first trip. He's soooo cool.'

Erin glanced at me, an unspoken question requiring an answer.

I wasn't sure whether Destiny meant that Ray Winstone was cool or Cecil was. I winked at Erin to indicate I'd seen her quizzical look and changed the subject. 'Right, let's get some drinks in.'

'Our shout Matt,' Jasper said. 'It's your birthday.'

Jasper ordered more Champagne. Cecil pulled me to one side.

'That Erin bird's sharp mate. You can tell. It's in the eyes. You got a handful there.'

'I haven't got her Ces. I'm just having a drink with a...with a friend.'

'Friend? Who you tryin to blag geezer? You known her five minutes. That ain't a friend. That's a hot bird mate and she's up for the old hashmadishmalacka.'

'Ces, I'm with Louise. I'm not going to screw that up for a drunken bang.'

'Nobody's askin you to screw anything up with your bird mate but I'm tellin ya, she's a bit of alright. And she's no bimbo either. More to her than meets the eye, trust me. Where'd you meet her?'

'On the plane coming over. She's the one I told you about that gave me the flower for luck. Remember?'

'Yeah, you did mention that. Well a right bit of luck meeting her then,' Cecil said, elbowing me playfully in the ribs. 'And you reckon she's a friend.'

'Yes, but what I didn't tell you was I'd met her before that. You remember that speed course thing I went on? Well she was on that. That's where I first ran into her. And then when I got chucked off your flight I ended up by co-incidence on the one she was working.'

'There you go then geezer. Fate. All karma, see. You was meant to be on that flight and meant to end up shagging her.'

Cecil had a way of over simplifying things when he wanted to, especially where women were concerned, that would inevitably justify his logic for why sex was on the agenda.

'Ces, I told you. I'm with Louise. Sure it was co-incidence running into Erin but I'm just having a drink and a laugh with her. No agenda.'

'Mate, don't try blaggin a blagger. That bird's interested in you. I'm tellin ya.'

I was about to make another protest at Cecil's assumptions when we were interrupted by Morgan.

'You coming to dance with me Cecil?'

'Yeah, be right over luv. Just doin a bit of business.'

Morgan pouted, licked her red lips and left Cecil to his *business.*

'What are you on about Ces? What business?' I asked.

'Mate I'm blaggin it. They love all that London gangster image.' He tugged at both cuffs of his shirt as if straightening them up. 'Told ya mate, didn't I? It's my get it shirt. I reckon I'll be going medieval on that later. You'd do well to do the same mate. What happens in Vegas and all that. You get me?'

The night dissolved into a timeless blur of music, lights, laughter and dancing. We made our way to the upper Rooftop Gardens, a huge outdoor nightclub that stood under the Eiffel Tower. In the shadows cast by the dance floor lighting it looked surreal, looming high above the bar like a giant automaton, accepting the adoration of the hundreds of revellers who cavorted at its massive metallic feet.

'Are you ok, Matthew?'

'Yeah...yeah fine. I was just staring at the tower. Impressive isn't it.'

Erin laughed and tugged at the sleeve of my jacket. 'Let's slip away Matthew. I'm done now.'

'You are? Ok, it's been a long night but great fun. You must be tired,' I said.

'I was thinking more along the lines of perhaps getting another drink somewhere...somewhere quiet,' she said, her eyes bright and intense.

'Somewhere quiet? What in Las Vegas? That's unlikely,' I laughed.

'Well, what about your room, Matthew? That would be quiet, wouldn't it? Have you got anything to drink?'

The latter part of her question seemed to register more than the fact that she had mentioned my room.

'Err...yes. Yes, I picked up a bottle of gin at the airport on my way out. A bottle of Bombay. I think there's some tonic in the fridge.'

'Excellent. Let's do that. And I have a little surprise for you too.'

It was the word *surprise* that suddenly made me focus on the fact that she had invited herself back to my room. What was the surprise? A birthday gift? She reached out her hand and took mine, leading me away from the noise and lights towards the exit. We crossed the casino floor, passed the Central Lobby Bar and reached the lift area. I pressed the button and watched as the red highlighted arrow switched from up to down. The gold coloured doors slid open and we stepped in. The silence was almost intense. Erin leant against the wall and stared at the panel above the door as it clicked off the floors. My mind began to race. The motion of the lift rising, so slowly it seemed, taking me to my room with a very attractive woman. A situation I should not be in. I felt the helplessness of it all, the unknown, as if I was being controlled by a force that organised the inevitable and anything that happened as a result was not my doing. Yet there was a feeling of anticipation enveloping me, a feeling that was at odds with my desire to convince myself that I was doing nothing more than simply going for an innocent drink with a friend. I was being driven by fate but led by my own failure to decide what I wanted. The *ding* of the lift cut through the conflict in my head.

'Is this you?' Erin asked, as the doors glided open.

'Err...yes...it is.'

We walked along the corridor and reached room 1164. I fumbled in my wallet for the keycard and slipped it into the reader. The green light released the door and I led the way in. I walked straight to the fridge where I had left the bottle of Bombay gin, my nerves not allowing me the politeness of showing Erin to the sofa and asking her to take a seat. Erin didn't seem too put out. She dropped her bag on the floor by the table next to the wardrobe and sat down on the end of the bed.

'This is it Erin...the room, I mean. Err...a drink then...gin is all I have...that ok?'

'That's fine Matthew,' she said. She leant back on the bed, her arms placed behind her, propping herself up on her elbows in a half seated, half-lying position. As she did, the hem of her dress rode up. She crossed her legs, one shoe dangling on the end of her toes.

I busied myself with the gin and tonic.

'I haven't got any ice I'm afraid.'

'I'm sure it will be fine. Come and sit down,' she said, reaching out for the glass.

I turned back to the table to pick up my drink. I felt flustered, unsure. I remembered the surprise.

'So, what's the surprise you have Erin, if you don't mind me asking?'

'Oh yes.' She sprang up from the bed, placed her glass on top of the silver bin that Cecil had left where it was when he had tidied up, and reached for her bag. 'Have you ever tried coke, Matthew?' she asked as she searched through the contents of her bag.

'Coke?' I hesitated. Coke. I suspected that she didn't mean the drink. 'Coke, you mean –'

'Yes, cocaine. Charlie. You know...a line,' she said as she pulled a small paper wrap from her bag. 'A friend of mine got me some.

It's a bit of fun. I don't do it that much but it's great to liven up a party.'

Party. There were only the two of us. I felt the tension shiver through me. I had never tried coke. I was pretty straight laced. Conflict again surged through my head, a fear of the perception I had of drugs and a concern that Erin would think I was an uncool, out of touch nobhead.

I watched as she unfolded the wrap and tipped a heap of white powder onto the table surface. She pulled a credit card from her purse and began to manoeuvre the powder around with the edge of the card until she had shaped it into two distinct, long thin lines. I grabbed my gin and tonic and took a slurp. My anxiety caused me to tip the glass back too far and the mouthful I took was far too much. I tried to swallow it but my throat didn't cope with it all. A gagging, coughing splurt sent half the drink from the back of my throat up to my nose, causing a loud sneeze, which ejected the contents forcefully over the back of my hand.

Erin was busy rolling a dollar bill into a tubular shape when my sudden coughing and sneezing fit caused her to look towards me.

'You alright?'

'Yes,' I said through a semi-choking cough, my eyes watering. 'Too big a mouthful that's all.'

She laughed. 'Greedy boy. Here try this. If nothing else it will clear your nose.' She handed me the rolled dollar bill.

I knew what to do. I'd seen too many movies not to know but I had never done it myself. My heart raced as I took the rolled note and stood over one of the lines. With the end of the note poised, I inserted the narrower end into one nostril.

'Squeeze the other side shut, Matthew,' I heard Erin say.

It can only have been that it was still sensitive from the coughing fit. As the dollar bill touched the lining of my nose I felt the tickle. My body must have still been in eject mode. Before I could control it my face exploded in an almighty sneeze. The perfectly groomed powder lines didn't stand a chance. They both disappeared as if a magician had performed a mesmeric trick, a sleight of hand that the eye could not detect. I heard Erin gasp with surprise. A subconscious reflex caused me to lurch to my right in a futile attempt to chase the fast disappearing white powder. I had no chance. My foot landed on something firm as my momentum took me sideways. I had no idea what it was until I saw Erin's glass launch into the air, the liquid contents flying ahead of the glass, as the pedal bin lid catapulted it forward. My heightened reflexes shot me into an involuntary dive, like some demented goalkeeper attempting a penalty save. My fingertips caught the side of the glass and I managed to push it against the wall where it shattered into several large chunks. Unfortunately the gin and tonic it had contained hit Erin full square across her chest, soaking her olive green dress. I landed in a heap, crumpling a waste paper basket under my weight.

'My god, Matthew, you eejit. What the feck are you doing?' Erin shouted, more in shock than anger.

For a moment I lay dazed on the floor. All I could do was look at the ceiling. Erin held out her hand towards me. I scrambled to my feet as the embarrassment kicked in.

'I'm so sorry Erin. Your drink. Let me get you another one,' I said.

'My drink? What about my fecking coke?'

'Oh...god...sorry. It was an accident. I couldn't help sneezing. I'll get a pan and brush. Maybe I can find it and sweep it...sweep it up.' I got down on my hands and knees and began to look under the table. 'I can't see anything Erin. Can I get you some more from somewhere?'

There was no reply from Erin, just a fit of giggles.

'What's up?' I asked.

'Matthew. Don't worry. You are far too nice. The stupid coke was given to me anyway. We don't need it. Come here.'

She stood facing me her arms outstretched. I noticed the damp gin and tonic stain across the front of her dress.

'I'm really sorry about your dress too Erin. It's soaked.'

She dropped her head and looked down at her chest.

'Oh, it is, isn't it? I will just have to take it off then won't I?'

I wasn't sure she meant it but she did. One hand tucked up

behind her back seeking out the zip as the other pushed it down from behind her neck. The dress dropped to the floor in a fluid, graceful descent. She stood there for a moment in nothing more than a black lacy bra and matching knickers. I was rooted to the spot, speechless, immobilised by the suddenness of her action and then by the perfect body that was displayed in front of me.

Her eyes twinkled. A semi pout flickered across her lips. She knew that despite her state of undress she controlled the space between us, controlled the moment.

'Ooooh, I think my bra is wet too,' she said, as she reached around behind her back.

I realised what was about to happen.

'Erin, hang on. You...' My sentence hung in mid air, too late to change anything.

Her bra dropped to the floor. She stood hands on hips, her breasts heaving as the excitement of her near nakedness took hold, her nipples firm, emphasising her growing desire.

'Come here Matthew,' she said, her voice suddenly deeper, huskier, 'it is your birthday after all.'

I hesitated feeling the warm drops of sweat forming on my brow. I took two steps towards her, almost involuntarily before I had time to consider what I was doing. Erin came to me, her arms outstretched. There was no hesitation on her part. Her arms went around my neck, pulling against me as she raised her face towards mine. My hands were around her waist pulling her to me, feeling her breasts flatten against my chest and her hips press against my groin. She nuzzled her face into my neck, a deep sigh emerging from her lips. The fresh smell of her hair was invigorating, seductive. For a moment I let the sensation wash over me. I lowered my head into her neck, breathing in her scent, feeling the heat of her body as my hands slid slowly up the smooth curve of her back until they reached her shoulders.

And then I caught sight of my watch. Five o'clock in the morning. For some reason my head did an automatic calculation. One o'clock in the afternoon back home. Louise. Louise would be having lunch with Sheryl or something. Laughing, joking, having fun, unaware that the man she cared for was in a clinch in a hotel room several thousand miles away with a stunning, eager woman.

The guilt hit me, hard, shocking my senses. What was I doing? I pulled back, pushing Erin away.

'I'm sorry. So sorry Erin. I can't...I shouldn't be doing this. I have someone...someone back home.'

She looked stunned for a moment. Disbelief in her eyes.

'Are you serious? You don't want me?'

'I do want you, yes. Of course I do. You are gorgeous Erin...but I can't. I mustn't. I couldn't face it back home. I can't do this... to...to Louise.'

'Louise?' Erin asked, a frown clouding her features.

'Yes, Louise is...is my someone. I did mention a girlfriend when we first met. Remember. You teased me about it. When the cat's away, you said. It's not as if I was hiding it. I can't risk...it wouldn't be fair. I would feel so –'

Erin raised a finger to her lips, hushing me.

'Hey, Matthew. Take it easy. Have you not heard the saying, what happens in Vegas stays in Vegas?'

I had heard it. Everyone had heard it.

'Of course I have Erin. I even know what it means. But this isn't about you. You are absolutely stunning. Any man would want you. But what happens in Vegas doesn't always stay in Vegas. Not if you carry it home in your heart. Do you understand that?'

She didn't answer. She picked up her bra, looped it over her arms and fastened it at the back. When she had it done up she said, 'I do understand. I'm tired now.' She turned away.

'I know. It's late Erin. I'm sorry. You have my bed. I'll crash on the sofa.'

She climbed on to the bed and was asleep in an instant, exhausted by the night and the emotion. I eased her shoes from her feet and pulled the sheet up over her shoulders.

14

I was woken by the sound of movement. My back ached and my neck hurt from being scrunched up on the sofa. I stared at my watch. Nine forty-five. I reached over the back of the sofa and tugged one of the curtains partially open. It threw a shaft of light into the room. Erin was up and dressed and looking through the wardrobe.

'Morning,' I said croakily. A dull throb swirled through my head. 'What you lost?'

'Good morning Mister.'

She pushed one of the drawers back in and turned to face me.

'Lost? Oh, my shoes. I can't find my shoes. Have you seen them?'

'Your shoes. Yeah...I have. I took them off for you when you crashed out. They should be down by the side of the bed.'

She walked back to the side of the bed where she had slept, crouched down and found her shoes tucked between the bed and the cabinet.

'Found them. Looks like you hid them, Matthew,' she laughed. 'I don't want to lose them. They were expensive. Louboutin's.'

'Who's?' I asked as I swung my legs onto the floor and sat up.

'Christian Louboutin. The shoe designer. Do you like them?' She held up the pair of green suede shoes with the pencil thin heels that I had carefully placed on the floor the previous night.

'Yes. Yes, I do. Very nice.' My throbbing head and lack of sleep had seriously diminished my powers of appreciation at that time of the morning. 'Talking of losing things, I didn't tell you but I lost my camera. I have got to try and find it somehow.'

'Really? You lost it?' Erin's eyes gleamed and for a moment her face took on a serious look, as if she was sharing my disappointment. She picked up the kettle that stood on a tray on the table with a variety of coffee and tea sachets. 'Coffee? I'm parched.' Without waiting for my reply she disappeared into the bathroom. 'So where did you lose it?' she called out.

I stretched my arms high above my head to release the stiffness in my shoulders. The movement turned into a long, deep yawn.

Erin came out of the bathroom, placed the kettle on its stand and flicked the switch.

'So where did you lose it?' she asked again.

'No idea. If I knew where it was it wouldn't be lost,' I said, smiling at her so she would appreciate the irony.

'Well someone may have handed it in somewhere. Have you been to the police?'

'Err...no. I lost the whole bag on my first night. I thought I'd search around a bit more. No sense in involving the police. I don't think they'd be too interested in a camera.'

'I'm sure I saw you with a bag when you left Caesar's the other night. Can you not remember where you put it?'

'Did you?' I said, suddenly assured by some confirmation that I did have the bag at a specific point in time. 'Are you sure?'

'Well, I didn't take too much notice but I'm almost certain you were carrying a bag...yes, a black bag.'

'Yes, that's right. It was black. So that means I had it when I left Caesar's. So it must be in the Bond bar or the hotel here.'

'Oh, I see. You don't remember bringing it back here then? Do you need any help to look for it? I've arranged a lunch today but I could cancel.'

I didn't want to involve Erin in the complications of my lost bag. I hoped that when the camera bag was discovered it would be handed in but I still had no idea how I would deal with the other bag if I was confronted. It seemed to me that I must have picked up the money bag by mistake but I hoped that perhaps a bar worker had found the cameras in either the Bond Bar or the Paris. I intended to check both of those.

'No, no need Erin. I will ask around. I am sure it will turn up. It had my video camera in it too but the main camera was brand new. A birthday present from Louise…you know, who I mentioned last night.'

'Oh yes, Louise' Erin looked up from the kettle which had begun to spout steam.

I watched as she tore the tops off two coffee sachets, tipped the contents into two cups and began to pour the water from the kettle. I had expected a reaction. There was none.

'And talking of last night, I am really sorry. I didn't mean any –'

'Ssshhhh Matthew. Leave it. I understand. It doesn't matter. We had a good night. Here take your coffee. It will clear your head.'

I stood up and took the coffee from Erin's hand. As I caught her eye, I noticed the glaze, a wetness pooling above her lower eyelids. She turned away and walked to the bathroom. I sat down on the end of the bed not totally comprehending what was happening. Surely she couldn't be upset. We had both been pretty drunk with all the Champagne and gin. It was just one of those situations that can happen, but we hardly knew one another. I sipped the coffee and felt bad.

Erin came out of the bathroom, her make-up freshly touched, her face light and smiling.

'Right Matthew. I have to go back to my hotel, shower and make myself look passable for my lunch appointment.'

'What about your coffee,' I said, as if it was critical.

'Oh, I will get another. Don't let those big important things worry you too much, eh.' She smiled, a rueful little twist of her lips and came towards me. She placed a hand on my shoulder. Her warm lips pressed against the side of my face in a soft kiss that was more than just a *see you later*. I felt a sense of finality imparted by the lingering touch of her mouth. She whispered into my ear.

'Take care Matthew. I've tidied up, cleaned up the glass you were throwing around last night and any traces of, you know, the white stuff.'

I stood up as she pulled back.

'Thanks Erin...and thanks for the evening out. Have a good day. Catch up again,' I said, more a question than a statement of intent. I reached out for her fingertips but she slipped away.

'Byeeeee Matthew. Good luck finding the bag.'

My phone rang as I stepped out of the shower.

'Geezer. How you doin? You awake?'

'Hi Ces. Just out of the shower. You ok? How'd you get on with the Texan girl? Morgan, was it?'

'Mate. She's still asleep. What a night. Hot little lady. What about you? How'd you do with the air hostess?'

'Tell you later Ces. I have to go and see if I can find my bag this morning.'

'Mate, we're all thinkin of going up to Denny's for breakfast later. I arranged it with Jas and Carlos. Meet you in reception in twenty and we'll go get some food. You can do the bag thing after that.'

'I got to sort this out first Ces. It's a worry. The sooner I find out what happened to my bag then the sooner I can maybe sort out the missing money thing. I'm going to check out the Bond Bar this morning soon as I'm dressed.'

'Your call mate but I'd give it half an hour or so. They'll still have the cleaners in them bars. Give 'em a chance to get sorted.'

'Maybe. Ok, I'll pop down stairs, get a coffee, kill some time.'

'Ok geezer. See you down in the Central Bar. Mine's a Bloody Mary.'

I dressed in shorts, polo shirt and trainers trying to ignore the dull thud that had developed in my head. I was beginning to realise that partying and jet lag were not compatible. Getting to bed at five-thirty in the morning was the equivalent of going to bed at one-thirty in the afternoon back home as far as my body clock was concerned. That was not something I did. Not something most normal people did. And now I had managed it on two consecutive nights. I dismissed the thought and told myself that I was on a once in a lifetime trip to Vegas and if I couldn't have a few wild nights there where could I have them? As Cecil often reminded me, nobody lies on their deathbed saying *I should've stayed in more*.

I was first down to the Central Lobby bar. I checked my wallet, pleased to see I still had some dollars from the night before and ordered two Bloody Marys. My throbbing head had changed my focus from coffee to a hair of the dog as I rode down in the lift. The first sip hit me, a sharp spice attack that zinged over my tongue burning my mouth and lips. I scooped out an olive and chewed it to counteract the bitter after taste of the alcohol. In the background, noise from the casino blurred into a steady hum of bells, chimes and old rock tunes, an irritating cacophony of sound for someone in a delicate condition.

Cecil made an appearance just before eleven, grabbed his Bloody Mary and took down half of it in one gulp.

'Thirsty then Ces?' I said.

'Gives you an appetite mate. So, c'mon then. Give us the mumble.'

'There's no mumble, Ces. Nothing happened.'

'Nothin happened? You're winding me aren't you mate? You both looked pretty cosy in that bar. Then you go disappear without sayin a thing so I reckoned you were game on. She was well into you.'

'Well I'm telling you. Nothing happened. I can't pretend I wasn't tempted. She's a good looking lady, very sexy. But I have Louise back home. You know that. I can't screw it up Ces. You're younger than me...what, nearly ten years? You're playing the game still so it's ok for you.' I felt the agitation grow within me. Perhaps it was the hangover or perhaps it was natural male regret at passing up an opportunity with an attractive woman. I grabbed the Bloody Mary, almost putting my eye out with the cocktail stick as I raised the glass. 'Bollocks. That hurt.'

'Alright, mate. Take it easy. You're right though. There's something about her. Wouldn't mind a crack at it myself.'

A hefty slap on my back interrupted any further talk of Erin.

'Matt. How you doing, chap? Good night last night?'

Jasper Kane was all smiles. Clearly he had indulged in a good night and was about to tell us all about it. Carlos followed behind him an obvious limp in his gait, his eyes red with sleeplessness and jet lag.

'So where'd you get to Carlos,' I asked, 'and what's up with your leg?'

'Och, I got talking to two wee Mexican lassies. They like to do the Bachata –'

'What the fuck's the Bachata, Carlos? Not one of your nob dances is it?' Cecil interrupted.

'The Bachata, Cecil, is a dance of South America. Too complicated for you amigo. Only for men with rhythm. It's all in the caderas. You dance the Bachata and the ladies know what you're like in bed.'

'So did you get laid then Carlos or not?' Cecil asked bluntly.

'It's not about getting laid amigo –'

'So you didn't then,' Cecil grinned, as he stabbed the celery stick into the Bloody Mary soaking up the remnants at the bottom of the glass. 'And it's all in the what?'

Carlos began a twisting movement in which his upper body remained almost motionless and his lower body snaked from side to side.

'The hips, Cecil. It's about the rhythm of the hips.' He stopped abruptly, his face contorted with pain.

'What's up, mate?' I asked.

'It's my knee. A wee pain in it. Overdid the dancing with the senoritas last night. It'll be alright.'

'Geezer, yer too old for that boogying now. You should stick to pullin pints not trying to pull the birdies.'

Carlos scowled at Cecil, eased himself onto a stool and held his troublesome leg out in front of him. 'I can dance better on one leg than you can on two Cecil. Don't you worry yer heid about that.'

I'd had enough. I could see the banter about to break out, each of the boys still in high spirits from the night before and I had a pressing issue to deal with.

'Look, guys. I'm going to see if I can find my bag. I'll leave you to it. Where are you going to be? Give me your room numbers in case we miss one another.' I pushed a white napkin across the bar towards Carlos and Jasper and grabbed a pen from my pocket. They both jotted down their room numbers.

I folded the napkin and put it in my pocket. 'So you'll be in Denny's right?'

The Bond bar was open for business but it was still quiet. A couple sat at the bar. A barman was polishing glasses with a white cloth and placing them on a shelf. He saw me approach and came towards me.

'Good morning Sir. How's your day? What can I get you?'

'Morning. Fine thanks. Just a coffee, please.'

'Cream and sugar?'

'Oh...yes please.' I pulled up a stool and waited until he had poured the coffee. 'Thank you. Listen, you wouldn't happen to have found a bag at all in the last few days?'

'A bag Sir? What type?'

'A back pack...sports bag, rucksack style. It was black with the Nike logo on it. I may have lost it on Friday...Friday night. Well early hours of Saturday.'

'I was off on Friday and Saturday, Sir, so I can't really help you out on that.' He must have noticed the disappointment in my face. 'But I could call my colleague who was in charge those nights. We're not too busy so I can go call him now if you can wait. I'll be right back.'

I waited patiently, sipping my coffee, hoping that the barman's quest would prove positive. It was five or ten minutes before he returned. His expression gave nothing away.

'Sorry to keep you waiting, Sir. Can I ask your name?'

'Err...yes. It's Malarkey. Matthew Malarkey.'

'Do you have any ID Sir?'

'Yes, I think so. Hold on.' I fumbled in my pocket for my wallet and pulled out a credit card. 'This any good. It's got my name on it.'

'Ok. And what did you have in the bag, Sir?'

I felt a wave of optimism. He hadn't said he hadn't found it and now he was asking questions that suggested he had something.

'Have you found it then?' I asked.

'Sir, you need to answer my questions first. Did you have anything in the bag that you say you lost?'

'Yes. Yes I did. If it's all still there. I had a camera. A canon. I mean...a Canon camera...err...not an actual...err...I had a lens. A telescopic one. I mean, you know, a telephoto lens. I can't remember the make. My video camera. A JVC make. And a book...by John Grisham.'

'Well then I am pleased to tell you Sir, we seem to have that very bag. You're the gentleman that came in yesterday and left your details with my colleague?'

A wave of relief swept over me. My throbbing head suddenly felt lighter. I could have hugged the barman.

'I am. Yes. You have it. Fantastic. But where was it?'

'It was handed in late last night Sir. Jaime, my colleague, was working the bar. He said some guy handed it in. Wouldn't leave his details. Jaime remembered you because the bag had the Nike swoosh on it. But we were so busy last night he didn't get a chance to call you. I woke him just now when I called.'

'I'm so grateful. Thank you,' I said. 'The camera's brand new. A birthday present. It's a shame the man who found it didn't leave his details. I'd love to thank him.'

'Ok, you wait there Sir and I will go get it. Jaime put it away for safekeeping. You'll have to sign for it.'

I sat back down on the stool feeling elated. The first bit of luck I had had on the whole trip. I finished my coffee and dialled Cecil's mobile. It went to voicemail. I decided I'd sooner tell him the good news in person. The barman returned a few minutes later carrying my bag. He handed it to me and asked me to check the contents. I pulled the zips apart and looked inside. Everything seemed to be there. I lifted out my camera. All intact. Next, I pulled out the telephoto lens. It seemed fine. Then the movie camera and the book.

'It's all here,' I said, 'thank you.' I signed a lost property book that the barman put in front of me, hoisted the bag onto my shoulder and walked out into the bright morning sunlight of the Strip.

15

The traffic on Las Vegas Boulevard, the Strip, was heavy, a mid-morning stream on both sides of the wide carriageway trying to beat the lights that controlled the junctions by the Bellagio and the Paris.

'Mister Malarkey.'

I heard the voice as I stood on the corner looking across at Planet Hollywood and the Paris, further along. Instinctively I turned around. A short stocky man in a dark suit, an open neck white shirt and thin framed sunglasses was walking towards me. His dark hair was slicked back and he had a small dark goatee beard. He stopped right in front of me, his legs splayed slightly, his hands joined in front of his waist.

'Is that your bag?' he asked.

I was taken by surprise by the question but my first thought was that perhaps he was the guy who had handed it in.

'Yes, it is.'

'You got it back then. I'm pleased for you.'

'Err...thanks. Yes, I'm glad I got it back. It's got my cameras in it. Did you find it?'

As I spoke, he took a pace nearer so that the space between us was now an uncomfortably small gap. I went to take a step back but he reached forward as I did so and grabbed my right wrist with his left hand. I felt the tug on my arm preventing me from moving away. My blood seemed to freeze as the shock of what was happening rooted me to the spot, rendering me unable to react. His voice dropped to a low whisper, his face just inches from mine.

'You got some goddam cojones coming back for that. Problem is, we're not glad. In fact, we're pretty pissed. See you may have got your bag back but we don't have our bag back. And the thing is, we think you know where it is. And you don't need me to tell you that we're talking about a lot of money, Mister Malarkey. Our money. Putting yourself up as the bag man...not very clever. You have made some bad people very angry pulling a stunt like that. Now I need you to take me to where you have our bag and I need you to let me have it back. You do that and maybe no questions will be asked. Capiche?'

I hadn't really comprehended most of the last part of what he had said. As soon as I heard the words *bag* and *money* Cecil's own words flooded my mind - '*you got some villain's wedge.*' Panic and sheer terror overwhelmed me, followed quickly by an instinct to flee. The sensation caused me to tug against my assailant's grip but he squeezed tighter.

'It's no use trying to run motherfucker, we know who you are now. It doesn't take much to find these things out if you know the right people in the hotels. You understand? And we know who your little lady is too. That camera has got a lot of interesting stuff on it. Now you might be thinking that your lady friend is all safe tucked up in lil 'ol England but we got people everywhere. And if we don't get our money back, well you can just imagine...' His voice tailed off.

My panic heightened. I remembered the pictures I had taken before I left London, when Louise had given me the camera. They must have been through them. That also meant they knew about the other lads too. I was scared. I had no way out. I looked around me. Hundreds of tourists, people all around, many heading for the Bellagio walkway, yet no one seeing anything odd about my situation. Rational thought escaped me. It didn't occur to me to tell him that the bag had been stolen. Cecil's advice did not materialise. I tugged again to get free. As I did so, I caught sight of his other hand clenching into a fist. Adrenaline began to course through me. My mind started to race with wild thoughts. I recalled the Kung Fu lessons I had taken in my early twenties and with the confrontational situation in front of me, the detail began a slow, hazy journey from my sub-conscious. My first thought was to try to remember the correct stance to take when in danger of an imminent attack. Was it left foot forward, weight back on the right with the right hand shielding the left side of the face and the left hand protecting the groin? Was it the other way around or was it none of those? Would any of that free me from his grip? The vague memories of those early lessons scrambled around in my brain trying to organise a picture I could relate to and put into action. The adrenaline pumping through my system did not help my clarity of thought. I could hardly stop and ask my assailant for time to organize my thinking. *'Excuse me, could you just hold on a second while I get into position.'*

It was irrational blind panic that finally made me do it. From the depths of my sub-conscious an instinctive response triggered. I dropped my left hand in front of my groin for protection and jerked my captured right hand upwards, catching my assailants own wrist between my thumb and forefinger and clasped my fingers around it. The impetus of my sudden movement carried his arm back towards him and, as it did so, I brought my left hand down into the crook of his elbow, just below the bicep, forcing my elbow towards his throat. His surprise stopped any immediate attempt to defend himself and I took full advantage. I pushed harder against his forearm so that his hand was now almost past his head at the same time pushing down hard on the elbow. The leverage against his arm had the desired effect. I heard something tear at the shoulder as he arched his back in an attempt to alleviate the stress on the joint. He let out a guttural yelp of pain. With my left elbow firmly against his neck, and his lower arm forced upwards and hard against his shoulder, he could no longer maintain any balance and I eased him to the floor onto his back. In total surprise at what I had done I let go of him, but he was in no position to react. Rolling into a semi-foetal position he

144

grabbed at his shoulder, clutching it tight to his upper body and stayed on the ground.

My legs began to wobble. I became aware of my pounding heart. I had never had to defend myself before. It was not a natural state. Passers-by on the ramp that led to the Bellagio had stopped walking and were looking across at the incident. Fight turned to flight. I started to run towards the road junction and straight across the Strip. Despite my state of panic I had the presence of mind to glance to my right to check the traffic as I ran out into the highway. The screech of burning tyres against the dry tarmac, accompanied by the blare of multiple car horns, reminded me that traffic in America comes from the left as you step off the sidewalk. The shock of the sudden uproar startled me so much that I stopped abruptly in the middle of the carriageway.

'Aaaaaassshoooooole,' seemed to be the preferred greeting of most of the drivers in an array of cars spread out across the highway like Formula 1 racers on the starting grid. Several were leaning out through their windows to make their expletives more emphatic. Clenched fists accompanied many of the adjectives used to describe my existence on the planet. I had seen enough clenched fists. I turned away and ran for the safety of the central reservation. For a brief moment I leant against a traffic light to compose myself and tried to mingle with the crowds who had turned back to the business of getting across to the other side of the Strip. I glanced back at my attacker who had managed to get himself into a seated position and appeared to be waving in the direction of the Paris with his good arm. I clutched my bag tight to my shoulder and began to run across the far side of the carriageway once the light had turned green, this time taking care to check in the right direction. I reached the other side and legged it towards the Paris. As I turned into Paris Drive, the short avenue that led to the Arc de Triomphe and the main entrance to the hotel, I spotted who my attacker had been waving at. A similarly dressed man, in a dark suit, same dark glasses, was standing about fifty metres ahead of me, directly on my route to the entrance. I slowed down to a walk and turned North again on the Strip but he had already spotted me and began to move towards me.

I had a head start and began to run. My breath was coming in short bursts as I sprinted along the sidewalk, not through any lack of fitness but simply from the overwhelming realisation that I was in a severe mess. I weaved in and out of pedestrians who were going about their daily business, oblivious to my predicament. Ahead of me I saw the sign for Bally's. To one side of the sidewalk was the footbridge with its twin escalators that crossed the Strip. I glanced behind to see how close my pursuer was. The instant I looked behind me I felt the jolt. I was spun around in a 180-degree arc, a hailstorm of French fries raining down on me.

'You goddam jerk. Whaddya doin?'

I tried to gather my senses wondering why my progress had been stopped so abruptly and turned round to face the way I had been running. A young couple were standing open mouthed, staring at me. Both were holding what appeared to be empty take-away boxes. The guy had his hands splayed away from his side in a questioning gesture.

'That's our goddam brunch dude. What's your rush?'

I took a step forward, as the awareness of what had happened kicked in. My shoe squished against the sidewalk and for a moment I thought the sun had melted the concrete.

'That's my dorg, dude,' the guy said, pointing at the floor. 'Look whatcha done.'

'Your...your...dorgdude? Sorry? What?'

'Yeah, my dorg. You stoopid or what?'

My gaze fell to the spot he had pointed at. I eased my foot away to see the sticky mix of ketchup and mustard that had glued a half flattened frankfurter to the sole of my shoe.

'Your...dorg...dorg...oh, hot dog. I'm sorry.'

I glanced around to my right. My pursuer had gained a good thirty metres on me and, to my horror, I noticed that he was accompanied by another guy. The new guy was taller and heavier than his companion, his eyes also shielded behind dark glasses.

They had both slowed to a walk as they got closer. I turned back to the young couple.

'Look, I'm sorry. Sorry about your dorgdude…I mean, your hot dog but I haven't got time for this.' I tugged my wallet from my shorts pocket and grabbed a twenty-dollar bill. 'Here take this... for the...the food.' I didn't wait for either of them to react. I kicked the sticking frankfurter from my trainer. It flew into the road and stuck to the door of a passing taxi. I dropped the twenty dollars on the ground in front of the couple and began to run again.

My intention had been to cross the footbridge and disappear over the other side of the Strip but the two guys chasing me were too close and would have seen where I had gone. I decided to keep running ahead. The sidewalk was swarming with people and I thought that if I could get amongst them it would enable me to disappear more easily and evade my pursuers. I ran ahead to the junction with Flamingo Road. There was another bridge for pedestrians to cross but I ignored it. The junction had a red light and traffic was stationary. I vaulted the small balustrade wall that was in place to direct pedestrians to the bridge crossing and ran straight across the carriageway. On the other side I clambered over the low wall, stopping just long enough to glance behind me. I couldn't see either of the guys who were chasing me. The lights on Flamingo Road had switched to green and traffic was moving. That must have prevented them following me across the road. I looked towards the pedestrian bridge and there they were, running up one side, the heavier guy lagging behind. The traffic had given me an advantage as they had to take the longer route over the road. I looked around me to get my bearings. Familiarity influenced my next decision. Across the Strip, the Caesar's complex stood in all its pristine white glory highlighted by the pale blue of the cloudless Vegas sky. Just ahead of me was the escalator that led onto the bridge crossing to the other side. It was the route I had taken with the lads on the first night. I knew that I was temporarily out of sight. My pursuers were still round the corner crossing the Flamingo Road Bridge. I had to take advantage. When they reached this point they would not know whether I had continued north along the Strip, or taken one of the side turnings or disappeared into one of the many casinos or shops that lined the route. I decided to head for Caesar's. I could wander through the maze of the complex, make my way back down the other side and head back towards the Paris where I could hook up with Ces and the boys as backup should I need it. My only vulnerable point would be on top of the road bridge. It was exposed on all sides but I reckoned I had put some distance between us and even if I was seen, I could lose them in Caesar's Palace.

I raced up the moving escalator. At the top I turned left and sped across the bridge, weaving in and out of the crowds ambling their way across in either direction. Below the traffic raced along the Strip, a low rumble of sound and flashing colour. As I reached the end of the bridge and the down escalator, I spotted them again. The two guys, standing on the corner of Flamingo Road and the Strip contemplating their next move. They had also seen me. One of them had an arm raised and a finger pointed in my direction. I lowered my head and ran down the escalator. Next, I turned right at the bottom and made my way into the complex, stopping once to check signage. The whole complex looked bigger and more confusing in the daylight. I made my way down the Spanish Steps and followed the signs for reception, thinking that it was best to go to where I knew, even if that knowledge was based on just one brief visit. When I reached the main entrance I stopped to look around and see if I was still being followed. The two guys were nowhere in sight. I walked through the lobby, my breathing heavy with exhaustion from running in the heat and the adrenaline-fuelled alertness that had crept over me now that I was in a more confined space. Sweat began to drip from my brow onto my shirt and arms. I walked on into the Palace Casino retracing the steps I had taken on my last visit. Even in the middle of the day the slot machines were fully occupied with hopeful punters, the blackjack tables crowded and roulette wheels spinning out their eagerly awaited randomness. I passed the table where I had played poker with Arturo, Martha and Pete. Maria was entertaining a group of gamblers. She didn't see me.

I came to the end of the casino. The air-conditioned atmosphere had helped me cool down and I had begun to feel more confident that somehow I had lost my pursuers. I decided I would risk making my way back out of the complex and work my way round to the Strip and head south back to the Paris. I didn't want to retrace my steps just in case I ran into the bad guys. To my right a sign indicated the Appian Way shops. Shops should take me through to another exit. I had started to walk towards the sign when I heard voices and footsteps. What was different from the normal relaxed tourist chatter was that these voices seemed more urgent, angry even. My heightened instincts caused me to stop. Ahead of me, I caught sight of my two pursuers, walking towards me, deep in conversation. Alarm shot through me, preventing me from making a calm decision. Instead of turning slowly and walking away I began to run. The sudden movement clearly caught their attention. I heard a shout, just one word. 'There!'

I ran blindly, not knowing where I was going. Ahead a sign indicated the Temple Pool. I raced through a set of doors out of the main building, down a flight of stone steps and found myself outside in a huge, breathtaking pool complex. The sudden emergence into bright sunlight blurred my vision and I stopped running, indecision overcoming me at the complexity of the sight before me. At first all I could see were the soaring Corinthian style columns, their fluted shafts encircling a tall domed rotunda. As my eyes focussed I realised that the rotunda was the centrepiece of a huge circular pool. In the middle of the columned rotunda, a golden statue of Caesar stood on a white stone plinth overlooking a sea of sunbathers stretched out on blue sun loungers around the full circumference of the pool. Behind the main deck area of the pool, tall palm trees threw shadows across the paving and white sculpted statues of Roman horsemen fronted the elaborate temple style structures that formed the outer buildings of the complex.

My hesitation had cost me time and the small distance advantage ahead of my adversaries. I looked around the pool hoping to see somewhere obvious to shelter. There was nothing. I knew that if I ran towards any of the buildings I risked being spotted such was the openness of the area. Impulse took over. On the right side of the pool I spotted two sun loungers one of which had a huge red towel draped over it so that it hung down on either side almost touching the ground. It was my only chance. I ran towards it, weaving between sunbathers who were stretched out unaware of my presence. A short distance away, by the edge of the pool, two king sized day beds, with huge blue mattresses, were positioned close to one another with just a small round drinks table separating them. I shoved my camera bag in between them and under the table. I ran back to the sun loungers, laid down on my back at the base of the one with the towel on it and shuffled my way, feet first, beneath it. I was completely concealed by its full length and the towel hanging down either side. There was no room underneath to do anything other than lie flat. My chest heaved with short bursts of breath and the thump of my heart. I couldn't see a thing other than the blue base of the lounger. Trickles of sweat began to roll down my face into my ears. From the poolside there was laughter and chatter as children and bathers splashed around in the water.

With my vision restricted and an inability to move, my hearing took on an acute sense of awareness. Over the chatter I heard the voices again that I had heard near the Appian Way shopping area.

'He musta gone out through one of them buildings. He can't have gone no further through here. You get through here and there's just two pools right up ahead. There's no way out unless he comes back this way. You go check'em out and we meet back here. If he ain't there we go back through the casino. We don't get the motherfucker today, we get him tomorrow.'

I lay as still as my shaking body would let me. They weren't going to give up. Within ten minutes they were back but this time further away it seemed, nearer the front of the pool. I couldn't make out what they were saying but within a couple of minutes the voices stopped. I remained where I was, too scared to move in case I came out too soon. I decided to give it fifteen minutes and then risk it. Unable to look at my watch in the restricted space I lay there, eyes closed, counting off the seconds.

My estimation of time was brought to an abrupt end by a

downward force that almost broke my ribcage. A massive weight above me bulged the canvas of the lounger so far down that it was rubbing against my chest. I realised immediately what had happened and then I heard the voice.

'Great lunch honey. They certainly know how to feed you here.'

Above me the occupant of the sun lounger fidgeted again clearly trying to get comfortable. The canvas of the bed rumbled and rolled under the weight. I managed to move my head to one side to gain some breathing space. I tried to push myself backwards but the space was now too confined to move. I was trapped. Why did I have to pick the sunbed that belonged to the fattest bloke in Las Vegas?

'You wanna another beer sugar?' a female voice asked.

'No, I'm fine honey. Gonna sleep that lunch off. Maybe get one later.'

I couldn't believe what I had heard. He was going to go to sleep. I could be trapped for hours. I didn't want to risk saying anything. It wasn't a good idea to be caught creeping around under someone's sun lounger. I tried again to push myself out. It wasn't happening. Within seconds I heard the snoring. And then he broke wind. Right above my head. A poisonous, sulphuric stench that burst around the lower half of the bed where my face was. I couldn't stand it any longer. I jerked my right knee hard into the top half of the bed and connected with something solid.

'What the...chrissakes...what the hell was that?' I heard. 'My goddam head. Jeez... I just been pole axed.' His weight shifted as he sat up and rolled his feet to the side of the bed.

'It's ok, honey. You were asleep. You must have been dreaming. The beers maybe? Give you a headache, did they?' the female voice said.

'Goddam, pack a punch if they did.'

'Hey, c'mon sugar. Let's have a swim. It'll clear your head. C'mon.'

The weight shifted off the lounger and I felt able to breathe again. I waited a minute or so until I felt the couple were well away from the bed and I slid out from under it. I grabbed my bag from between the day beds and legged it.

16

I made my way out of Caesar's back on to the Strip and stopped to catch my breath. I pulled out my mobile and called Cecil. This time he answered.

'Hello mate. How'd you get on? Any luck with the bag?'

'I got it Ces but it's all going tits up. Where are you? You left Denny's?'

'Just on my way up there mate. The Bloody Marys turned into a bit of a sesh. Jas has gone back to bed and I think Carlos won't be far behind him.'

'Listen, Ces, we got to talk. I'll meet you there. Where is it?'

'It's on the way up the Strip opposite the Mirage, just before you get to the Venetian. I'll be there in about ten.'

'Ok. I'm up that way already. I can see the Mirage from here.'

I made my way north along the Strip. I spotted Denny's on the other side of the carriageway and crossed over in front of the Venetian complex, with its impressive replicas of the St Mark's Basilica bell tower and Rialto Bridge.

A queue had formed in Denny's main doorway. I booked a table for two. Five minutes later Cecil showed up. We took a seat in the waiting area and waited for our names to be called.

'So you got the bag geezer. What's the story then?'

'Ces. It's not good. You were right. I think we may have crossed some villains.' I started to tell Cecil what had happened just as my name was called out.

'Party for Malarkey.'

A waitress led us to a table by a window on the far side of the restaurant.

'It's gone one-thirty, I haven't had any breakfast and yet I don't feel that hungry Ces,' I said, as I browsed through the menu.

'Mate, you gotta eat. You can't party all night and not eat.'

He had a point. I felt exhausted and needed to build up my energy. I ordered steak and eggs. Cecil had steak and an omelette. The waitress poured two coffees. At the table next to us, four people were chatting animatedly in Spanish, their conversation loud and interspersed with raucous laughter. Their noisy presence made me feel that I could talk to Cecil without too much fear of being overheard.

'So, Ces, what I'm saying is that I'm now being threatened and I reckon they would've done me some harm this morning if they'd got hold of me. I'm going to have to check out of the Paris and go somewhere else.'

'Calm down mate what did they say?'

'Well the bloke I talked to said he wanted me to take him to where I had the bag and he wanted it back. He used the words *our money.*'

'Ok. Let me think. So you got your bag back. That means that either somebody honest just found it and handed it in, or the geezer who attacked you had it and handed it in to flush you out. So, let's assume it was him and he's worked out that you got his bag with the money, how'd he know where you'd look for it and where to hand it in?'

'I don't know if he did. He seemed surprised I'd come for it.'

'D'you ask him if he found it?'

'I did but he didn't answer. Maybe it wasn't him that found it but he was just there because they know where I'm staying.'

'D'you say anything about the other bag? D'you tell him you'd seen it?'

'Of course not. I could hardly go, don't worry mate we did have your bag with half a million dollars in it but my mate went and spent some of it and then let a hooker walk off with the rest. But don't worry we'll get it back.'

153

'Alright geezer. Keep your fucking hair on. I didn't let no hooker walk off with it. She took it, didn't she. But I did tell ya if you got fronted up to say it'd bin nicked. Then give them the ten kay we got in the hotel, yeah?' Cecil stared at me intensely, his brown eyes looking for a response.

'I wasn't thinking straight Ces. It was just all very sudden. The bloke caught me by surprise and then when he grabbed hold of me...'

Cecil stroked his chin between thumb and forefinger for a moment.

'So what else did he say?'

'Not a lot. I didn't get into a deep and meaningful conversation with him. He just said that I'd made some bad people very angry.'

'People?'

'Yeah, people. And he threatened Louise.'

'Louise? How the fuck did he know about your bird?'

'He'd looked through the camera and seen some pictures I took before I came away.'

'Mate, that means he must've had your bag, right. So he was trying to flush you out. Somehow he knew you'd been in the Bond Bar otherwise he wouldn't have gone there. Unless he was there that first night and made the mistake of picking up the wrong bag and he's had to work out what might have happened from your camera. So, he gives it back in and then, when he sees you pick it up, he knows it's you that's got his.'

'Maybe. He said something about me having cojones, almost as if he hadn't expected me to come back for it. But he could've found out it was me earlier. Somebody broke into my room and took my passport. Remember? So he could have found me without waiting for me to show up.'

'Yeah, you're right. Unless...unless...' Cecil continued to rub his chin, deep in thought. 'Unless it was somebody else who broke into your room,' he said, as if talking to himself. He paused for a moment his fingers rapping the tabletop. Finally, he broke the silence. 'People? He ain't on his own mate.'

'What do you–?'

I was interrupted by the waitress. Her name badge announced that she was Loretta.

'Steak 'n omelette?' She placed the plate in front of Cecil and the other one in front of me. 'More coffee?' We both nodded and she topped up our mugs.

'So what do you reckon Ces?' I asked, hoping he had a solution but doubting it very much.

'Well if he ain't on his own it looks like there could be somebody else who's looking for the money too that ain't keeping him in the loop.'

'What do you mean?'

'Well, look at this way mate. Let's say there's more than one geezer interested in this wedge, then by the sound of it they ain't working together. Somebody finds out who you are, breaks into your room and don't tell the other geezer. So he still has to track you down by handing your bag in. That means he ain't bin told nuthin so they can't be on the same team.'

'Sort of. But the bloke called my name out.'

'Mate, he'd seen your photos on the camera right. Don't take a lot to print off some shots from the memory card. Then all he has to do is ask round the hotels to see if anyone can identify you. And you'd reported your bag missing to the Bond Bar anyway, yeah? It ain't hard. All these guys are connected geeze.'

'So then they could be working together. Yeah, I'd left my hotel details with the bar the morning before my room was trashed.'

'But the Bond Bar ain't gonna give your details out just like that. Nah. I reckon there's more than one of them on the case. I mean, mate, we're talking half a million bucks here.'

It was bad enough to have one guy after me but now that Cecil had raised the possibility of two, I was even more concerned.

'Hang on Ces. If there was somebody else interested in the bag why break into my room to find out who I am and then not come after me?'

Cecil chewed on a mouthful of steak before answering.

'Geezer, think about it. Why do people break into places? To nick things, right? So, I reckon whoever broke in your room is definitely looking for the bag with the cash too. Tumble?'

'But why my room? You had the bag in your room.'

'I dunno. Unless he knows you took it. He breaks in thinking you got it, finds it ain't there, trashes the place looking for it and then, when he gets no joy, he dumps your passport so you can't leave the country. Makes sense to me.'

'Bit of a long shot Ces. The bloke who got hold of me said something weird...about putting myself up as the bag man. But if you're right, that would mean there are two different villains looking for the same bag and they're not working together. The bloke who attacked me mentioned making *bad men* angry so he's got to be part of a gang or something. And if he's part of a gang and there's a second bloke looking too, then he could be part of another gang. Bloody hell Ces, I reckon I'm in right deep shit.'

'Mate, I was just speculating, yeah. It don't mean you got half the low life in Las Vegas on your case. Just stay cool.'

Staying cool was easier said than done. 'So who does the bag belong to?'

'No fucking idea geezer.' Cecil jabbed his knife at my plate. 'You eatin that steak?'

I had started to pick at the steak but with my stomach churning, my appetite was not that good. I took a mouthful, ate one of the eggs and pushed the plate aside. Cecil slid the steak across onto his own plate. He pointed his fork at my bag.

'Give us that camera a minute mate. Let's have a butchers.'

I pulled the Canon out and handed it to Cecil.

'How d'you switch it on? I wanna play back the pictures.'

I pushed the small lever at the top of the camera. It powered up. I pointed to the playback button on the bottom right at the back. 'Press that one there.'

'Got it mate.' Cecil flicked through the pictures. A grin cracked his face as he looked over the top of the camera directly at me. 'Nice tits.'

I shot out a hand and grabbed the camera, realising what he had seen. I had forgotten the one I had shot of Louise when I had playfully pulled her dressing gown open the night before the trip.

'Hey, give me that Ces. You're not supposed to see that.'

'Geezer, it's just a pair of tits. I've seen plenty of tits, trust me.'

'Maybe, mate, but not Louise's.'

'You reckon,' he said, a wink creasing his eye. He noticed my puzzled expression. 'I'm winding you geezer. All the same, great pair of bangers.'

I scrolled through the other pictures. The only other ones I had taken were on the first night before I had lost the bag. I slid out of my seat and sat next to Cecil.

'Look Ces. The photos we took in the Paris at the bar. Ok. Then the ones going up the Strip and then the ones in front of the statue in Caesar's. So, we know I had the camera going into Caesar's which means I had my bag with me. That's the last place we know I had it for definite based on the photos. Carlos reckons I had it in the Bond Bar but I didn't take any more shots. Apart from the few of Louise the rest are all us guys.'

'Mate, I can't remember if you had it or not but if Carlos has seen you with it then the geezer who's fronted you up must've cocked up and gone off with the wrong one. Stands to reason. But what the fuck is he doin in a bar with half a million bucks?'

'God knows. But once he's seen these pictures, why didn't he come straight after me instead of waiting for me at the Bond bar this morning? He knew who I was from the photos.'

'Yeah he's seen the photos but we're all in 'em at one time or another. How's he know who's the one who might have his bag?'

'That's a point.'

'More coffee gentlemen?' Loretta stood next to the table, coffee jug poised.

Cecil turned to face her. 'Couldn't get me a small beer could you Loretta, darling? I'm all coffeed out. And one for my buddy.'

'No problem. I'll be right back with your beers boys.'

Loretta went off to fetch the order, a broad smile on her face.

I flicked through the pictures again, enjoying the brief lighthearted moments we had experienced before the trip had gone pear shaped.

Cecil shot out a hand. 'Hang on, scroll back again, mate.'

I scrolled back three pictures.

'Yeah, there. Hold it there.'

We stopped at a group shot of the four of us that the waitress had a taken in the Central Lobby bar of the Paris.

'Yeah that one. Can you zoom it?'

'I dunno Ces. I haven't had the camera that long. Hang on.' I fiddled with the buttons on the back of the camera.

'Fuck's sake mate. We gotta do a course to work the fucking thing?'

'Easy Ces. Here it is. Top right. Button with the square on it, next to that...snowflake image button, or whatever it is.'

Cecil pressed the button once and the picture enlarged. He did it again and it zoomed in further. Several more presses and the picture was too close to make out the main subject matter, the four of us in the bar.

'What are you trying to do?'

'I wanna check the background. If you look close enough at the picture you can see some people in the background. I'm tryin to zoom in on the detail.'

I took the camera and tried to recall what was in the instruction book. Next to the viewing screen there was a button marked SET. Around this were four arrow buttons. I pressed one and the picture moved left. Another scrolled the picture up.

'Got it Ces. Here. Try that.'

Loretta returned with two cold beers. 'Enjoy.'

Cecil took a slurp straight from one of the bottles and then began to manoeuvre the picture around using the zoom and scroll buttons until he had picked out some figures in the deep background of the photograph.

'There. See that geezer on the slot machine there. That looks like the geezer you was talking to when we left you in the casino at Caesar's. See.'

'Who?'

'The geezer that was giving you the poker tips. The South American, yeah?'

I took a close look. The image, having being zoomed in so

much, was grainy and not clear at all but I could see what Cecil meant.

'Arturo. You mean Arturo?'

'No idea what the muppet's called. We didn't get acquainted.'

'Well, that's who I was talking to. Arturo...Arturo Magana something or other. The poker player.'

'Well what's he doing in your picture then mate?'

'He's not in my picture Ces. It's just some bloke in the shot. There's other people further back too. It could be him. Looks a bit like him sure, but he's not in it, like he's posing in the background or something. He gambles. We're in Las Vegas. The Lobby Bar is right on the end of the casino. It wouldn't be unusual to find a gambler in a casino, would it?'

'No, but you know what I'm saying. Bit of a coincidence in my book that a geezer you was chattin to on that night is also in one of your pictures. Do you know who the birds are further back there?'

'What birds?'

'Mate, there's two birds right at the back there. Bit blurred I know, but any ideas? You gotta check these things.' He stared more closely at the image on the tiny screen. 'Come to think of it, that looks like that bird you squirted by the pool. I thought she looked familiar when I saw her. Seen her somewhere before. Here, check it out.'

I took the camera from Cecil and stared past the large image of the four of us in the centre of the picture. There were people in the background but it was too dark and grainy to identify anyone.

'Not a clue. It's too vague. Look Ces, the casino's full of people... gamblers, boozers, escorts...could be that bird that nicked the bag for all we know. Talking of which, we got to find her. What was her name? The bird you had in your room. Can you remember?'

Cecil took another look at the picture.

'I dunno, I spose it could be her. Dunno though. Definitely not the other one. She's too short.'

'Yeah but what was her name? We need her name if we're going to find her. We have to get that money back.' I reached out for the beer and took a long pull from the bottle. 'You have to remember Ces?'

Cecil scratched his head, his face a mix of concentration and irritation.

'Alright mate. Leave it. It'll come to me. I was pissed don't forget.'

I looked around the restaurant. Happy faces enjoying a meal and their break from the humdrum of everyday life. I was supposed to be doing the same but it was turning into a nightmare.

'Party for Sylvia,' the waitress on the front desk called out. A stout, middle aged woman answered and was led to a table along with three friends.

Cecil turned towards the group. 'That's it mate. That's her,' he said, as he ran both hands through his hair.

I glanced across at the group as they took their seats. 'That middle aged woman? She's got to be fifty odd Ces. That's her?'

'No, you twat. Not her. The name…Sylvia.'

'What? Her name's Sylvia?'

'No mate. You're not listening. Krystal. It's Krystal. The escort bird. Her name was Krystal.'

'Krystal? How did you get that then?'

'It just came to me. That bird's shouted out Sylvia. Reminded me of silver. It's all metal, rocks and shit. Silver, crystal…all the same. Yeah Krystal.'

I dismissed what I was thinking about Cecil's logic. 'Great. Well that's a start but I wouldn't be holding out too much hope that it's her real name.'

We paid the check and left a tip for Loretta.

Out on the Strip I told Cecil that I wanted to take some shots of the Venetian. He said he was going back to the hotel.

'Gotta get some kip mate. Got a big night out.'

'Where we going then?'

'Dunno yet, geezer, but you gotta keep the dream alive. Ain't gonna let no villains spoil the party. You on it mate?'

I nodded agreement but inside I wasn't so confident.

17

I turned right out of Denny's and walked along to the Venetian. My mind was in turmoil but I wanted to enjoy my Las Vegas experience. Part of that enjoyment was to take back some memories. The memories I was likely to take back were not the pleasant ones of a fun holiday. Cecil's words echoed in my head. He was right. Why should I let villains spoil the party? My immediate solution was to capture the experience on camera. I stood in front of the St Mark's Basilica bell tower and clicked off some shots. Further into the piazza an escalator led onto the Rialto Bridge. I crossed the bridge into a long covered balcony that ran the length of one side of the building. Its highly polished red, white and black patterned floor caught the bright shafts of daylight that streamed through the gaps between the columns. From this vantage point there was an excellent view of the exterior part of the Grand Canal, the entrance road to the Venetian and out across the Strip itself. I leant on the stone balustrade at its front and took a few more pictures. Beneath me a wide pedestrian bridge split the two sides of the canal. On either side, tied to their red and white mooring poles, several gondolas bobbed gently on the turquoise water awaiting their next paying customers. At the bridge entrance, the winged Lion of St Mark and the warrior like figure of St. Theodore stood atop two tall columns keeping a watchful eye on the bustle of activity below. Across the Strip a wide curved ach straddled the road that wound its way to the golden facade of the Mirage hotel. I rolled the lens of the camera and focussed on the gondolas below.

'Great view.'

I glanced in the direction of the voice. A dark haired man, his face lightly tanned by the sun, leant on the balustrade next to me. I hadn't seen him approach. Unlike the throngs of tourists he was not wearing weekend, casual clothes but looked quite out of place in a grey, lightweight business suit and a pale pink open-necked shirt. He stared out across the Grand Canal almost as if his comment had been directed at one of the gondoliers.

'Yes it is,' I said, turning towards him. 'I was just taking a few shots for the holiday album.'

'Of course, you're on holiday.'

'Well, yes. Is it that obvious?' I said, slightly surprised by the certainty in his statement.

He turned to face me for the first time, a smile on his face but a cool, intense look in his eyes.

'The camera is often a giveaway, Matthew. You don't mind if I call you Matthew, do you?'

An icy shiver ran through me despite the warmth of the afternoon. I grabbed my bag ready to take flight.

'How do you know my name?' I managed to stutter.

'Hey, easy Matthew. Don't be alarmed. I just want to talk, ok. I know your name because it's my job to know these things. I'm a lawyer and I work for some people whose financial interests I look after.'

Financial interests. I heard the words and immediately thought of the missing five hundred thousand dollars. I said nothing in the hope that I was mistaken and perhaps he was just selling life insurance.

'It has come to our attention, Matthew, that you may have something that has caused my clients a degree of inconvenience.'

My heart sank. The first time ever in my life I had actually wanted to hear something about life insurance. Again I said nothing.

'A little matter of half a million dollars,' he said, 'and it needs to be recovered. His tone was calm, cool and measured, his eyes focussed directly on mine as if seeking an immediate reaction.

I stared back at him, unsure how to respond. He let the silence remain for a moment, his face expressionless. Then he turned away and looked out across the Strip.

'It's a lovely day Matthew, don't you think.'

The unexpected change of tone threw me. It was a lovely day out there for sure but my day was far from lovely. He had referred to half a million dollars as an inconvenience. As far as its impact to me was concerned it was an unmitigated bloody catastrophe.

'Inconvenience?' was all I could say.

'Yes, Matthew. An inconvenience. My clients were hoping to conclude a business deal on Saturday night and that has now been delayed by your unexpected intervention.'

A couple of tourists had come to the balcony edge and were pointing across at the Mirage. I waited until they had moved on. Crowds of sightseers were moving in and out of the doors of the building behind us. My instinct to flee flared up again. I resisted it. I realised that I had to get more information if I was to solve the difficulties I found myself in. Running earlier on had only delayed matters.

'What intervention? I don't know what you mean. I haven't done anything. Look, I know about the bag. I know about the money but I don't know how I have come to be involved in all this. That's the truth. There must be some mistake...I don't know how but...you have the wrong guy.'

'So you know about the money?'

'Well, yes but –'

'So, there can be no mistake. If you know about the money Matthew, you are involved. You understand?'

I immediately regretted my candid admission.

'I meant I know something about the money but I don't have it. We did have it –'

'We? Who's we?'

The hairs on the back of my neck prickled as I realised I might be implicating the whole holiday crew, Jasper and Carlos as well as Cecil. I decided I had to tell him what little I knew. When I had finished my account of how the money came to be in our possession he remained silent for a few minutes as if considering whether to believe me.

'An interesting story Matthew. But, you see, it could just be that's all it is. A story. Nothing more than a story. Let's just say I believe you...you seem like a regular guy...the thing is, the people I represent are not quite as accommodating as me. They work on results. It doesn't really matter to them who did what to who. They won't be interested in some little lady that you say might have stolen the money. These guys just wanna know why their deal has gone wrong and who is responsible. How they'll see this right now, is that you are that responsible person Matthew. They are businessmen.'

'Businessmen. Oh, ok, so why don't we just go to the police and sort this all out?' I said.

The reaction I got was not what I had expected. A burst of laughter greeted my question.

'I like that Matthew. You're a funny guy. Let's just say that my clients sort their own problems out, if you know what I mean. One of our team was robbed on the way down here for this deal on Friday afternoon. And you know, I wouldn't want to think you were involved in that.' The laughter had disappeared from his voice and had been replaced by a more menacing tone. It crossed my mind that it was unsuited to a lawyer.

'Friday afternoon? I wasn't in Vegas on Friday afternoon. I was still on the flight,' I said, a burst of optimism washing over me.

'We know that. We've checked. But that doesn't mean you couldn't have been involved. Personally, I don't think you are. I think you're just some English tourist schmuck who got in the way. Somebody else is responsible for our man. And you know what? We will find the sonofabitch and deal with that little matter ourselves. You understand? Now we got this additional problem and my clients do not like being taken for patsies. We need to get that bag back so we can get this deal back on and sort things out from there. You understand?'

He didn't wait for any acknowledgement.

'So here's the deal. You got forty-eight hours to sort out our little predicament so we can get our business back on. That's being generous. Nobody gets forty eight hours as a rule but the boss is attending to other matters right now. You are scheduled to go back to UK on Wednesday, right?'

'I am,' I said, wondering how he knew but not totally surprised by then.

'Well I am sure you want this matter all tidied up by then so you can get on that flight back home, all safe and sound, don't you Matthew?' His eyes widened and he nodded his head as if encouraging me to say yes. Again he didn't wait for any affirmation. 'I will contact you in forty-eight hours from now... that's, let's see...' He raised his left arm and glanced at a watch with a silver bracelet, '...it's three o'clock right now...so make that three on Tuesday.'

I nodded agreement. I realised I had no choice. I had no immediate idea how I was going to recover the money but at that moment I could only acknowledge his request.

'So how do I get in touch? Do you have a business card?'

He smiled condescendingly. 'I don't do business cards Matthew. Don't you worry about getting in touch. We'll find you.' With that he turned and began to walk away.

'Wait...wait...Mister...err...hang on,' I called after him.

He turned around and waited as I walked towards him.

'Just one thing. I'm confused. This morning I was confronted by a guy demanding that I take him to where the money is. Then two of them came after me. I assume these guys are with you?'

'Not exactly Matthew, but we know who they are. They are keen to sort this little deal out too. They stand to lose out if it's not. But they won't bother you in the next forty-eight hours now. I will make sure of that. The people I represent, let's just say they are not two bit street punks. But if you don't deliver by our deadline I can't guarantee you anything...except....' His voice tailed off. He pointed an index finger at me. Before I could decide whether he was mimicking a gun or giving me a *catch you later* salute, he had turned on his heel and disappeared along the crowded walkway.

I got back to the Paris and headed straight for Cecil's room. There was no response to my frantic hammering on his door. Either he was asleep or he wasn't in. I decided to try the others. I pulled the folded up napkin from my pocket and checked room numbers. Carlos's room, 1155, was closest. No reply there either. My knocking on room 1189 met with the same lack of response. Jasper appeared to be out too. The only other option was the pool. I dumped my bag in my room and raced back along the corridor to the lift. When I reached the pool floor I ran straight out onto the poolside, stopping briefly to scan the immediate area. As luck would have it I spotted Jasper near the pool sitting on the edge of a sun lounger in deep conversation with a woman. Carlos was lying flat out on Jasper's far side. I couldn't see any sign of Cecil. I ran towards them keen to unload my news and called out Jasper's name. He looked up in my direction as did his female companion, Kimberley. Her face screwed up into a concerned frown at my hasty approach. It turned out that her concern was well placed. Such was my hurry I failed to see the camera on the ground next to her bag. My momentum took me on a direct collision course with it. At the last second I caught sight of the camera but too late. My left foot caught the lens with an inadvertent kick that propelled it in a whirling, sliding spin across the poolside directly into the water. For a moment Kimberley was dumbstruck, her mouth agape, her eyes wide in disbelief. Her muted moment didn't last.

'You freakin goddam sonofabitch. Look what you done to my fucking camera. I told you to stay the hell away from me, didn't I?'

She jumped up from her sun lounger, her face incandescent with barely restrained rage. In my fraught state of mind I didn't cope with her reaction.

'What the fuck is it doing on the floor anyway you stupid bitch?' I shouted. 'And who are you calling a sonofabitch. It's a frigging camera. That's all. It's not life or death. Get another one. I don't need you mouthing off at me.'

For a moment she stood stock still, my reaction sending her into a state of inertia. Then she flew at me in a leap that would have been more appropriate for a predatory puma than a human being. Jasper was on his feet in a flash. He grabbed her from behind, catching her arms above both elbows to restrain her wild attack. Such was her rage that even in Jasper's grip she managed to get both feet kicking out in my direction. Her frustration at being unable to get at me resulted in a stream of expletives directed with all the venom she could muster. The commotion woke Carlos and alerted everyone in the immediate vicinity including three of the lifeguard staff. Jasper held on to Kimberley's arms until she had exhausted her rage.

'What's happened here?' one of the staff asked.

'This jerk just kicked my camera into the pool,' Kimberley said, jabbing a finger in my direction, her eyes bristling with bad intent, her face as red as her hair.

'Did you Sir?' the lifeguard asked. 'What did you do that for?'

Kimberley's camera was the least of my worries at that moment. As far as I was aware I had two sets of criminals intent on doing me some sort of damage if I did not return half a million dollars that I had never had in the first place, and, compared with that, Kimberley's camera was not high up on my list of things that I had to deal with. My response to the lifeguard was fuelled by anxiety and frustration at being unable to resolve the serious predicament I found myself in.

'What did I do that for? Look, it's not as if I took a running pot shot at this woman's camera and decided that I wanted to launch it into the pool. Do I look like someone who's practising for the Super Bowl? It was an accident. They happen. It's why we have insurance for holidays. Why would you leave a camera on the poolside floor anyway and that close to the edge? It's just asking to be booted up in the air. Serves the stupid...serves her right if you ask me for being so careless.'

Kimberley's eyes blazed.

'Careless. I'll sue you, jerkoff. You've ruined my fucking camera. It's soaking wet. You won't hear the end of this.'

'Well go ahead, lady, sue me. I suppose it could have been

worse. It could have been your big pink dildo I booted into the water couldn't it? No problem with that getting wet though, eh?'

Kimberley's mouth dropped open again and then shut just as quickly. She stared at me as if she wanted to say something but her eyes softened slightly as if she wanted to ensure I said no more. The moment was interrupted by a female lifeguard approaching with the waterlogged camera.

'There you are,' she said, holding it out towards Kimberley. 'It might dry out.'

Kimberley snatched it away from the lifeguard, grabbed her bag and marched off.

Carlos, who had been quiet throughout the whole episode, spoke first.

'Hey Mateo, what was all that about? It's not like you to get so upset. Que pasa amigo?'

I pulled up a sun longer and took off my shirt. The sun was warm on my back and the sensation immediately soothing. I buried my head in my hands for a moment, kneading the tension from my forehead as I soaked up the warmth on the back of my neck.

'This man needs a beer,' I heard Jasper say. 'Three Bud's please darling.'

I looked up to see two expectant faces watching me, waiting on an answer.

'Not having much luck with cameras this holiday am I?' I said, smiling as I thought of Louise's birthday gift to me and the latest incident. 'Listen boys, I've had a shit day. I'm sorry about losing it there. Just, that woman winds me up. What's going on with her anyway, Jasper?'

'Nothing mate...well not yet anyway. She just came over and started chatting, you know, after the sun cream thing and all that the other day. And what's all that about a dildo?' he asked, breaking into his gleaming smile.

'Oh nothing. I'm sure you'll find out for yourself sooner or later. Anyway, where's Cecil?'

'He's hooked up again with that Morgan. I saw him this afternoon heading back to his room with her,' Jasper replied.

'Well he's not there now or at least he's not answering. I've just been there.'

'Maybe he's gone to her hotel. Her and Destiny are staying up at the Wynn.'

The waitress returned with three cold beers. Carlos paid her and handed them round.

'Get these down you lads and quit ya bletherin about women,' he said, raising his bottle in a salute. 'So what's happened then Mateo?'

I took two large sips from the bottle, enjoying the fizzy sensation of the cold beer as it slipped down, the first bit of light relief I had felt since I had experienced the brief elation at recovering my camera.

'It's just been a total crap day to be honest guys. I got my bag back this morning but I'm in serious bother.' I took a deep breath and began to tell them about my encounter with the two villains earlier and then my meeting with the lawyer. When I had finished I realised I had absent mindedly peeled most of the label off the beer bottle.

'So what are we gonna do now then?' Carlos asked.

'We?' I said. 'Thanks Carlos but it's me they're after and to be honest, I don't know.'

'Hey Mateo. We are all in this together. You have a problema, we all have a problema. Right Jasper?'

'That's right,' Jasper confirmed, as he raised his bottle and clanked it against mine.

'Thanks boys. I appreciate it. Somehow I have to track that money down so I can get it back to whoever it is that owns it.'

'We could try winning it,' Jasper said.

'Winning it? You must be aff yer napper Jasper. He cannae win half a million dollars? If it was that simple we'd all be at it,' Carlos said, staring at Jasper as if he was a total lunatic. 'No, we have to find the woman who took it from Cecil. She was an escort, right?'

'That's right. Ces reckons her name was Krystal.'

'It's not gonna be that easy is it guys? There must be hundreds of escorts in Vegas,' Jasper said. He shrugged in a dismissive manner and took a long pull from his beer before continuing. 'I reckon we'd have more chance gambling and winning than finding some escort.'

'Hang on. That's it,' I said, as a thought flashed through my mind. 'Hundreds of escorts. Brooke!'

'Brooke?' Jasper repeated.

'Yeah. Brooke. You're right. There must be hundreds of escorts in Vegas, sure, but I have a number for one of them. It has to be a fairly tight knit thing. There has to be a network. That's a start. Brooke. You remember guys? That hot looking babe that gave me her card in the Bellagio? Las Vegas Barbie Doll.'

18

I sat at the desk in my room and pulled the card from my wallet. I punched the numbers *712 631 7643* into my mobile and waited. It rang three times and went to voicemail.

'Hi this is Brooke your Las Vegas Barbie Doll. I'm busy right now but leave me your number and I will get straight back to you.'

'Bollocks.' I let out the expletive just as the beep on the voicemail kicked in. My annoyance was driven by my urgency to get some sort of clue as to where I might begin to sort my predicament out. I had to be patient.

'Hi, my name is Matthew. You gave me your card the other night in the Bellagio and I wondered if we could meet up for a chat. Please call me at the Paris, room 1164.'

I threw myself onto the bed and lay there for a moment trying to make some sense of it all. The chat with Cecil at Denny's had made me think. What if Cecil was right and someone had broken into my room just to see if I had the bag? I had run into two sets of villains now. It was possible they were connected. My conversation with the lawyer had suggested they might be. On the other hand they may not be connected at all and both were simply competing to get the cash. What if there was a third person? The one that had entered my room? But he could also have been connected with the first lot of villains or even the lawyer. Or they could all be connected. I had to break things down in to small pieces otherwise I was in danger of being overwhelmed by my own thoughts. I jumped off the bed, picked up my camera from the table and laid back down. I set the button to playback and looked through the pictures. The last pictures I had taken were in Caesar's but I hadn't taken any in the casino, even though we were all together there for a while. But that was because it wasn't allowed and I recalled Maria saying so. I thought back to the moment I had gone to take her picture, just after she had pinned my flower to her blouse. And then I remembered. It was Arturo who had actually stopped me taking the picture, not Maria. *'You can't take pictures in the casino,'* he'd said. Maria had just confirmed it, but it was Arturo that had stopped me. Had he been stopping me or just telling me?

I scrolled through the pictures again stopping at the group shot of all four of us lads. I zoomed in trying to see if there were any clues as to who the people were that Cecil had spotted in the background. The image of the man was definitely the clearest. He stood at a slot machine seemingly engrossed in what he was doing. He was tall but his features were not easily discernible. It could have been Arturo as Cecil had suggested but it could also have been anyone. With the two women further back it was impossible to gather any likeness since both were partially turned away from the camera and the more I zoomed in the more grainy the image became.

I decided that perhaps I should seek out Arturo. He was the last person that had seen me with the bag in the casino. I had no idea how he could help but it was a part of organising my thoughts. Then I remembered Erin. I had met her as I left Caesar's but all we had done was practically pass one another. And in any case I had seen her since and she didn't seem to know anything. I decided that I would also talk to Maria, the croupier at Caesar's. It could all help piece my evening together. It crossed my mind too that the whole thing may have simply been a stupid mistake by Cecil. I was beating myself up about it all but it may have been that he just picked up the wrong bag after I had left mine behind.

My scrambled thoughts were brought to an abrupt end by the

bedside telephone. I reached across and grabbed the receiver. 'Hello.'

'Hi. Is that Matthew. This is Brooke, your Las Vegas Barbie Doll. Thank you for your call today. How can I help?'

'Oh...hi Brooke. Thanks for calling me back. You gave me your card in the Bellagio and I wondered if we could get together for a short while. I wanted to talk to you.'

'Ok. You want me to show you Las Vegas? Maybe party a little?'

'No, it's ok. I just want to talk to you.'

'You just wanna talk? That's cool. A lot of guys just wanna talk. When would you like to meet? I'm free this evening.'

'Well, right now would be good if you can do that Brooke.'

'Oh you are eager, aren't you? Say, are you from England? I just love that accent.'

My ego experienced a seismic jolt and as a result my accent inadvertently took on a more pronounced English emphasis. 'Yes, indeed. I am from England, London actually. Do you know it?'

'London. How cool. I would love to go to London. You guys are all real gentlemen over there.'

Again, I took her remark personally. My day had been dreadful and it must have been because I needed the boost. However, I decided I ought to stick to the point rather than get carried away chatting up an attractive blonde.

'So Brooke, when could you meet?'

'I'd love a little time to get ready first Matthew. I always like to look my best for a date. How about six-thirty?'

I glanced at my watch. It was five o'clock. 'That would be fine.'

'How long will you want me for?' Her voice had dropped an octave, the question practically oozing over the phone, full of enticement and raw seduction.

'Oh, not too long. I just want to talk. Half an hour or so. I am in room 1164.'

There was a pause on the other end of the line. Brooke's voice came back, this time her tone a little more matter of fact.

'Ok, Matthew but we need to get a few things straight first. I don't meet in hotel rooms. I'm happy to meet you in the bar at

your hotel. It's five hundred dollars for the first four hours – that's a minimum charge – and one hundred dollars an hour after that.'

I stifled the gasp that instantly caught in my throat. Stupidly, I hadn't even thought of payment. She was an escort after all.

'Err...well as I say, it should only take a half an hour. Is there a discount?'

'Like I said, minimum charge Matthew is five hundred whether it's five minutes or the full four hours. You want to meet?'

Confusion blurred my thoughts for a moment. Five hundred dollars was a lot of money. I was trying to retrieve money but it looked like I was going to have to spend some in order to make any progress. That seemed to be the unwritten law of Las Vegas. The law of the gambler. If you were going to make big bucks you had to speculate in the first place. It was all a risk. I decided I had no choice but to go for it. It would be the same for any escort. Their time was money. My first step to finding Krystal depended upon getting some answers.

'Sure, no problem. Do you know the Central Lobby Bar in the Paris? We can meet there. Six-thirty. I will definitely recognise you. Oh, and you'll recognise me - I have an English accent.'

I heard the little giggle before she replied.

'Fantastic Matthew. I will look forward to it.'

I showered and shaved and then stood in front of the wardrobe trying to decide what to wear. If I was paying five hundred dollars for what could turn out to be no more than a twenty minute chat with a stunning young lady I might as well look the part. I chose a pale pink Paul Smith shirt for no reason other than it would contrast well with the black suit I had in mind. I checked my look in the mirror, picked up my wallet from the bedside table and made for the door. As I slipped the wallet into my jacket pocket I realised that I did not have enough cash to pay for Brooke's time. It was turning into an expensive trip. I had already paid out over fourteen hundred pounds for my flight and lent Cecil four hundred dollars and that was without my own spending money. The thought of Cecil gave me an idea.

I made my way to his room, hoping he would be in, and rapped on the door. He opened it, a towel tight around his waist and his hair still wet from the shower.

'Alright mate. How you doin? Where you goin all dressed up anyway?'

'I'm good Ces,' I said as I walked into the room. 'Listen I need a favour. I'm meeting up with that escort that gave me her card in the Bellagio and I need –'

'Oh yeah mate? Nice one. Yeah, bit of a stunna weren't she?'

'Yes...no...err...I mean, it's not what you're thinking Ces. Look, you know you said that escort you met was called Krystal. Well, I thought if I make some enquiries one of the girls in the business may know her. So I thought I'd start with Brooke.'

'Brooke?'

'Yeah, that's her name. The one that gave me the card. It's a long shot but all I can come up with at the moment and you won't believe what happened this afternoon after you left. I was walking round the –'

Cecil held up a hand in front of me.

'Whoa...slow down. You'll give yourself a seizure mate. Sit down there,' he said, pointing to the armchair by the window. 'I got some Jack in the cupboard. Let me do a coupla JD and cokes.' He unscrewed the Jack Daniel's bottle, poured two large measures, flipped the ring on a coke can and poured the fizzing contents into both glasses. 'There you go mate. Now start again.'

I sipped my drink slowly and told Cecil all that had happened that afternoon with the mysterious lawyer I had met at the Venetian. When I had finished Cecil sat for a moment looking into his glass.

'I reckon the geezer you met then is the real deal. With the proper villains. There's some shit goin on mate that we ain't tumbled. He's mentioned some deal that was going down on Friday and he thinks that somehow you got in the way of it. Maybe that villain that's grabbed you has nicked their money then lost it in the Bond Bar. Who knows? Yeah, your lawyer friend is representing the real players.'

'Well he was the one issuing the forty-eight hour ultimatum. And he more or less said he'd call the first lot of guys off. So who are those guys?'

'I dunno mate. Maybe they were part of the original deal he was on about. Anyway, I reckon you got it about right hooking up with that escort. If you can get some info from her on that Krystal bird that's a start. I'd be interested in finding her myself after she stitched us up. And anyway you probably need to get to her before the villains do. They'll be asking around too.'

'I didn't mention she was an escort. I just said it was some girl you met in the bar. I didn't think of it. It was all a bit of a panic.' I swigged back the last of my JD. 'Look, I got to get going Ces. I'm meeting Brooke in fifteen minutes downstairs. Where you going to be?'

'We're starting out in The Bond Bar then over to the Hyde bit later. Then we're heading up to the Wynn. That Morgan bird reckoned the Tryst club was kickin. Keep your mobile on mate.'

'Blimey Ces. A proper little itinerary you got there.'

'Yeah, well geeze, when you're going for the title you gotta be on top of yer game.' He dropped into a boxer's crouch and threw a left, right, left combination into the air. 'And what's that favour you was going on about?'

I'd almost forgotten the money. 'I need five hundred dollars to pay Brooke.'

'What the fuck? What you paying her for? She shelling out?'

'She's an escort, Ces. I told you. I got no choice, have I? It's her time. If she's with me she's not earning somewhere else. If I want to get that information I'm going to have to do this. It's five hundred minimum charge up to four hours. So I was thinking, the rest of that cash you have in the safe…the eleven and a half grand. Well I need the five hundred. The way I see it is we have to find the best part of four hundred and ninety grand so another five hundred isn't going to make a lot of difference. It's like an expense of the job now so it may as well come from what we have.'

'You're right mate. No probs,' Cecil said, as he went to the wardrobe where the room safe was tucked away on an upper shelf.

He pressed four buttons on the front and clicked the door open.

'So, look mate, I reckon if you're paying for four hours, it ain't gonna take you that long to ask the question...does she know this other bird or not. So, once you done that mumble you may as well take advantage of the entertainment you're paying for.'

19

I took a seat at the Central Lobby Bar, ordered a beer and waited for Brooke. At exactly six-thirty I saw her approach. There was no mistaking her. All of the men facing her direction stopped drinking and stared. Those who weren't facing the right way turned to see what the guys were looking at. Most of the men and even some of the women walking by on the replica boulevards were distracted by Brooke, the guys rolling into a head swivel as she passed, the ladies casting a surreptitious glance. She was probably no more than five-six tall but high black, silver studded heels, accentuated her smooth, shapely legs creating the impression that she was taller. Her emerald green, one shoulder, black polka dotted tunic dress, was short enough to emphasis her legs even more. She walked towards the bar area, a purposeful smooth elegant gait that made her look like she was sliding over the mock cobblestones. A black handbag swayed gently with her movement. She walked up the three steps to the bar and stopped in front of me.

'Matthew?' she said, the southern drawl elongating my name. Her blonde hair was pulled back tight over her ears and set in a French plait. The style enhanced her fresh good looks and gave her a stylish grace that counteracted the boldness of her dress. Her lipstick, a shade darker then when I had first met her, was carefully applied with just a hint of gloss.

'Yes…yes it is. Brooke?'

'Nice to meet you Matthew,' she said holding out a hand. 'A

pleasant surprise. No calling card this time,' she said, with a meaningful wink.

'No,' I laughed, 'but how did you know me?'

'You just look English. That English style. It's right out there, you know.'

I was taken aback. 'Oh, that bad eh?'

She slipped onto the seat opposite me, her green dress sliding along her thighs as she did.

'Not at all Matthew. I love it.'

'Well thank you for coming Brooke. I appreciate it.'

'And you English guys are so polite. Not shooting your mouth off all the time. And I love that accent too. I think we could have fun.'

I swallowed hard trying to dismiss the prospect of fun with Brooke.

'Err…yes…well…err…what can I get you to drink Brooke?'

'What do you recommend?' she said as she crossed her legs.

I was very taken by Brooke's good looks. I knew that she was only here because she was being paid. Yet already I felt she had a natural manner, an easy, relaxed, style and that made me feel at ease. I knew what she did but sometimes you can connect with a person instantly. I was paying five hundred dollars so lemonades all round would probably have been my recommendation with anyone else, but something made me want to impress. She had flattered my ego.

'Champagne,' I said in as decisive an English accent as I could muster. 'Any particular one you fancy?' I read a few from the bar list.

'That sounds nice, the Veuve Clicquot Rosé. I like rosé.'

I hadn't bothered to look at the cost in my enthusiasm. I checked the list - $150.00. One hundred and fifty dollars. The price rattled through my head. It would be an expensive evening.

Brooke noticed my hesitation. 'Everything ok, Matthew?'

'Oh…err…yes, fine. I was…was just, you know, checking their full list. The Rosé is fine.' I closed the drinks list, caught the barman's attention and ordered. 'Err…put it on my room please…1164.'

The Champagne was presented in an ice bucket and we moved to one of the tables. Brooke was relaxed, very laid back and unhurried. In the soft lighting, the stem of her Champagne glass held elegantly between slender manicured fingers, she had an innocence about her that, in my mind, was at odds with her work. She entertained for money, which had to require a hard edge, yet her natural persona seemed gentle and unpretentiousness. She sipped her Champagne slowly and asked questions about England. I was doing an awful lot of talking about myself but despite enjoying the relaxed conversation I realised I had to address the real purpose of my meeting with Brooke.

'So where are you from then, Brooke?'

'I was brought up in Jacksonville, Florida. My father was in the military, based at Jacksonville Naval Air Station. Then we moved to Atlanta when he came out. He joined the police force and was a cop in the Atlanta Police Department. He moved back to Jacksonville with Mom when I was in college. He's an FBI agent now.'

'An FBI agent?' Alarm bells began to ring in my head. The last thing I needed was to be involved with the police, let alone an FBI agent.

'Yes, FBI Jacksonville Division on the Evidence Response Team. Does all that crime scene stuff. He loves it. He likes being part of a team, like he's back in the military.'

I was beginning to have second thoughts. I realised that what Brooke's father did was nothing to do with her and he was based on the east coast in any case. But it worried me. I sipped the Champagne to give my thoughts time to assemble into some sort of rational order.

'Do you see much of your parents…your father?' I wasn't doing a very good job of getting around to the subject I really wanted to discuss.

'No, not really. My mom phones once a week and I get back home when I can. I'm going to go see them this week actually. My mom knows what I do out here but my pop thinks I'm modelling.'

My mind ticked over. Perhaps I was worrying too much. So her father was a cop. I only had a few days to solve my predicament and then I'd be gone. I had booked Brooke at five hundred dollars and I couldn't very well pull the plug on our date without causing a commotion of some sort. I'd have to pay her even if I decided not to pursue my original intention to get information on Krystal. I couldn't afford the time nor the money involved in booking someone else. I decided I had nothing to lose. I only had to tell her what she needed to know.

'So, how did you end up here in Vegas?'

'Well when I was in school everybody kinda said I should go into modelling so I got that in my head and decided to try out. One of my friends in college was from Vegas so soon as I'd finished college I came here. I've done a few shoots here and there but it's real difficult to get signed up with the big agencies. They all want so much money for everything, like pictures for your portfolio and stuff. So I kinda got into the escort thing because it pays well and that way I can get enough together for an agent and get some high class pictures done, you know. And it pays the bills right now as well.' She laughed and sipped her Champagne.

'Well, talking of pictures I've got a camera. Maybe when I get good enough I can do your pictures for you.'

'Really?'

'No, I'm only teasing. I am no expert…err…but that's what I wanted to talk to you about.'

'What pictures? You into pictures?'

'Oh no, nothing like that. You remember I said I wanted to talk, you know, tonight, on our…well, what do you call it…date?'

'Yes, a date. I like that. A date. Sure. But you really just want to talk?' She frowned, a look of sheer puzzlement crossing her face.

'Yes I do. Look you are gorgeous. No doubt about that but I am just here to talk. That's it.' I stared for a moment at the bubbles fizzing to the surface of my Champagne. 'I have someone at home…back in England…a girl and –'

'Hey, a lot of guys have someone at home Matthew but when they're in Vegas –'

'I know. I know…but I'm serious. Listen, I don't want to sound weird or anything but I can't talk here in public. I need somewhere private. Can we go to my room? It's peaceful there and I can tell you why I have arranged the date.'

She looked around her. The bar had filled up and the whole area was now a mass people on the move, heading for restaurants, bars and shops. I couldn't risk being overheard and I needed to convince Brooke that I was genuine.

'I have only just met you Matthew. I get booked by a lot of guys and sometimes it's no fun at all. You do seem like a nice guy but…I don't know…it's –'

'Look Brooke. I will tell the bar tender where we are going ok? All above board. He's seen us together. I've even signed for the Champagne so he has my room number.'

She pursed her lips and glanced at the bar tender who was busy shaking a cocktail for a customer on the far side of the bar. Then she looked back towards me, her blue eyes holding my gaze in a searching stare. After a moment she reached out and patted me on the knee, a gesture of reassurance after the brief hesitation.

'I have to make decisions all the time in this game. Judgement calls, you know. My whole well-being depends on it. You get guys who think they own you just because they paid for your time. But I like you. You have an honest face.' The serious look was replaced by a warm smile. 'Ok, let's do it then.'

I ordered another bottle of Champagne and told the bar tender to send it up to 1164. Another one hundred and fifty dollars but what the hell I thought. This had turned out to be no ordinary trip. Back in my room Brooke sat on the sofa. I paid her the five hundred dollars straight away, for reassurance, and decided to get to the point.

'Brooke, I need some information and I need it in a hurry.'

Her smile changed to a more serious frown but I decided to press on.

'I need to know if you know anyone in your circle that goes by the name of Krystal.'

'Why?' she asked, her face betraying no sign of recognition at the name.

'Well because on Saturday night my friend met her in the bar here and, well to get to the point, she ripped him off.'

Brooke's expression clouded even more and she stood up.

'Hey, Matthew, I can't get involved in that sort of thing. It happens all the time. Guys get guilty and then say they got ripped off and stuff. That's between your friend and Krystal.'

'Do you know her…Krystal?'

'I just said…I can't –'

'Brooke…this isn't about a guy thinking he's been ripped off. This is far more serious. Listen to me. Krystal…whoever she is, took a bag from my friend's room. That bag contained a lot of money. And I mean a serious lot of money. It's best you don't know the details but as a result of what she has done I am in a serious amount of trouble with some very nasty guys.'

'You're in trouble? What do you mean?'

'Let's just say I was the one who was supposed to have the bag and get it back to these guys. So it is me they are looking for. But the problem now is that if they find out Krystal has the money she will be in very serious trouble too.'

Brooke sat back down on the sofa, her face ashen. Behind me there was a knock on the door. I opened it expecting to see a waiter with the Champagne. Instead I saw Erin Farrell.

'Hello Matthew.'

I was stunned into silence for a moment.

'Can I come in?'

'What are you doing here, Erin?' I said finally.

'Pleased to see me then,' she said, a slight roll of her eyes underlining the sarcastic tone. 'I'm on my way out, don't worry. I just called by on the off chance. I wanted to speak to you…about last night. Can I come in or not?'

On her way out. The red cocktail dress did seem a bit dressy for a quick visit.

'Yes, sorry. Come in Erin.'

I closed the door behind her and she walked into the room. When she had passed the bathroom she caught sight of Brooke. She turned back towards me, her eyes narrowed into two small slits, tightness in her lips.

'Oh…you have company I see,' she said in a low whisper.

'Err yes…Erin, this is Brooke…she's a…a…you know… friend.' I gestured towards Brooke who stood up and held a hand out towards Erin.

'Brooke…erm…this is Erin…she's a friend…a friend of mine…too.'

'Pleased to meet you Erin,' Brooke said, her smile warm and open.

I was pleased to see that the colour had returned to her cheeks.

Erin shook Brooke's hand but before anything else was said there was another knock on the door. The Champagne had arrived. One bottle, two glasses. The waiter made a show of pouring it.

Erin turned to me. 'Looks like three's a crowd Matthew. I should go.'

'Hang on,' I said as I ducked into the bathroom and grabbed the glass that my toothbrush was standing in, 'have a glass of Champagne. You haven't told me what it was that, you know, you wanted to say about last night.'

Brooke picked up both glasses that the waiter had poured and handed one to Erin. I poured a measure into the toothbrush holder.

'It's ok Matthew,' Erin said, 'it was nothing important. Did you find your bag by the way?'

'Yes, I did thanks. Someone handed it in, luckily.' I caught Brooke's eye when Erin mentioned a bag. I winked at her. She said nothing.

'That's good. Wouldn't want you to lose your present from Louise, would we?' Erin said and shot a glance at Brooke.

Another knock on the door interrupted us. I opened it. Jasper Kane stood with a broad grin on his face.

'Hi mate. Just calling to let you know we are on our way out,' he said, peering past me into the room. 'Cecil said you were entertaining tonight. Looks like he was right.'

'Well, yes and no. Look, I'm a bit busy Jasper. You going to be with Ces?'

He leant in close and began to whisper. 'I can see that mate.

Couple of super hotties you got there. Bit of a dark horse aren't you. Give 'em one for me. Yeah, heading out with Ces and Carlos so if you got any energy left we'll be in the Tryst club at the Wynn.' A playful punch and a wink confirmed his total misreading of my situation.

I shut the door. Brooke and Erin were both standing looking at me as if I had to make a decision. Quite what that was I had no idea. All I knew was I had to get my money's worth from Brooke. 'Any more Champagne anyone?'

Brooke held her glass out. Erin placed hers on the table.

'I have to go Matthew. Nice to catch up. I'm back to work soon, flying out later this week so I don't suppose I will see you. Enjoy Vegas.' She leant towards me and kissed me gently on one cheek. 'Bye Matthew.' Her contact was cooler than I had expected, almost distant. It disturbed me but I didn't know why. It was as if I had upset her in some way.

'Are you having some more?' Brooke said, waving the Champagne bottle at me.

I offered my glass and she filled it but I knew it was time to focus on what I wanted to know.

'Brooke, are you going to help me here or not? I need to know whether you might know who Krystal is. I need to get in touch with her before…well, before anyone else does, because if I don't somebody else will and they won't be so patient. Bottom line is that whoever Krystal is, she's taken something that belongs to some very dangerous people.'

Brooke stared at me for a moment, as if she was trying to determine how sincere I was.

'Are you serious Matthew?'

'I'm deadly serious. Do you think I would pay five hundred dollars to play private detective if I wasn't?'

'Oh, so that's why you booked me. Just for info was it.'

'Well…yes…but… Look, you are stunning. Beautiful. I told you that. But be fair, you are just using me for the money you earn so it shouldn't matter to you what my motive is.'

She bowed her head and focussed on her glass as if she

was counting each bubble that fizzed to the surface before it disappeared. After a moment she looked up and smiled.

'You know something Matthew. It isn't about using. Us girls do our work. We escort guys who want a good time in Vegas and want to be seen on the arm of a pretty girl. We have to put up with some very tricky situations and some goddam creeps. It isn't us using them. They have the money and they are buying… buying a commodity. Most of the time they don't even see us as people. They just see the Las Vegas Barbie Doll. But that's not who I am. I'm not Brooke. That's not my real name. I don't know why I'm telling you this. My name is Claire. Not so glamorous… just Claire. All I'm looking for is a nice normal guy, you know. Maybe someone like you. Someone who doesn't want anything from me other than to get to know me. These guys out there who pay five hundred dollars for my time are not interested in me. Sure they want to be seen with me. But that's just so they can be the big guy. Hey, dude look at the babe I got. Aren't I the big guy. You know what? I'd only just met you and you asked about me. Most guys don't do that. Sure they do at some point but not right away. Usually they're just trying to impress. You know, talk about themselves. That's what I'm looking for. Somebody interested in me…a normal guy. Maybe that's why I am telling you this stuff… because you seem normal.'

I walked over and sat on the sofa next to her. The conversation was not going where I wanted it to but I felt for her all of a sudden.

'Hey, Brooke…Claire. Look, first off *looking for* is when you have lost something. Sometimes it's best just to explore. Exploration doesn't have a pre-meditated outcome. When you explore you don't know what you're going to get. No expectations. That way you find out about people.'

She looked into my eyes. I wasn't sure she got me. Five hundred dollars for a gorgeous girl and I was behaving like a social worker.

'Now listen to me. I don't have much time to sort things out here. I need to know if you know Krystal or if you know anyone else who might. It's urgent, Claire…Brooke.'

She drained her glass and reached for the Champagne bottle.

186

'It's not her real name either…I mean, Krystal. That's just her, you know…her name is Pauline.'

'You do know her then.'

'Yes. I do…but I don't know anything about money or a bag. Krystal's only been on the circuit for about six months. She lived in Dallas before she came here. She has a daughter, Emma…ten months old. Emma needs medical treatment. Some sort of eye operation.'

'Brooke…I mean Claire, I –'

'Matthew, just call me Brooke for now. It's ok.'

'Sure. Yes. I don't have any right to call you Claire.'

'It's not that. It just might be simpler at the moment. If we're out in public it's easier. I know a lot of people in Vegas most of whom I don't want knowing anything about my private life.'

'I understand. Now, I need to get in touch with Pauline. As soon as possible. Do you have any contact details you could let me have?'

Brooke reached out and touched the back of my hand.

'I can't give you her details Matthew. Not without telling her. Look, why don't I try contacting her tomorrow. I'll tell her that she needs to get in touch with you urgently. I have your number.'

I was relieved at getting something positive.

'Ok, thanks. But please make sure she knows just how urgent this is.'

Brooke left my room at precisely 10.30. Four hours exactly. We had shared a couple of gins from my fridge and chatted about Pauline, life, relationships and London. I parted company with her at the Central Lobby Bar. I was exhausted by the events of the day. I decided that an early night was what was needed.

'Hey, buddy. How you doin?'

I wheeled round at the greeting. Richard Heydon, the gun salesman, stood beaming at me.

'I thought we were gonna hook up? What you been up to?'

'Oh, hi Richard. Just been you know…hectic.'

'Yeah, I bet. All those pretty ladies.' A slap on my back

accompanied his conspiratorial wink. 'So what you up to tonight? Any action?'

'I was thinking of going back to my room...long day. Exhausted to tell you the truth.'

'Not surprised. Just seen that little hottie you were with. How d'you get them chicks buddy? Is it the accent or what?'

I smiled at him and said nothing. Not because I wanted him to think that I was some sort of superstud but mainly because I did not want to get into that conversation. My smile seemed to satisfy him.

'Yeah, I get it. Listen, let me get you a drink before you go. Yeah?'

His exuberant manner and slightly slurred speech suggested that he'd had a few drinks already and although I didn't really want another drink at that point, I decided it would humour him if I joined him for one. Two Buds were ordered. He began a series of questions all related to the art of seducing the opposite sex. Finally I got tired of it.

'So, Richard, how have you been getting on then with the ladies? Didn't you have a date the other day?'

'Oh yeah...lunch. With Kate. Yeah, went ok. Nice girl. From New York. Works in the jewellery trade. Didn't get anywhere if you know what I mean.'

'Well it was only a lunch Richard,' I said, wondering if he expected women to fall at his feet in restaurants. 'You not seeing her again?'

'Yeah, well, kinda. She said she might be around tonight but she was meeting a girlfriend. Hey, you don't think she's...you know...'

'She's what?'

'You know. The girlfriend bit?'

I had to laugh. 'It's just an expression Richard. It's a friend who happens to be a girl.'

'Oh ok. I guess I'll look her up again. Hey, you don't fancy it tonight, do you? Me and you...look Kate and her friend up. Whaddya say?'

I had to admire his enthusiasm. 'Another time Richard. I'm whacked.'

'Hey buddy, you're in Vegas. We don't do whacked in Vegas. The night is young.' He glanced at a gold braceleted watch. 'Ten forty five. Man, only children go to bed at this time in Vegas. A couple of beers. That's all. Maybe run into your pals.' He reached across and slapped me heartily on the shoulder. 'C'mon. Whaddya say?'

I slugged half the Budweiser and gave in to persuasion.

'Ok, ok. But just an hour or so. Not much left to bring to the party.'

'Attaboy Matt. Whaddya need to bring? Just yourself and a good attitude. That'll take care of the goddam party buddy.' He smiled, picked up his beer, the bottle poised in front of his face. 'Say, where are your friends tonight anyway?'

'They're over at the Hyde bar then going to the Tryst Club up at the Wynn.'

'Well no sense in us sitting here buddy. Let's get our butts over the Hyde. There could be some hot ladies in town tonight. Get in amongst them. They won't be able to resist once we all hook up.'

I knew Richard's bull in a china shop was not the way to impress the ladies. I'd made too many mistakes myself in the dating game. I felt the need to dispense a little advice.

'Maybe you just need to chill a bit Richard. Play it cool, you know.'

'What, like you English guys?'

'Yeah, maybe,' I said, thinking back to my dating days that had been anything but cool. 'You don't need to try and impress. Just be yourself. Chill a bit.'

'You know, you could be right buddy. Let's go show them ladies exactly how we chill.'

I finished my beer. Perhaps Richard Heydon was one of those guys who would never get it.

20

As I headed towards the hotel exit I caught sight of him. His outline was unmistakeable, an instant recognition that turned all my in-built sensors to flight mode. One of the two guys, the taller, heavier one that had pursued me through Caesar's earlier in the day, was standing just inside the entrance looking to his right as if searching for something. Why he was still wearing the same dark glasses in the twilight world of the Paris casino puzzled me but I didn't feel the need to ask. Perhaps the shaded vision they afforded had limited his observations skills, which was just as well for me, as he hadn't yet spotted me. I recalled the chase earlier and decided evasive action was more agreeable than a wild pursuit around the hotel floor. I grabbed Richard by the arm.

'Err…Richard, you go on ahead without me. I left…my… erm…I mean, I need to pick up some more cash…from my room. I'll catch up, ok?' My gaze remained fixed on the guy in the doorway. I heard Richard's reply.

'Oh, ok buddy. No problem. See you in the Hyde.'

I turned in my tracks and began to walk away slowly, trying not to attract attention. I had gone no more than a few yards when Richard's voice boomed out.

'Hey, Matt. Wait. You wanna borrow some bucks ma man? Save time.'

I turned instinctively on hearing my name. I wasn't the only one who had heard it. Ahead of me the guy in the dark shades spun round in the direction of the voice. In the time it took him to focus I ducked between two rows of slot machines. Too late. I realised he'd spotted me. I broke into a trot and headed across the casino floor, through the crowds milling around the roulette and blackjack tables. A glance behind me told me I was being followed. I continued to the far end of the casino and then turned right towards the Central Lobby Bar. With its location right in the middle of the floor there was nowhere to hide and I had no time to take stock of my next move. I was simply focussed on putting distance between me and my pursuer. So much for trying to avoid a chase around the hotel. I headed straight on, past the elevators into the shopping boulevard, without a backward glance. The long narrow boulevard eventually took me into an open space. To one side, a sign across a square balconied entrance said '*Les Centres Des Conventions.*' I hesitated just long enough to see if I had lost my pursuer. There was no immediate sign of him. My next decision was influenced by the need to mingle with people. A convention centre meant meetings. Meetings meant people. People remaining in one place. Easier to mingle.

The main hallway of '*Les Centres Des Conventions*' was lined on both sides with ornate mirrored arches, its floor covered end to end in a highly elaborate blue patterned carpet. A gold leafed moulded ceiling held a continuous line of crystal chandeliers. I had no idea where I was or where I should go next. Ahead of me a sign indicated directions to a number of ballrooms – Rivoli, Champagne and Concorde. I made my way to the nearest, the Champagne Ballroom.

I entered the room to find hundreds of people standing around in a variety of groups, chatting, drinking and generally enjoying some sort of social interaction. I paused for a moment. Most of the men were in business suits. The women in evening wear. The room was massive, its presentation continuing the old world French décor theme of the main hallway. At first glance it seemed an ideal place to lay low for a while, but doubt began to creep over me. Whatever the event was I could well be revealed as a gatecrasher. It was cover I needed, not attention. I turned back towards the door. Just as I stepped outside I caught sight of my pursuer at the end of the hallway. There was no way I could get past him. I ducked back into the ballroom, closed the door and turned to see what my options were. A waiter in a white jacket and white gloves approached, tray in hand, several glasses of Champagne balanced perfectly on its surface.

'Champagne Sir?'

I took a glass. If I was going to mingle I had to look inconspicuous.

'Your ID pass Sir? Have you lost it?' The waiter pointed to my chest.

'ID? Err…no…no…I must have…err, forgotten to collect it. I was, you know, running late.'

'Not a problem Sir. I have them back here. Follow me.'

'It's ok. Don't worry. It's fine, I'll just stay here out of the way.'

'Everybody must display their ID, Sir, otherwise security get nervous.'

Security. I glanced around. There was no security in sight but perhaps that was the point. Keep a low profile and spot the gatecrasher. I decided I had better conform. Better to style it out than to get kicked out. We stopped by a small cloakroom in one corner of the room. The waiter pulled a box from a shelf. Inside lay seven or eight laminated ID passes, each attached to a gold ribbon.

'These are the ones that were not collected Sir. Mostly no shows and those who couldn't make the event. Shall I check the guest list for you?'

'Oh…no…no. Don't worry. There's mine.' I pointed totally randomly into the box. The waiter held the box out towards me. I picked up the first one I saw. *Jack Hathaway (South Carolina)*.

'Let me help you with that Mister Hathaway, Sir.' He took the pass from me and placed it around my neck. 'You have a good evening Sir.'

A good evening. Unlikely. I was caught between getting roughed up by some villain who was on my tail or trying to style it out as a guest at some sort of convention. I decided to sip the Champagne quietly in a corner and then try to make an exit later on. Twenty minutes or so should be enough. My pursuer was bound to go looking elsewhere by then. Maybe, if I was really fortunate the message from my lawyer contact may get through to stop him coming after me.

'Hey, you from the Charleston office, buddy? Do I know you?'

The voice took me by surprise. I turned to see a portly, middle aged man, his hair almost white and curling over both ears, standing to one side. In his right hand he held what seemed to be a whiskey glass. His left pointed to my pass.

'The Charleston office? Well, South Carolina, yes...yes. That's what it...err, yeah...Charleston.'

'I didn't know you guys were comin. I'm Rubin Gorestanger, area manager mid-west division. Originally a Noo Yorker but took over mid-west three years ago. How you doin?' he said, the words elongated by a distinct drawl.

'Err...good to meet you Robin. I'm...I'm...err...Jack Hathaway –'

'Rubin. It's Rubin. You mean, your Jack's representative?'

'Err yes...his representative. Jack Hathaway's representative. I am...him.'

'He didn't say nuthin about you comin?'

'No...all a bit last minute. They couldn't even get me my own security pass it was so...err, as I say, last minute. I stood in, you know...once he got...err, sick.'

'Sick? Jeez, he's had some rough luck then. Once he cried off I didn't think nobody was comin to collect the award. He'd had a flight booked an all. But glad you made it. So, how's the old bastard doin?'

'Well...you know...not so good. Not...since he...you know, he got the...the flu thing–'

'The flu? Funny, he didn't mention that. On top of everything else, fer chrissakes. His poor wife, eh?'

'Of course, yes, tough them both getting it.'

'What? She got it too? That's rough. He phoned to say he couldn't make it tonight. We knew his wife was pregnant but then he called to say she'd gone into labour. And now she's got the flu? Man that's real tough.'

'You know how it is. It's not…not uncommon to catch the… err…flu when you're pregnant. It's the immune system. It gets… you know, gets…down.'

'Hey I didn't know that. That sucks. Still, Jack's normally right on the money. I'm surprised he didn't say nuthin about you comin over to Vegas.'

'Well, you know, he…he had a lot on his mind. What with the fluey…err, pregnant…wife, thing. Probably why he didn't say I was coming…with everything going on. Can't have been thinking straight.'

'I guess not. So he sent you to represent South Carolina. What's your name buddy?'

I took a gulp of Champagne. 'It's err…Malachie…err…Martin Malachie.' I had no time to think but somehow I knew I shouldn't give my real name since I was registered in the hotel.

'You must be a new boy in that office. You Australian by any chance? Your accent…'

'Err, no…I'm not. Been there, in the office…six weeks. I'd been working overseas before that.'

'Anyway, glad you could make it. Shame you missed the dinner and the awards ceremony. But what the hell. You're here.'

I breathed a sigh of relief and ignored the beads of sweat forming on my brow.

'Yes, great to be here even last minute…you know. Jack's… err…flu…pregnancy thing, gave me an opportunity I hadn't expected. Been fairly low key, up until now.'

'Well, you can't have been that low key buddy. Your goddam office just won realtor of the fuckin year. Record sales. Hit the condo market big time. Record sales. Exceeded all targets. Condominium targets for the region blown right out the fuckin water. Hell of a performance. And as Jack said, all of you guys made it happen. So congratulations to you Martin.'

'It's Matt…err…I mean, matter of fact…Jack's right, yes. And thank you Robin…sorry Rubin.'

Realtor of the year? It went over my head. I resisted the urge to ask what a realtor did. My focus was on looking for a way out.

The last thing I needed was Rubin Gorestanger. Another waiter approached with more Champagne. I grabbed a glass and took a hit.

'Very impressed Martin. Just shows when you go for it what can be done. Got a hell of a fuckin year to look forward to. Whaddya say?'

'Sounds good, Mister...Mister Gorestanger. The market's growing daily. No reason why we shouldn't beat them...err... condom minimum levels again this year,' I said, by way of small talk and in the hope that he would move on.

'Hey, I told you. It's Rubin. Call me Rubin. Now listen up buddy. You missed the dinner and all the award stuff. Big disappointment for all these hard working sales people here. They wanted to know how you did it. Tell you what, let's get you up there. Nice surprise for the company now you made it.' He grabbed me by the arm.

'Sorry Rubin. Where are we going?'

'You're gonna tell these people out here how you took the condo market by storm. Unprecedented sales this year, in fact... ever. They need people like you to keep them motivated.'

'That's ok, Rubin. I prefer to play it low key, you know.'

'Low key? You outta yer fuckin mind? You guys bring in the biggest numbers in company history and you wanna go low key? Buddy, you schlepped all the way over here. You gotta tell it like it is, you know? This way buddy.'

Rubin Gorestanger was clearly some big cheese in the room. As he led me forward the crowded floor parted to let him through. I took a deep breath. Style it out. He obviously wanted me to meet a few people and tell them some stuff about the sale of condoms. I knew nothing at all about the condom business but it couldn't be that difficult to talk about. Five minutes glad handing some execs and I'd bluff my way out and get back to my room. They'd all had a few drinks so it couldn't be too tricky.

We reached the front of the room. Rubin beckoned a member of staff towards him. The staff member handed him a microphone.

'Ladeeees and genelmen. Can I have your undivided attention for a moment please. We have a surprise visitor here tonight. We gave out the awards earlier during our sumptuous dinner but we were not able to give the top award to our sales team of the year. But better late than never, we now have a representative for our realtor of the year award. All the way from the South Carolina office in Charleston would you please welcome Mister Martin... Mister Martin Malachie.'

I had no time to be shocked. As he introduced me an assistant pinned a radio mike to my lapel and led me up a low flight of steps to a raised platform. On the wall behind, a large blue and gold banner announced that I was at the '*Sure Condos Realtor of the Year Awards 2013.*' Another glass of Champagne was thrust into my hand.

'For the toast, Sir.'

A spotlight swung round and captured me in its circular light. I glanced down to see several hundred faces looking in my direction. The applause gave me time to think but my thoughts were not composed and focussed. What the hell was a realtor? What could I tell them about condom sales? I checked to my right and then to my left. Stages usually had exit wings, a curtain to slip through, somewhere to make an escape and leg it. Not this one. It was nothing more than an extended, raised platform, specially constructed for the event and neatly tucked into an alcove in the wall. Legging it was not an option. I was about to come clean and announce that there had been a major mix up when I saw him again. Right at the back. The dark glasses, a sinister touch in the low lighting of the room, focussed my attention. Somehow my pursuer had found me and slipped in unnoticed. He stood, arms folded, his gaze directed straight ahead. The applause began to quieten until a complete hush had descended on the room. I had no choice. The safest place for me at that point seemed to be the stage. One word reverberated through my head. Improvise.

'Good evening ladies and gentlemen. Err...well first of all, it's quite a surprise for me to be here...I mean as my...err... my colleague, Jack...Jack Hawthorne...' I noticed one or two surprised faces. 'Sorry Hathaway...it's the Champagne. Gets you in the end. Yes, Jack...he sends his apologies. He was struck down suddenly with pregnancy…I mean flu…and his wife struck too…she caught it, the err…pregnancy bug…sorry, the flu bug, as well as going into labour.'

I raised my glass and took a long slurp. The bubbles fizzed in my nose. I took a deep breath. It seemed I just had to go for it.

'Obviously, it seems our Jack's not been making use of his own products then, what with his wife up the…err...I mean pregnant. He sells them by the bucket load but not to himself it would seem.'

My attempt at humour went right over the heads of the audience. No reaction, apart from puzzled faces. Obviously English humour was different from what Americans were used to. I decided to play it straight. At the back of the room my pursuer continued his staring vigilance. I took another gulp of Champagne, cleared my throat and decided to go for it.

'Anyway, erm…first of all, on behalf of the Charles…erm… Town office in…Carolina, I'd like to say thank you for the award that Mister Gorestanger has presented tonight. It's fantastic to be the real…real thing of the year…' I glanced over my shoulder for help from the banner. 'The real tor person…oh and did anyone else notice the typo.' I jabbed my thumb behind me in the direction of the banner. 'Condos. Hey, can't get it right every time, eh?' There was no response. I carried on, again regretting my attempt at humour. 'Anyway, the…the err…condom market is bigger than ever before. We in the Charles Town office had record sales and exceeded our condom minimum targets because we focussed directly on the customer. More and more people are having it… err, sex, that is…having sex and the quality of our product is what they need in order to feel comfortable and confident. Our product is about the materials. We use the best quality rubber, aware of the need for sensitivity.'

I noticed a murmur and a lone voice. 'Rubber condos?'

'Yes, indeed. Essentially our product is nothing more than rubber but we focus on the experience.' My mind raced. The stress of the situation seemed to drag everything I had ever heard about condoms from somewhere in my deepest subconscious. 'So in the Charles Town Office we place the focus on the fact that what we sell is an ultra-fine product with extra lubricant for increased sensitivity. We provide variety too. Our narrower than standard product line provides a tighter fit for those who like… err…snugness. So by giving our customers what they want, by focussing on the experience alone we have managed to exceed, way beyond even our own expectations, our condom minimum sales requirement. So on behalf of the Charles Town office I'd like to thank everyone for recognising me…err…us…with this award tonight.'

I stood back to denote that I had finished and waited for the customary applause. Total silence until a heckler piped up from the floor.

'You selling real estate too, buddy?'

The audience broke out into a ripple of laughter. At the back of the room my pursuer stood and watched. There seemed to be no way out.

'Err, thank you Sir. That reminds me. Has anyone got any questions?' I paused, eyes fixed on the dark glasses at the back. 'What about you Sir, back there?' I pointed at my pursuer. All heads turned. 'Yes, you Sir, without the ID security pass? I know you came in late so happy to answer any questions you might have.'

I saw him shuffle towards the door as the spotlight swung onto the audience, but too late to avoid the sudden attention of two uniformed security men who emerged from behind a screen to one side. As they escorted him towards the exit I raised my Champagne glass. From my right I saw Rubin Gorestanger approach the stage carrying a glass sculpture.

'A toast then to Sure Condoms and our Charles Town office. May they have continued success in the coming year. Err… coming being the…the operative word. I'm afraid I will be unable to participate in that success as I have just, this very day, decided to resign my position…err…for personal reasons.'

I drained the Champagne glass and left the stage.

21

I got up early. I had things to do. I had to get some order into my thoughts. My first task was to track down Arturo Magana-Gallegos. It was probably too early to find him in a casino but this was Vegas where time doesn't exist.

The call came through at 10.30am as I walked up to Caesar's Palace.

'*Matthew. It's Brooke. I've spoken with Pauline. She will see you. Have you got a pen?*'

'No. Text me her number.'

'*I can't. She doesn't want you to have her number. She said she'd meet you.*'

'Ok. Where?'

'*It's a diner...on East Tropicana Avenue. It's called Coco's. Any taxi driver will know it. It's not far from the MGM Grand.*'

'Can you text me the details? What time?'

'*An hour or so...say eleven thirty? That good for you?*'

'Sure. No problem. Oh...and how will I know her?'

'*She'll be wearing a red jacket, jeans and sneakers. She's about twenty four, same height as me, black hair...oh and big boobs.*'

'Err...ok...well, I should be able to find her then. Thanks for your help with this Brooke. I appreciate it.'

'*No problem Matthew...but hey, go easy with her. She's very nervous about all this. I'll text you now. Good luck.*'

My mobile rang again.

'*Mate, where are ya?*'

'Hi Ces. Just on my way up to Caesar's. Looking for that Arturo bloke. What are you doing?'

'Just woke up mate. Where'd you get to last night? You didn't show. You doing the mumble with that bird?'

'No, Ces. Don't ask. I was going to come up but I ran into one of the villains again so let's just say I took a little detour and then decided I'd have an early night.'

'Mate...an early night? What's the matter with ya? So what happened with the villain then? You ok?'

'Oh, nothing happened. I gave him the slip. Hopefully he'll get the message from the lawyer bloke to lay off now. So how was your night?'

'Blinding mate. You missed a good one last night. Ran into your mate, the gun geezer.'

'Richard? Yeah, he said he was going to look you up.'

'He did mate. Got him off his face. He was tryin to chase birds all night. Matter of fact he was even trying to chat your bird up.'

'My bird? What bird?'

'You know, the bird at the hotel.'

'What Erin?'

'Oh right mate. Is Erin your bird now then?' Cecil chuckled.

'No, I mean...I meant...I don't know any bird from the hotel.'

'Yeah you do. Jaz reckons you had a few run ins with her.'

'Who Kimberley? The American? She was there?'

'Yeah. Kimberley. She was asking for you?'

'Asking for me? Only so she could get out of my way I reckon. She doesn't like me Ces.'

'Maybe not mate. She was asking where you were. Looks like she's into Jaz though. Couldn't leave him alone. As for matey boy...what's his name?'

'Richard.'

'Yeah, he didn't get a look in. He left there about half twelve. Couldn't take the pace with us Brits. Reckons he was gonna look up his dinner date, Kate. Not that he was in any fit state to do the mumble. Anyway, you get anything off that little hottie you was with last night?'

200

'Matter of fact I did Ces. I'm meeting up with Krystal around half eleven, at some diner called Coco's. I'll let you know what happens.'

'*You tracked her down then? Nice one geeze. Keep me posted. Catch ya later.*'

I arrived at Caesars and headed straight for the casino. There was no sign of Arturo but Maria was behind her table. She had no punters right at that moment so I was in luck. She seemed pleased to see me and after the usual pleasantries I asked about Arturo. He had been in the night before and played until about three in the morning. He normally came through around lunch time. I asked Maria whether she had noticed my bag on the Friday night. She said she had seen me with a bag. It was her job to be observant but mostly she focussed on what was happening on the table. If she remembered correctly I had put it down on the floor when I began to play. I asked if she remembered me leaving with the bag. She was sure that she did. She was discreet enough not to ask me any questions. I thanked her and asked her if Arturo came by could she get a message to him for me. The problem was I didn't know how I could reach him but I needed to see him as soon as possible. I told Maria that I was off to Coco's Diner but that Arturo could find me at the Paris later on.

I hailed a taxi on the Strip and headed for the diner. It took ten minutes in the traffic. The taxi pulled off the busy highway into the car park and dropped me outside the entrance. Cocoa's was a typical American style diner, rows of fixed tables and leather back to back sofa style booths, many of them occupied already. I spotted Pauline's red jacket straight away. She was early and sat alone, nervously fiddling with a coffee cup. I slid into the seat opposite.

'Krystal...Pauline?'

'Yes...it is. You must be Matthew. Claire said you'd be coming?'

'Yes. Thanks for meeting up.' I held both hands out in front in a calming gesture. 'Look, before we do anything let me just assure you I am not here to cause you any trouble. I assume that Brooke...Claire told you some of what this is about? It's just that

I'm in a lot of trouble myself. I'm only meant to be here on a holiday and somehow I've got mixed up in this. It's not good.'

Pauline looked down at her coffee cup, her eyes filled with tears.

'I know...I know. I'm sorry. I've been worried about this. I knew I'd made a mistake when I saw how much money was in the bag. I wasn't thinking straight when I took it. It's just that... it was there...it was...a chance. I didn't realise it was so much. Just that the guy I was with seemed to be throwing cash around and I didn't think he'd miss it. But it was a mistake, I know. I was worried he'd come after me.'

'Who Cecil?'

'You know him?'

'He's my friend. It's not his money. He isn't after you. He found it and thought...look, Pauline, I haven't got much time. There are people after me and I need it back. I won't involve you. There is no need to mention anything as long as I get it back. I have until tomorrow to return it otherwise there will be some serious trouble. You do still have it?'

I saw the expression on Pauline's face tighten as I asked the question and the colour desert her cheeks.

'You still have the money, don't you Pauline?' I asked again. 'You only took it the other night. You must still have it, surely?'

Her voice began to shake. My heart began to thud. She had to have the money.

'Yes...but...not...not all of it.'

'Not all of it? What do you mean?'

A waitress interrupted. 'You wanna order something Sir?'

'Err...yeah...erm...I'll take a coffee. Cream...sugar. Thanks.' I turned back to Pauline who was sniffling into a tissue. 'The money, Pauline. How much have you got?'

She wiped away a tear and squeezed both eyes tight shut, stifling a sob.

'I needed money. My daughter...for my daughter...Emma. She needs an eye operation. She's only three and...' The tears came again.

I reached out a hand to comfort her and placed it on her arm.

'It's ok. It's ok. Tell me.'

'My daughter…she was born with a degenerative muscular problem in her right eye. I had been trying to save for an operation but it's so difficult. And she needs constant treatment. If she doesn't have the operation soon she may lose the sight of her eye completely. I took a loan a few weeks ago to pay for it and for other treatment that she's had. I couldn't get a loan from my bank. So, I borrowed it from a loan company. It was recommended by a guy I met in a casino. But I was having trouble paying it back. Their payment terms are so tough. And now the operation is all booked and paid for by the loan money. So when I saw the bag with all that cash….I just…it was the answer. It meant I could sort out the loan and I could just focus on Emma. I didn't really think it through.'

The waitress placed a coffee on the table. My hand shook as I pulled the cup towards me.

'Ok. I understand that Pauline. But when you say you haven't got all of the money what have you done with it? How much have you spent?' I kind of knew it wasn't going to be good news by the way she hesitated before she answered.

'Thirty-five thousand–'

'Thirty-five grand!'

As the number registered my right hand shot forward in an involuntary spasm catching my coffee cup. A large slop of coffee splattered over the table top causing Pauline to jerk back in her seat. The waitress was at the table in an instant, a napkin at the ready to soak up the spillage.

'You wanna refill, Sir?'

'Err…yes…thank you…sorry about the…the spillage.' I turned back to Pauline. 'Thirty-five?'

'Yes. I owed thirty-five thousand...with the interest. I took it straight round to the loan people on Saturday. I wanted to get it sorted. I panicked. I had the money and I just thought, I've done it now…taken it. So I went and paid them back. I am so sorry but I was desperate.' She wiped her eyes again with the damp tissue.

I let it sink in. I knew we could not go to the dodgy loan company and ask for thirty-five grand back and tell them it was a mistake. My mind slipped into calculation mode. If Pauline had spent thirty-five thousand and Cecil had blown eight and a half thousand that meant I had forty-three and a half grand to make up. Then I remembered the five hundred to Brooke. A nice round forty-four thousand dollars short of the half million I had to return. And that was with the eleven thousand left in the room. Terrific. How was I supposed to raise that amount? I didn't have the time to work it out at that point. First of all I had to make sure Pauline had the rest of the cash.

'Pauline, look I understand your predicament. It's your daughter. I know that. Nothing we can do about the money you've spent but you have to let me have the rest back. Can you get it?'

'I have it. I brought it with me. I just want to be rid of it.'

'You have it here?'

'Yes, in my car. I have the bag. There's four hundred and forty five thousand dollars in there. I counted it. I'd never seen so much money.'

'Seriously? You're carrying that much money in your car? You weren't followed, were you?'

'It's in the trunk. Nobody followed me.' She frowned and leant towards me. 'Why would anyone? They don't know I have it. It just looks like a rucksack anyway. I'll go get it.'

She slid out of her seat, her face a bit more relaxed. I assumed that was because I hadn't gone ballistic about the spent cash. But what could I do? I had no idea. I sipped my coffee and waited for Pauline to return. She came back within five minutes carrying a black rucksack with a Nike logo emblazoned across the front. It was identical to my camera bag. The blood drained from my face as the full impact of what appeared to have been a very costly mistake hit me. Clearly Cecil had picked up the wrong bag. Pauline slipped into her seat and placed the bag on the table.

'Here it is Matthew. Do you want to count it?'

'Count it? What here? Right in the middle of the diner? Do you think I'm nuts? Pauline, I'm going to have to trust you on this.'

'You can trust me Matthew. I just want rid of it. I hope there is no comeback to me. I just want things to be right for Emma...' Her voice tailed off as she wiped her eyes again. 'The money... it's all there. I promise.'

My heart said I could trust her but my head reminded me that I had never seen her before in my life and I could not afford to be stitched up. I needed to be certain. I pulled the zips of the rucksack apart and looked inside. It was filled with bundles of dollars similar to the wad that had been left in Cecil's room. I lifted out two wads of notes and flicked through them below the table level to avoid looking conspicuous. They seemed to be intact. I stuffed them back into the bag and pulled the zips closed. As I placed the bag on the seat next to me I caught the quizzical gaze of the waitress. She looked away quickly and walked to the back of the serving area.

I turned to Pauline. I felt sorry for her. I realised why she had done what she had. In that moment I knew I had to trust her and that the rest of money was all there just as she said. Well...all but thirty-five thousand dollars.

22

The mid-morning sun bathed my face in a warm glow as I stood outside Coco's on East Tropicana Avenue staring at the traffic. I held the black rucksack tight to my shoulder grateful that I had at least got the bulk of the money back. I would worry about the rest later. My first task was to get what I had back to safety.

I had thought of asking Pauline if she would drop me back at the Paris but her haste to leave after she had handed the bag over suggested that she probably didn't want a lot more to do with me. I scanned the carriageway for a taxi. There were none in sight. I began to pace the sidewalk, my eyes glued to the traffic. Thoughts came in random cycles. I had nearly half a million dollars on me and couldn't get a taxi. How was I going to make up the forty-four thousand dollars difference? If I did find a way was there enough time? Perhaps the villains would be happy enough at getting most of the money back. Unlikely. Maybe the lawyer who represented them would be reasonable. He'd said I was a *regular guy* so maybe he would understand. Even more unlikely. He'd also called me an *English tourist schmuck* so clearly he didn't hold me in any great regard. My thoughts were interrupted by a voice behind me.

'You were looking for me, Matthew?'

I wheeled round.

'Arturo. Oh…hi.' I was completely surprised to see him even though I had wanted to catch up with him. 'What are you doing here?'

He ignored my question. He stood square-on to me, legs slightly apart, one hand in the pocket of what seemed an overly smart grey suit for that time of the morning. In his other hand a half smoked cigarette wafted pale blue smoke into the air.

'What can I do for you then Matthew?' he asked.

I wasn't sure Arturo could do anything for me at that point. I'd retrieved the bag and now assumed that Cecil had simply picked up the wrong one in the Bond Bar.

'I did want to ask you something Arturo but it doesn't matter now. I'm just getting a taxi back to my hotel.' I felt exposed out on the street. The cash was making me nervous, the open space uncomfortable.

Arturo raised the cigarette to his lips and took a long drag.

'So what was it you wanted to know?' he said, a plume of smoke emerging from his mouth as he spoke.

I stepped back into the diner parking area, where it was less exposed than on the street. Arturo followed. I wondered how he had known where I would be and then I remembered Maria. I had told her that I was going to Coco's. She must have thought I was going for breakfast and mentioned it to Arturo. Still, it surprised me that he would want to follow me down there.

'I wanted to ask you about my bag, Arturo. I'd lost it and I thought that you might have seen –'

'You seem to have found it now,' he said. 'Hand it over.'

'Sorry?'

'Hand it over Matthew. I want to see what's in it,' he said, his dark eyes cold and focussed.

I froze in disbelief. Why would Arturo want my bag…unless? My disbelief turned to utter astonishment at his next move. His right hand shot out of his jacket pocket, clasping a short pistol, which he pointed directly at me.

'I said hand it over. Now.'

The shock coursed through me. I shuffled the bag off my shoulder and held it out towards him. Just as I did so I caught sight of a taxi approaching in my peripheral vision but my gaze remained fixed on the gun. Five minutes earlier would have been good I thought. In the distance I heard the wail of a siren.

Arturo grabbed the bag, crouched on the floor and parted the zips. A satisfied grunt told me he had found what he wanted.

He never managed to rise from his crouch.

The kick came from his right and caught him square in the ribcage sending him sprawling across the ground. The gun flew from his hand and swivelled across the tarmac. My eyes were drawn to the gun and then immediately back to where the kick had come from. Cecil. He stood over Arturo who lay in a semi-foetal position gripping his side where the kick had done the damage. He stared up at Cecil, surprise and fear in his eyes.

'What's this got to do with you?'

Cecil raised his arm, his fist clenched.

'Plenty my friend. What's the next question you want the wrong fucking answer to?'

Arturo raised a hand to ward off Cecil's anger.

Cecil lowered his face towards him.

'Listen, mug, don't even dream about coming near me or my mate again. You hearing me?'

In the background the siren had got louder. Adrenaline, surprise, confusion and panic merged into a volatile cocktail within me. I grabbed the gun from the ground and threw it towards Cecil who instinctively caught it and then dropped it immediately.

'What the fuck you doin, you nob. Grab that fucking bag and get outta here.'

I scooped up the bag and stood looking at Cecil. 'Ces...how... what –'

'Geezer, shut the fuck up and get outta here. You lose that bag again you're in the shit. Go.'

The last thing I saw was Cecil throwing a punch at the rising Arturo as he tried to get to his feet. A crowd of people had stopped to stare. I started to run. Behind me the siren wailed loudly almost upon me. I reached the corner of a junction and turned into a side road. A glance to my right. A police car had stopped right outside Coco's, blue and red lights oscillating across its roof. I ran on for another hundred yards or so before stopping to get my bearings and my breath. To my left was McCarran Airport. In the distance away to my right was the gleaming blue tower of the MGM. I knew it was not far from the Strip. I ran in that direction using it as a landmark. As I reached the end of the road, I stopped dead in my tracks. It was part instinct and part recognition. A guy in a black suit and dark glasses. The suit was not appropriate and the look was familiar. The tall, heavy built villain who had chased me into Caesar's. I knew that wherever he was his accomplice would not be far behind. The mumbled shout confirmed there were two of them. The lawyer had said he had called them off but evidently not. I wasn't about to discuss this point with them either. I turned on my heels and began to run.

At the end of the road I turned sharp left and slipped into a quieter street across to my right. Ahead of me was a shop. A sign above it read '*Bellissimi Fiori.*' A vast floral display outside showed it was a florist shop. I didn't want another chase like I'd had the previous day. I was already exhausted. I ran through the shop doorway. I should have been looking where I was going but, blinded by panic, I didn't see the vacuum cleaner wire stretched across the floor. My foot caught it, sending me sprawling across the floor straight into the floral display next to the counter. Three vases of flowers pitched off the shelf at the impact, tipping what felt like half a gallon of water over my head and upper body. In shock, I jumped up catching my left foot on a metal display rack that held several rows of terracotta pots. The stand tipped forward hurling at least eight of the pot plants in my direction. I rolled to one side in the puddle on the floor but could not avoid a cascade of soil and plants landing on my prone body. I was covered in a congealing mess of mud as if I had just stepped off the rugby pitch on a November afternoon. I rolled onto my side and grabbed the bag that had slipped off my shoulder. I caught the look of horror on the florists face. She began screaming in Italian. I scrambled to my feet and headed for a door at the back of the shop.

'I am so sorry,' I called out, as I raced through the back door.

Outside, I found myself in a narrow fenced in yard cluttered with cardboard boxes and discarded plastic flowerpots. To one side, three large waste bins stood in a neat line, their lids unable to compress the contents into the available space. Ahead there was another building backing on to the property. To my right a metal staircase hugged the side of the building. With nowhere to go I started to run up it. Halfway up I could see the flat roof of a single storey adjoining building, an extension of the shop next to the florist. Further ahead, at the back of that property, there was a wall. I swung a leg over the iron railing of the stairs and clambered over. A short jump and I was on the flat roof. I scrambled over the edge and lowered myself down the side. Another jump and I was on the ground. I turned to run and remembered the bag. I had left it on the roof as I manoeuvred over the edge.

'Bollocks.'

There was no sign of my pursuers. Sweat rolled down my face. Fear gripped my stomach. I had to get to the bag. At the back end of the yard I found a waste bin. I dragged it over to the extension wall and climbed on top. From there I could just reach out and touch the bag. I tugged at it with my fingertips until it was within grip reach on the edge of the roof. Just as I was about to grab it the snarling, barking and yelping of what sounded like a very pissed off dog stopped me in my tracks. From round the side of the building a large Doberman bounded out into the yard. I stood stock still, perilously balanced on the waste bin, my legs shaking as I confronted this new predicament. From next door I heard the voices. A rapid, high pitched hysterical tirade in Italian, followed by the deeper tones of two males. I couldn't see them but I knew my pursuers had found my escape route. I had a choice. Confront the Doberman or confront the two villains and the near hysterical Italian lady. The Doberman seemed the better option. At least he had no personal agenda. I swung the bag off the roof and dropped it onto the floor. It hit the ground, distracting the dog sufficiently for me to pull my polo shirt off and jump from the waste bin. As I landed, the Doberman turned towards me, his top lip curling just enough to expose his teeth. I raised the polo shirt high into the air and threw it directly at him. It caught him on the head, covering his whole face. As he lost sight of me and became preoccupied with my sweat soaked shirt, I grabbed the bag and made a run for the rear wall. Adrenaline and fear got me over the head high wall in a one shambolic, scrambling vault. I slipped down the other side and ran. I hoped that the Doberman would deter my two followers from being equally athletic.

At the main intersection I managed to hail a taxi. The driver leant towards me, took one look at my shirtless, mud-covered state and declined to take me.

'Am real sorry buddy. Ah can't get ya'll in ma vehicle lookin like dat. Whas appen to you?'

I tried pleading. 'I had an accident. I can't walk. Please…I need to get back to the Paris.'

He wasn't having it.

'Am sorry dude. You git yo'self all cleaned up and then ah can take you. Ain't nobody can git in ma cab in dat state, ya hear. No driver gonna let you ride all wet an' covered in dirt like dat. Real sorry ma friend.' With that, he hit the accelerator and sped off.

I started walking, keeping to the back roads. In the distance I could see the rear of the Paris with the tip of its Eiffel Tower protruding over the top of the building. I was sure I was not too far from the hotel but felt reluctant to come right out into the open in my conspicuous state. I pulled out my mobile and dialled Jasper. Voicemail. Next I dialled Carlos. Three rings and he answered.

'Carlos. Just listen. I need you to get a taxi and come and get me…no, listen…can you grab a shirt and a towel or something. Don't ask… just do it for me. I'll explain later. I'm at…hang on...' I looked around to see if I could see a street sign. 'Yeah…I'm at somewhere called…Kishner…Kishner Drive. I'll stay here. Ok?'

I sat on the kerbside and waited, clutching the bag. The shock of realising that somehow Arturo may be involved was beginning to sink in. So too was concern for Cecil. I had no idea what may have happened to him.

23

I stepped out of the shower and rubbed my hair dry with a hand towel. I wrapped a bath towel around me and walked into the bedroom. Carlos sat in an armchair nursing a cup of tea. The Nike bag was on the bed but I was uneasy.

'I called Jasper when you were showering Mateo. He's on his way here. He's managed to lose that Kimberley woman for half an hour. I told him to get rid of her. She's a…una sanguijuela.'

'Sangi what?'

'You know…a sucker…one of them bloodsucker things. Hangs on to you.'

'A leech?'

'Exactamente. A leech. I told him, stay away. She's trouble. Asks too many questions.'

I threw myself onto the sofa. 'Well perhaps she thinks he makes a better toy than that bloody great dildo she had in her bag.'

'Dildo?' Carlos said, his eyes wide and questioning. 'You mentioned that before.'

I was saved an explanation by a knock on the door.

'So what's going on?' Jasper said as he walked in. 'Where's Ces?'

I stood up, walked over to the kettle and flicked the switch.

'I'm not sure. I think he may have been arrested.'

'Arrested?' Jasper shot a quizzical look at Carlos. 'You never said anything about that Carlos.' Turning back towards me, he asked, 'What's he done anyway?'

'Hang on, Jasper,' I said. 'I told Carlos not to say anything until you got here. I don't know exactly what's happened with Ces. Carlos doesn't know much either. I couldn't really say a lot in the taxi.'

I spent the next ten minutes telling them the details of what had happened to me that morning. When I had finished they both sat staring at me, neither saying a word. I poured hot water onto a tea bag and stirred the brew.

'Bottom line now boys...somehow I have to get the rest of the money that I am short of and deliver the whole lot back to the people who want it. Problem is, it looks like there are three different lots after it. I hadn't reckoned with Arturo but it seems he's in the equation too. I can't figure it out though. He was fine when I first met him. He didn't do anything that made me think he was up to something.' I paused for a moment as the thought hit me. 'Except...well except that...'

'What is it Mateo?' Carlos asked.

'I don't know. Last night I was thinking things over and it occurred to me that when I was in Caesar's on the first night, I wanted to take a picture of the croupier and it was Arturo who stopped me.'

'Stopped you?' Jasper said.

'Well, not exactly stopped. Just warned me... *You can't take pictures in the casino* he said. So I didn't. I didn't open the bag to get my camera out. It may be nothing but...well, if I'd opened the bag would it have been mine or would it have been the one with the money in? And if it was the one with the money, how the hell could that have happened? I may just be putting two and two together after what he did this morning. I mean he pulled a bloody gun on me. I've never even seen a gun before, let alone have one pointed at me.'

'Well he's definitely involved now. He's come after you this morning so he must have known you had the bag,' Jasper said.

'Or just followed me. I don't know. The thing I do know is that, whether he's with the two villains who keep chasing me or the lawyer I met, I can't stay here. It won't be long before somebody comes after me again. I have to keep this bag of money safe somehow if I'm going to meet the forty-eight hour deadline. And then I have to find another forty-four friggin thousand dollars by three o'clock tomorrow afternoon. How am I supposed to do that for god's sake?'

Carlos let out a deep sigh and massaged his knee with both hands.

'You ok Carlos? That dodgy knee playing up?' Jasper asked.

'Aye, it's sore but it isnae that. I was thinking. I dunno how you're going to find all that extra money Mateo, but I have an idea about the bag.'

'You have? Let's hear it then Carlos.' I reached for my tea.

'Well yer dinnae want the bag in your room in case it gets broken into again and neither of us can keep it in ours for the same reason. So…why not put it in lost property down stairs?'

Jasper and I looked at one another, neither of us sure whether Carlos had just had a brilliant idea or a totally stupid one. We said nothing.

'See, nobody will think to ask the lost property people will they? When you think about it, who would hand in a bag with over four hundred thousand dollars inside to a lost property office?' Carlos answered his own question. 'Nobody. It's perfect. I can stick the padlock I have for my case on the zips so nobody can open it and hand it in. I'll say I found it in the lift. Simple.' He shrugged as if it really was that simple.

'Hang on a minute, Carlos,' Jasper said, 'how's he supposed to get the frigging thing back? Just walk in ask for it and walk out? They'll want him to prove it's his and you know what that means don't you? They're bound to ask him what's in it. So what's he supposed to say? Oh, just four hundred thousand bucks. Can I have it back please?'

Carlos turned and looked directly at Jasper, a smile playing across his face.

'You Sassenachs, always finding problems, eh?' He took a deep breath and turned back to me. 'You have to be adventurous sometimes Mateo. You've not got many choices here. This is what you do. You stick your passport in the bag and –'

'My passport? Oh yeah right. Just risk that too I suppose.'

'Yes, your passport. Just listen. You put, say your passport in the bag and a few t-shirts and socks over the top of the money. So when they ask you what's in there, you say your passport and some dirty sports stuff. I give you a key to the padlock. You open it in front of them and sure enough, your passport is in there. You pull out a t-shirt and some socks and you're done. The bag's yours again. They're not going to want to search through a rucksack full of what they think is dirty sports kit once they see your ID is inside it. That's proof enough it's your bag.'

'Yeah, but why can't he just show up with his passport and claim the bag?' Jasper asked.

'He could amigo. But all the passport or whatever ID he shows up with proves is that the laddie standing in front of them is who he says he is. It don't prove it's his bag. That's why they'll want to search it. To make sure what he says is in it actually is. And we don't want no search. Four hundred thousand dollars stuffed in a bag makes people suspicious. You wimme? So, the ID inside the bag ties Mateo straight to it. Couldn't be simpler.'

I had a feeling that perhaps it could all be a lot simpler but I was not quite sure how. I needed a moment to think. Carlos was right. I had few choices. I had to stash the bag.

'You know something Carlos, it might just work. Brilliant. Now all you have to do for me is come up with a blinding idea to make up the missing money so I have the original half a million and we are home and dry.'

Jasper stood up and walked towards the window. He stared for a moment out across the rooftops towards the brown ridge of the desert mountains that cut across the clear blue sky.

'So what about my idea?' he said as if speaking to some other person out on the street.

'Your idea?' I said, 'What's that then?' I took a sip of tea and waited for a response.

Jasper turned around, his face intense with concentration. 'The one I told you about yesterday by the pool. Win the money back.'

'Win it?' Carlos said and burst out laughing.

I tried to keep a straight face. 'Well, yes, you did mention winning it back now I come to think about it.'

'Well what other options you got Matt? Maybe go to a bank and get a loan? I don't think so? Find some nice rich cougar who's got money to burn and just fancies having you as her toy boy? No, that's not happening either. I know, maybe try robbing the Bellagio like they did in them Oceans movies. Yeah, that might work if you're George Clooney or Brad Pitt and somebody has written the friggin script for you. No problem then. Yeah, perhaps I should've suggested that.' Jasper's dark eyes were ablaze. I realised he was serious.

'Hey, calm down Jasper,' I said. 'Look, I know I've got sod all options but what's the odds of me getting the money back by winning it? Slim to…well…fat chance, I reckon.'

'Yeah, but look at it this way. Yesterday when I made the suggestion it was about winning half a million but now it's only forty-four grand.'

'Only forty-four? Are you out of your mind Jasper?' I said. 'Only forty…you think people go round winning forty grand just like that?'

'Aye, if you think it's that easy Jas, you're a goon man,' Carlos chipped in.

'You Jocks, Spaniards or whatever friggin nationality you are Carlos…always finding problems, eh?' Jasper gave Carlos a smug smile as he threw his words back at him. 'I know it's not easy but what I'm trying to say is, well…it's just got easier. The odds of winning half a mil are greater than that of winning forty odd grand. Stands to reason, right? And since you have no other choice at all and the odds have just got better…why not? I mean, that's what people do in Vegas. Gamble. The whole place is geared up for winning money. Some people beat the odds some of the time, don't they? If every single person always lost nobody would ever come back.'

Carlos rubbed his chin as if deep in thought. 'Maybe he has a point Mateo. You don't have any real options amigo.'

216

Jasper jumped back in at the first sign of possible support. 'Let's just for a minute say you did try winning it. Ok. Right. You take ten or twenty grand from the money you have already as your working cash. That's what you play with. There's no point in doing ten dollar bets here. You got to speculate. Maximise the odds.' Jasper saw my face and held up a hand to stop me interrupting. 'Hear me out Matt. Let's just say that in the worst case scenario you lost the lot. Now you'd owe sixty-four grand. If you do nothing you still owe forty-four. The point is, you're in the shit if you do nothing and if you try something and it don't come off, you're still in same shit. You might as well take the chance.'

I scratched my head, trying to follow Jasper's logic. 'Great. That's made me feel a whole lot better,' I said. 'So, let me see, is getting shot in the head for forty-four grand better or worse than getting shot in the fucking head for sixty-four grand?'

Jasper rolled his eye in dismissal of my negative take on his meaning.

'I think I need a beer,' I said, as the tension seeped into my body.

Carlos grabbed three beers from the fridge. 'Hey, nobody's talking about getting shot Mateo. It's all the same. If you're short of the cash you're in the dog poo. I think you havtae give it a wee go. Jasper might have a point.' He flicked the top off one of bottles and placed the bottle on the bedside table.

'Oh right. Yeah, but I'm the poor sucker who stands to take the bullet...but I do understand the point. Yeah, definitely. Getting my brains blown out for being short by sixty-four grand won't feel too much different than getting them blown out for forty-four so I might as well take the risk. That it?'

I picked up the bottle that Carlos had left on the table and took three long gulps of the cold beer. Carlos and Jasper remained silent, sensing my turmoil. I paced along the room towards the bathroom. Leaning on the sink I stared at my reflection in the mirror. I had to make a decision. A decision that could turn out to be life threatening. Jasper's idea was the height of stupidity given the amount of losers that left Vegas potless. It didn't make any sense to risk what I had. But I had no solutions, no other bright ideas myself. My choices were limited. Maybe Carlos and Jasper had the only solution given the time we had left. I took another slurp from the bottle and walked out into the room. Mentally I had resigned myself to the gambler's route.

'Ok. Ok…you've persuaded me. Looks like we're going to have to go for it.'

'Good man. We won't let you down,' Jasper said, relief on his face.

I raised my bottle in a salute to Jasper.

'I know you won't but it isn't about us. It's all about Lady Luck so let's just see what happens. Now what about Cecil? What are we going to do about him?'

'I reckon the polis have nicked him or he'd have been back by now,' Carlos said.

'You try ringing him?' Jasper asked.

'I did. No answer. It was funny that cop car turning up. There were people about but I am sure I heard the siren before Cecil got out of that cab and lamped Arturo.'

'Well maybe somebody's called the cops thinking you were doing some dodgy drug deal with the bag. Who knows?' Jasper said. 'Look, why don't I contact the cops and see if they know anything.'

'No. No…you can't Jasper,' I said. 'He could well have been nicked. He'd just assaulted Arturo last time I saw him. Arturo's probably been nicked too. They're going to want info on that gun and what Cecil's involvement was. If he's been nicked there is no point in us getting ourselves known too. I know Cecil. He won't say anything. Let's wait a while. If we don't hear anything then…' The truth was I wasn't sure what we should do if Cecil didn't turn up.

'But couldn't you just go to the police now and tell them everything,' Jasper said, as he swigged his beer.

'And how do I explain the missing cash?' I said. 'I'd be dropping Pauline right in it…and her daughter. And we don't even know what this money is for or where it came from. You never know what we could get mixed up with.' The thought of Pauline sparked an idea.

'Got it. If Cecil doesn't show up we can assume he's been nicked. If that's the case I will ask Brooke to check him out. Find out where he is and go see him. She can't be connected to us so it will give us some time.'

'The escort?' Jasper said. 'Will she do it?'

'I think so…and then I'm going to spend the night with her.'

24

I took two bundles of cash out of the rucksack, twenty thousand dollars in total, and put it into the safe. Then I placed my passport in the bag. Next I pulled out a couple of t-shirts from one of the hotel laundry bags at the bottom of the wardrobe and placed them in the rucksack, making sure they covered up the remaining wads of dollar bills. I then stuck in a four of pairs of socks on the top and closed up the zips. Carlos brought a padlock from his room and locked the bag. He then gave me the key.

'So what's in there Mateo?'

'Most of the cash except what we need to play with tonight and my passport like you said.'

Carlos grinned, took the bag and made his way down to the lost property office situated close to the reception area. Jasper sat on the sofa and tried to reach Cecil but with no luck.

'It keeps going to voicemail, mate. I reckon the cops got him.'

'Well let's wait and see. It's nearly two o'clock. If we've heard nothing in an hour we'll assume he's been arrested and take it from there. You don't think he's gone off with that Morgan again do you?'

'Unlikely mate. She goes back home this afternoon. No, I reckon…well from what you said happened, he's been nicked.'

'Well, we'll see. First of all I got to get some things organised. I have to check out of this hotel for a start and I have to call Brooke see if she will do me a couple of favours.'

'I'm sure she will,' Jasper said, winking at me. 'What you checking out for?'

'I told you. I can't stay here. Somebody will come looking for me sooner or later.'

Jasper stood up and began to pace the room. 'Where you gonna go?'

'I was thinking of asking Brooke if I could crash at hers.'

'Ok, don't blame you mate. Good shout. But hang on. I understand you have to lay low but why check out of here? If you check out you set a new trail for anyone who wants to find you. You're all paid up for the full stay so keep the registration. We only have two nights to go. You lay low at Brooke's but make it look like you're still here at the Paris.'

I liked Jasper's thinking. 'Makes sense. No, you're right,' I said. 'Now if we are going to win back this money we need a plan. I need to sort this stuff with Brooke. Let's say we meet in your room at seven o'clock.'

'Ok. Good luck Matt. Catch you later.'

As Jasper opened the door to leave I called him back.

'Oh Jasper. Just a thought. You seeing Kimberley again? Carlos said she was a bit of a hanger on.'

'Well, no plans to but she keeps showing up. We had a bit of a one off. As far as I was concerned it was a one off anyway. Why? What's up?'

'I don't know. She just seems to be around a lot and it was something Cecil said. He said she was asking for me, you know, when you guys ran into her last night. Just seems a bit odd to me after all the run ins we've had.'

Jasper shut the door and turned back to face me.

'Yeah, come to think of it she does mention you a lot. I did comment on it but she just said you were…how'd she put it…oh yeah, an asshole. Sorry Matt. Yeah, and she wanted to keep out of your way.'

'What's she asking?'

'Just stuff…where you are, what you're doing.'

'Did you mention my lost bag at all?'

'Well, yeah. I said you'd lost your camera bag but I never said anything about the money.'

I felt my fingers clench tight. 'Are you sure Jasper? Nothing?'

'No. Nothing Matt. She asked a couple of times if you found your bag. I just told her that you did but I said nothing about any money. Straight up. What're you thinking?'

'Not sure. It's just a feeling. Seems weird to keep asking stuff like that just because we had a couple of incidents. The thing is Jasper, I have just over twenty-four hours to get this money together and the less said about anything at all the better. You know what I mean?'

'I gotcha mate. Not a word.'

I spent the next hour lying on the bed trying to get some rest. The drama of the morning had left me feeling drained. My instinct was to lock my door, hole up and wait until it was time to get the flight back to London. It couldn't come quick enough for me. But I knew I could not ignore the situation. At three o'clock I tried Cecil's number again. Still no response. That was unlike Cecil. If he knew there was a problem he'd be there. I resigned myself to the thought that the worst had happened and he had been arrested. I wondered what had happened to Arturo too. Had he been arrested? Was he back out looking for me. I had to do something to cover myself. I sprang up off the bed and grabbed my wallet. I pulled out Brooke's card and called her.

'*Hi, this is Brooke, your Las Vegas Barbie Doll. How can I help you today?*'

'Brooke. It's Matthew…from the Paris. How are –?'

'*Oh Hi Matthew. Great to hear from you. I was just thinking about yo*u.'

'You were?'

'*Oh yes. I heard what you did for Pauline. She called me up. You are such a nice guy. I just knew you English guys were cool.*'

'Sorry. What I did for her? I didn't do anything?'

I heard the giggle in Brooke's response. '*That is so cool. You know. You let her have that money for her daughter's operation. She is so grateful Matthew.'*

Let her have the money. I flopped back down on the bed. I had no real choice. She had already spent it. What could I have done? Forced her somehow to pay it back? And if so how? A cold sweat broke out on my face. I sat up abruptly.

'She does *have* a daughter, Brooke?'

'Yeah, I know she does,' Brooke replied, misreading my meaning. *'Emma's so lovely. I'm her godmother. I just hope they can fix her eye for her. Poor little thing.'*

A sigh of relief escaped my lips. For one horrible moment I thought I had been duped again. Maybe I had. I would never know. I just had to believe I hadn't. Whatever the case time was running short and I had to sort my problem out.

'Brooke, listen. I need a couple of favours.'

I explained what had happened to Cecil and that I wanted her to contact the local police department to see if she could find anything out.

'Of course I will. We owe you for your kindness. So what's the other favour Matthew?'

'I need somewhere to stay tonight. I can't stay at the Paris and I can't risk checking in somewhere else. I just wondered…err… I wondered if you had somewhere…if I could stay with you… maybe? Happy to pay for the time.'

'Of course you can. I have a nice apartment just out of town. There's no charge to you Matthew. It's not a date. You're a friend now,' she said. *'Tell you what. I have the night off. I will call the Metropolitan Police Department and see what I can find out and then get back to you. We can meet up later, let's say at the Central Lobby Bar again tonight. Ten o'clock, OK?'*

'Let's make it midnight. I have work to do first.'

'Ok, midnight it is. What's your friend's full name again?'

'Cecil Delaney. Just make up some story about knowing him. Don't mention me….and thanks Brooke.'

At seven o'clock, carrying a hotel laundry bag, I knocked on the door of Room 1189. Jasper let me in. Carlos was already there.

'Any news amigo?' he asked.

'Nothing. Looks like Cecil has been arrested. I'm hoping to get some information later. Brooke's on the case. How did you get on with lost property Carlos?'

'Piece of cake. They signed it in, labelled it and stored it. Done in a flash…en un dos por tres.'

'Err…right. Nice one Carlos.' I said, feeling relieved to have got rid of the bag. 'What about you Jasper? Any news?'

'Nothing mate. That Kimberley came knocking but I told her we were planning a trip to the Grand Canyon. Might keep her outta my hair for a while.'

'Good. Ok, now listen. We have to hit the casinos tonight and somehow win this money back. It's a long shot but it's all we have.' I put the laundry bag on the table and pulled out two bundles of dollar bills. 'I've got twenty thousand large ones here lads. This is our gambling money. If we lose this lot we are screwed. We have to set some limits. If we lose it we call it a day and let fate play its hand. I can't keep dipping into the rest. So, you take five grand each and go play whatever it is you think you are more comfortable with. It's your call…blackjack, poker, roulette…whatever. I'll take the other ten grand and do the same. I got us into this mess so I feel the responsibility to get back as much as I can. There are no rules…well, maybe one. Minimum bet is two hundred and fifty dollars.' I pointed to Jasper. 'As you said, mate, there's no point in doing ten dollar bets. Too safe. If you have ten dollars on at four to one you get forty back. Two fifty on you get a grand. Makes sense to go large then. The risk is the same in terms of the odds. It just means if you lose, your money disappears quicker. Chance we have to take though if we're going to crack it. Everybody cool with that?'

They both nodded.

'Great. We meet back in the Central Lobby Bar at midnight at the latest, win, lose or draw. We must rendezvous at that point. That's key.'

'Why?' Jasper asked.

'We have to be disciplined about this. We have to see how close or not we are to what we are trying to do. Look lads, we're not out there gambling for fun. This is work. So we have to treat it dead seriously. When we meet we take stock. If we're way off the mark we can call it a day. If we're close to what we need then maybe we can try and close the gap. But we can't have each of us going off doing our own thing just totally randomly all night. We need to know what the cumulative result is. How much we have made between us.'

'You make it sound like Mission Impossible, Mateo,' Carlos said as he rubbed his dodgy knee.

'Hey, Carlos. No negatives. I had time to think this afternoon. We got to rise to meet the challenge,' I said, trying to convince myself as well. I took a deep, nervous breath. It was hardly a *'Once more unto the breach dear friends'* moment but I hoped I'd said enough to ensure that my two gambling partners knew exactly how much was at stake, quite literally as far as the cash was concerned.

Jasper walked across to Carlos and slapped him heartily on the back.

'C'mon mate. You're up for it. Use that old Spanish charm to lure them dollars into your hands.'

'Peruvian mate. Peruvian.'

'Whatever. That knee gonna stand up to a night of hardcore gambling?'

'Lads…no negatives,' I interrupted. 'Let's get going. We'll get a shot each at the bar downstairs to kick the night off, then go take Vegas out of the equation…as Ces would say.'

High fives all round and we left the room on our mission.

25

We split up. Jasper headed for the Bellagio, Carlos stayed at the Paris. For no reason other than it had been the first casino I had gambled at when I got to Vegas I headed straight for Caesar's Palace. It had also been lucky for me. I had made five hundred dollars profit at my first attempt. Perhaps things would turn out that way again only this time for higher stakes. The casino seemed just as busy at six fifteen in the evening as it had been when I had arrived a lot later on that first night. I looked for Maria's table. Familiarity made me feel comfortable. She was there but the table was busy. I waited ten minutes until one of the punters left.

'Hi Matthew. You come to play tonight?' she said, her smile broad and welcoming.

'Sure. My lucky night I hope.' I cashed five thousand dollars into chips. Maria didn't bat an eyelid.

Something was happening. My first hand threw up a flush and I won a thousand dollars. The next two hands were both pairs paying evens. Another five hundred dollars. I couldn't believe it. I stuck with the Pair Plus bet for a while. It seemed simple. Get a pair or better. I won a few more at evens and dropped a few but overall after twenty minutes I was two thousand dollars ahead. A waitress took a drinks order. A simple beer was sufficient. I needed to keep my focus. I decided to try the Ante bet, against the dealer. My luck changed on a pair of Jacks. Maria had a pair of Kings. Matching a two hundred and fifty dollar bet meant I lost five hundred in an instant. I played and folded on two more hands then lost another five hundred. I was now just five hundred ahead. I sipped my beer and took a breather. At least I *was* ahead. Somehow I needed to win at bigger odds. I started to play both the Ante and the Pair Plus. I was wagering five hundred dollars at a time, two-fifty to play the Pair Plus and two-fifty to play the Ante and if I wanted to bet on my hand, I had to match the Ante wager with another two-fifty. It started to unravel when I played on a Queen, Jack and a five. Maria had an Ace, a Queen and a three. I lost seven hundred and fifty dollars. One hour later I had gambled away five thousand dollars.

I walked away from the table. I had to slow down. Be more clinical with my bets. It wasn't happening with three-card poker. They say the odds favour the house. I had just proved the point. I took another beer and wandered around the casino floor trying to decide what to do next. I just hoped Carlos and Jasper were winning. I cashed another five thousand, stopped at a Blackjack game and watched for a while. As far as I was concerned it was Pontoon but with big bucks. I'd played Pontoon at home…twist, stick or bust. The table had a twenty dollar maximum bet. No good for my requirements. I strolled around and found one with a three hundred dollar limit. Big mistake. One hour later I had lost another two thousand dollars. It was only just nine-thirty in the evening and I had lost seven thousand dollars of my ten grand stash. If Carlos and Jasper were doing as badly as I was, with just five grand each, we were in serious trouble. I dismissed the thought and went looking for a different option. A game of craps looked too busy and the table looked too complicated. I decided to go back to three-card poker. At least I had a basic idea of what was going on with the game and felt optimistic that the luck that had come my way earlier could return.

I pulled up a stool at a different table. A fresh table may bring good fortune. It did. For a while. I won five straight hands with a pair each time. I folded on four consecutive hands after that, each fold costing me two hundred and fifty dollars but I decided I had to be sensible. There was no point in pursuing a dud hand. My biggest success was a straight, three cards in sequence. At six to one it paid fifteen hundred dollars. I needed a lot more of those. I won several more hands at evens and at one point had recovered some four thousand dollars. But I just couldn't seem to get a consistent run and gradually the winning hands began to become few and far between until the tide began to turn against me. As I lost one hand after another the sweat started to run down my face. I loosened my shirt collar, ordered another beer, took a deep breath and ploughed on. More losses followed. When fate drags you down the path of a losing streak it makes sense to dig your heels in and turn away, turn back. But I had no choice. I had to play. I had to win. So I kept on playing. And steadily, inevitably, slowly even at times, I slid down the loser's path until my ten thousand dollar stake had become no more than one hundred and fifty dollars.

I stood up from the table, my head pounding, my brow gripped in a knot of tension, fear and total bewilderment, neck muscles tensed into a solid mass of pain. For what seemed like an hour I stood and stared at the walls. Ahead of me was the cashier's desk, a queue of excited people changing money or cashing in chips. I had lost nine thousand eight-hundred and fifty dollars in just over four hours. I knew I would have to suffer the humiliation of facing the others in roughly another half an hour. I just hoped they had fared better than I had.

26

Carlos was already sitting in the Central Lobby Bar when I got back to the Paris. An ominous feeling crept over me as I got closer and saw his hunched over body language. His face, a grim, inert mask, confirmed my worst fears as I approached him. I asked the question all the same.

'How did you do Carlos?'

He turned his gaze away from the whiskey glass he had been staring into and sighed heavily. 'I'm sorry Matthew…no es bueno. No good amigo.'

'How bad is no good, Carlos? I can take it,' I said, as I sat down at the table.

'I will be straight Mateo. I have one hundred and eighty dollars left.' He smiled, but there was no fun in his eyes. 'How about you?'

My heart sank as the enormity of our losses hit home.

'That much Carlos? Well it looks like we've got…three hundred and thirty dollars left between us.'

'What? You lost –'

'Lost? Almost ten friggin grand. Gambling's a friggin mugs game. But we knew that already, didn't we?'

Carlos ignored my question, drained his whiskey and stood up.

'Looks like we both need a drink. What you having?'

'Jack and Coke mate. Let's just hope it's worked out for Jasper. It's just gone midnight so maybe he's on a roll.'

'Aye, mind you he'd have to be winning an extra fifteen grand to cover our losses too so I wouldn't be holding out too much hope amigo. What you gannae do?'

I didn't answer. I didn't know but for some reason, once I had heard that Carlos had lost all of his cash too, I felt strangely calm. Perhaps it was the realisation that it was far easier to lose in Vegas than it was to win, no matter how positive you felt. It was also an acceptance that, whatever the outcome of that evening, fate would play a bigger part than anything we could do.

Carlos returned with the drinks just as Brooke made an entrance.

'Hi Matthew.' She kissed me lightly on the cheek, her loose blonde hair brushing against my face. Its freshly washed fragrance hung in the air, instantly intoxicating, penetrating deep into my senses. 'Oh, hello,' she said, as she spotted Carlos.

'And hello to you too, Senorita.' Carlos reached for Brooke's hand and raised it to his lips. 'Pleased to meet you.'

Brooke giggled. I noticed the slight tilt of her head as she glanced at Carlos, like a lady of the manor accustomed to accepting the praise of underlings. Perhaps she was used to adoration. Her smile showed that she was enjoying the interaction rather than deliberately adopting any pretentious demeanour.

'What a charming Englishman,' she said.

Carlos absent-mindedly stroked his bald head as if correcting a hairstyle that remained in his memory but that had long ago deserted his head.

'Englishman! Young lady, my heart beats with Spanish blood and my mind possesses the cunning of a Scotsman.'

I felt the need to interrupt. 'Hey, Carlos, we have bigger issues to sort out than what nationality you are,' I said. I turned to Brooke. 'Any news on Cecil?'

She placed a hand on mine, a gentle touch of her fingertips. 'Yes. But give me a moment. I will be back. I must pop to the washroom...lipstick...you know?'

I didn't know. Lipstick. I was waiting to hear critical news but a woman needed to ensure her appearance was just right. Carlos didn't have the same view.

'Una señora caliente,' he said, under his breath.

'What's that?' I asked.

'Mateo. That girlie is a stunner. A hot lady. Where did you find her? Did you see that shape? That red dress amigo. Like a toreador about to seduce the bull? Her legs…magnifico.'

'I know, I know. You remember her? From the Bellagio. But never mind any of that. We got bigger issues here.' I glanced at my watch. Nearly a quarter past midnight. 'Where the bloody hell is Jasper?'

'Maybe it's a good sign. Maybe he's on a roll,' Carlos said, his wide-eyed look trying to convey some encouragement but his body language not supporting it.

'Let's hope so.'

Brooke returned and sat between us. She sipped a glass of Champagne and told us that she had been to see Cecil. She had discovered that he had been arrested and was being held at the Clark County Detention Centre on suspicion of assault and battery and possession of a firearm.

'That's all we need. Cecil arrested,' I said. 'As if we haven't got enough aggravation. You said a firearm Brooke. The gun. But that belonged to Arturo. Did he not tell them that?'

'He did. But he has told the cops nothing other than that he'd just been trying to help a tourist who was being mugged,' Brooke said.

'A tourist? What tourist?' I asked, as I tried to recall the incident. And then it dawned on me. I was the tourist. Cecil had told me to run after he had thumped Arturo. So now he was using that as his defence. 'I had better go and see him and sort this out. I can't leave him in jail.'

Brooke shot out a hand and placed it on my arm. 'No, no Matthew. Cecil told me you'd think that. He said you must sort out your other business first. Going to see him would only complicate matters. He said he's fine and not to worry. He can handle it.'

'But they think it's his gun. Why?'

'They found three sets of finger prints on it. One of them belonged to your friend and another set to the other man.'

'Arturo,' I said.

'And the third set?' Carlos asked.

'Must be mine. I picked it up. Don't know why and then gave it...well threw it, to Cecil. It all happened so quick. It was a shock. I sort of thought Ces was trying to get the gun off Arturo so when he dropped it I went after it. Stupid.'

Carlos frowned. 'Then the cops will be looking for you too, amigo.'

'Well, yeah, they will. But they won't know it's me, will they? They only have prints.'

'But you were printed at the airport when you came in, right? Won't take them too long to track you down.'

'Oh great Carlos. More good news.' I downed the last of the Jack Daniels. 'Then we have to get things sorted here fast. God knows how. Where the bloody hell is Jasper anyway?' I turned towards Brooke. 'Did Ces say anything about Arturo? What he's doing in all this?'

'He just said that the other guy told the cops that *he* was assaulted by Cecil and that the gun didn't belong to him...that it was Cecil's. But, it turned out that it was stolen. When the cops checked the registration and serial number they found that it was registered to a gun dealership in Chicago. They contacted their offices and found out that their rep is here in Vegas and –'

'Richard Heydon,' I said, under my breath but loud enough for Brooke to question it.

'Who?'

'Richard Heydon. A guy we met in the Bellagio. He's a gun salesman or something. It may just be co-incidence.'

It had to be him. Vegas couldn't have been swamped with gun salesmen all of a sudden. But if Arturo had one of his guns he must be connected to Richard somehow.

'Stolen Brooke. You said the gun was stolen and the police traced it. If it was stolen I wonder why the rep didn't report it? Seems odd to me,' I said.

Brooke shrugged. 'I don't know. I am only telling you what Cecil told me.'

'So does Cecil need a lawyer?' Carlos asked.

A lawyer. Sounded like Cecil did need a lawyer and oddly

enough I had just met one. However, I didn't think he was perhaps the right lawyer to be asking for help.

'He may well do mate, but we can't do much about that now. Cecil is right. If I go down there now the police are going to want me as a witness. Arturo will probably try to implicate me in some way and it won't get our cash problem sorted. And if I don't manage to sort that I'm toast. They will detain Cecil while they investigate things as I reckon assault and possessing a firearm is quite serious over here. Knowing Ces he will say very little until he knows we got the cash problem sorted out.'

'Well it won't take long to trace him back to the hotel and identify him fully,' Carlos said.

'I know. But he won't be linked to me straight away will he? We came in on different flights.'

The conversation ended at the sight of Jasper strolling towards the bar, jangling a handful of chips between both hands. A moment's optimism created the hope that they might be in five thousand dollar valuations. They were not.

'How did you do, amigo?' Carlos asked.

Jasper swivelled a chair around from an adjoining table and sat down.

'Screwed up guys I'm afraid. I was up by ten fucking grand at one point. Then I went too big. Lost it again. Tried to get it back by going large. Blew the fucking lot.'

I felt the panic rise within me. I wasn't interested in what Jasper had nearly won. I needed to know what he had left.

'So how much have you got left Jasper?' I asked, trying to keep the tremor from my voice.

'Six hundred and twenty dollars is all I got, Matt. What about you guys?'

The question didn't need answering. Jasper must have seen my expression.

Carlos stood up. 'Let me get you a drink Mateo.'

I took a deep breath hoping the intake of oxygen would quell the rising dread. My earlier calm had clearly been as a result of hanging on to the hope that Jasper would save the day.

'Fucking drink, Carlos? Oh right, that will sort it. Yeah, get me a large Jack and Coke and a fucking morphine chaser. Bring on oblivion. We've got, what… nine hundred and fifty dollars left out of the twenty fucking grand that we started the night with. So a drink will definitely sort out all this shit. I'm supposed to have half a million friggin dollars by three o'clock tomorrow afternoon and I'm now short of that total by over sixty-three grand. Then just to put the cherry right smack bang on top of the icing of this fucking mess, I now find out my best mate is in jail. Do you not realise that these guys are going to tie me up by the bollocks and loop the rope round some fucking cactus out there in the Nevada wilderness tomorrow? I'm done guys. I might as well go out big style. So, yeah, let's do it. Let's get smashed.'

I felt a hand on my shoulder and turned to see one of the waitresses.

'Sir, could you keep your voice down please. There are people here trying to have a nice evening. If you don't mind…please.'

I looked around to see several faces staring in my direction. 'I'm sorry. Sure. My apologies.'

Carlos sat perfectly still, totally taken aback by my outburst. Brooke played with her glass and stared at the table. Jasper leant towards me.

'Hey, mate. Calm it. We'll sort it. There's no need to panic.'

'I'm not panicking. I'm fucking panicking,' I hissed, trying to keep my voice down. 'We'll sort it, will we? Yeah? Sixty odd grand. So tell me Jasper, when was the last time you just stumbled over sixty grand? Regular occurrence for you is it?'

'Hold it, mate. Don't be having a go at me. I didn't lose the fucking bag did I?' Jasper shouted, his face flushed.

'Nor did I lose it come to think of it. It was nicked, remember… from Cecil,' I shot back.

'You can't blame Cecil, Mateo,' Carlos chipped in.

'Boys! Boys. Hey. Cool it.' Brooke's tone was sharp and insistent. 'What's the matter with y'all? You're not going to solve your problem fighting each other are you? That's not helping. You're like a bunch of kids. You have to stick together.' She stared at us one by one, unhurriedly, waiting for order to be restored. 'That's better. Ok. Now, tell me, how much money have you got left?'

'Nine hundred and fifty dollars,' Carlos said.

'Ok. Well why not try roulette. If you just play the colours or odds and evens you have a fifty-fifty chance. Play twenty dollars you win twenty. And if you start winning you can raise the bet. Who knows. Falling out with each other isn't getting your money back nor is it getting your friend out of jail.'

There was a moments silence and then everyone started talking at once. I waited until the chatter had subsided.

'Brooke's right. We have to stick together on this. It's my neck I suppose so I'm willing to give anything a try. And I'm sorry lads. I didn't mean anything. It's just a bad situation, you know... what with Ces being banged up now. It's thrown me. You know what he's like. If he was here he'd have some sort of answer. I'm sure of it.' I turned to Carlos. 'Sorry mate...yeah, a drink would help.'

He smiled and slapped me on the shoulder.

'No problem, Mateo. I understand.' He nodded towards the casino floor. 'It's worth a go boys. Let's give it another crack on the roulette tables. If we're gannae lose it, we might as well go for it.'

It wasn't the most helpful thing I had heard but with no other options I was ready to try.

27

There were several roulette stations scattered around the far end of the Paris casino. Each one had a crowd around it. We took three hundred dollars apiece and went to different tables. Brooke stayed with me. I played the even numbers at first, ten dollars at a time. After half an hour I had made no more than fifty dollars. I raised my bets from ten dollars to twenty but with no great change in my fortunes. I decided to switch bets and just play on red but with similar results. I won some and then lost it again. I needed a consistent run on the red. It wasn't happening. My three hundred dollars had halved in an hour. I knew it was an impossible task but once I had walked to the table a flicker of optimism had arisen within me. As I watched my dollars deplete that optimism blew out completely. Jasper and Carlos came across to my table to see how I was getting on. Brooke disappeared to the washroom.

'How we doing lads?' Jasper asked.

Jasper had managed to turn his stake into a twenty dollar profit. Carlos was ninety dollars down.

'We've got six hundred and eighty dollars left between us. Not exactly high rollers are we? And even if Lady Luck showed up herself it would take a friggin miracle to turn six hundred odd dollars into sixty thousand. I think we're done boys, well and truly cooked,' I said, the dejection causing the final words to catch in my throat. I turned away from the table. Jasper and Carlos both stared straight ahead, not knowing what to say.

And then the voice came from behind my right shoulder.

'Hello Matthew. How are you?'

I turned on hearing my name. Erin Farrell stood there looking stunning in a silver cocktail dress.

'Erin, hello. What are you doing here?'

'Doing what everybody else is. Enjoying Vegas. Are you winning?' she asked, nodding towards the roulette table.

'Err, well…not exactly. Playing catch up actually. So, are you playing?'

'Oh no, I don't waste my money. Gambling's not for me. I think I prefer more certainty. They say gambling's for mugs…present company excepted. It's my last night so just meeting some friends for drinks.'

'Ok, you off home tomorrow then?'

'No. Day after but I never go out the night before a work day. Have to be fresh and on the ball for our lovely passengers.' She smiled, her green eyes twinkling with mischief.

Our conversation was interrupted by Brooke's return.

'How are you doing Matthew? Winning yet?'

'Err…no, not yet. Erin, this is –'

I didn't get to finish the introduction. All the mischief and sparkle had disappeared from Erin's eyes. Her tone was matter of fact.

'Yes, we've met, remember?' she said, as she gave Brooke no more than a cursory glance. 'Good luck with your, erm… investments. Enjoy the rest of your stay.' She turned and walked away.

'Your friend not staying?' Brooke asked.

'Err…no, she's busy…meeting friends…other friends I mean.'

As I watched Erin walk away I felt a strange sensation of disappointment at the prospect of her departure. She wasn't really a friend. I barely knew her. But I liked her. She always seemed positive and she was fun. My mind shot back to the day I had met her at the speed awareness course. She had walked right up and asked to join me as I sat there sipping a coffee. It was odd how fate had thrown us together. One minute in the leafy suburbs of Surrey and the next in the bright lights of Vegas. And all because we were breaking the speed limit. Me by six miles an hour and Erin by nine. Not much in it but an odd symmetry in the two numbers. Two numbers that had caused our paths to cross. I smiled to myself as I recalled her response to my comment that it was unfortunate. '*Yes. Very unfortunate. Nine…my unlucky number.*' There was some irony in that phrase occurring to me as I stood in a casino with a whole evening of unlucky numbers behind me.

And then in a glaring flash, brighter than any neon light in Las Vegas, a vision cut through my jumbled thoughts.

'That's it,' I shouted and headed back towards the table .

'What's it, Matt?' Jasper said, his face revealing his curiosity at my sudden animation.

'Lady Luck.'

'What are you on about? You're losing it mate?'

'No, Lady Luck. You remember what I said? That it wasn't about us. That it's all about Lady Luck? Well she's here.'

'You've lost it. You're stressed out mate. Let me get you another –'

'No, listen Jasper. Numbers. Numbers, right? If I'm going to get this money back I should be playing the numbers. Just the numbers.'

'What, a single number? The odds are thirty-five to one. You got no chance the way things have been going.'

'That's the point. We need the long odds now. Trust me Jasper. I have to take the risk.'

It was time to gamble and gamble properly. My eyes were drawn to the six. Six miles an hour. Six miles an hour over the limit. It made no sense. My logic was flawed but there was something burning into my soul.

Fate. Erin. Me. Six. Nine.

I leant over the roulette table and placed fifty dollars right in the middle of the black number six on the green cloth. I pulled my hand away instantly before I could change my mind.

'Straight up, number six,' I said unnecessarily, as if trying to convince myself that I was doing the right thing.

I turned away. I didn't want to watch. Jasper and Carlos stared at the table. I heard the ball clacking around the wheel. A moment's silence. Then the shouts.

'Six! Jeez, Matt you won. It's come in.'

I spun round to catch the last few turns of the wheel. Sure enough the small white ball nestled in the black six slot. I tried to suppress my elation.

'What's that worth? How much? How much we got?' I shouted out.

Carlos pulled his mobile from a pocket and punched in the numbers.

'Fifty dollars…at thirty-fives…one thousand seven hundred and fifty, amigo.'

'Plus you get your fifty back,' Jasper added. 'Eighteen hundred.'

I knew what I had to do but I wasn't sure I had the nerve. My head tried a quick calculation. Put it all back on and I could win…

'Carlos, what's eighteen hundred at thirty-fives?'

Carlos punched in the numbers again. 'Sixty-three thousand. You going for it?'

My cautious side kicked in. I couldn't make the play. Too risky. If I just bet a hundred I still had plenty left for more bets.

'No, mate too risky. I can't afford to lose it.'

Jasper grabbed me by the arm.

'Matt. Listen to me. This isn't about losing. This is about winning. Nothing else. You can't afford not to *win* it. If you think like a loser, you lose. You gotta go for it.'

'That's all very well for you to say Jasper. It isn't your bollocks that will be hanging on the end of some cactus tomorrow is it?'

And then I spotted the number nine. The red nine. It jumped out at me, almost as if it was twice the size of the other slots. Nine, Erin's unlucky number and my unlucky six. The numbers that had thrown us together in the first place.

It was Brooke that convinced me.

'Go on Matthew. You're in Las Vegas. It's where the big boys come out to play.' She kissed me playfully on the cheek. 'Good luck.'

I felt the beads of sweat prickle my brow. A knot in my stomach.

Palms clammy with apprehension. The decision had been made in my heart but my head held me back. I swallowed hard and took a deep breath. *The big boys, yeah. C'mon, Matthew. Time to join the high rollers.*

Eighteen hundred dollars worth of chips went straight down on the red nine.

This time I had to watch. The croupier took the ball and placed it under the rim of the wheel housing as the wheel span anti-clockwise. He held it there for a second. With a deft flick of the fingers he sent the ball careering clockwise round the circumference of the wheel, like a speeding cyclist on the wall of death. All eyes around the table stayed glued to the ball as it hugged the tilted wheel edge. All those eyes willing it to fall in a specific place. As it began to lose momentum it dropped down and bounced across the slotted chambers. The bounce took it up again onto the track. It slewed around the smooth wooden surface and dropped again. Each bounce slowed it some more. As it lost its impetus it hovered above the numbered chambers, clacking off the edges and then falling again. It bounced on zero. I held my breath. It rolled across twenty-eight, balanced briefly on the edge. And then it dropped.

'Nine! Oh my god, nine.' Jasper was on me before I had time to register what had happened. 'You fucking did it, Matt. You done it. Go on my son. Fill yer boots! Get in there. Reeeeee....zult!'

'Mateo. Sonofagun. You did it.' Carlos shook my hand frantically, his own relief clear. 'Bravo Mateo, I knew you'd do it. Legend.'

Brooke flung her arms around me. 'The big boys are in town. Whoohoo...'

I was still in shock. I glanced round at the table to make sure it had happened. The wheel had almost come to a standstill but the little white ball was firmly placed in the number nine slot. My next thought was to see if I had covered the debt.

'How much Carlos?' I asked. 'How much? How friggin much? What we got?'

'Easy, Mateo. Calm down. Hang on.' Carlos pulled out his

240

mobile again. 'I told you…sixty-three grand. Plus you get your stake back so…sixty-four thousand eight hundred dollars.'

As Carlos uttered the numbers, an enormous weight shifted from my shoulders. I punched the air in relief and with the elation of the moment.

'Then we've done it. I needed, what…sixty-three and a bit after we blew nearly all of that twenty-grand. So we've made up the difference and got some over.'

Carlos did some quick calculations. 'About fourteen hundred up, amigos.'

I stood for a moment and took in the atmosphere. Around me the casino was packed, animated faces, chattering and cheering but for that brief moment I heard nothing. My eyes were drawn to a distant point across the room. Erin Farrell walked towards the hotel exit. Lady Luck was leaving the building.

A slap on the back brought me back to reality.

'Champagne anybody?' I asked.

At three o'clock in the morning, I left the Paris. Exhaustion had taken hold both emotionally and physically. Carlos took possession of the winnings and said he would keep the money in his room. I took a taxi with Brooke back to her apartment, a one-bedroom bungalow style residence near the Rhodes Ranch Golf Club. Even though I now had the money, it still made sense for me to lay low. There was still the possibility of one or other of the interested parties coming to look for me.

Brooke disappeared into the kitchen to make coffee and I wandered around her front room. I picked up a photograph that stood in a wall unit - Brooke, with a young blonde haired girl sitting on her lap. The girl had a dark eye patch, pirate style, over her left eye.

'Nice picture,' I said, as Brooke came into the room carrying two cups. 'Don't tell me. Pauline's daughter?'

'Yes, Emma. Lovely isn't she.'

'So what's with the patch? Must be her bad eye, I guess.'

'No, that's her good eye. She has to wear the patch from time to time so that she can develop the eye muscle in her bad eye. It makes her use it more. We pretend it's a game.'

I was relieved at seeing the picture. It made me realise that Pauline's story had been true and I hadn't been taken for a sucker. Brooke sat alongside me. We sipped coffee and chatted for an hour or so. Then she brought out a duvet and two pillows and made up a bed for me on the sofa in the front room. With the events of the day taking their toll, I undressed and fell into a deep sleep.

The light was just beginning to break through the blinds when I heard the noise. I woke with a start, nervous tension still clearly a problem. In the half-light of the morning I saw her, standing almost naked by the sofa, in nothing more than a tiny pair of white knickers. What all of us guys had imagined was clear to be seen. She was beautiful, tanned and toned. I rubbed my eyes to focus and shake myself into wakefulness, fully expecting the vision in front of me to melt away into the early dawn. I raised myself on one elbow and sat up.

'Brooke. What…what are you doing?'

She sat down on the edge of the sofa and rested one hand on the duvet over my knee.

'I couldn't sleep Matthew. I was thinking and it kept me awake.'

'Thinking…about?' I said, trying not to stare directly at her firm breasts, her nipples pointed directly at me.

'I am going to see my parents in Florida tomorrow. I arranged it yesterday before I met up with you and, well, you know, I won't see you again before you go home.' Her hand had begun to move gently over the duvet, stroking my leg. 'And I didn't want to leave it like this.'

'Leave it? Leave it like what?'

'You know what I mean. You're a really nice guy. I like you. I meet so many jerks. It's just nice to be with someone who doesn't want anything from me.' Her hand moved to my bare chest, the tips of her fingers sending shivers through me. 'And we may never see each other again….'

'We can keep in touch,' I said, taking a deep breath as I felt

myself react to her touch. I swallowed hard. 'That would be…
err…good…I'd like that. Brooke…what are you doing?'

She ignored my question, slipped the duvet to one side and lay
down beside me, her head on my chest, her right leg across my
lower body. Her fingers continued to trace patterns over my chest
and shoulders. Her warmth, perfume and sensuous touch had
started to wear down my resistance. I felt her hand slide up to my
face, turning my head towards hers. Her soft lips touched mine,
in a gentle caress of a kiss. She pressed her groin into my thigh.
It was at that moment all of my resolve melted away. The tension
of the day, the pressure, the alcohol and now the soft caress of
a stunning woman combined to defeat any thoughts I had about
resisting. What man could? It was a moment, the present and I
was sinking into it.

The high-pitched jangle of my mobile cut through that moment.
Three loud rings signalled a text message that brought me abruptly
back to reality.

'I have to get this Brooke,' I said. 'It could be important…Cecil
or something.' I clicked the message icon and watched as the text
appeared on the screen.

*'Hi Matthew. I hope I didn't wake you up. Not sure what time
it is there. I was just having lunch and thinking about you. I hope
you are having a great time and have won loads of money. Ha
ha. Unlikely. Can't wait to see you when you get back. Take care.
Love Louise.'*

I sat for a moment, silently. I had nearly slipped up again.
Slipped up on the girl I had taken so long to find.

'What's wrong Matthew? Is everything ok?'

'Err… yes… just family…you know, back home.'

I stood up and paced across the room, my mind racing. I didn't
want to upset Brooke and I knew I was wrestling with my own
conscience. I turned back towards the sofa. In the low light that
struggled to filter through the blinds, I saw Brooke in a half-
seated, half-lying position propped up on both elbows, the duvet
just reaching her navel. I tried to focus on her face.

'Look Brooke I can't do this. It's not you. I just think we'd

243

spoil our little adventure. You have been so nice to me, helping me out and everything. I have too much on my mind still. Lots to get through. I don't want to spoil it by…err…you know, getting it wrong. Another time, another place, eh?'

The surprise was clear on her face. I walked towards the sofa and sat down on the edge. I saw that she was about to say something and placed the tip of my finger on her lips. I had no words at that moment that would adequately explain my thoughts. I also knew that if I got into a discussion my resolve might not last. Best to say no more. Leaning forward I kissed her gently on the forehead. As I pulled away, I looked her straight in the eyes, a long lingering look. Another time, another place indeed.

She seemed to understand. She got up and walked slowly back to her room.

28

Contact came earlier than I had expected.

On my return to the Paris, the receptionist handed me a note when I collected my room keycard from the desk. I walked to the Central Lobby Bar, took a seat and opened the folded piece of paper. It had a single line typed message.

'*Venetian. Same place. Midday. Come alone. No baggage.*'

Midday. No baggage. That meant they didn't want the money there and then. I ordered a coffee and thought about what was likely to happen. Why the early contact? They said I had until three in the afternoon. However, it made no difference now that I had the money. I was just relieved that I had been able to get it. I decided to leave the Nike bag where it was in Lost Property until I knew what the next move was.

'Hi Matt. How you doing this morning?' Jasper strolled towards me, his usual cheeky chappy, cheery grin back in place.

'Good Jasper. And you?'

'Not bad mate. Right result last night. Unbelievable in fact. Who'd have thought it would fall like that, eh?'

'I know. I was sweating a bit when that ball was flying round the wheel. I couldn't believe it when it dropped.'

'Yeah, blinding. Glad you got the dosh sorted. Bit close to the wire, that's for sure. So anyway, how'd you get on with that little hottie, Brooke? She's a right babe. You get a result there too?' He pulled out a seat and sat down.

I decided my night with Brooke was not worth the debate or the denial.

'That's your trouble,' I said, tapping the side of my nose. 'Let's just say it was all cool.'

'You're a bit of a dark horse, I reckon Matt.'

I changed the subject. 'Any sign of Carlos? I hope he stuck that money away safely last night. I can't go through that palaver again. Where is he anyway?'

'No worries Matt. He put it in the safe in his room. I went with him. We had a couple more drinks after you left. Last I saw of him he was out on the dance floor doing his groove thing. His knee seems to have made a bit of a recovery although I reckon he just anaesthetised it with booze. He's a right party animal when he gets going.'

'I know.' I leant forward, my tone more hushed. 'Listen Jasper. I've been contacted about the money. I have to meet up at midday at the Venetian.'

'Have you? I'll come with you.'

'No, I have to go alone. I had a note. It said to come alone. I'm just telling you so you know where I am. As soon as I know what's happening I'll let you know. But don't say a word to anyone… well apart from Carlos. Oh, and especially not to that Kimberley woman. I'm still not sure about her.'

'I won't. Funny enough I saw her by the pool this morning and she never said a thing.'

'Good, let's hope she keeps it that way.' I finished my coffee and left a tip for the bar man. 'Right, I'm on my way.'

'You gonna be ok, Matt?'

'Who knows mate.'

I was at the Venetian just before midday. I stood on the balcony walkway looking out across the hustle and bustle of another tourist day below. Taxis pulling in and dropping excited holidaymakers. Gondoliers ferrying their passengers into the mysteries of the Venetian's palatial depths.

The lawyer came and stood next to me, much as he'd done before. This time in a dark blue suit.

'Matthew. Glad you made it. A lovely morning again. So how's your day?'

I wasn't sure about the small talk. I needed him to get to the point.

'It's fine,' I said, 'and in case you're wondering, I have the money. All of it.'

'Shhhh…Matthew, Matthew. What's the hurry? You always that keen to get down to business?'

'In the circumstances I am,' I said. 'To be honest I just want to get this business sorted out. It's ruined my trip and to be straight with you, the sooner it's done the better. Anyway, talking of rushing I thought I had until three o'clock today?'

'Things change. I'm hearing things coming back to me. Seems to me there have been one or two developments. It appears one of our contacts has got himself arrested and that makes us vulnerable. So there's been a change of plan.'

'Arrested? You mean, Arturo?'

'No names Matthew. Just we heard things, you know and I don't want our operation jeopardised, you understand.' He reached into his pocket and pulled out a pack of cigarettes. He opened it and offered me one. 'You smoke?'

'No thanks.'

He slipped a cigarette from the pack and tapped it on the front of the carton, his gaze firmly fixed on me. His direct stare had a slightly unnerving impact as if he was deciding my fate. I watched him light the cigarette and blow a plume of smoke over the balustrade. His dismissal of my question had confirmed that Arturo was involved more than I had realised. But I still didn't know how.

'A change of plan. What plan?' I said.

'Always a plan my friend. Here's what I want you to do. You travel to a place called Tonopah tomorrow. You take the bag with you. You come alone, no friends. When you get to the first gas station going north, a Texaco truck stop, you pull in. You get your gas, and then once you've paid, you go behind the building. There are two blue dumpsters there. You check underneath and you will find an envelope stuck to the base. You got that?'

'Yes, but…Tono…what? Where's that? '

'North west outta the city, Highway 95. You look it up. By the time you get there you're gonna need gas anyway. You open the envelope and read the detail carefully. Then you do exactly as instructed.'

'Need gas? I don't have a car. How far is it?' I asked, wondering why the mystery.

'It's about two hundred miles out of Vegas. I suggest you get a car. You're gonna need one.'

'Two hundred miles? I'm supposed to be going home tomorrow night. Can't I just bring you the bag here or something? What's all the mystery about?'

'Fraid not Matthew. We can't do this in Vegas now. I can't be seen taking a bag nor can I risk being involved. You're just gonna have to follow instructions and the more you know the more risk there is for us. I suggest you start out real early if you wanna be back in time for your flight. You keep your end of the deal and you'll get back to Vegas.'

He blew another cloud of smoke into the air, dropped the half-finished cigarette on the polished red, white and black patterned floor and flattened it with his foot. He turned to walk away.

'Wait a minute. Hang on,' I shouted. 'Those other guys are still after me. They followed me the other day. I thought you said they'd leave me alone.'

'Yeah, I heard about that. Dumb assholes. Opportunists. Trying to impress their bosses and make a name for themselves. It's taken care of. Our clients know the deal now. They know you'll be making a drop. You'll be ok.'

29

I walked back to the Paris, my head a jumble of confused thought. I had expected to hand the bag over to whoever it belonged to and that would be the end of it. Now I had a two hundred mile drive to contend with, a journey the equivalent of London to Manchester, and a load of mysterious instructions to follow. I needed to focus. First, I had to hire a car and then I had to reclaim the bag from Lost Property. Back in my room, I checked to see if I had my driving licence. It was in my wallet along with the business cards I had collected on the trip. I flicked through them. Brooke, Richard Heydon, William Earp. Bill Earp, the businessman I had met on the flight coming out. WEN Car Rental. Just what I wanted. I picked up the bedside phone and dialled the number.

'Hey buddy. Good to hear from you. Sure, we got cars available. What you got in mind? I can get you a nice top of the range Cadillac.'

I had no idea what I wanted. I just needed a car.

'Whatever you recommend Bill. I'm in your hands. Something practical will be fine, you know. I only need it for one trip.'

'Ok buddy. I'll take care of ya. Practical you say? Hell, ok, I'll get you something suitable and have it delivered to your hotel at five o'clock tonight.'

A practical Cadillac. Well, it was one thing less to worry about. Next, I called Lost Property.

'Hi, this is Matthew Malarkey, room 1164. I've lost a Nike rucksack, a black one. I left it by the lift...err, the elevator. I wondered if anything had been handed in?' I waited while a check was made.

'*Yes, Sir. We have a bag here that fits that description. You'll need some ID to claim it.*'

The Lost Property office was located to one side of the reception area along a narrow corridor. Behind the desk, a young woman sat with an open ledger.

'Hi. I'm Mister Malarkey. I rang about a Nike bag.'

The woman fetched it from a shelf at the back of the room and placed it on her desk. A brown paper tag with a number on it had been tied to the strap.

'Do you have any ID Mister Malarkey, Sir? I need something to connect you to the bag.'

'I do. My passport and my driving…err…driver's licence. That ok?'

'That's fine Sir. Just one will do and I will need you to tell me the contents for extra verification. If you could let me have the ID first.'

'It's actually in the bag. If you let me open it I can show you.'

She pushed the bag towards me and I reached into my pocket for the padlock key that Carlos had given me. It wasn't there. I tried the other pocket. Same result. The key had to be there. They were the same trousers I had on the night before when Carlos gave me the key. I hadn't had time to get changed when I returned from Brooke's place.

'I can't seem to find the key,' I said, as I stuffed my hand down into my pockets again, my search getting more frantic. 'It's definitely my bag. It's…err…got my dirty sports kit in it.'

The woman looked at me strangely and pulled the bag towards her side of the table.

'I'm sorry Sir. I can't let you have the bag without ID.'

'Look, I promise you. It is my bag. I have dirty socks, sweaty tee shirts…the lot in there. I need to get it back right now. I mean… err, you know. The laundry…it all needs washing…urgently.'

I went to grab the strap but she pulled the bag right off the desk.

'Sir, you have to have ID. I can't let you have the bag without it. They are the hotel rules ok. Now if you try to grab the bag again I will have to call security.'

Not bloody security again. 'Ok, ok. I'm sorry. I will get the key. Just hold onto it for me. I'm sorry.'

I raced back to my room. A search of the drawers and my other clothes proved fruitless. I almost knew it would, as I could not recall removing the key from my pocket. I hadn't taken the trousers off either. Except...in Brooke's apartment. I dialled Brooke's number.

'*Hi, this is Brooke, your Las Vegas –*'

'Brooke. Brooke. It's Matthew. Where are you?'

'*Oh hi Matthew. I'm at the airport. I'm about to go through for my flight to Jacksonville. What's up?*'

'Oh, I'm sorry but it's an emergency, Brooke. I think I might have left the key to that rucksack with the...err...goods in it at your apartment. Did you find anything?'

'*A key? No, no I didn't.*'

'I need to get the rucksack back tonight or I am back in the mire Brooke. It has to be at yours. I took my trousers off there, when I crashed on your sofa. It must have fallen out of the pocket.'

'*There's not a lot I can do Matthew. I need to get this flight. It leaves at 3.15. My mom is picking me up tonight. Can you get down here? Right now? I could give you my apartment key. I'm at McCarran. But you'll have to hurry. I've checked in but still the right side. I can wait if you're quick.*'

'Ok. I'm on my way.'

I was in a taxi outside the Paris within three minutes and at McCarran Airport ten minutes later. I asked the driver to wait and ran straight into Departures. I got lucky. I found Brooke straight away.

'Here Matthew.' She handed me a key. 'It's for the front door. You know where to go? It's Rhodes Ranch. Head for West Warm Springs Road and Durango. Near the golf club. All the drivers know it.'

'Ok, yeah, I'll recognise it.'

'Great. Good luck. I gotta run. Just leave the key with my

neighbour on the right when you're done. I hope you find your key. Good luck.'

'Thanks Brooke. I won't forget you.' I kissed her full on the lips, turned, and began to run back to the taxi.

'Matthew. Wait. The alarm. There's an alarm. Just inside the door. It's eight, three, six, seven. Then hit the hash key.'

'An alarm. Ok. Eight, three what?'

'Six, seven…eight, three, six, seven. You have thirty seconds to deactivate it once you're in.'

I made a mental note and raced back to the taxi.

'Rhodes Ranch, please. West Warm Springs Road and Durango, near the golf club.'

I recognized Brooke's street as the taxi cruised around the maze of avenues at Rhodes Ranch. The driver pulled up at the end of the road and I asked him to wait at the junction. I cut across the neatly mown front lawn to the front door and slipped the key into the lock. As the door opened a series of intermittent high pitched pulses kicked in from the alarm. I found the keypad and punched in the numbers…8, 6, 3, 7 and hit the hash key. Nothing changed. The pulses stayed exactly the same. I tried again 3, 8, 6, 7 and the hash key again. Still nothing. My hands began to shake. What had Brooke said? I poked at the buttons again…6, 7, 8, 3, hash.

'Shit…come on, come on.'

I was on my fourth attempt when the pitch suddenly switched to a banshee-like deafening wail. At the same time, a flashing light above the porch shot beams of orange across the lawn. I slammed the door shut and ran towards the front room where I had slept, my heart beating wildly. The wailing noise seemed to get louder, heightening my sense of anxiety. With the blinds down, the room was in semi-darkness and I couldn't see clearly. I scrambled around on my hands and knees next to the sofa, feeling underneath it for the key. As my eyes became accustomed to the dimness, I found a lamp switch. I flicked it on. There was nothing on the carpet around the sofa. My heart pounded. The alarm wailed. I knew the whole neighbourhood had been alerted by the noise. I shoved against one side of the sofa, pushing it back slightly. Underneath, highlighted against the beige of the carpet, was the black plastic top of a key. Another heave and the key was fully exposed.

I wasted no time. I shoved the key in my pocket and ran into the kitchen straight towards the back door. It was locked. It seemed that I had no choice other than to go back the way I came. The siren's oscillating wail seemed louder than before. In the hallway, I stopped in my tracks. Through the frosted door glass I spotted three shadowy figures highlighted by the orange glow. I wiped away the beads of sweat that had formed on my forehead. Neighbours? Security guards? Police? I had no idea but the alarm had definitely attracted investigation. For a split second I hesitated. I had Brooke's key. I could explain why I was there. The key was proof. But what if whoever it was that was outside didn't believe me? What if it was the police? I didn't have the time to explain myself and I couldn't end up questioned by the cops. Too risky in the circumstances. It wouldn't take them long to associate me with Cecil. Even worse to connect me with Arturo. And the last thing I needed was to be connected to half a million dollars that sounded dodgy at best and illegal at worst. I made my decision. There was no way I could exit through the front. I ran back through the hall. Brooke's bedroom was on the right. I made for the window. It was locked. An en-suite bathroom at the far end of the room had no windows and no exit. I ran back through the sitting room to the kitchen again. This time I tried the windows but just like the back door, they too were locked. As I came back into the hall, I heard a loud banging on the front door followed by a deep booming voice above the siren.

'C'mon out buddy. We know you're in there, ya hear.'

At the end of the hallway I knew there was a bathroom. I had used it to freshen up before I had left that morning. It was my last option. I opened the door and went straight to the window. I stretched across the small sink that stood beneath it and pulled on the blind release cord. A shaft of light shone through the square opaque piece of glass, highlighting the brightly tiled room. To my right, a shower cubicle. On the other side of the sink a toilet. With the blind rolled up I tried the window catch. It opened but it wasn't designed for anyone to get through as it moved a mere six inches, enough to let air into the room and nothing else. I could hear the banging on the door in the background. It seemed I was trapped, no easy way out. If I went out to face what I now perceived as a mob outside the door, I'd be lynched or at best, arrested. I didn't fancy a vigilante mob and if I were to be arrested, apart from the obvious implications, I'd never make my rendezvous with the cash.

I walked across the room and shut the door. Better to block out as much of the noise as I could. I needed to think. And fast. There was no choice. I was in a room with a shower, a sink, a toilet and a window that didn't open fully but the window was my only hope. If I could force it back, it may open sufficiently to squeeze through. I could pay for repairs to the frame later when Brooke returned. I stood on the toilet seat to my left, and stretched my right leg across to the sink. A small shove against the side wall propelled me across onto my right foot, shifting my weight onto the edge of the sink. As I grabbed at the frame of the window to lever myself up onto the ledge, I heard the crack. Instinctively I glanced downwards. Before my eyes a hairline split had begun to work its way from right to left across the white sealant where the sink joined the tiling, like a fissure opening up in the ground after an earth tremor. I froze, mesmerised, my left leg dangling in space. I realised what was happening and tried to step back but the toilet seat was too far across. As the fissure reached the end of its line, a splintering fracture slowly opened up between the wall and the sink. To my horror it widened enough for me to see almost through to the floor. In an attempt to stop further damaged I jumped off the sink edge. The sudden thrust on my right foot had a cataclysmic impact. In a ripping, rupturing motion the sink tore away completely from the wall and crashed to the floor, the porcelain shattering into two large chunks, showered by a multitude of smashed fragments.

As I hit the ground with the debris, a jet of water shot towards the ceiling from the remnants of a fractured copper pipe still pinned to the concrete wall. In a burst of adrenaline-fuelled panic I dived at the pipe, covering it with both hands in an attempt to quell the deluge of water. To no avail. The powerful jet simply squirted through my fingers soaking my hair, face and shirt. I jumped to my feet and ran out towards the kitchen. The siren still wailed continuously outside, the shadows hovering around the door. Pulling open a cupboard beneath the main sink, I found the stopcock valve. I twisted it frantically, hoping I had the right one. Back in the bathroom, I was relieved to see the water had stopped but horrified to see the mess. The ceiling was soaked. Chips of broken porcelain floated in a huge pool of water that trickled slowly towards the door.

There was no time to do anything about the mess. I had to get out. I reached for a towel and mopped my wet shirt, face and hair. I then tied it turban style around my head. Vibrant pink would probably draw a bit of attention but I reasoned that it was sensible to have my face partially covered as I made my escape. With the sink out of the way it was easier to hoist myself up onto the ledge. I grabbed the window frame and leant hard against the white PVC frame, shoving it with my shoulder. Slowly it moved against its hinges. I pushed more of my weight against it. All I needed was ten, maybe twelve inches to squeeze through. Below it was a straight hop onto the back garden and a six foot fence out into an alley. I pushed harder and felt some give. But not the give I had expected. A large crack shot across the windowpane in a diagonal line. As the resistance in the glass diminished, the frame started to bend. As it did the glass exploded, sending shower of splinters back into the room. Instinctively I recoiled from the sudden burst and clutched the window edge to stop myself falling off the sill. My improvised pink turban had protected me from the flying splinters. The shock of the exploding glass caused me to hesitate. I glanced back at the disaster scene that was Brooke's bathroom. For some reason my mother's scolding when I was a child shot into my head. *'Don't leave the bathroom in a mess.'*

Adrenaline gave way to a sudden wave of depressed guilt. But there was no time to spare and it was the wrong time for self-reproach. I pushed out the glass that remained in the rectangular frame and clambered through. A running jump at the fence and I managed to scramble over and drop down into the alley. Hidden between two boundary fences I crept along the alley to the end. I peered to my left. It seemed clear. The commotion was at the front of the property. In the distance I heard the wail of a police car siren. No time to lose. I shot out of the alley and headed for the road junction.

When I got back to where I had left the taxi, the driver had gone, clearly a sensible decision given the ensuing commotion. I headed back into the estate, through a maze of quiet roads, Hacienda style properties and manicured lawns, unsure of my direction but desperate to find the main highway. I kept running until eventually I found myself by a service station on the junction of West Windmill Lane and South Durango Drive. A taxi driver was filling up his car at a pump.

'I need a ride to the Paris,' I said.

'Nice turban,' he said, pointing at my pink headgear.

I pulled the towel from my head. 'Just got out of the...err... shower. Running a...you know...bit late.'

'What, you got in the shower with all your clothes on?'

'Err...no, just...just grabbed the shirt out of the washing machine. In a hurry. It'll dry out.'

'Jump in then buddy. Just gassin up and I'll be right with you.'

I slumped into the rear seat and pulled my mobile from my pocket. Brooke wasn't answering so I left a message. Better that she found out what had happened to her bathroom from me first rather than the cops.

Back at the hotel I went straight to Lost Property. Carlos's ruse worked a treat. I opened the bag, pulled out some socks and a t-shirt and uncovered my passport. The receptionist recoiled on seeing the items of clothing given what I had said earlier. I held out the passport for her but she asked me to open it rather than risk any contamination that had come from my dirty clothes. She checked the ID and that was sufficient for me to get the bag back without any need to delve further through its contents. I stuck the passport in my pocket and went straight to room 1155.

'Carlos, you there? It's Matthew,' I said as I banged on the door.

'Hang on amigo. I'm coming.'

Carlos opened the door, wearing a pair of shorts and looking red-eyed and hung over.

'You alright mate? It's nearly four in the afternoon,' I said.

'Och, had a wee bit of a late one. Think I hit the wall last night. Still trying to get over it. It's higher than I expected. This jet lag and late nights thing is a killer,' Carlos replied as he rubbed his forehead as if to alleviate some deep-seated ache. 'Come in Mateo.'

'Well, sounds like you had a good time anyway. You're limping again though.'

'Wee bit of boogying and drinking celebrating our win. Went out to–'

'Hang on. Celebrating? You still got the money Carlos, haven't you?' I said, my heart suddenly thumping at the prospect that it might have financed another night out.

'Aye, Mateo. What you saying? It's in the safe.'

'Nothing. Nothing, mate. Just that I've picked the bag up from Lost Property and I need to put the rest of the cash with it to make up the half a million. I need to deliver it tomorrow to somewhere called…Tono…Tonopah or something.'

'Where's that?'

'Not completely sure just yet. Somewhere north of Vegas. Need to be there tomorrow morning. The contact has been in touch.' I gave Carlos a quick rundown of my meeting with the lawyer.

'So you got the bag alright then? See, you listen to Carlos, things go smoothly.'

I wiped my damp brow remembering just how smoothly the afternoon had not gone.

'It worked fine but I had a bit of a palaver with your key. I left it in Brooke's place and had to rush over there and get the bloody thing. She's gone away and I've set off her alarms, the lot. The neighbours think I'm a friggin burglar.'

257

Carlos stared at me for a moment, walked across to his wardrobe and pulled open a drawer.

'You shoulda come to see me amigo. I have a spare one.'

30

William Earp's idea of a practical car was a 1954 Series 62 Cadillac Convertible Coupe. Bright red, with silver trim and white wall wheels, it boasted huge chrome bumpers and a chrome front grille. The interior was a mix of red and white trim, white leather seats and a red and white steering wheel. It had to be over twenty feet long and it was far from subtle. It was a cool car but I wasn't sure it was practical. Bill delivered it himself. We did the paperwork and he handed me the keys.

'Part of my personal touch for a new customer all the way from England,' he said.

Carlos and Jasper were very impressed by my new set of wheels.

At 5.45 on Wednesday morning, dressed in shorts, t-shirt and trainers, I loaded the black Nike rucksack, with its half million dollars, into the boot and locked it securely. I jumped behind the wheel of the Cadillac and checked the Nevada map I'd bought downtown. Tonopah seemed to be in the middle of nowhere but then since Las Vegas was built in the Nevada desert, leaving town was like heading to nowhere. I had checked the journey the night before on the Paris internet. Tonopah was two hundred and fifteen miles north.

The first part of my journey took me towards North Las Vegas. At the intersection I turned left onto US Route 95, signposted Reno. I followed the wide carriageway through the outlying areas of Vegas, properties and buildings disappearing into the distance behind me as I headed north. Further on, as the road snaked its way through vast expanses of scrubland that was the Nevada desert, it merged into one endless tarmac ribbon that extended out ahead of me towards distant sandy-brown mountain ridges. The scenery remained much the same along the whole route. Either side, dry desert scrubland, with a thin covering of green brush-like plants breaking up the grey-brown dusty surface and the occasional solitary cactus. Ahead, hazy blue sky spanned the landscape where it met the mountaintops. For sections the road stretched in a long arrow straight line with not another vehicle in sight. Then, breaking the monotony, a heavy truck would trundle out of the distance and disappear again in my rear view mirror. I was heading into unfamiliar, hostile territory. Alone. No back up. The further I drove, the more a sense of isolation grew within me.

I had been driving for just over three hours when I noticed the speed limit signs, each one taking the speed down another ten miles an hour. Ahead was Tonopah. I slowed to just under the advised thirty-five, not wanting to miss my rendezvous point. As the road curved left I spotted the Texaco petrol station on my right. I pulled in and stopped. The garage stood just back off the road, a normal covered petrol filling point with what looked like a convenience store at the back of it. Behind the building and to either side, a huge expanse of wasteland bordered the desert scrub. A large road-train style truck was parked up to the left of the building and a couple of cars were parked a bit further back. To the right of the building, close to the scrubland, a black four-wheel drive vehicle was parked facing the desert. I could just make out that it was a Subaru. Now that I had reached the rendezvous point, my earlier feeling of isolation had been replaced by a sense of unease. I wasn't sure why. I was just doing as I had been instructed.

I swung the Cadillac in front of one of the pumps, got out and filled up. I walked into the store picked up a bottle of water and went to the pay desk. An elderly man with a drooping moustache took the transaction. Apart from him, the store was empty. Once outside I stood for a moment in the warm sun and checked to see if anyone was around. There was no one. The trucker must have been asleep in his cab. I assumed the two cars parked right at the back belonged to staff at the garage. The four-wheel drive vehicle was too far away to see if anyone was in it. I walked round to the back of the building. Just as the lawyer had said, there were two blue dumpsters backed up against one of its walls, their paintwork scuffed from use. One had a heap of building rubble piled up inside and the other had what appeared to be bits of engines and car parts. I walked slowly round them bending down to see if I could find an envelope. There was nothing obvious. I crouched down to get a better look and ran my hand under the raised base. Again nothing, just grime and rust. I followed the edge right the way around until I reached the adjacent dumpster and did the same thing along the front edge. Still nothing. I moved to the far side. As I traced my way around its right hand edge, I felt it. A cardboard flap. I knelt down in the dirt and checked underneath. A plain brown hard-backed envelope was stuck to the underside of the metal dumpster. I pulled it away to find it had been attached with four bits of Blu Tack.

Straightening up, I checked to see if anyone was around. There was no one. I waited until I was back at the Cadillac before I opened the envelope. Inside was a folded plain white sheet of paper containing a typewritten message. I leant against the back of the car and began to read.

'Go north on Highway 95 to Carson City. At Carson City go to the Gold Lace Casino and Lap Dance Club. Bring the luggage. Ask for Rodrigo. This matter is confidential. If you divulge information or fail to deliver there will be consequences for you and your friends. You have until 4pm.'

I read it again, my mind trying to absorb the information and make sense of it all. Where was Carson City for god's sake? Gold Lace Casino and Lap Dance Club? How was I supposed to find that? And why did it sound familiar? I grabbed the map from the Cadillac, traced the line of Highway 95 and looked for Carson City. South of Reno, it looked to be at least the same distance that I had already travelled. That would take another three and a half to four hours at least. It was already nine-fifteen. My flight home was at nine o'clock that night. I had to travel well over another two hundred miles to deliver the bag, then get back to Vegas and somehow get Cecil out of jail. It was impossible. I had no contact with these people. If I had done, maybe I could have arranged for them to meet me half way. But even if I did, I doubted that they would see things from my point of view and be reasonable. And now they were threatening my friends. For a moment I contemplated trying to get the Gold Lace Casino and Lap Dance Club number on my mobile from enquiries. Maybe Rodrigo was a reasonable man. But why did the club sound familiar?

The voice took me by surprise when I heard it, but as soon as I did my question was answered.

'Nice car.'

'What are you doing here?' I asked, as soon as I'd recovered from the shock.

'A good question.'

I threw the map onto the passenger seat of the car.

'I'm confused. Why are you here?'

'You don't know?'

'No...I don't. I'm on my way to...' I paused mid-sentence as the thought struck me. '...the casino I'm meant to be going to... it's got the same name as –'

Erin Farrell took three paces towards me.

'That's right. The primrose I gave you. Gold Lace. Good name for a casino and lap dancing club though, don't you think? Kind of sums it all up.'

'I don't understand. It's a bit of a co-incidence. And you...here. It's the middle of nowhere. What's going on?'

'Co-incidence Matthew? Maybe,' Erin said. A light breeze fluttered her loose, white cotton dress as she spoke. She smiled and brushed her hair away from her face. 'I want to show you something. Pull your car in next to that black Subaru over there,' she said, pointing in the direction of the four-wheel drive.

I jumped into the Cadillac and pulled in alongside the Subaru, my head full of questions. Erin waited until I got out of the car and then walked to the passenger door of the Subaru, leant in and pulled out a brown leather satchel-style shoulder bag. She then went to the back of the vehicle and flicked open the rear hatch door.

'Ok, now you. Open the boot, Matthew.'

I stood rooted to the spot, unable to comprehend her request.

'Sorry?'

'Open the boot of your car Matthew,' she said, her voice more insistent. 'I want the bag.'

Her request was clear but, for a moment, it seemed incomprehensible to me. She wanted the bag that had caused me so much aggravation over the whole trip. The bag with half a million dollars in it. There had to be a mistake. My lack of action caused her to repeat the request.

'Matthew, do as I ask. Open the boot and give me the bag.'

'I don't understand Erin. What bag?'

'Matthew, don't try playing games. I want the bag you have that has the money in it. Am I clear enough now?' She must have noticed the shock on my face. 'Yes, the half a million dollars.'

I had been chased around Vegas by two sets of villains, lost the bag once already, threatened at gun point by Arturo and now someone else was after it too. Someone I had least expected. The thought of Arturo stopped me in my tracks. Surely Erin was not connected with him. Then I remembered the flower again. The Primula Gold Lace that Erin had given to me on the flight. The name of the casino I was meant to be going to. It didn't make sense but somehow it was all connected.

'I can't give you the bag Erin. I am being pursued by some very bad people and if I don't deliver it to them I'm in a lot of trouble.'

'Not my problem right now Matthew,' Erin said. Her green eyes had narrowed as she stared at me, her face now a cold detached mask, focussed and determined. 'So, are you going to open the boot and give me the bag or will I have to make you?'

'Make me? I can't Erin. I don't understand. Why you are doing this?'

There was no response to my question. She reached into the leather shoulder bag, pulled out a short black gun and pointed it directly at me.

'You see this Matthew. I don't know if you know anything about guns but this is a Ruger SR9c Compact Centrefire Pistol. In the wrong hands it can do a lot of damage and right now, it's in the wrong hands. Mine. It is in the wrong hands because you have something I badly want and you are not co-operating. I am asking you one more time. Open the boot of your car. Take the bag out and put it in here.' She waved the point of the pistol towards the rear of the Subaru.

Momentary paralysis kept me rooted to the spot. Jaw dropping disbelief coursed through me. Erin Farrell, who had stood semi-naked in front of me just a few days before, had a gun pointed somewhere in the region of my mid-chest. It occurred to me that Erin semi-naked and Erin pointing a gun had caused more or less the same reaction – a stupefying inertia that removed my powers of speech. My lack of activity provoked another wave of the gun.

'The bag, Matthew.'

The movement of the gun, the second one that had been pointed at me in two days, galvanised me into action. I couldn't be sure whether Erin intended to use it or not but her face had lost all the warmth, charm and humour that I had seen before in the brief time I had known her. I pulled the Cadillac keys from my pocket and unlocked the boot. Erin stood back, the gun still pointed at me. I picked up the bag and transferred it to the rear of the Subaru.

'Ok. Now give me your keys and your mobile phone.'

'What?'

'Your car keys and your mobile. Place them there.' She pointed at the rear of her car where I had put the bag. 'Now close the boot of your car and get into mine, in the driver's seat.'

I was focussed now. I had lost the money again and with a gun pointed at me I decided to co-operate fully. I could not be sure what she might do. I shut the Cadillac's boot and got into the front of her Subaru. She climbed into the back and sat on the passenger side.

'That's better Matthew. Glad you see sense. Ok, now we're going for a drive. Lock your door.'

I pushed the lock switch into place.

She reached over from the rear and handed me the keys.

'Now, don't try anything clever, brave or stupid. I have the gun pointed directly at the back of your head. Don't forget that. Start the engine. The next stretch heads west but just follow the highway.'

I swung the Subaru back onto the road.

'Where are we going Erin? Carson City? This is the way I was going.'

'Never mind that right now. Just keep your speed to fifty and keep going straight.'

31

I took the Subaru through the urban area of Tonopah and back out on to the desert road. The scenery ahead and to both sides was identical to that before Tonopah but my focus was not entirely on the road. I was acutely aware of Erin and her gun in the back seat. There was nothing I could do to get myself out of the situation. She had the upper hand. We had been driving for almost five minutes when I decided I had to ask.

'Erin, I don't know what you're doing involved in all this and nor do I know how it's all going to turn out but don't you think you owe me an explanation? I just came here to celebrate my birthday. That was all. Now I'm involved in whatever you, Arturo and those goons in Vegas and Carson City are plotting.'

'What do you want to know Matthew?' she answered in a matter of fact tone, almost as if I had asked her something as innocuous as what she had been doing in Vegas so far.

'All of it,' I said. 'For a start…Arturo. He pulled a gun on me the other day, now you have. You're connected to him, aren't you? Is he your boyfriend or something?'

I heard a deep, resigned sigh from behind me. It was a minute or so before she spoke.

'I don't suppose any of this matters too much now Matthew but, sure, maybe I do owe you an explanation. Just you stay focussed on the road ahead and keep your speed to fifty. Remember I have a gun here in the back so no funny business, ok.'

She lapsed back into silence for a few minutes and then she spoke again.

'No, Arturo's not a boyfriend. I met him in a hotel in New York about eight months ago. He's just a cog in the wheels of a bigger machine out there on the east coast. But he thinks he's a big shot. He likes to flash the cash, talk big. He was ambitious but sometimes, like a lot of these educated types, he has no common sense.'

She paused for a moment as if collecting her thoughts, perhaps even to consider how much she should tell me. Then she continued.

'He knew the Baltimore job was coming up and –'

'The Baltimore job? What's that?'

'It was a two million dollar payroll heist. A robbery. In Baltimore. A team out there had been planning it for months. Arturo had connections with a few of the guys involved so he knew about it. You wouldn't have heard much about it in the UK.'

Baltimore. A robbery. It came back to me in a flash.

'No, I didn't but…I think I read something on the flight out. In the Washington Post or somewhere but I didn't take too much notice. You're involved in that?'

I heard Erin's laughter. 'Not me exactly. I'm no armed robber. I had nothing –'

'Really? Well from where I'm sitting, with you making off with my bag of cash and that gun pointing at me, it kind of looks like you could be.'

'You know what I mean Matthew. I had nothing to do with the actual robbery. Anyway, after too much Champagne one night Arturo practically told me all about it. He indicated that the proceeds of the heist would be shifted across the country and washed through a casino where big volumes of money are the norm. A few weeks later the gang carried out the robbery and made off with the two million. The FBI are still following up leads but even all these weeks after it happened they don't seem to be any closer to solving it.'

I was surprised that Erin was telling me so much but I didn't want to stop her flow. I kept the Subaru at fifty.

'So you mean after the robbery they had to clean up the cash… what's it called…money laundering?'

'That's right. They needed people to make it happen. Arturo's a gambler. He knows people, especially in Vegas. He's dabbled a bit…drugs, petty stuff, you know. So he put them in touch with some guys he knew out here who could do it. In return he said he might get some of the action, as he called it. I asked him what his cut would be. Five thousand dollars for each drop. It didn't seem a lot for such a risk so I told him that he should be looking for more. But that was their price.'

I listened in silence, allowing Erin to talk while she was on a roll.

'It was a massive risk for him to be connected to such a high profile heist. It was all over the papers in the States. So, I just got to thinking about it and came up with a way of cashing in on the opportunity. The cash for the Baltimore robbery was being exchanged on a two for one basis. The stolen cash was being delivered half a million dollars at a time in four drops. In return two hundred and fifty thousand of clean money would be handed over at each drop. Arturo stood to make twenty thousand dollars from all four exchanges but I knew he could make at least ten times that amount if he managed to pull off just one switch. I mean what's the point of being small time? To be honest I didn't think he'd have the balls to go through with it. But I kind of planted the idea in his head about the switch. Made it look like his idea.'

A cold shiver ran through me when I heard the word.

'Switch? What switch?'

'Well, first of all it was a courier thing. You know, exchanging the heist money for the laundered money. Two million dollars from a very public robbery is difficult to hide. The only way to conceal it and filter it back out is through organised crime links. The big crime organisations have the ways and means. They have outlets. One of them is the Gold Lace Casino and Lap Dancing Club in Carson –'

'So, that's why you gave me the primrose. It was some sort of sign or –'

'Hang on Matthew. You asked me to explain. Let me finish will you. So the guys Arturo knows out here are running a casino operation up in Carson City but really it's just a front for their organized crime connections. They take the proceeds of a robbery or drug deal and wash it through the casino. The guys who carried out the payroll heist would get a million dollars for off loading two million in stolen cash. It's a tough deal for them but they don't have a lot of options. Not many will handle that amount of cash from a heist. So they do the deal and then the money going back to them is clean as it has passed through lots of casinos in Nevada. The Gold Lace Casino guys make a nice profit for their bosses and the team that handled the Baltimore job get legitimate cash for their efforts.'

'So what is this switch then?'

'Once I knew Arturo would be involved in moving the money as a go between, I realised that there was proper money to be made if an exchange could be intercepted. I just saw a once in a lifetime opportunity if somehow we could switch one of the drops and get hold of the clean cash. It was a bit of a fantasy. You know, one of those things when you dream of what you would do if you had a million dollars. A Champagne fuelled fantasy. It was always meant to be a one off. Just take two hundred and fifty grand. That's plenty, especially with the risk involved. But I wasn't sure how.'

I stared straight ahead at the road, only glancing away occasionally to check my speed.

'After they pulled off the heist the East Coast team had to lay low for a while. The robbery was over two months ago so they had to start shifting the cash eventually. Arturo told me when he would be running the courier thing for the exchanges. The idea started to take hold and I began to think it was possible to pull off a switch if I could get a foolproof plan together. Arturo was keen. He thought that it would set him up after all his gambling losses. He wanted to go to Europe. Spain or somewhere and wanted me to go with him. He's just a foolish romantic. But it was a chance for me too so I fuelled the idea, gave him the plan.'

'And how exactly was I part of that plan then?'

'We had to find someone we could use to replace the real courier from Carson City. Make it look like Arturo had been tricked and push the blame onto someone else. I'm sorry now Matthew that it was you. I really got to like you. I kind of wish I could have used someone else. There was something about you, you know. Something likeable. I didn't want to put you in any danger. I guess I thought it was all a game, a part of the fantasy.'

I felt anger well up inside me.

'You did put me in danger Erin. And Louise. They threatened to have her kidnapped back in London. They saw her photos on my camera. You put us all at risk.'

I heard the deep sigh before she responded.

'I realise that now. But when you showed up in that speed awareness course late, I could see you had an air of naivety, a sort of innocence. I needed somebody like that. When you said you were going to Vegas it crossed my mind that you'd be ideal and maybe we could pull off the switch on that drop. It seemed too much of a coincidence that one of the exchanges was due to take place in Vegas. I just didn't know how I could make it happen with you at first.'

'You mean you needed someone you could dupe.'

'No, not dupe. Just someone who was right. Someone in the right place at the right time. Someone who could fit the plan. And the beauty of it was, you were only going to be in Vegas for a short while.'

'So how was the plan supposed to work exactly if I took the money away in the exchange?' I asked, feeling more dumb than innocent.

'Simple really. The money exchange involved the courier from Carson City meeting Arturo in Caesar's Palace. Arturo was supposed to give him the half million instalment from the robbery in exchange for the two hundred and fifty thousand laundered money. He had to get the courier out of the way so we could make it look like you were the contact. So he arranged for him be waylaid on the way down to Vegas.'

'Waylaid?'

'Intercepted. He was stopped by a bogus highway patrol car

just north of Hawthorne on US 95. You don't need to know the details Matthew.'

I did want to know the details. I thought that if I knew how they treated the *waylaid* driver it might give me an indication of what would happen to me.

'You might as well tell me Erin. It makes no odds to me.'

'Look, I didn't get involved in that. All I know is what Arturo told me. They had to make sure he couldn't let anyone know what had happened. So he was drugged, blindfolded and taken to a safe apartment back there in Tonopah. The following day he was driven back to where he'd been intercepted, still sedated and blindfolded and left on the back seat of the car. They took his mobile. He wouldn't have been able to contact anyone until long after Arturo had done the switch. The bag the courier was carrying with the two hundred and fifty thousand, was delivered to Arturo well before the rendezvous time. The guys had no idea what they were delivering. Amazing what you can get done for five thousand dollars.'

I felt my hands tighten on the steering wheel.

'So it *was* Arturo that switched bags with me in Caesar's Palace that first night?'

'Well, yes. It was. He's a bit of a con artist so it wasn't difficult for him. He's never settled since the fame of his polo playing days so he's always after an adrenaline rush.'

'So why did he need to switch the robbery money with me if he'd already taken the clean cash from the casino courier?'

'He had to cover his tracks. He couldn't take the risk of stealing directly from the guys working out of the Gold Lace Casino. They're dangerous men. He was never going to take their money without some sort of cover to back up his story. He had to direct the focus away from himself. His plan was to store the legitimate cash, the two hundred and fifty grand, until he had secured the bag switch with you and had your camera bag. Then, once he'd delivered the bogus bag to the East Coast guys and made it look like you'd hijacked the whole deal, he was coming back to sort the robbery proceeds. If it had gone to plan it was simply a matter getting the half million back from you and tipping off the Gold Lace boys where to find it. Then all we had to do was get out of town with the clean money he'd stashed back at his place. The robbery team would be left high and dry thinking that you'd hijacked their deal but by then you'd be back in London.'

My head had begun to swirl with the information and each bit of detail raised a question. I stared straight ahead at the road, a jumble of questions forming in my mind. In the distance I saw a truck approaching. For a moment it occurred to me to flash the headlights in some sort of emergency manner to attract attention but something stopped me. I needed to know how and why I had been duped. Another question.

'But, it doesn't make sense for somebody to switch bags for a quarter of a million dollars and leave a camera in the other bag with their picture on it, does it?'

'Maybe not Matthew. But as I said, Arturo had to put the focus on you. A distraction. It was meant to give us time to collect the money and be on our way.'

'Yeah, but once Arturo switched bags with me how was he supposed to get the money back for himself?'

Erin let out a long sigh, as if weary of the whole thing, before answering.

'He had to go through a proper switch. The exchange was planned for Caesar's Palace and he couldn't risk not doing it properly. There are CCTV cameras all over Vegas and these guys have contacts too. Where there's a large cash transaction the trust factor isn't that great. So, once he'd done the bag switch with you, he planned to break into your room and retrieve the five hundred grand when you were asleep. But of course you went and lost the bloody bag which really upset the whole plan.'

'Well he did break in. Or someone did. Practically trashed the whole room.'

'I know but he'd tried the subtle approach earlier. We thought you were taking the bag straight back to your room. You remember I saw you as you were leaving Caesar's that night? I asked you if you fancied a drink but you said you were going back to the hotel. I was just keeping an eye on your movements. Anyway, after you got back to the Paris Arturo got into your room to get the bag back as planned. You were out of it and –'

'The sleeping pill.' Out of it. Of course. 'Arturo gave me that pill. I remember now. All a bloody set up.'

'Well, yes, he knew with a few drinks, jetlag and the sleeping pill you'd never stir. That was the plan. But he couldn't find the bag. He couldn't do a thorough search. Too risky with you in the room. So without the bag he couldn't leave town.'

'But he already had the other money, the clean money and –'

'I just told you. You don't mess with those guys running the Carson City operation. They'd track him down no matter what. They're well connected and dangerous. They would not tolerate losing two hundred and fifty grand and would've come after everybody connected with the deal. So we had to make sure they got their end of the deal before we left. They get their half a million and they're happy.'

The mention of the well-connected Carson City villains focussed me on my predicament. The word *dangerous* served to heighten the impossible situation I was in. They were expecting a delivery. I was supposed to make sure it happened. It seemed very unlikely the way things were going that I could fulfil that expectation. I recalled the note in the envelope. '*...consequences for you and your friend.*' Panic began to take a grip. It seemed to me I had more to fear from them than from Erin.

I pulled the Subaru across to the right and braked hard, pulling up off the tarmac in a cloud of dust.

'What are you doing Matthew?' Erin shouted.

My mind raced. I had acted on impulse. Somehow I had to find a way out and get the bag back. I had no idea how I would do that but I knew I had to separate myself from Erin and her gun first.

'I…I err…need to go…err to use the facilities.'

'What facilities? There are no facilities out here?'

'You know…a…I need the washrooms, the gents. I've been driving all morning. I just need…you know.'

Erin laughed out loud. 'Why didn't you go back at the service station?'

'I didn't…I don't know. Can we go back we're only…what, ten minutes or so away?'

'Oh sure Matthew. Do you think I'm stupid? Sure, we go back. You pop in the washrooms and tip off the guy in the store that you're being held at gunpoint? You think that's a clever plan? Really? I had you down as a bit brighter than that?'

Although I hadn't quite got the detail of a plan I realised that Erin was right. She'd never fall for something so lame but with the lack of any better idea I tried again anyway.

'No, I really do want to go…to the…gents.'

'Really? Ok. No problem. Take a wander out there,' Erin said, waving her hand in the direction of the desert. 'There's nobody around. You'll be fine. But make it quick Matthew. I haven't got all day. Now hand me the keys and get out of the car.'

I hesitated. It wasn't going the way I thought.

'Err…but there are no…wash basins…and no…loo roll.'

'Oh I see. You want creature comforts too. I'm afraid not. You're going to have to rough it. There'll be a cactus or two to clean up on.' Erin threw back her head and laughed. 'Now go on. Do what you have to do. Oh and don't stray too far. I was the All-Ireland under fifteen pistol shooting champion back in the day.'

32

I had walked about a hundred yards from the car before I stopped to consider my options. As I stood on the dusty surface of the desert floor underneath the blazing sun, I realised that I didn't seem to have that many. The bag was still in the back of the Subaru. Erin was leaning casually against the front of the vehicle. She had a gun and the car keys. She knew I could go nowhere. There was nobody around. Nothing but scrubland. I had no plan. There was no way out. If I was going to deliver the money my only hope was to stay with the vehicle and stay near the bag. I also needed some answers.

I walked back towards the car. As I approached, Erin called out.

'Changed your mind then?' Her right hand held the gun down by her side. Her other hand had bunched the folds of her cotton dress so that she could raise it up above her knees to let the sparse breeze cool her legs.

'Err...yes. I don't want to go now. Must be...you know, stage fright.'

'C'mon then Matthew. Get back in the car. We've wasted too much time already.'

I did as I was told, started the engine and pulled back out onto the road. I tried to dismiss any thoughts of the dangerous men from Carson City and focus on the road ahead. As I did, my mind returned to Erin's explanation of how I had been duped by her and Arturo. At that moment I would have gladly taken one of Arturo's sleeping pills and hoped, that when I woke up again, all I had been through would have been nothing more than a nightmare. The thought of Arturo fired up the questions I still had that needed answering. For the first time since we'd been on the road, I stared directly at Erin in the rear view mirror. I caught her gaze, focussed right back at me.

'So tell me. How did he do it? How did Arturo get into my room in the first place?' I saw the fleeting little smile as she answered.

'Kimberley.'

'Kimberley?'

'Yes, Kimberley. You know, the woman you had the run ins with. It made me laugh when I heard about them Matthew. She wasn't very ha–'

'You mean, Kimberley…with the vibrator? The one in the lift. Whose camera I kicked in the pool? How did *she* get into my room?'

I heard a giggle behind me. 'Vibrator? I didn't know about that. What's that about?'

'Nothing. Just…how did she get in my room?'

'She didn't. She got your keycard for Arturo. That first night, when you collapsed in the Paris bar. She was the one who got you back to your room.'

I tried to recall the detail of that first night. I could barely remember walking back to the Paris. Everything had been a blur and had got worse as the sleeping pill had kicked in. And then I remembered the voices. The bar tender…'*two dollars, Sir.*' Two dollars for what? I had tried to order something…must have done. A coffee. That was it. The woman's voice came back to me too… '*We met in Caesar's. Are you Ok?*' Kimberley. So it was Kimberley that took me back to my room. That gave her the opportunity to take the keycard from my wallet. I vaguely recalled scrambling around on the floor trying to pick it up. '*We met in Caesar's.*' No wonder Kimberley had looked familiar at the poolside.

'It was her in Caesar's wasn't it?' I said, as the memory of the woman in the black cocktail dress and vampish makeup swirled into focus.

'Well she was hanging around Arturo,' Erin replied.

'But why would she take my card? She's working with Arturo, right? She helped him switch bags? Is she involved too?'

'No. Not really. She knew nothing about the money. Arturo can be a bit of a charmer. He met her a few days ago. She's on holiday. He noticed she'd lost quite a bit on roulette so he offered her five hundred dollars to pass him information on your movements and another five hundred to lift your keycard. It was an easy option so his cover would not be blown. That bit hadn't been planned before. He just saw an opportunity for him to keep a lower profile rather than following you himself. He told her he worked under cover for a security company and was investigating credit card fraud on hotel payments. He said you were suspected of running up hotel bills fraudulently and he needed to get into your room. So it wouldn't have seemed too odd to her if she'd seen him switch the bags.'

'Very nice. Stitched me right up.'

'Then when things started to unravel he offered her more cash to keep an eye on you, as she was staying at the Paris too.'

'Oh so that's why she was so keen on Jasper.' I should have known when he said she was asking questions.

'Yes, but you, Matthew, you nearly drove her to distraction. In the end she didn't seem to want much to do with Arturo's little under cover job.'

I felt stupid. I'd been taken for a sucker. Erin, Arturo, Kimberley. And I hadn't seen any of it. Now I was in real trouble. I wondered if any of this would have been possible if I had managed to stay on my original flight with the boys.

'You know what's puzzling me,' I said. 'How did you know I'd be on your flight?'

'I didn't. Fate threw us together. I couldn't believe it when you came on board. They had already started moving the money. There was one drop off two weeks ago in San Diego and another the week before in Dallas. They had to be careful and move around, different cities, different locations. I knew the next one was in Las Vegas. There was only going to be four drops in total to exchange the full two million so I knew we had to get involved in one of them sooner or later if we were going to pull off the plan. So when I ran into you for the first time and heard you were going to Vegas it seemed like it had to be the one. So I volunteered for the flight out here so I could be in the right place but when you stepped on the same plane it just made things easier. And you'd already said you'd be at the Paris so I kind of knew your movements but it was just a bonus that you happened to get the same flight.'

'But how did you get Arturo to find me? And...hang on, how did you know I'd have the right bag for the switch over anyway?'

'I took your picture on my mobile when you were asleep on the flight so Arturo would be familiar with you. He didn't have to find you. If you remember as you left the plane I suggested you go up to Caesar's. We just needed you to be in the right place.'

'Yes, you did. I remember that.'

'As for the bag...you didn't have the right bag.'

'I didn't?' I glanced back at Erin.

'No. You didn't need the right bag. We did. I made sure we got the right one. You mentioned the bag you mislaid. When I took your picture I also checked the overhead locker. Nobody takes any notice of a stewardess opening a locker. I got the description of your bag and sent a text to Arturo along with your picture once we'd landed. He had plenty of time to find an identical bag and place the cash in it. Nike is big in Vegas so it wasn't difficult to get one like yours. It worked out right too that you had that type of bag. All the exchanges are made using backpacks. It's an inconspicuous bag because tourists carry them about and it just blends in. And it's natural for a tourist on their first night to take a camera out with them. They all do it. It was a gamble, a sort of evolving plan with you. To be honest, we were not quite sure how the bag switch would work. If you'd not taken it with you to Caesar's then we would have had to step in and encourage you to do so.'

I glanced again at Erin in the mirror. I saw her glance at her watch.

'Encourage me? How?'

'I don't know. We'd have found a way but as it happened we

278

didn't need to. The point was to get you to Caesar's with the bag. We only had a small window of opportunity. Arturo had to make sure he delivered the clean cash to the East Coast team by the following evening. They'd arranged a rendezvous in Flagstaff, Arizona. If we were to make you look like the courier, we had to ensure you were in Caesar's that first night. We tracked you in the Paris when you met up with your friends to make sure you had your Nike bag with you.'

'I didn't see you.'

'You wouldn't have done. Arturo played the slots in the casino and kept watch. I stayed pretty low key but was around in case I was needed. Then once we saw you had the bag we followed you up to Caesar's when you left the Paris.'

'So it *was* Arturo in my picture,' I said, almost in a whisper, as I remembered Cecil scrolling through the camera.

'What picture?'

'Oh nothing. So you just knew I'd take the bag out. All too easy, eh, Erin?'

'Well sooner or later you'd do the tourist thing and take pictures. I saw you had a video camera in the bag too and I guessed you'd take the whole lot out with you at some point.'

If I had not been driving, I would have hung my head in shame at my predictability.

'So I just went right ahead and did exactly what you expected like some dumb, sad sack tourist. I walked right into Caesar's carrying the bag just as you predicted.'

'Well, yes, I suppose. But you *are* a tourist, Matthew. And let's face it, Vegas works on predictability. Punters do the same old predictable thing and the casinos take their money. But your predictability ended when you lost the bag. I hadn't expected that, not after you'd told me you'd already mislaid it when you missed your flight.'

'Pity I didn't miss your one too Erin.' My fingers gripped the steering wheel hard as my first night at Caesar's flashed through my mind. 'I can't believe it. I must have stuck out like sore thumb wearing your stupid flower.'

'Hey, don't be too hard on yourself. You were set up. The couriers from Carson City all wore the Gold Lace primrose. It was the way they were recognized as coming from the Gold Lace Casino for the collection. They don't use the same guy twice as a courier for their own security. And it meant that Arturo had an explanation for the mistake he told his bosses had happened. When he gave them your camera bag, they were able to see you in your pictures in the Paris wearing the primrose. So his story was believable.'

'And I thought that the primrose was for luck. I thought it was really nice of you. So all the time you were setting me up.' I felt cheated. Erin's dishonesty had offended me. And then I remembered something else. 'Didn't you tell me that some old lady had given you the flowers? Made a bouquet or something. That was bullshit too then?'

'I said I'm sorry Matthew. You're right. There was no old lady. I had the primrose on the flight because it was part of the plan. It had to be done. If I was going to go through with it, it had to be done properly.'

I sat in silence for a moment, not knowing what to say. The desert flashed by in a blur but I was driving on autopilot. I listened as Erin continued.

'Arturo had to deliver the clean money to his contacts at the drop off point in Flagstaff the following evening so they could move it on to the East Coast. After the switch he stuffed wads of newspaper into your camera bag to give it some bulk and make it look like you'd pulled a stunt to trick him. When they opened the bag they realised they'd been double-crossed. He had a hard time explaining what had happened. He told them he'd never opened the bag because the contact was wearing the primrose. He couldn't tell them your name or that you were staying at the Paris. It would have blown his story to know all that. He had to make out that he genuinely thought you were the real Gold Lace Casino contact. He said that you sounded English or Australian or something and that he was sure he had seen you a little while later going into the Cosmopolitan as he was driving down the Strip. So he kind of sowed the seed that you might still be hanging around Vegas and set up a false trail to buy time. He asked to keep the bag with the camera because it had your picture on it and he could use it to identify you. The contents of your bag were worthless to them so they let him have it back. They gave him time to see if he could locate you. But unbeknown to Arturo they also sent their guys over to Vegas. There's not a lot of trust in the greed game.'

'Yeah, that goon who accosted me on the street and his mate who chased me round Caesar's.'

'I guess so.'

'But why did he take the camera bag back to the Bond Bar? What was the point? I don't understand why it was left in the Bond Bar?' I asked, still trying to piece together the picture that Erin was creating for me. 'And how did he know I'd gone to the Bond bar anyway? I never said anything to him…I don't think.'

'Kimberley again, I'm afraid. She was eavesdropping. Your friend Cecil said he was going there that first night and might see you there. And you did mention it to me too later. So when Arturo realised you didn't have the cash in your room he thought that you might have hidden it somewhere once you'd seen what was in it. There was always the risk that you might have got greedy. If so, he guessed you would have to get your camera back as your picture was on it and you couldn't risk being identified. So if you were searching for your own bag perhaps you'd lead him to where the cash was. Either that or when you realised that you had the wrong bag you would go back to the Bond Bar thinking that you had mixed the bags up there and could exchange them back. So when he got back from Flagstaff he kept tabs on you to see if you would go back to the Bond bar and lead him to the money. He couldn't follow you too closely as he couldn't risk being seen to have contact with you and not dealing with the lost cash. He needed to wait until you led him to the money if his plan was to come off.'

'Yes, but I was hardly going to hand half a million dollars in to the Bond bar was I? So how was that supposed to help Arturo get the robbery money back?'

'Keeping tabs on you was the only choice he had. Then when the other guys turned up it made it difficult. So our plan had clearly gone wrong by then. Arturo had to keep up the appearance of not knowing anything and appearing to have been tricked. He had to answer some pretty stringent questions from the East Coast gang. He thought that, if he could buy some time, he might be able to locate the bag you'd lost and get it back to the Gold Lace contacts. But then he found out that a representative of the Gold Lace Casino had approached you and they'd warned off the other guys. So he got desperate as he could see the whole plan collapsing. He's not really a violent man but desperation made him get the gun. And then your friend Cecil interfered and he got himself arrested.'

The whole complex plan was unravelling around my ears. I couldn't believe I had been such a dupe. As I focussed on each aspect of Erin's story, I tried to go over what I could have done differently. But hindsight is the mother of regret and I knew there was no point in dwelling on it. I was brought back to reality by Erin's cry from the rear seat.

'Hey, watch your speed Matthew. Keep it at fifty. We don't want to get stopped for speeding.'

I almost laughed at the irony of her comment but I wasn't feeling too light hearted just at that point.

'So what happens now, Erin? Where are we going?'

'I told you I was never going to be with Arturo full time. I intended to make the break after we got to Europe with something to show for it. But things change. Arturo can't get the money now where he is.'

'What are you going to do then?'

There was a long pause before she replied.

'Well…there's always you and me Matthew?'

'What do you mean?'

'You know. You and me. We could make a run for it. Head off somewhere sunny in Europe. I like you. I told you that. We have the cash to start again somewhere nice. What do you think?'

I was totally taken aback. A woman who was holding me at

282

gunpoint wanted me to run away with her. I shot a look in the mirror.

'I have someone Erin. I told you that. Someone I want to be with. Someone who doesn't place material things above love and respect. Do you understand that?'

I saw a brief glimpse of sadness sweep over her green eyes.

'Love and respect?' There was anger in her voice as she replied. 'Is that what you call it? So what about that blonde bimbo you've been hanging around with in the Paris. She was even in your room. And you seemed very friendly the other night in the casino.'

'You mean Brooke? She's a friend. She was helping me find the bag. That's all. I'm with Louise. I don't need anyone else.'

Erin was silent for a moment. I felt her hand on my shoulder and then she spoke, her tone a little softer.

'I'm sorry Matthew. I was teasing. I know you have your lady. She's a lucky girl. I knew after you rejected my advances in your room that it could never happen. And then when I came to see you, that girl was in your room. I had come to apologise…you know. Just to say that it had all been a bit quick. When I saw the girl there, I thought you were just giving me a line about the girlfriend. It was then that I decided I had to go through with the plan. I'd thought better of it once I got to know you a little bit. Losing the bag changed things. Gave me time to think about what was important. Made me doubt what I was doing. When I realised you were not that interested in me I decided I had to go for it. Go through with the plan one way or another.'

I felt the need to assert my masculinity.

'I was tempted, the other night I can tell you that. You are a very attractive lady. But I couldn't do that to Louise. Anyway, you haven't answered my question. What now?'

'I shall take the money myself and run.'

'But the money we got here is the robbery money? You can't take that. That was the point wasn't it? To clean it up so it isn't traceable. And you can't take the other cash or you'll end up in the same position that Arturo was concerned about. You know, being tracked down. And if you run out on Arturo he'll reveal all. You won't get away with it Erin.'

She took a deep breath. 'I'm not worried about Arturo. He doesn't really know anything about me. For a start he thinks my name is Caitlin O'Hara.'

I turned my head to the right and for a moment faced Erin.

'Caitlin O'Hara? Caitlin?'

'Yes, Caitlin…Katy…Kate. Whatever you like. I used them all.'

'So, Arturo doesn't know who you really are either?'

'I would never give my real details to some complete stranger I met in a bar.' She chuckled softly. 'Well, maybe I would in your case, Matthew. Anyway, it's not that difficult. Once I get back into Vegas, I'll simply switch the money over myself. Don't worry, I have a plan.'

'But suppose Arturo does talk?'

'I doubt he will. First of all he won't know I've made the switch. Why would he? If he does find out, I will be long gone in any case. And he can hardly reveal that he was part of the plan to hijack the money as that will mean him exposing his involvement to the guys at Gold Lace. His only choice if he wants to save his own skin would be to tell the cops everything and hope he gets protection. But he'll do time for that.'

'So what *is* the plan?'

'Ah…that's my business. The less anyone knows the more likely it is to succeed.'

'Well I wouldn't want to be in your shoes when the Gold Lace guys find out what you've been up to with their money.'

'Well you won't be saying anything, will you Matthew? Otherwise your friend is not getting out of jail. I'll make sure he's implicated if you do.'

I had no answer to that. Instead, I focussed on the team from the East Coast in the hope that it would make Erin rethink.

'But what about the guys who did the Baltimore robbery? They are going to want their two hundred and fifty grand.'

'Don't worry about them. They'll back off for now. They have made two exchanges already and have one more to go. And right now, they think that you were the one who pulled the whole switch so they are still expecting to get their cut tonight after you've delivered the money to Carson City. By that time I'll be gone.'

I felt the beads of sweat on my forehead.

'You mean the East Coast villains think I've got all the money? All seven hundred and fifty grand?'

'I would think so. They still suspect that you've organised the whole thing to cream off the whole pot. But don't panic. You'll be out of town long before they realise what's panned out.'

The blood had drained from my face. I felt cold right through and it wasn't from the aircon.

'It's all one big gamble Erin.'

'Gamble? Of course it is.'

'But didn't you tell me that gambling was a mug's game? That you preferred certainty.'

'I did, but we're in Vegas, Matthew. Gambling is what you do in Vegas.'

33

I had driven for just over half an hour when Erin told me to slow down. I slowed to around thirty miles an hour. I had no idea why and began to wonder what she was planning. I shot a glance at her through the rear view mirror. She was staring out across the landscape to her right as if looking for something. She then told me to pull over off the road and stop. She hit a button on the door console, eased down a rear window and pointed across the scrub.

'Ok Matthew, I want you to drive across there and keep going until I tell you to stop.'

'But there's no road there. Where are we going?'

'Just do as I say. It's an off road car. It will handle it.'

It wasn't the car I was worried about. There was nothing around, just miles of desert scrub as far as the eye could see. No landmark of any description. The absence of any life started to worry me. For a fleeting moment, it crossed my mind that it would be a good place to shoot someone and leave them for dead. Out in the desert it would take a long time for anyone to find a body. A body was more likely to be discovered by a coyote than a human.

We continued to drive, clouds of dust and dirt trailing behind us from the wheels. Just as I was beginning to think that perhaps I knew too much of Erin's plan and it would make sense to silence me, she told me to stop.

'Switch off the engine Matthew and get out of the car.'

As I stepped onto the dusty ground, a blast of searing heat hit me. Erin walked around to the front of the car, in one hand the gun held in front of her and pointed directly at me, in the other a large canvas bag. She placed it on the ground and stepped back. Above us the sun burned blindingly hot in a cloudless blue sky. This was no place for a picnic.

'This is where we part company.'

A fearful tremor shot through me.

'Part company. What? What do you mean?'

'Don't worry. It's not as bad as you think. Open the bag,' she said, smiling and pointing to the canvas bag.

I had no idea what she had to smile about but I bent down and opened the bag.

'There's a baseball hat in there, some sun screen and half a dozen bottles of water. You'll need them. It's about half an hour walk back to the road. Just follow the vehicle tracks and you won't go wrong. From there it's about twenty-five miles back to Tonopah where your car is. When you get back to the car you'll find your keys and your mobile.'

'You're leaving me here?' I said, not quite believing the situation I found myself in.

'You'll survive. Just take your time. I need a head start. Oh, and I want your wallet.'

'My wallet? I only have fifty or so dollars in it. I can't believe you want to rob me as well. Haven't you got enough?'

'You are funny, Matthew,' she laughed. 'I'm not robbing you. I just want your wallet. You won't need money out here. It's just a precaution. You know, in case you have phone numbers or try to bribe someone into giving you a ride or making a call for you. You'll get it back. It'll be in the boot of your car. I will leave the keys on the inside of the passenger side front wheel. OK.'

I threw my wallet on the ground in front of her.

'You know it's going to take…I don't know…five hours or more to get to my car.'

'Perfect. Suits me.'

I realised she meant business. A careful plan that she was putting into place.

'Tell me something, Erin. How did you know I would be coming out here today? Nobody else knew, except my mates.'

'Simple. I got Kimberley to visit Arturo in jail. Gave her five hundred, told her that Arturo had gone undercover in the county jail as part of his investigations into the hotel fraud. His contacts had been in touch to tell him what was going on. He obviously knew you had the bag. The Gold Lace guys had told the East Coast lot to stay off your case as you were making the drop. Arturo gave Kimberley a note. He said that, as you were heading to Carson City with the money, the plan had changed. He told me to back off and lay low. Once you got the cash to Carson City they'd be after you for the rest. Then when he got out of jail we could make our move with the other money. He said that he'd be cool with the East Coast guys because he could show he'd try to recover the bag from you, which is how he'd ended up getting arrested. Too dangerous in my book and I can't wait on him.'

'But how did you know where to find me?' I asked.

'Well, once I found out where you were going I knew you'd stop at Tonopah for fuel. I just got a head start on you.'

'And if I hadn't stopped there?'

'You'd have had to stop at one of the gas stations down there especially driving that big Cadillac. If you hadn't stopped at that one I'd have caught up with you at the next.'

'I was told to stop there,' I said, to avoid being seen as predictable again.

'Maybe, but I didn't know that. Anyway, we're wasting time here Matthew. I have to get going. Things to do.'

She turned towards the car door and pulled it open. She was about to step in behind the wheel when I called out to her.

'Erin. Wait. One more thing.'

She turned to face me, a quizzical look crossing her face.

'I don't understand. If this is about making sure the casino guys get their money why have you stopped me? I was delivering it anyway and you obviously know where the other money is.'

The quizzical look gave way to a smile.

'It's about control. We have lost control of this whole plan in the last few days. I need to be sure things get done now. I can't risk anything else going wrong. You're track record is not exactly great is it? I can't afford to have the Gold Lace guys coming after Arturo and finding out about me.'

'But you said Arturo doesn't know who you are. He thinks you're Kate, or Caitlin, whatever name you used.'

'Caitlin. Yes, that's right. Arturo knows nothing about me but it wouldn't take much for one of the Gold Lace guys to ask around in the casinos and check out their CCTV cameras to see who he's been with, would it? They are resourceful and they are connected. They have people all over Vegas. If Arturo did start talking I need to be well out of the way. So I need to know that they'll definitely get their money. And as far as they are concerned the East Coast guys can take care of their own business. They kept their end of the deal.'

'But, that's the point. I was delivering it to them. If you'd just left me alone I –'

'But I can't be sure you would deliver, Matthew. You'd have time to think on a long drive out here. Suppose you changed your mind and decided to go to the cops now you have the money. For all I know you'd see it as a way of getting Cecil out of jail and being rid of this whole thing. You're an honest guy after all. And if that happened I reckon Arturo would have come clean on the whole deal in return for police protection. That could put me right in the frame and that little stash of cash I'm going to collect would be history. Can't risk that having come this far.'

Little stash? A quarter of a million dollars. I wiped the sweat from my brow as the sun blazed down on my head.

'But Erin, these guys threatened me. I wouldn't have risked not delivering, would I?'

She let out a deep sigh and shot a glance across the open desert away to her right, collecting her thoughts before she answered.

'Look, I have no idea what you'd do. As I say, it's about control. I can't take any more chances. I can hardly turn up in Carson City with you to deliver the bag, can I? Get real. I have to stay below the radar. So this buys me time too. Let's me tidy up things my end. And right now standing in the desert chatting to you, much as I enjoy your company, is using up that time.' She turned again towards the Subaru.

I tried one last attempt to avoid being left out in the wilderness.

'Erin. The other guys are sure to come after you. They won't be too happy about losing their little stash as you call it and getting ripped off too.'

'I told you Matthew. They won't know anything until it's too late. I'll be long gone. Bottom line is they're a bunch of amateurs compared with the Gold Lace guys and they don't have the clout to come after me. Oh, and you know I'm doing you a favour leaving you out here.'

I scratched my head as the sweat tickled through my scalp.

'A favour? You are? Why? How?'

'Because I like you and I don't want to see you come to any harm. Some of the East Coast guys could be waiting for you up there in Carson City too. Once you hand over the half million at the Gold Lace they could be looking for their money. As I said, Arturo thinks they will be. They're all villains Matthew. You just don't know how they cut these deals.'

I hadn't thought of that. Erin had it all worked out it seemed. Perhaps wandering around in the desert was the best option after all. But I needed to get back to Vegas at some point.

'So you're just going to leave me out here in the middle of nowhere?'

The cheeky smile creased her face.

'You'll survive. You'll get back ok, I have no doubt.' Then the smile dropped away, replaced by a sterner expression.

'So listen carefully. If you happen somehow to get out of here faster than I expect you to, you make no phone calls to anyone. If I am contacted in any way I will make sure you friend Cecil does not get out of jail. I will implicate you both in the scam. Do you understand that?'

'I got it,' I said, resigned to the fact that she was serious about leaving me in the desert.

'I need time to sort things out my end. So if you want Cecil on that flight home you do as I say.'

'Ok…ok. I got it.'

'Oh and one more thing Matthew. Don't forget, if I don't get to tip off the Gold Lace guys where to find their money, they are going to come looking for you. They are expecting to get their half a million at some point today, although perhaps not in the way they'd arranged.'

She jumped into the driver's seat of the Subaru and fired up the engine. The car rolled forward and then stopped. The window came down.

'It's been great knowing you Matthew. Good luck…and thanks a million.'

34

When faced with isolation it is easy to panic. But there was a moment of calm that washed over me. Out in the desert nobody could get me. I had safety. I was alone. Nobody knew where I was. The bad guys that had been pursuing me couldn't find me. But that also meant that my friends wouldn't know what had happened to me either. I realised my feeling of safety was nothing more than temporary relief from the stress I had been going through.

I stood and stared at my surroundings. From the comfort of an air-conditioned vehicle, it was easy to watch the open landscape rush past, see none of the detail and feel no sense of the harshness of the environment. To accept that it was a scrubland as we cut through it was an undemanding thought, but the only one that meant anything without first-hand experience. On foot things seemed much different. Around me, tall yucca type plants, short, spiny cacti with thick fleshy shoots, and low-lying green, sagebrush plants were scattered randomly in sparse patterns across the brown dust and rock of the desert floor. Above me, the blue of the sky held a few light, white wispy threads of cloud but nothing that provided any shade from the golden glow of the sun that was rising towards the peak of another hundred degree desert day. Hot dry air burned against my face, causing the sweat to run down in continuous rivulets. The sense of abandonment was suddenly heightened by the stillness of the landscape and the lack of anything on the horizon that was familiar to my normal existence.

For a moment I was tempted to sit on a nearby rock and hope for rescue. A rancher's passing plane perhaps, like I'd seen in movies. But the only sign of activity was the single white trace of a passenger jet, tens of thousands of feet above my head, as it painted a trail across the blue sky. Resigned to my predicament and spurred on by the threatening nature of my surroundings I picked up the canvas bag, pulled out the sunscreen and smeared a generous helping over my legs, arms, face and neck. Next, I stuck the baseball hat on my head and started to walk in the tracks left by the Subaru. The sun blazed overhead. Perspiration continued to pour down the sides of my face. My mind started doing calculations, conscious of the fact I had been given a four o'clock deadline to deliver the bag. I checked my watch. Just gone ten-thirty. Half an hour to the road Erin had said. And then a twenty-five mile walk. The deadline was not going to happen. I didn't even have the bag. My only hope was that Erin would do as she said and make sure the money was delivered to the Gold Lace team somehow. Otherwise I had a better chance of surviving the day alone in the Nevada Desert.

Erin's estimation had been accurate. I reached the road within thirty-five minutes. My arms glistened, damp with sweat, my feet boiled in the trainers but I was relieved to reach the road. With no sign of any vehicles, I crossed to the right hand side of the road, turned south and began to walk. After five minutes a large truck passed me by, ignoring my attempts to flag it down but acknowledging my presence with a blast from its horn. Two cars going north were of no use to me. A mini-bus full of tourists sped past, several of its occupants feeling the need to catcall and wave in a demented fashion. Perhaps I was just a strange sight, trudging down the side of a desert road, swigging from a water bottle, carrying a canvas bag. Erin crossed my mind again. The interaction with her. How had I not seen anything in her that would have given me a clue about the side of her character that had driven her to do what she had done? I thought back to our first meeting and the significance of her words when she had compared the extent of our two speeding misdemeanours. '*Oh I am much*

more of a villain than you. Still it's much more fun breaking the law than being a goody-two shoes all the time. Don't you think?'
I had to smile. She had proved her point.

I resigned myself to the walk and focussed on Tonopah. I had been through a hellish experience already. This final leg could be no worse.

I had been walking for over an hour, my shirt stuck to my back, wet with sweat, when I heard the sound of a car horn coming from the opposite side of the road. A long white open topped Cadillac, its sharp, angular front housing a shiny grille that looked like a metallic milk crate, cruised up, twin headlights flashing. I stopped and stared. As it got closer I saw a familiar face. Carlos MacFadden.

'Hola, hola Mateo,' he shouted, a broad smile cracking his face.

The vehicle slowed as it passed me, then swung around on the carriageway in a single U-turn and pulled up off the tarmac next to me.

'Hey, Mateo, what you doing out here on your own?'

'I could ask you the same Carlos but I don't care. Glad to see you, mate. How'd you find me anyway?'

'Tell you in a minute but why are you wandering round in the desert?'

'Long story mate. You won't believe the shit that's happened.' I jumped in to the front seat of the car, a seat big enough for two, and began my story of how Erin had hijacked me, taken the half-million dollars and left me alone in the desert.

'Puta!' Carlos shouted when I had finished.

'Puta?'

'Aye…she's a whore, Mateo. A double crossing whore.'

'Bit strong mate…but…I don't know.'

I had no idea why I felt protective of Erin. Perhaps it was a secret admiration for the fact that she had…balls. The balls to attempt such an audacious scam. Carlos broke my thought pattern.

'So what you gannae do…about the money?'

'Nothing I can do, mate. Erin's got it. She has some sort of plan all figured out but god knows how that's going to work. I only hope for my sake that it does. I really don't want them gangsters chasing me down if they don't get their money. Had enough of it all.'

'I bet you have. Anyway, where too Mateo? Where we heading?'

'Back to Vegas I suppose. I've no bag to deliver now. Got to sort this somehow and get Cecil out of jail. I'm going to have to keep a low profile though until we get on that plane. As soon as these villains realise there's no delivery they'll be asking questions. I just hope Erin's gamble pays off.' I wiped the sweat from my brow and wondered how far ahead of us Erin might be. 'By the way you didn't happen to see a black Subaru pass you on the way up, did you?'

Carlos swung the car back onto the tarmac. 'A Subaru? What's that?'

'A four-wheel drive, off road thing. It doesn't matter. Just wondered if you'd seen it. Erin's car.'

'I seen a few cars Mateo. Not many. Didn't take any notice in the end. I was busy looking for you.'

Even if he had seen the car, he wouldn't have known it was her. There was no point in worrying about it. Carlos squeezed the accelerator and the Cadillac picked up speed. I stared out across the desert, the cool breeze rushing through my hair as we raced over the tarmac.

I turned back towards Carlos. 'So how come you are out here anyway? You didn't say.'

'I didn't like the idea of you going out on your own to do the bag drop to be honest Mateo. I talked to Jasper about it. Neither of us was happy but we knew you had to go alone. We knew we couldn't be seen with you or following you, so I decided to come after you later on, just in case. Jasper stayed behind to check us out of the hotel and keep tabs on what's happening with Cecil. Then when I got to where you said you were going…Tono…'

'Tonopah.'

'Aye. When I got there I saw your car parked up…hard to miss it. But no sign of you. I asked in the store. The man said he'd

295

seen an Englishman come in but didn't know where you'd gone. I thought for a minute that maybe you'd dropped the bag off at the petrol station and were on the way back to Vegas but I couldn't work out why you would've left your car there. Something odd about it. I thought maybe you must've met somebody and gone with them but if you did, I guessed you would be going north still. No sense in coming all the way out here to meet somebody and then going back towards Vegas with them. So I thought I'd keep going, see what I could see. I didn't know it would be so far.'

'Yeah, bit of a trek mate. And thanks Carlos. Glad you came looking. No fun being left in the desert.'

'That's what friends are for Mateo. Now we just got to get back and get Cecil out of jail and then stop that woman.'

'We'll see mate. We need to free Cecil but to be honest I just want to get out of Vegas now. Let's get back to my car first,' I said. I unscrewed another bottle of water from the bag and took a long swig. 'So where'd you get this motor anyway?'

'I called up your man. Where you got yours. He was happy to help. It's a 1973 Eldorado.'

'It's massive Carlos. Look at the size of that bonnet. It's way out in front of us. Looks like it'll get to Vegas well before we do.'

'Aye, it's a wee beastie. Never driven a column change automatic. In fact I never drive automatics. Took a bit of getting used to coming out of the city but once I hit the highway here it's just sit back and cruise along.'

Carlos laughed and hit the accelerator. The big Cadillac lurched forward and picked up pace.

'Easy mate. There's a speed limit out here,' I said. 'We don't want you ending up on a Speed Awareness Course.'

35

We hit the outskirts of Tonopah at around twelve-forty and ten minutes later we were back at the Texaco filling station. My car was exactly where I'd left it but not in the same condition.

Carlos noticed it first.

'You got two flat tyres, Mateo.'

I walked around the Cadillac examining the tyres. They had been fine when I pulled in. There was no explanation other than that Erin had let them down. Why would she do that? She had left me in the desert to walk back. She could only have done it as a precaution, to buy time. If for some reason I had managed to hitch a lift back it would ensure I was delayed further. I went to the front of the car, crouched down by the passenger side wheel and felt around in the gravel until my hand came to rest on the keys, precisely where Erin had said they would be. I moved to the back of the car and unlocked it. My wallet and mobile were placed neatly in the centre of the boot. The battery had been removed from my mobile. I picked them up and shoved them into the pocket of my shorts.

'Looks like we better get to work and change them wheels,' Carlos said.

'I spose so. That's all we need and we only have one spare,' I said.

Carlos scratched his bald head and stood for a moment staring at the rear of the car.

'We'll have to take them both off. Get them both pumped up.'

The nearest air line was at the far side of the service station entrance.

'We can stick the spare on but they've both got to come off. Right, let's get to work.'

I pulled up the matting in the boot and lugged out the spare. Carlos grabbed the wheel brace and began to loosen the wheel nuts. The first two loosened up fairly easily but the next proved a problem. Positioning the brace on one of the nuts, he placed his foot on the extended arm and pushed down hard.

'Ow...bollocks, that hurt,' he shouted, as the wheel brace slipped off the nut and his foot stamped hard against the ground. The nut hadn't budged.

'What is it, mate?'

'My dodgy knee. Jarred it a bit. I'll get the bugger though.'

He picked up the wheel brace again and made another attempt. This time the wheel brace span forward, bounced off a section of concrete and flew up towards his face as he pitched forward with the impetus of his failed attempt. The metal brace caught him square on the left eyebrow. A short gash opened up sending a trickle of blood into his eye and down across his face.

'Hijo de puta!' he shouted and clutched his face. The feel of his own blood must have sparked the rage that caused him to seek retribution. In a flurry of movement and accompanying Spanish expletives, he grabbed the wheel brace and slammed it down on the rear wing of the Cadillac in three successive blows.

For a moment I stood frozen to the spot with disbelief. As I began to comprehend what was happening to the car I sprang forward and tried to grab the wheel brace.

'Carlos, what the bloody hell you doing? Have you gone nuts? Look at the friggin car.' I managed to intercept his fourth swing, catching his arm below the elbow. 'What're you doing you nutter? Calm down...easy...easy.'

He dropped the wheel brace to the ground, a blank look on his face as if he too didn't quite understand what had happened.

'Sorry Mateo. Sorry, amigo. My bastard knee and now my eye. I just lost it. It's been a –'

'Lost it? Too bloody right you did,' I said, staring at the three deep indentations he had left in the bodywork of the Cadillac. 'Look at the state of that. That's going to cost a bloody fortune.'

'I'm sorry,' he said again as he stared at the blood on his fingers.

'Forget it. Let's get you cleaned up.'

I ran to the store and bought a small pack of tissues. Carlos held one to his bleeding eyebrow and apologised at least five more times.

'Best get these wheels sorted Mateo.'

By now I had given up on the wheels and was more concerned with getting back to Vegas to sort out Cecil's predicament.

'Forget it. We haven't got time. We're going to have to leave it. Come on, we need to get going. We have to get Cecil out of jail and then we've got a flight to catch tonight. I need to get out of here before these villains come looking. Have you got your mobile with you? We need to check with Jasper and see if there's any developments.'

'I have but it's out of charge. I forgot to plug it in.'

I took a deep breath, resigned to the fact that everything seemed to be loaded against us and I would just have to see what fate had in store.

'Ok, ok. Forget it. Let's go, mate.'

We jumped back into the Eldorado and drove back onto the highway. I handed Carlos a bottle of water and sat back in the seat to try and relax and enjoy the ride. The combination of an early start to the day and the smooth, undulating motion of the car soon began to make me feel drowsy. I slid further down in the leather seat. My eyes drooped, a trance like state overwhelming me.

My sleepy stupor lasted approximately two minutes. The loud curse shocked me into a startled wakefulness. I shot bolt upright in the seat.

'Carajo!' Carlos spat the word again.

This time I heard it clearly and knew it was an expletive even if I didn't understand it. I turned to look at him. Fear and pain were showing on his face in a wide-eyed grimace.

'What's up Carlos? What's going on?'

'My knee has locked up Mateo…can't bend it…foot's stuck… on the pedal,' he said, as the Eldorado sped along the open road.

'What d'you mean stuck? On the accelerator?'

'Aye. I can't bend…' His grip on the steering tightened as he squirmed in the seat trying to free his right leg. Sweat ran freely down his cheek.

'Shit, Carlos. You have to…how are we going to…?' My thoughts merged into one rapid, jumbled muddle. The road ahead rushed towards us. 'Can you not pull your knee up or something… with your hand?'

He let go of the wheel and tucked his right hand under his knee. The car lurched to the left. Instinctively I shot out a hand towards the steering.

'Bloody hell man. Watch it. Keep hold of the wheel.'

'You just said –'

'Forget it. Keep hold of the wheel.'

The big Cadillac raced on, the landscape on either side careering by, the road arrow straight in front of us. I pushed at the automatic gearshift to try and get it into neutral. It wouldn't move. I shot a glance at the speedo. Eighty. I turned to Carlos. His face was a frozen mask of terror.

'Carlos,' I shouted, 'listen, can you not get your other foot on the brake? Your left foot.'

For a moment he seemed to register what I was trying to say. I watched as his left foot lifted off the floor, hovered for a moment where it was and then went straight back down again.

'You need to slow down, Carlos. The brake. Hit the –'

'Stop shouting at me Mateo, I'm trying.'

His left foot hovered again but never made it more than a couple of inches off the floor. It was as if he could not comprehend the concept of braking and accelerating at the same time. The stress of the moment, the concentration he was exerting in trying to keep the Cadillac steady as it hurtled forward, seemed to have stopped all rational thought. His gaze remained fixed ahead in a glazed tense look. I realised I had to do something.

'Right. Listen, I'm going to try and step on the brake, ok. Keep it steady.'

I slid along the leather passenger seat until I was right next to him and hoisted my left leg over his right thigh and down between his legs. I managed to press against the brake pedal but the angle was all wrong and the motion of the car prevented me from staying still long enough to get any stability. Carlos's right arm formed a rigid barrier as he gripped the steering wheel in a desperate attempt to keep the speeding vehicle steady. I increased the pressure but only seemed to be pressing against the side of the pedal. I leant across further to get a better angle.

Carlos's right elbow jabbed me hard in the ribs. 'Away tae fuck. I cannae see the road.'

The car swerved to the left, his vision impeded by my shoulder. He pulled the steering back hard to the right in a reflex response. The sudden lurch threw my weight further across him.

'Jeez, get the fuck off me Mateo. You'll get us killed.'

I tried to halt my movement by bracing my left foot. It slid back off the pedal and jammed sideways under what little space there was between the brake and the floor. At that same moment, in some sort of panic stricken reflex action, Carlos finally managed to bring his left foot hard down onto the brake. With my foot stuck underneath it, his sudden action had no impact at all on the car's speed. The car rocked again as it slewed first left, then right.

'Ahm telling you. Yer gannae get us killed.'

'I'll get us killed? You're the one with your bloody foot on the friggin gas. And now you've got my foot trapped. Get your foot off the brake.'

'I told you Mateo, I cannae move my leg.'

'Your other foot you moron. The one on the brake.'

'You told me to brake. Santo dios…we're…I cannae slow down…'

The sensation of speed coupled with lack of control was unbearable. I leant back trying to release my trainer. The pressure from Carlos's foot on the brake kept it stuck fast. I realised he'd gone beyond rational thinking, such was his fear.'

'Holy shit!'

Carlos's sudden exclamation caused me to look away from the brake pedal. A sharp bend ahead. I glanced back at the speedo. Ninety. We had increased speed. Approximately a mile to the bend, a curve to the left. At that speed we would reach it in well under a minute. I saw the sweat roll down Carlos's face. The noise of the wind rushing by, as the car cut through the air, heightened the sense of lost control. I had to think clearly. I reached down towards my jammed foot. I tried to push Carlos's foot off the brake. His leg had gone into some sort of spasm and remained fixed. I started to scrabble around with my fingers, trying to reach the lace of my trainer. The Eldorado lurched left and right again.

'Hold the fucking car straight Carlos,' I shouted, adrenaline pumping as I fought to free my foot.

'Ahm tryin…what you doing?'

I ignored the question. There was no time for a debate. My fingers stretched forward. I couldn't reach far enough. Carlos's arm blocked my way. I ducked under it and managed to reach further down and feel the heel of my trainer. My head was turned almost at right angles facing under the dashboard.

'Hurry up for chrissakes, whatever you're doing Mateo. I cannae take that bend at this speed. An wi'you stretched across me, I cannae hold her.'

I felt the loop of the lace. I tugged. It didn't give. Despite the excruciating stretch in the back of my left leg I managed to reach forward a bit further and tugged on the lace again. This time I felt movement. My head was now almost down on Carlos's knees. Even if he had come to his senses it was doubtful that he had room to raise his leg off the brake.

'Jeez, this is no time for a siesta, Mateo. What, the hell you doin?'

'Just keep calm, you nob and hold onto this friggin car. I'm trying to get my trainer off.' I pulled the lace again. It slid back. I caught the loose end as it came free and pulled harder. It untied. I ducked back under Carlos's arm and shot up into an upright position. The bend was now about half a mile away. About twenty seconds and we'd be on it. I wriggled my foot from side to side. The trainer loosened. Another frantic wriggle and my foot slipped out but with the trainer lying sideways it continued to block the brake pedal.

'You better hold on Mateo. I'm gannae have to take this bend.'

'Ok. I'm out. Get a friggin grip, Carlos. I'm going pull my trainer away and then try and free your leg off the gas. When I get the trainer out push down hard on the brake with your other foot. Got it? Now, keep your hands on the wheel. Keep this friggin car straight. Ok.'

'Ok. Ok. I got it.'

I raised my leg out from its awkward position between Carlos's knees and leant across his lap. Next I hooked my finger into my trainer and pulled hard. It shot back from under the pedal. The sudden release caused Carlos's foot to stamp downwards. The tyres screeched across the hot tarmac but we were at the point of no return. No amount of braking would stop us reaching the bend. We would have to take it.

'The gas Carlos. Get your foot off the friggin gas,' I screamed.

His reaction was the wrong one. His left foot came off the brake, his right still firmly planted on the accelerator.

'What're you doing? I said the gas, Carlos…get off the friggin acceler –'

His eyes were fixed, trance like, on the bend as we sped towards it. I knew it was no use. He hadn't heard me. We were seconds from the bend. I placed my hands either side of his right leg, tucked under the crook of his knee, and pulled hard. I heard the scream of pain and the crack as his knee bent sharply. It pulled up and off the accelerator pedal. The sudden movement caused Carlos to jerk the steering. The Eldorado rolled and bounced on its suspension. We were right on top of the bend.

'Hit that bloody brake Carlos. Now!'

At the last minute he reacted. His left foot came down hard on the pedal. A frantic yank on the steering wheel, in an attempt to steer into the bend, was to no avail. The Cadillac's speed was still too much for the curve. The rapid deceleration and hard pull on the wheel sent the car into a tailspin. The rear end swung hard to the right kicking up a cloud of dust and gravel as it swerved off the road into a three hundred and sixty degree spin. Our sliding, slipping momentum was brought to an abrupt stop with a booming thud against the rear end of the vehicle. Just as it came to rest in a bouncing, undulating skid, I heard the deep resonating blare of a horn. Through the dust and debris from the desert scrub, I could just make out the outline of an articulated road train as it swept around the bend in the opposite direction.

I sat back in the seat, my body suddenly limp as the tension left it. I glanced across at Carlos who had blood seeping from a small gash across his forehead. The silence of the desert was suddenly unsettling and weird after the manic mayhem that had gone before.

'God…that was a close shave. You ok?'

'Aye…ok. Did you see that truck?'

'I did Carlos. Our luck was in. Few seconds more and we might have been…head on.' The enormity of that close shave suddenly unsettled me. My whole trip appeared to be close shaves. I turned on Carlos.

'So what the fuck were you doing Carlos? Why didn't you hit that brake when I said? You nearly got us killed man.'

For a moment Carlos just stared, the adrenalin seeping from his body. He appeared not to have the will for a row.

'Easy, amigo. My leg, It seized up. I couldn't move it. It must've been the long drive out here, you know…my leg in the one position.'

'Your other one you nob. Your left. Why didn't you brake?'

'I tried. It didn't make sense. The speed…trying to keep the car straight too. I panicked a bit, I think. Didn't make sense to brake and speed at the same time. My brain wouldn't…no, no sense. And…well, I told you I never drive automatics. I'm sorry Mateo.'

The apologetic look on Carlos's face stopped any response. I knew it had not been his fault. My own fraught situation had frazzled my nerves.

I took a deep breath of the warm desert air and held out my hand. 'Hey, Carlos, still mates, eh? No apologies needed. I know it wasn't your fault. An accident, mate. I'm sorry to lose it. Just the whole thing, you know. Some fortieth birthday.'

Carlos smiled and shook my hand.

'Do me a favour Mateo. Take more than a little runaway car to break up a good friendship. Anyway, you're right laddie. Some birthday. You'll nae forget it will you?'

'Definitely not.' I pointed to his face. It seemed he had caught his head on the rear-view mirror as the car spun round. 'Nice cut. You got a matching pair now, mate.'

Carlos felt his head and stared at the blood on his fingers. This time he stayed calm.

'Flesh wound, I reckon. C'mon Mateo. Let's check the damage to the car.'

I stepped out of the car, the dust still billowing and falling onto the scrub. Carlos limped round the Cadillac from the driver's side. At the back of the car we found the reason for our abrupt halt. A low, spiny cactus, half of one side sheared off by the impact, was jammed underneath the boot. One of the front tyres had a gash across its sidewall where it had hit one of the many rocks and boulders strewn around the desert floor, but it was still inflated. A closer inspection of the vehicle showed that, apart from the tyre, the only other damage was a dent to the rear bodywork where it had hit the cactus.

'More expense,' I said. 'Let's get this wheel changed. It's not going to last the trip back like that.'

It took twenty minutes to change the wheel. When we had done, Carlos wiped the dust and sweat from his face and looked directly at me.

'You're not gannae get back in time to catch her now Mateo. What will you do?'

'I don't know, Carlos. I'm more worried about getting Cecil out than catching up with Erin. I'm not even sure I want to catch her. We need to get out of town and we have a flight to get too. I'm done with this birthday trip to be honest.' I wiped my grubby hands on my shorts and opened the car door. 'Get in. I'm driving. Can't risk your bloody knee again.'

305

36

We reached Las Vegas at twenty past four, twenty minutes past the drop off deadline in Carson City. I hoped that Erin had done what she had said and had contacted the Gold Lace casino team, but I had no way of knowing. Carlos dropped me outside the Paris.

'Drop the car back to Bill, Carlos. Just tell him where mine is. Here, take the keys. The insurance should cover the cost of the damage. I'm going to get cleaned up. See you back here.'

Covered in dust and sweat I walked back into the Paris. I didn't get far. Standing just inside the doorway of the lobby was the lawyer from the Gold Lace Casino. This time he had company. Two large shaven-headed accomplices stood on either side of him, their presence clearly signalling no way past. I froze on the spot.

'Matthew. I wasn't expecting to see you here. I thought you would be taking advantage of our hospitality right now in Carson City.'

I looked behind me, the instinct to run suddenly surging through me. There was no escape route. Standing on the far side of the door, arms crossed in front of him, was one of the tallest men I had ever seen. His dark glasses added to the air of menace that his wide legged, solid stance portrayed.

'I can explain,' I said, not entirely sure how I could, as the thought kicked in of Erin's threat to make sure Cecil stayed in jail if I said anything.

'Be my guest then Matthew,' the lawyer said. 'I'd love to hear your explanation.'

'My car broke down…in Tonopah. Flat tyres.'

'You mean where you picked up our message, Matthew?'

'Yes…in the garage. That's right,' I said, taking his response as acceptance of what I had said.

'So you were in a garage and you couldn't get a wheel fixed?' He eyed me up and down looking at the dust and grime that covered my clothes, face and hands. 'So let's see, you decided to walk back to Vegas, right?'

'No…no…I…err…hitched a lift…back.'

'It would have made more sense to hitch a lift to Carson City surely and keep your appointment. That's what a gentlemen does, Matthew. And I thought you Englishmen were gentlemen.'

I had no response but he didn't wait for one.

'Nevertheless, I assume you have brought our luggage with you. You have, haven't you?'

The blood rushed from my face, my head spun, dizzy with trepidation as I realised Erin had not kept her promise to deliver the bag. I had no explanation. I heard myself speak but did not feel that I was voluntarily offering the information.

'I left it…in the boot…the trunk…of the car. It was too heavy to carry all the way back…and…err…you did say that you can't be seen taking a bag nor could you risk being involved…err…if you remember.'

There was no verbal response. A nod of the lawyers head galvanised the two accomplices into action. I was lifted bodily off the steps of the Paris and dragged backwards across the pavement. The tall villain flung open the rear door of a waiting car and shoved me head first across the back seat. He then got into the driver's seat. The lawyer and one of the two accomplices got into the back and sat either side of me.

'Now listen carefully Matthew. I warned you not to fuck us over. I represent some very serious businessmen and they do not like to be fucked with. We are driving up to Tonopah right now to get that bag. If it's not where you say it is you will be feeding the coyotes tonight. Now, you sure you don't want to tell me anything else?'

I hesitated. The car sped off. I considered that feeding the coyotes didn't mean handing them chunks of food like you would a pet dog. My mind was a scramble of panic stricken thoughts. Save my bacon, shop Erin and ensure Cecil stayed in jail. Erin was clever. She would implicate Cecil somehow and even if whatever story she invented didn't stand up, it could be months or even more before he got out. If I said nothing, in three hours or so, the game would be up. They would discover that there was no bag in the car in Tonopah. I didn't even have the keys with me. I'd just given them to Carlos. What would Cecil have done in the circumstances? Probably clumped them both and tried to make a run for it. We were out on the freeway now and the car was picking up speed. That wasn't an option even if I could remember any of my old Kung Fu moves.

My hectic brain activity was interrupted by the jangling of a mobile.

'Yeah, Davidson.'

So that was the lawyer's name. A mistake I guessed. He must have been used to answering his mobile that way.

'Yeah. When?'

I listened as he spoke. I could only hear one side of the conversation.

'At the airport? The whole lot?'

I stared straight ahead.

'The bag...'

I tried to make sense of what I was hearing. Had they caught Erin?

'Ok...ok. I'll see to it. Send me the number. Ciao.'

He cut the call, placed the mobile in his jacket and called out to the driver.

'Pull over at West Sahara.' He turned and looked at me, a look of dismissal.

The car swung off the freeway, took a right turn and then pulled into a side road under the flyover we had just crossed. The driver cut the engine. I sat staring ahead unsure what was to happen next but feeling fearful. Davidson turned towards me.

'You been bullshitting me Matthew,' he said, a statement more than a question.

I didn't reply.

'I don't like bullshitters, you know that. Meet them all the time in my job.'

I felt I had to say something. 'I'm sorry, I don't understand.'

'Yeah you do. The money. You been bullshitting about the money. You haven't got the money in Tonopah have you? No, you haven't. We've recovered it. Not exactly as we had expected but recovered all the same. One of our people is downtown right now. We have what we want so I don't need you anymore, do I?'

A question I couldn't answer.

'You're nobody. Get out of the car.'

I looked at him. I suddenly felt safer in the car. He didn't need me. I was nobody. Dispensable. If I left the car I had no idea what was going to happen. The driver got out and came round to the rear passenger door. He opened it. The villain to my left got out.

'I said get out of the car Matthew. Now.' The command was insistent.

I felt a rough tug on my left arm and I was dragged out onto the tarmac. I landed on my back. I sat up, the driver towering above me. As I did I felt the cold, hard edge of something touching my head. Immediately I knew what it was. The third time a gun had been pointed directly at me only this time the long narrow silencer on the end of the barrel meant business. This time I had no doubt that it was to be used. Arturo had wanted something. Erin had wanted something. They had both used a gun to try and get what they wanted but these guys wanted nothing from me now.

I took a deep breath to quell the fear.

'You were warned there would be consequences, Matthew,' Davidson said, his eyes stern as he looked down at me from the back of the car.

Consequences. I remembered the note in Tonopah. I hadn't expected to find out what the consequences were. This was not how my fortieth birthday trip was supposed to end. I saw Davidson nod towards the gunman. I felt the tip of the barrel push more firmly against my head as the villain cocked the trigger. My body was taught with fear. Sweat poured freely down my face yet my throat burned bone dry. Whatever my vital systems were doing as they faced up to their last moments, my brain clung to one instinct. Survival. With the money delivered and Erin now out of the picture I had nothing to lose.

'Wait…wait,' I shouted, 'I know what happened to your money.'

Davidson's eyes narrowed. He glanced up at the gunman and then back at me.

'What money? What are you talking about.'

'Your other money,' I said. 'The money for the exchange.'

'The money our courier had?'

'Yes…yes. When we first met at the Venetian, you know, you said one of your team was robbed. And you said you'd get the… err…the sonofabitch…I think that's what you called him, right? Well, I can help.' Perspiration continued to pour down my face but I didn't move a muscle.

Davidson edged across the seat and stepped out of the car.

'Ok, Matthew. Tell me what you know.'

'I will…but first…first you have to give me your word that you won't shoot me.' The muscles in the back of my neck tightened with fear as he moved towards me.

Davidson laughed. 'You wanna bargain with me now?'

'I can help you, that's all. I can help you so this doesn't happen again to you and your…your businessmen colleagues. You know…so your business can operate without…without people trying to upset things. It's information…but I need your word… as a gentleman…an American.'

It was then I felt the stirring in my shorts. I couldn't believe it. I was sitting on the ground, my life in the balance a gun pointing at my head and I was getting a hard on. I glanced downward. I was definitely getting an erection. Nobody had noticed. Davidson had started to pace. I swallowed hard but my mouth was too dry for it to make any difference. I thought about the gun at my head but that didn't work. I had developed a full-blown hard on. Possibly people react in different ways to fear. Why I couldn't just piss myself like normal people when facing sheer terror, I had no idea. It was not a reaction I could have expected. Perhaps it was a combination - fear and the sudden feeling I had of a shift of power. Despite my precarious position, I had definitely gained a small bit of control over some seriously dangerous people. I knew something or at least they thought I did. The aphrodisiac of power began to raise its head, demonstrating its emotional potency. Maybe at the point where a life is about to be terminated, nature fights back, a phallic display, a symbol of life. A reminder that it will not be extinguished.

I shuffled slightly hoping to re-arrange the obvious bulge in my shorts. It didn't work. I had gained a moments control over my assailants but not over my dick.

Davidson stopped pacing and stood in front of me.

'You bullshitting me again Matthew?'

I held a hand up in front of me.

'I swear, no. Look, I am just offering you information. Information that will make sure your business deals run smoothly. That's all. When somebody's working against you, you need to know. I've nothing to lose. I'm nobody. You said so. I don't care what you do. It's none of my business. I just got mixed up in it through no fault of my own…and right now I just want to go home. Back to England…I will be gone tonight. You won't ever see me again. Rest assured.'

Davidson turned towards the car and leant on the open door. He raised his head and stared at the flyover above him. I waited for his next move, with the same apprehension that had overwhelmed me when I had waited for the roulette ball to drop in the right slot. I had placed my bet. I no longer had any control of the outcome. The seconds ticked. My headed pounded. I waited.

Finally, he turned back towards me, his right hand wiping an imaginary speck from his lapel as if freeing himself of an insignificant irritant. He stared at me for a while, his eyes cold but a spark of curiosity just seeping through.

'Ok, tell me what you got.'

I tried to speak with a clear and assertive tone. 'I need your word…as an American…and a gentleman that you won't shoot me.'

'You got it. My word. You can walk away when you tell me what you know.'

'Ok. Tell him to put the gun away first.'

Davidson nodded at the gunman. He lowered the weapon and stood back. I got to my feet, subtly adjusting the discomfort of my shorts so it was not as obvious. I realised I had only one bargaining tool and that was to give them something. Something concrete, something realistic. I also knew that where the culprit was, he was out of reach.

'Your man is the go between, Arturo Magana-Gallegos. He set this all up. He used me to try and cream off a cut for himself.'

I watched Davidson's face change colour.

'Sonofabitch,' he screamed. He turned towards the car and for a moment stared skywards. Then he turned back towards me.

'You bullshitting me again, you limey punk?'

'No. It's straight. He set me up. How could I plan all this? I'm on holiday. There's no way I could've known about your business deals. I just got here Friday. You said yourself that you knew that.'

Davidson's face changed from scarlet to a greyish white pallor. 'He will pay for this, I swear.'

'You know he's in the detention centre already,' I said. 'He won't say anything. He'll keep his mouth shut. Once he knows that you know he's crossed you, he won't say anything. It's not for me to tell you what to do but –'

'No it's not,' Davidson said, his eyes ablaze with anger. 'The sonofabitch knows too much.'

'But…maybe he's best off where he is for now.'

'Senor Magana-Gallegos is our problem not yours.' He signalled to his accomplices and pointed to the car. 'Get in.' He turned back towards me. 'Goodbye Matthew Malarkey. Make sure you are on your flight tonight and don't let me see your face in Vegas again.'

The two villains jumped back into the car. The engine fired up. The car disappeared in a screech of rubber against tarmac.

I fell back down onto the ground, my legs having turned to jelly along with my adrenaline fuelled hard on.

37

Jasper Kane met me in the lobby of the Paris as I trudged across the elegantly patterned black and white tiled floor.

'Mate. You ok? You look like shit.'

'Feel like it Jasper. I just want to get a shower.'

'Yeah, Carlos told me about your trip. What's happening?'

'I don't know. We need to get Cecil sorted.' I checked my watch. 'It's quarter past five already. You checked out?'

'Yeah, we did but your room's still available. They wouldn't let me in. There's a surcharge on yours.'

'I don't care. I just need to get cleaned up. I'm going to get my key.'

At the reception desk I picked up my keycard. I had another hour on the room if I needed it. As I went to walk away, the receptionist handed me a package.

'This came for you Mister Malarkey.'

I turned to Jasper. 'Get hold of Carlos and meet me upstairs.'

Back in my room I sat on the bed and opened the parcel the receptionist had given me. To my utter shock, wrapped up in a money band was a bundle of dollar bills. I picked it up and flicked through it, each one a hundred dollar note. Underneath the cash was a sealed envelope with my name handwritten on the front. Inside, the battery for my mobile phone along with a folded note. I unfolded it and stared at the type.

'*Hi Matthew. It's done. By now you will realise I made the switch. The bag has been handed over and I am on my way. Our friends'*

money was safely tucked away in a deposit box at the airport. Thanks for keeping quiet. I hope you get your friend, Cecil, out. I don't know what will become of Arturo. I guess he will feel safer inside than he will outside. I expect he will come up with some story about me but I will be long gone. I have enclosed a little something for all your expenses and trouble. Don't be a fool and feel guilty. Walk on the wild side. The money is clean, fresh out of the casinos. It isn't unusual to take money out of Vegas, you know.
Take care. E. x.
   p.s. I have no idea if there is such a thing as an All-Ireland under fifteen pistol shooting championship!'

I folded the note and put it in my shorts. Erin Farrell. Clever. Thoughtful. Opportunist. Survivor. Somehow she had pulled it off. Pulled off what she had set out to do in the first place. There were casualties of her actions, not least of all me. But nothing gets done without consequences, as I nearly found out to my cost. I picked up the money and counted it. Ten thousand dollars. She was right. I did feel guilty. It was money that she had come by through criminal actions. But I was past caring.

I stood under the hot shower and tried to wash away the negativity along with the dust of the desert. Carlos and Jasper came up to the room. I told them the news.

'Lads. I have to get Cecil out and I need you to do a few things. We don't have a lot of time. Carlos can you do me a favour mate and chuck all my stuff in my suitcase and then check me out.' I pulled five hundred dollars from the wad and stuck it into one of the hotel envelopes. 'Jasper, there's a little florist down near where Carlos picked me up on Monday. It's called Bellissimi Flori or something –'

'Fiori...it's fiori. Italian for flowers,' Carlos interrupted.

'Ok, thanks for that Carlos. Anyway Jasper, can you take this envelope to them and just say it's for the damage. They'll know what you mean. Carlos, tell him how to get there.'

Next I peeled off ten one hundred dollar bills and put them in another envelope. I marked it *Pauline* and placed it inside a larger envelope. On the front of that one I marked *Brooke*. Inside

314

I put three thousand dollars, her key and a note – *To help with the damage. Sorry.*

'Carlos, when you get down to reception can you tell them to store this on my behalf and it will be collected later in the week. Ok?'

'What's it for, Mateo?'

'I'll tell you later. Let's just say I'm helping ease my guilt. Don't forget we were over fourteen hundred up on the winnings and now we still have the best part of five and a half grand left. I'll split it between us all. It will cover our costs. Now I have to get going. Cecil's waited long enough. Let's meet over in the Bond Bar for around six-thirty. Ok?'

I walked into the Las Vegas Police Department, South Central carrying a black Nike rucksack. I told the officer in charge that I was the victim of an attempted mugging outside Coco's Diner on Monday afternoon and that I believed they were holding someone who had foiled a potential robbery. I opened the rucksack and showed them my camera, lenses and video camera. I described the man who had accosted me and had held me at gunpoint and who had attempted to steal my bag. I described the man who had intervened. The officer checked the file. Witnesses had said they had seen a man attempt to take a bag at gunpoint and that another man had intervened. I was asked if I wanted to press charges for attempted robbery. I said I didn't and that I was going back to England. It was of no concern to them whether I did or not as they were holding my attacker on suspicion of handling a stolen weapon and using it without a permit.

Within half an hour Cecil was delivered to the police department free of any charges. I was pleased to see him. He greeted me with a back slapping bear hug.

'Geezer, took your fucking time. Thought I was going to be banged up with all them crackheads and fucking loop jobs. You sorted the other mumble?'

'I have Ces. Long story mate. I'll tell you over a beer but you were right about that Erin,' I said, as we walked out onto the street.

'The hostess? Yeah…what's she done?'

'Oh not a lot mate. Just set this whole cash caper up. Switched bags so I'm walking around with the half million dollars that you found. Sharp alright.'

'You're winding me mate. Straight?'

'You wait till you hear the half of it. Yeah, she's behind it all.'

I gave Cecil the condensed version of Erin's escapade as we stood on the street corner watching the road for a taxi. When I had finished he looked genuinely shocked.

'Well fuck me, geezer. I knew there was something about that bird. Told ya she was sharp, didn't I? Must admit though I wouldn't have had her down for a villain.'

'Not sure she is. I think she was winging it. An opportunist. Anyway, it's good to see you Ces. And thanks. You got me out of a scrape the other day with that Arturo bloke.'

'Mate, you know the mumble. That's what mates do, right?'

'So what made you turn up at that diner anyway?'

'I got worried geeze. When you said you hadn't showed up at the Wynn that night cos you'd ran into one of the villains again it bothered me, you know. So when you reckoned you were one your way down to meet up with that Krystal bird at Coco's, the old alarm bells started. If they was following you they'd be very interested in finding her as well. I didn't want them getting to the cash before we did, not with them other geezers after you too. Then when I got there I just saw that mug with the gun.'

'Well, all the same it was brave Ces. I mean with him having the frigging gun.'

'Well, you know. Just reacted mate. And the cops gave me a load of grief over the gun. Had my prints on it cos you went and threw the fucking thing at me. They tried to make out it was mine. Like I'm a Brit tourist who comes to Vegas and wants to play the gangster. They listen to too much fucking rap if you ask me.'

'I was trying to figure out how the cops managed to turn up just at that point. I thought somebody must have called them when they saw they gun.'

'Nah mate. It was the waitress. The feds told me. She's called them up when she's seen you holding two bundles of dollars in the diner. Mate, she wasn't thinking you was gonna order the whole menu and just checking you had enough cash to pay for it. Nah, she's clocked the dough and called the cops thinking you're some scumbag dealer. She's seen the bird in tears and bang, put two and two together and made fucking five. That's why the old bill showed up.'

'Blimey. Bad timing for you, what with the gun and all that.'

'Mate, the laws over here are well complicated. They reckon you don't need a licence for a gun in this state. Can you believe that?'

'Well it is America Ces.'

'Yeah but then they reckoned I needed one for a handgun unless it was in full view. Either way I told them it weren't my gun. They had me both ways, trying to stitch me for a felony of some sort.'

'So what about Arturo? Did they not try to pin it on him.'

'Yeah, big time mate.' Cecil waved at a passing taxi. It didn't stop. 'They were playing both of us. Bottom line is they didn't know who to believe. The geezer's got a bit of a record. He was done for possession of controlled substances a couple of years ago and had bin on a rehab program. So no way was anyone giving him a permit for a fucking gun.'

'He's a dabbler then. Must be where Erin got the Charlie,' I said, thinking back to that night in my room.

'What, the air hostess? She's doing the old candycaine?'

'Sort of. You know, just the recreational thing I reckon.'

Cecil laughed and ran a hand thorough his hair.

'So anyway, I've told them that this Arturo geezer has tried to mug some tourist and nick his bag. He reckoned it was the other way round. Fucking nobhead. Tried to frame me right up. As far as I'm concerned I hope he stays in nick. Twat can spin on the rough end of a fucking pineapple. Tryin to stitch me. So he tells them all this bollocks about me trying to mug him, then what's complicated the whole mumble was they found out the gun was nicked. They reckoned it was traced back to whasisname…you know, your mate from Chicago. The gun salesman.'

'What, Richard? He's not exactly my mate Ces. He chatted to me in the Hyde.' I pulled my wallet from my pocket and took out the card. 'Richard Heydon. I thought it was too much of a co-incidence when Brooke said the guns had been stolen from a rep in Vegas. So he's in on it too then? Supplying guns?'

'No he ain't in on anything. But according to the old Bill he reckons he had a couple of guns nicked from his room. Thinks it's some bird he hooked up with. The cops are checking him out though.'

A taxi pulled up and we got in.

'Two guns you said? Nicked? But he said he kept them all under lock and key in a case?'

'Yeah, I know. But he thinks it happened when he met up with some Irish bird…Kate. The cops were trying to tie me in with her as if I set it up, but I don't know who the fuck she is.'

The cogs of my mind clicked and whirred until the information hit me like one of Vegas's neon banners. Kate? Irish?

'Caitlin O'Hara,' I said out loud, but as if I was having the conversation with myself.

'Who?'

'Caitlin. Caitlin O'Hara.' I turned towards Cecil. 'Erin Farrell. Erin. Same person.'

'What you on about geeze?'

'You said yourself that Richard was going to look up his dinner date…Kate. You know, when you got him pissed up the other night in the Wynn. Well, Erin told me that Arturo knows her as Caitlin O'Hara, not by her real name. That's it. I remember when we met Richard he said he had a lunch date with a Kate. So they must have met up again. What else did he tell the police?'

'They said he'd told them he'd gone back to his room with this Kate bird for a drink. He'd told her what he did. Well, you know what a mouthy nob he was. I mean, he'd told us all about his mumble that first night. And mate, if you're in that business you gotta at least keep your mouth shut, right. One minute he reckons he tells people he's flogging textiles or some shit and then he's telling you about his fucking gun models. No wonder the geezer's got stitched by some bird. He reckons all he did was show her the samples he was carrying in the case. Nobhead.'

'Right. So, all Erin had to do was open the case and lift a couple of guns. One she gave to Arturo and one she kept. And if the cops were trying to link you with *Kate* they'll be doing the same with Arturo.'

'I reckon so,' Cecil said, leaning back in his seat and staring at the passing traffic. 'If he got the gun from her, sooner or later he'll shop her otherwise he's gonna wind up in front of the Clark County District Judge.'

'I don't know Ces. He's already up to his neck in it with some proper villains. He can't let on about Erin without having to tell them about his involvement in the bag scam, can he? And there is no Kate, no Caitlin O'Hara, so it's a dead end. I think he'll play dumb and take the hit. He's better off inside right now for his own safety. But what I don't understand is why, when Richard found his guns missing, he didn't report it?'

'Yeah the cops wanted to know that too. Turns out that he's had something slipped in his drink. Knocked him right out and then –'

'Something put in his drink?' The memory of my first night with the bourbon and pill concoction flashed into my head. 'Bloody hell. One of Arturo's little sleepers like the one he gave me, I bet. Dropped it in his booze and then, when he was out of it, Erin's opened the case.'

'Yeah, but he didn't report anything cos he gets a text message with a coupla pictures sent to him from what turns out to be one of them throwaway phones. You know, some SIM card loaded with ten dollars and then ditched. First picture has him laying stark bollock naked on the bed with a line of coke across his chest. Then there's another one, him lying there and you can just see two stockinged thighs either side of him. She's done him right up mate. Texted him to tell him that if he said anything, the photos would be sent to his missus. Cops showed me them cos they thought I'd set him up with this Kate bird.'

'His missus? The bloke has a wife? You wouldn't have thought

319

it the way he was chasing birds. What a stitch up.'

'Told ya mate. Sharp bird. Wouldn't have taken much to memorise the combination of his case either. I bet the nob opened it right in front of her. Showing off his big macho gun image. What a prick. They shouldn't put geezers like him in charge of a water fucking pistol.'

'You're right Ces. One smart lady. And the thing is, she's improvised it all. You know, their whole plan went tits up when I lost the bag that night so she's had to adapt all along. She's duped Arturo, duped Richard and –'

'Stitched you too by the sound of it, geezer,' Cecil laughed.

I couldn't argue. There was no doubt I had been taken in by Erin from the start but somehow I didn't feel any bitterness. I was disappointed. Disappointed in myself for being so naïve but also because I quite liked her. She had personality and a love of life. She probably saw it all as an adventure. The fact that she'd left me in the desert but gave me sunscreen and water to cope told me she meant no harm. She did what she had to do. Then she'd left me cash to cover my expenses. Was I just making excuses for her? And if so why? Was I just too forgiving? Maybe, but in many ways I admired someone who had the audacity and the intellect to try and pull off such an audacious caper.

'You know what Ces, I'm thinking. I bet there were no bullets in either of the guns. Richard said he carried ammo but it wouldn't have been in the display case would it? Not likely anyway. Erin would have just lifted the two weapons and disappeared. She had no intention of using them.'

Deep inside I hoped that Erin had meant me no harm. And by leaving me in the desert to avoid going to Carson City, I suppose, in her own strange way, she'd proved it. I smiled to myself as I recalled her crack about being All-Ireland pistol shooting champion and the subsequent note.

'I mean it wasn't as if she was used to handling guns. She's an air hostess for god's sake. I remember how she even described its make as she pointed it at me. No normal villain who's used to carrying a gun would do that.'

'You're probably right about the bullets mate but you'll never know.'

The taxi pulled up outside the Bond Bar. Cecil slapped me on the back. 'C'mon geezer. Let's get a quick a beer. I'll check out later.'

'Be right with you mate. I have a call to make.'

Cecil grabbed me in one of his bear style manhugs.

'Good to see ya. Glad you got it sorted.' He turned to walk away.

I called after him. 'Hey Ces. Thanks mate.'

'For what?''

'You know. You had to put up with being banged up and questioned and all that. Can't have been any fun. Not the way to spend your days in Vegas. A lot of people would have told the police everything just to get off the hook.'

'Fun? Mate, you have no idea.' He paused for a moment, staring out across the Strip towards the Paris Hotel before continuing. 'I'm not a flaky geezer. You know me. I'm either in or I'm out. Yeah?'

I could only smile. As far as I was concerned Cecil was in and many a time it was good to have him on my side.

'I'll stick a large one on the bar for ya geeze. Help you sleep on the plane. Keep the dream alive.' A final slap on the back and he disappeared into the bar.

I watched him walk away. No matter what happened, Cecil never lost his swagger.

I had one more thing to do. I had made a decision. A price had to be paid. Arturo was safer inside than outside and, despite what he had done, I wanted him to stay that way. He would have two sets of villains on his case now. I was due on a flight in just under three hours. I stood outside the Cosmopolitan and reached for my mobile. I punched in Brooke's number. She sounded pleased to hear from me. I told her about her alarm. I apologised for the damage I had caused to her home. She was cool about it. The police had been in touch in any case, soon after my call. I told her where her key was. Her parents had a spare.

'Brooke, I am really sorry about the damage and the inconvenience. I'm paying for it.'

'I'm insured Matthew. Don't worry. I understand what you were going through.'

'I want to pay Brooke. It's up to you how you solve it but I want to pay, ok? So when you get back to Vegas there's an envelope, with your name on it, waiting for you in the Paris. If you don't need it for the repairs put it towards the photos for your portfolio. Maybe you'll make the cover of Vogue one day.'

'Wow, yeah, that would be something.'

'Oh and there's also a little something in there that I want you to give to Pauline…for Emma.'

And then I got to the point.

'Listen Brooke, you might want to give your father some information. Don't say where it came from. Grab a pen and take this down. Tell him he might want to get his colleagues to check out the Gold Lace Casino and Lap Dancing Club in Carson City. Tell him that it may help with Baltimore.'

'Baltimore?'

'Yes. Baltimore. Tell him that there's a guy by the name of Arturo Magana-Gallegos being held in a Las Vegas detention centre and that he has some important information that might be of interest to the FBI. But make sure you let him know that Arturo's life could be in danger and he will need protection. I am sure the FBI will be more than interested. And don't mention any of it until the morning, ok. I want to be out of town when you do.'

'Very mysterious Matthew. I'll tell him. Thanks.' She paused for a second. *'Are you going home now?'*

'I am,' I said.

'Well, it's been great meeting you. I'll miss you. You take care now.'

'Goodbye Brooke. It was a real pleasure meeting you. Oh, and just one more thing.'

'What's that?'

'Can I call you Claire now?'

I heard the soft giggle.

'Why, sure you can Matthew. And if you are ever back in Vegas, look me up won't you.'

I hesitated for a moment.

'If I ever come back…yes, I will Claire.'

38

The roar of the jumbo's powerful engines signalled its take-off. As the giant aircraft thrust itself along the runway, gathering momentum, I had a sense of no return, a feeling of my destiny being in the controlling hand of fate, much as it had through the whole Vegas trip. I sat back in my seat and stared through the window, allowing the sensations of take-off to wash over me. The sudden lift as the aircraft heaved itself off the ground; the landscape falling away beneath me; the sub-conscious awareness of the space that was developing between the aircraft and the security of the ground; the vibration in the cabin as the jumbo bounced over an air pocket and then banked steeply to the right in a curved turn. I watched the ground tip away as we levelled out again and climbed past clusters of puffy cloud. Below, streams of traffic snaked across the landscape in thin lines, as the lights of Las Vegas burned brightly all around, like the dying embers of a fire. Soon the aircraft was absorbed into the blackness of the night sky.

Next to me, Cecil and Jasper had already slipped into a half sleep. Carlos was across the aisle engrossed in a book. I sat and stared into space. Ahead of me was the first class section but I was seeing nothing. My thoughts were focussed on the eventful, disturbing but exciting days that I had just experienced. A fortieth birthday that I would never forget. I thought of Louise and how much I was looking forward to seeing her. My head lolled to the right as sleep crept upon me. A curtain at the first class entrance flapped open just as my eyes had begun to shut. The movement caught my peripheral vision but the first thing I saw was an outstretched hand holding the Champagne. I heard the familiar tone, the soft Irish lilt.

'Hello Matthew. I thought you might like a glass of bubbly.'

With Vegas Pursuit, Patrick Shanahan continues the adventures of Matthew Malarkey, the central character from his first novel, Cupid's Pursuit. Although a keen scribbler and story teller in early life Patrick only began to write seriously in recent years. However, serious writing was not the main aim as he found that his preference lay in humour, directed at an audience who just occasionally wanted a light, undemanding read that injected a bit of fun into a world full of serious books.

Patrick was born in South West London and currently lives in the Surrey area.

Also by Patrick Shanahan

Cupid's Pursuit

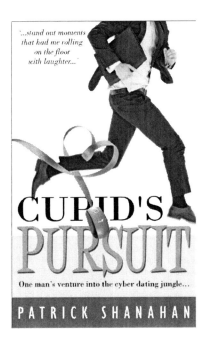

Matthew Malarkey is a man on a mission. To find a soul mate. His first problem is where to start looking. He has tried pubs and bars, all without success, just a sore head and an empty wallet to show for it. Now it's the turn of technology. The internet. Cyberspace could be the way to that meaningful relationship that Matthew is seeking. He signs up on line in the pursuit of love and embarks on a series of dating escapades, with a variety of ladies, only to find that Cupid does not make the quest for love easy. As Matthew searches for that elusive spark, he finds himself becoming involved in a succession of comical entanglements, culminating in a date he doesn't want – with the law.

www.cupidspursuit.co.uk

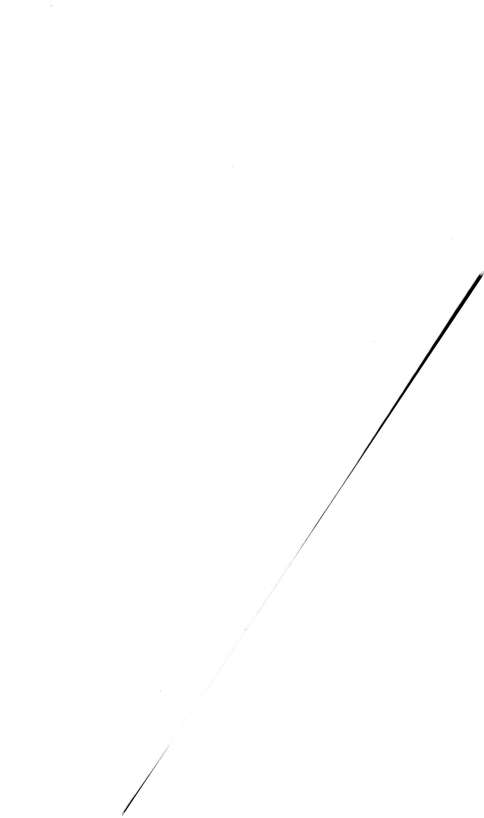